PASSPORT TO EVIL

PASSPORT TO EVIL

by

B.L. HUGHES

Blackie & Co
Publishers Ltd

A BLACKIE & CO

PUBLISHERS LIMITED PAPERBACK

© Copyright 2002

Bertram Hughes

The right of Bertram Hughes to be identified as Author of
this work has been asserted by him in accordance with the
Copyright, Designs and Patents Act 1988

First published in 2002

A CIP catalogue record for this title is
available from the British Library
ISBN 1 903138 24 8

Blackie & Co Publishers Ltd
107-111 Fleet Street
LONDON   EC4A 2AB

Printed and Bound in Great Britain

Dedication

To Nick, who is always ready to help.

About The Author

Bertram Lionel Hughes was born in Sawtry, Huntingdonshire in 1920. Educated first at Sawtry Primary, he won a scholarship to Fletton Grammar in Peterborough in 1930, where he gained his Oxford Senior School Certificate.

Bert was employed by the British Sugar Corporation until 1940 at which time he joined the Royal Air Force. He served for six years, five of them abroad and was 'Mentioned in Dispatches' in 1941. In 1946 he turned to accountancy, a profession to which he belonged until his retirement in 1986.

Bert has been involved in numerous public activities: he was a founder member of Huntingdon District Council, the Chairman of Governors of Sawtry Village College and four other schools, the Registrar for Births, Marriages and Deaths, a member of the Marriage Guidance Council and of the Inland Drainage Board.

Passport to Evil is his first novel.

Chapter One

Bradbury

Heading for the meet that bright March morning in 'thirty-two I never dreamt life as I knew it would be stood on its head by lunchtime. Never committed to chasing foxes I nonetheless loved the woodlands and was fascinated by hounds in their nose-down pursuit of the ginger-red bundle of fur townies love to love when it's threatened, like they loathe the morons in pursuit, with their lunatic cries of 'tally-ho' and 'clear the bloody way...' I didn't give a toss whether or not they caught the ruddy fox or broke their necks in the attempt.

Shoving my bike by the cowshed I crossed the road, edging my gawky frame into the paddock via the tradesman's gate, anonymous and unobtrusive, sidling to the less-populated far end. The enclave was filling fast for the West Thorncliffe's seasonal highlight – Bradbury's spring meet – *super-toffs* on parade.

I melted into the usual mix of foot-followers, mostly locals, absorbed in the screwball antics of a mounted brigade busy doffing their bowlers and stovepipe-toppers, baying non-stop a series of 'how-dos' and 'glad to see you outs'.

I quickly scanned the bigwigs but learned little, apart from noting a few familiar faces, like our MP Walter Strangward, Farndon's quack, Simon Mould, the vet Harry Childs.

Suddenly I found myself focused on a disgruntled Bob Grundy. He was fussing and fidgeting like his arse was ablaze, his nag unusually twitchy. An ornery sod at the best of times, his nose turned white when he was rattled, and it already looked decidedly pale. His face reddened, his snout blanched further, he began cursing in earnest, first *sotto-voce*, then way up the scale to crescendo. He called the gelding everything from a big ugly bastard to a stubborn old shit in a recital of classic sobriquets.

"You bugger, you're overfed, that's the problem – but we know how to deal with that!" His fuse shortened, his eyes narrowed and his jaw set fast, as snatching at the reins he abruptly upped his stick, fetching the nag a belter between the ears. Had he *prayed* for fireworks he'd never have done better! Instant and impressive, starting with a nifty pirouette, the incensed beast launched into space, hurtling full-bore to wherever its legs cared to take it, teeth bared, ears flat, eyes wild and wacky... then finally on a beeline for *me!* Mind you I'd asked for it, elbowing my way up front, when I could see well enough from the back.

Two options – stand and be pulped *or* – do a shimmy and jump the six-foot hedge. I did neither – no time. Inches from extinction (mine), the bay dug deep, divots flew, its rump swung clockwise – he'd twigged an escape-route. Down went its head, and it rocketed to the gap in overdrive, scattering the crowd like rice at a Chinese wedding, when a further change of heart had it swing right-handed, clear the hedge by a mile, then scorch up the road with Grundy clutching its mane.

Spitting bottle-tops, I scrambled swiftly across the tufts into safer territory.

"Crikey... that ole bugger's a bit fresh, Dick – Grundy must feed it dynamite," quipped a cloth-capped guy alongside. He cackled at his own smartness, then turned to me, yawping, "Watch it, Matey, 'less you want yer 'air parted. You never know what's comin' next!"

"He's had his share o' corn all right," replied a smirking Dick. "But Grundy never could ride. He should stick to his cart 'osses... silly old sod."

What a pair of beauties! Outsiders, yet somehow familiar, their faces the colour of creosote, a khaki muffler was half-choking Clothcap, before plunging down a faded overcoat bearing the logo of the London and North Eastern Railway. Ready-made roll-ups hooked from a lozenge-tin fed his craving for nicotine, though they petered out faster than he lit them, saliva dribbling onto the flimsy rice-paper, turning it dark oak. They stuck to his lips like mascara to tear-drops, riding up and down with his insane chatter. Dick was tidier, though hardly in dudes, his foxy eyes straddling a beaky nose above an Oundle tie he'd probably nicked from a scarecrow. A raincoat brushed his ankles, fastened with unmatched buttons and a safety-pin. He tugged restlessly at the collar in bids to extend its protection, yet wore neither hat nor scarf.

"It's gettin' nippy Dick... time they moved off." Clothcap hunched his shoulders, stamped his feet, shaking the ground with his hob-goblin boots. "Why they 'ave to muck about so long gets *me* beat – they should 'ead for the woods straight off and get stuck in. Can't they 'unt without a gutsful of booze?" Dick ignored the rhetoric, his supine features near-angelic, the ritual held him spellbound, but eventually he managed a non-committal "Ah." My 'take it or leave it' view of hunting never affected my appreciation of the stirrup-cup, to me a worthwhile ceremony. The sky was all-over blue by now though the north-easterly was evidently finding holes in Clothcap's 'stationmaster' coat.

Cornered by the duck-pond the hounds grew ever more restless, the 'whips' doing their damnedest to make sure they stayed bottled. It took little to set 'em alight. They eyed the old huntsman with a quirky mix of wariness and affection, keen to bound up to Briarsdale and begin probing.

The two dusky know-alls announced to all in earshot the best place to 'find', Charlie's escape-route, how to corner him, or where, in the end he'd turn, grinning with derision at the weary hounds as he scrambled to earth.

Seventy-odd riders were milling around an elm-lined arena stretching from the walled-in courtyard of the Big House down to the bottom hedge, where two field-gates accessed the narrow by-road, one 'tradesmen' the other 'private'. This tiny highway led to a Briarsdale famed for its foxes – speedy as greyhounds, artful as the Pope. In awe we once more studied the nobs in scarlet, wondering where their space-ship had landed, and which planet they were from? *They* eyed *us*, but we wouldn't register.

The waiting began to pall. Restless mounts with edgy riders started jerking about in untidy snatches, turning, twisting, kicking, tossing their heads, scattering foam around like pissed-up Indians making an hilarious mess of dropping their cotton-heads in the basket.

Autumn meets drew the crowds, but the March 'do' topped the bill. Promise of spring prompted a lively buzz amongst the foot-followers, the men deferential, women prim and proper, knowing their place, and oozing subservience. They'd trudged two long miles to reach Bradbury. It wasn't reckoned fashionable to pedal to such grand occasions. But the footsloggers were crafty, acquiring a giant thirst with which to attack the free ale on offer once the chase got under way. Huge ceramic jugs swathed in linen already rested on trestles by the ivy-clad courtyard entrance.

The milling halted – all went quiet – liveners on the way. Seven sprightly damsels in snowy bonnets and lacey aprons, emerged like magic from the courtyard, fanning out briskly into the jostling throng, neatly side-stepping the touchy nags, and plying their pilots with firewater. Few females rode with the West Thorncliffe though the hunt would have gone under without the Finmore sisters. Locals had it they were twins – not so, Elsie being two years Emma's senior. She invariably led the way when the pair set off. If not popular the spinsters were nonetheless grudgingly admired, scrunching along on their skinny old screws, sticking two fingers at an impoverished background. Mid-sixties, with blotchy faces and bottle-blued noses, they downed sherry faster than blacksmiths guzzle cider, but they'd hacked right from Granleigh, so maybe their thirst was understandable?

"Clear the way, damn it... keep hold o' that bloody pony!" A spotty youth on a paunchy piebald whipped round fast, dismayed to see Freddie Fishwick, the Granleigh Grinder, bearing down at speed, desperate to join the show-offs barging up and down the hedgerow. A sneering Fishwick finally missed the lad by a whisker. The local miller, he was eternally unpopular, yet boasted a knot of sycophants ever ready to pander to his vanity – mostly his employees and their families.

At last the 'Field' began circling the paddock in some sort of order. The hounds grew ever more restless, clambering about in bunches in resentment at the restraint. Suddenly Miss Emma displayed her scrawny features again as, ignoring the cries to 'get organised' she snatched up her veil, edging slyly towards a serving maid, the scent of more booze tickling her nostrils. The poor girl twitched with astonishment as Emma suddenly stooped from behind, grabbing at her fifth stiffener with all the finesse of a goshawk. Down it went, and only then did she deign to join the throng, and take up station alongside Elsie.

"Here comes the boss-man, Dick – look at all 'is bloody cronies!" Clothcap waxed indignant as if the boss's hangers-on were somehow a personal inconvenience. Dick shook his head in sympathy, then, switching motions, nodded vigorously to suggest support.

"Ah... bet your life *their* tongues are hangin' out too... scroungin' buggers." He favoured Clothcap with a broad beam.

The 'boss', Colonel Grant-Wilton, rode less and less these days, content just to wander amongst his guests, nodding here and there, guffawing at jests he'd heard a thousand times, tugging his moustache in mock appreciation. His movements were kind of puppet-like, his thighs in control, though the military bearing was unmistakeable. This was the guy who would transform my existence before Christmas was out. A six-footer, spare though not skinny, he wore traditional get-up for swells – all cords and tweed – though his long, waisted jacket held more leather than 'Harris'.

From a distance he looked sort of raffish, but close-up you'd notice the eyes were sombre and distant, the boredom threshold low. His teeth gleamed white and even, every one original. Hatless, no grey hair nor threat of baldness disfigured him, though the unblemished skin looked strangely pale when the sun fell across it, and the mobile mouth could at times look anything but gentle. On top of which George was distinctly unlucky...

He'd suffered spinal damage in the final tank-battle that raged on his bloodied sector of the Western Front. He'd also been rash enough to challenge head-on debilitating doses of pox and clap in the knocking-shops of Roubaix. With his handful of unmounteds he drifted back to the Hall as maids scurried along with the empties.

Watching these VIPs, riders carefully ceding them elbow-room, a lone pony came bouncing along the hedge to my right at the very moment the Grinder tried barging his way through to re-join the parade. Talk about caught with my pants down – for the *second* time that morning. At the gallop, rider bolt upright, composed and confident, like she could clear a mountain if she wished, escape was never an option. I turned, tried a Houdini, Fishwick swung left, but Dick and Clothcap, plus half the village, chose that moment to surge forward, determined to miss none of the action. Smack on the ear she caught me – with her *knee*, luckily not with her boot, but damn it did sting. Ignoring this brush with some cloth-eared yob she charged on unchecked, but in that split-second I couldn't help but notice how beautifully she sat the pony... and how bloody cocky she looked. Hat pulled low, red hair curled beneath the rim, smartly-cut coat, exquisite waistline, shoulders firm and square, she presented an unforgettable image – and a perfect derrière (goddesses don't have bums). This was the handsome Estelle Grant-Wilton everybody knew of but few had had the privilege of meeting. She was around my age... coming sixteen.

"She'll kill 'er bloody self one day, will that young Stella," grunted Clothcap. Although livid, dignity crushed, my ear on fire, I uttered a quick-fire prayer she never would, but I could cheerfully have dunked her in pig-slurry that bright March morning. I bent swiftly, grabbing up chunks of earth, hurling them after her in aggressive gestures of utter futility. She galloped on out of range, oblivious to any havoc she might have caused.

Although sacred territory for this special day, the surrounds were ultra-familiar – I delivered the Hall's newspapers every Sunday. A track ran diagonally from the tradesman's gate to the courtyard, where the last of the maids finally retreated.

The Big House was no 'Luton Hoo' but to us locals, a palace, the gardens screened by giant evergreens, with box and privet protecting the multitudes of crocuses, snowdrops and aconites on display. Every inch was a carpet of brightness, with a backdrop of narcissi, and golden daffodils, the banks crammed with all varieties, their trumpets jostling for space, as they were in the ditches bordering the road to Briarsdale.

The Grant-Wiltons were a *part* of Bradbury, so it surprised me to learn they arrived only around the time I was born. The dynasty was apparently big in cotton, but this chunk of it deserted the satanic mills, shook the dust of Lancashire from their aristocratic feet, brushed up their county accents, and migrated south in clouds of dust, creating the umpteenth squirearchy of the East Midlands. Farndon sits close to the old county border, and Bradbury, the biggest estate around, stretched to five thousand acres, mostly pasture – ideal hunting country. It boasted two giant woods, Briarsdale and Cuckoo-pint Rise, the former a merger of three plantations, a rich mix of elm, oak, beech and the odd horse-chestnut.

Two miles across the valley sat Cuckoo-pint Rise, a circular wood of similar acreage, dominating its surrounds, looked down on a brook meandering east to the flat black lands they call the Fens.

"Look out – they're on the bleedin' move. About time too. *Wake up, Dick!*"

Clothcap coughed violently announcing the 'off' and the dog-end flew from his mouth like a dart from a blowpipe: he leaned forward to monitor progress. Coming slowly to life, Dick followed suit.

Hounds were under way, one 'whip' cracking on ahead, the second close behind, ready to stand point and watch out for strays, or for 'Charlie' slipping away. The hounds were ecstatic, romping along behind the old huntsman, a jostling mass of heads, ears and tongues, tails swaying like flagpoles in the wind. We shot from our slots, darting smartly for a close-up of the Field leaving the paddock. Not that we knew them, apart from the odd bigwig and one or two farmers like Grundy, glad to welcome the Hunt over their land in exchange for free membership.

The scarlet-clad Master led them on to the road. With glossy top hat well forward, he looked big and imposing, like his giant white gelding – a seventeen-hand weight-carrier. Pale eyes glared from beneath heavy blond brows, assuring untouchables his stick was always at the ready. But it wasn't just the face... there was the ugly thick neck, the heavy shoulders, swollen by an over-rich diet.

But his looks didn't bother me, for on his heels, riding as though part of the pony, came the delectable Grant-Wilton girl. Injury dismissed, I gawped in awe at this vision of loveliness. She *also* treated the world with disdain, plus a measure of dislike, doubtless prompted by the mass of foot-soldiers crowding an already congested exit. Somehow, though, she looked *too* aloof, *too* composed. A pose, perhaps? But the eyes were hard and unflinching – the lips set tight. She rose effortlessly for the trot, like on springs fashioned in heaven. Everything about her was spot-on, from the proud bust and tiny waist, to the slender legs sheathed in gleaming boots, with elegant, pinkie-gold tops. The rest I saw only through a golden mist, though more 'girls' were out than I thought, several astride and all weathered as leather.

This second sighting worked wonders, though how I dare think of her as 'Stella' I'll never know. That smack on the ear, burning like hell again, had created a kind of familiarity like a bond had been formed. Mind you, that was only *my* view. I assumed the formidable Miss Grant would dismiss her low-key brush with the peasantry at best as annoying, at worst, disgusting. As the Field tried to exit in a ridiculously tight bunch they all got jostle-itis!

Big fat men! Big fat horses! Big fat women! Big fat bums! Tiny little gaps... Every silly sod seemed intent on breaking their necks to 'get forrard' – pushing, leaning, backing, twisting, turning, cursing like grave-diggers, courtesy strictly on hold. To add to the jam-up a stubborn old mare with warts on her fanny decided to raise her tail, spread her legs, and flood the entrance with urine, while other playful creatures were content to just kick up their heels and treat the assembly to fanfares of flatulence.

"Whoa! *Whoa* there, Tudor! *Punch...* watch it! Steady, damn you! (*Thwack.*) Git on up."

Sorted at last the cavalcade began its uphill 'descent' on to Briarsdale, a giant, ever-shifting canvas against a backdrop of hills, valleys, woods and pastures, with heads bobbing up and down like corks on a tidal estuary. Grabbing my bike I tore in pursuit, swerving through the generous dollops of dung with precision born of experience.

I was a lucky one – I could *ride*. The farmer I worked for at harvest-time had three lusty sons, and to them I owed my prowess in the saddle – and *out* of it – for I conquered bareback first! Each owned a pony and, work permitting, they'd egg me to be Roy Rogers. I never argued.

The pace sharpened; a whistling from above, and the subtle mumble of airborne mallard, signalled ducks on the move. A dozen flashed across the road, and with just one circuit for a look-see, dropped to the water, paddles lowered, brakes applied with precision. Turning back to the hunt I suddenly felt a surge of envy. 'Why can't *I* come out on a horse instead of this pesky pushbike?'

I fondled my collar. 'How would I look in a stock? Where can I borrow a jacket to come a-huntin'? Would the Barfords help out – *they* never ride to hounds? Why not a bona fide fox-hunter, upsides the elegant, if aloof, daughter of the Grant-Wiltons?' Never before had I pondered such fantasies. 'Hell, it'd cost the earth. Ordinary members spend oodles to be on nodding terms with the toffs. Then there's that fierce looking Master! That's a bridge too far even were I stinking rich! Dream on.' The subscription stood at sixty guineas.

Briarsdale at last, hounds already diving in to scour the top sector, darting through the trees like four-legged demons, their black-and-tan coats lending a special air of menace to the search. To work on scent alone, never sight, baffles mere mortals. The chatter of the riders subsided. The Field began cantering up the outer ride, desperate to keep in touch, and avoid the wrath of the foul-mouthed, if fussy Fieldmaster, while Fred, the old huntsman, with the Master hidden somewhere close by, ploughed a lonely furrow along a cross-ride, his head swivelling like a well-oiled gun-turret. From time to time he'd call to his charges in an odd mix of discipline and affection, then crack his whip round their ears.

"Minster... Marvel... MARVEL! Hey... Mason... MASON! *Bugger* ya!" But the pack stayed mute... and there was no sign of Grundy's body – or of his fractious mount. I half-expected him dangling from an elm, or spread-eagled on blackthorn.

I took this in very slowly. Though deep into favourite territory, which sometimes admitted Joe Public, on this occasion neither the furry pussy-willow, nor the sunlit catkins,

10

could erase the memory of that brush with Miss Grant that landed me a very thick ear.

Dumping the bike, I stalked cautiously up the outer ride. 'Watch your step. Do nothing daft. Don't for Christ's sake head the fox, or cross the hounds.' The familiar, sickly-sweet smell of earthy growth, peat-fed roots, rotting leaves and squirrel-shit swamped me, and the woodlands sprang to life.

Pigeons exploded from the tree-tops, fluttering like mad before deciding the safest route. Indignant pheasants, knowing running yields few dividends, took to the air with alacrity, squawking their way across the valley in hell-for-leather bids for the sanctuary of Cuckoo-pint Rise. Fieldfares soared in hundreds; hordes of redwings, starlings, and cawking rooks rose to join them... plus a solitary, sinister, for-ever-on-the-lookout sparrow-hawk, climbing, turning, gliding, spinning, then diving rocket-like on to some unwary songbird. A handful of wiseacres joined me, Dick and Clothcap amongst them. Sure enough, Clothcap began spouting wisdom.

"The crafty ole bugger'll be gone by now. No wonder – the racket they kick up – talk about a bloody beer-garden – got nothing on this lot. Charlie's 'opped it."

He was mistaken. From somewhere behind, strident 'holloas' and shrill horn-blasts, signalled the Hunt 'away' – hounds back in the open.

Up ahead half a dozen thrusters turned like lightning, and came belting flat out for the ride-gate, desperate to savour a two-mile point to Cuckoo-pint. A rare feat lifting a fox *that* fast from a covert the size of Briarsdale. But that's what it's all about – gloriously unpredictable. And this fellow might do a bender, and by devious cunning scuttle back to the woods via some secret detour up near the Holt, or maybe by skirting Chucklecopse. We shrank to one side, giving the bunch a clear run, my heart thumping like mad when I realised Estelle led the way. Lips parted, cheeks glowing red, grey eyes alive and dancing, she pushed the chestnut to his limit, shoving him hard at the ride-gate, clearing it easily, as 'footmen' signalled the road clear, shouting that hounds were screaming on a 'fresher than fresh' line towards the Rise. Hedge and dyke opposite were conquered with disdain, and all six put their heads down in joyful anticipation of a real fast point.

At the gallop too we bike-wallahs gave chase. Pushing the gate aside we pedalled furiously after the tootling horn, thankful for the handy, if roughened, track linking the two great woods of Bradbury.

Breathless, my chest going like a frog's belly, I asked a biker the time. Mustn't be late on a Saturday. Only midday, but dinner was at one – on the dot. Mum blew her top if I was late. I hadn't intended 'following' – just a quick shufti then home, was the original idea. But it wasn't the Hunt I was after – only the goddess concerned me. Had *she* not been pounding flat-out for Cuckoo-pint, no way would I be pedalling like mad in that direction.

With a whoosh the Field came thundering abreast, pounding the weak, weed-ridden winter wheat bordering the track. 'Cocky' Gannett, the jockey-sized Fieldmaster, was in no mood for pleasantries, his wrinkled features brick-red, his neck plum-coloured. Estelle's breach of etiquette had sent him barking. She'd upstaged him, taking her bunch of thrusters ahead of the official entourage.

'God – she's overrun the hounds! *Unpardonable...*'

I spotted Elsie Finmore on Gannett's outside, scrubbing at her old screw, arms going like connecting-rods on a steam-engine. Emma rode close up, fuelled on Bradbury firewater. But somebody was due a bollocking... Cocky's *face* told us that, and being in front I was odds-on to catch the flak!

"Keep to the fackin' track, Ape! Can't ya see you're impedin' the *Hunt?*"

He shrieked his command in top C, retaining his posh accent, his eyes pinpricks, his mouth screwed up like a ferret's. I'd hardly left the wretched track. You can't pedal a bike on sprouting corn with morning dew still lingering.

About to tell him 'get stuffed' he swung his roan towards me, swapped his stick over and walloped it across my shoulders! It stung like buggery – it sent me ape. With back hunched, and chin buried, I somehow managed to keep the bike straight and made a grab at his reins. I missed. But I was lucky. By an outrageous fluke I got hold of the bit-ring and clinging like a limpet, gave it all I'd got, dragging the nag round in a scrabbling half-circle. The bike slid from beneath me and the startled creature took root, sending Gannett flying over its head, describing a perfect arc then ending up flat to the ground, face down, gurgling obscenities as he mouthed mud and cornstems. Taking a savage kick at its girth I sent his mount spurting on ahead, the empty stirrups clanking on its belly.

"Don't you ever try that again, Mister Gannett – I'll butcher you, then hang you out to dry – I *mean* it, you little swine." He clawed despairingly at the gooey soil. I wanted to stamp on him and grind him into the earth. The injustice of his attack had sent me crazy. I'd never before threatened an adult. But I meant it. Being big and strong can be handy.

The rest of the Field swept by, nearing the slope to Cuckoo-pint. Little Caesar somehow scrambled to his feet looking a sorry sight, his bleached breeches a darkish brown, his scarlet coat caked in mud. Waving wildly, then commanding a lift on a weighty cob he shot me a look of sheer malevolence, but that's all, and his embarrassed chauffeur kicked on in vain hopes of catching the unfortunate roan. Cocky's face was redder than a pheasant's at mating time.

Dick bellowed 'bollocks' to no one in particular, but it barely carried, though far enough to earn a censorial scowl from a white-haired old buffer cracking away at the rear, wearing a faded stovepipe and chewing a fat cigar.

I was lucky – nearer to Cuckoo-pint meant nearer to home. The Rise looked down on Farndon – in every way. A handful of ambitious bikers were still tagging along, and we'd collected a sprinkling of less gutsy equestrians, including a subdued Grundy, who feared the hedges looked a bit big, and maybe barbed-wire lurked?

It became clear 'Charlie' was winning. All went quiet, hounds were puzzled, finally hitting off on a different line, swinging left-handed short of the Rise intent on a U-turn to Briarsdale. Almost recovered from the fracas, with a sigh I let them go, carrying on to where the track joins the back road to Farndon. Then the piss-taking began...

"What's wrong? Not goin' *'ome?* Gannett put the wind up ya, 'as he boy?"

Clothcap tried winding me up, his rasping voice rankled. Then Dick put *his* oar in.

"You've had a rough ole mornin', Matey. Give huntin' a rest. Get yoursen a whip and top..."

"Oh... go to hell – the pair of you." I was stuck for something biting, and the snidery grated. I watched as they swung their bikes towards Briarsdale. I rested a while, then finished up having a laugh. The ribald humour was about par. So too was Cocky's rage – it gave the day gyp. I cruised home in time for dinner. Hungry as the clappers, in love or not, murderous threats shelved, I tucked into mountains of shepherds' pie steeped in Mum's finest gravy, followed by spotted-dick. We always had 'special' on Saturdays, as well as Sunday. Bread and lard left the menu. In the week I made do with a pack-up, grammar-school being ten miles off. But delicious though the meal turned out, I was in a different world, hardly hearing a word Mum said, occasionally muttering half-hearted replies. She spotted the abstraction – usually I was sharp as a needle, noting every word, every nuance.

"You're quiet today – too hungry to talk?" A dash of vinegar spiced the barb, plus more than a hint of sarcasm. The sharp black eyes in the smallish face, gave me a questioning look I'd ignore at my peril.

"No, Mum – I'm thinking, that's all."

"Not about your *dinner!* You're miles away. Where is it today, Shangri-La or Shanghai?"

I laughed. I'd never beat her in a battle of wits. As well she spoke out – to get me off cloud nine, though I couldn't understand being *so* off-balance?

"Oh, nowhere like that. Up in the woods – hunting. We just had a smashing run..."

"Where from... where *to?*"

"We fetched him out of the thicket and took him to the Cuckoo Fork."

"*He* took *you*, more like! No more than two miles – almost straight!" She dismissed the point with contempt.

"Francis! *Francis...* What's wrong with your ear? It's all torn. Smothered in blood! Go and get it washed – this minute. *Go on!*" I shuffled to the kitchen, squinted in the tiny looking-glass, surprised at the mess. I dabbed it with a flannel. It wasn't half as bad as it looked, but I welcomed the chance to disappear. Mum's probing was beginning to grate – and I wasn't prepared to spill the beans. Trouble was, I couldn't always read her thoughts, though mostly they were crystal-clear, and she could put the mockers on me without a word.

"That's better," she said. "It still looks nasty though." I thought it wise to fib.

"I caught it – coming out of Briarsdale – you should see the brambles! They're thicker than ever. It doesn't *hurt...*"

"Oh," she murmured, looking mighty thoughtful. She knew damn well I was lying. Then I got angry with myself. 'A cocky little madam decides to show off, bashes into you without caring tuppence, and you tell lies to defend her. Come to your senses, you mug!'

I did. At least I tried.

Chapter Two

Estelle

Next day was Sunday: paper-round day, nothing could change *that*, and being my sole earner the four-bob reward was a fortune – not a cat in hell's of upping the ante before harvest. Mum, along with thousands of others, was a war-widow eking out her army pension odd-jobbing – sewing, embroidery, maybe laundry. Dad had been a saddler, guided by a disabled Grandad, until the Squareheads got him, forcing the sale of the business. The proceeds helped buy a cottage, though it was still a scratch and scrape existence, typical of the hard-up Thirties.

Reaching Bradbury, the round about finished, I lobbed the bike on the tradesmen's gate and hopped over with their up-market newsprint, praying for a miracle. The ducks were kicking up hell – a harsh, ear-splitting ante-natal serenade coming from the pond – the fluffy yellow ducklings hatch in early April. The miracle would be a glimpse of the elegant, if elusive, Estelle, making my day, my week and my year. I'd smartened up a bit – flannels pressed, clean shirt, best sweater, my mop more or less tidy.

Church-bells were clanging, Granleigh's or Little Downton's, maybe both? It was hard to tell. Their music filled the valley as rooks circled aimlessly, bound for nowhere, doves fluttering fitfully in the treetops. The mournful lowing of cattle, the non-stop bleat of new-born lambs and the gabble of greedy geese, contributed to a familiar symphony... when the bells permitted. Another day of rustic pursuits under way. The sun shone bright, a repeat of Saturday, the sky blue-over, hawthorn displaying that delicate shade of green that darkens rapidly as it opens. Serving the Hall was no problem – nobody was ever around. Bung the papers in the letter-box and that was that. Aristocrats, they wouldn't dream of paying on the dot like normal folk, but settle monthly, including 'dailies' which didn't concern me – I'd have missed the school bus had I done them.

Turning into the courtyard, looking across at an east-facing wall rising sheer to the clouds, four heavy-looking doors confronted me – kitchen, scullery, store-room, and larder. A fire-escape abutted the wall five yards on from the larder. The yard was dead empty, like the stables, unless they housed Shetlands. Folding the papers (mustn't deface such rich material) I shoved them in the letter-box one at a time giving the second an extra whack to make sure they dropped. About to risk a quick sortie I turned away, when a voice suddenly cried, "Hey... boy! You dropped *this!* Look!"

"Eh?" I swung round fast, the strident hail startled me. 'Where did it come from?' Puzzled, I stood there goon-like, my face red (I can tell). She came round the corner waving a coin – a florin, or a half-crown, with about as much expression as a gargoyle. Hard and unyielding the big grey eyes looked right through me to some distant landmark. She was in a pink frock dotted with tiny blue flowers – I remember it well – sandals completed her rig-out. Auburn curls swirled around the shoulders, framing a face smooth as dairy-cream, and every bit as innocent. For the first time I saw perfection from close up. Small oval features, tiny straight nose, firm yet full lips, and a shapely chin – but the glare was drop-dead daunting, her neutrality obscene. We were from different worlds. Always had been, always would be – *plus ça change.*

"Here," she said, flicking me the coin. I went to catch it but the damn thing didn't carry, dropping smack into a blob of mud. Her nonchalance griped; I felt something go 'boing!'.

'Why should *I* pick up the blasted coin? So it's worth a bit, and probably belongs to Jack Rowell, but damned if I'll go on hands and knees for it.' My face turned ashen (I can tell that too). Her eyes didn't flicker, the face stayed cool, impersonal, uninvolved: without a word but with the grace of a Markova, she floated towards me, retrieved the coin in one silky swoop, and plonked it on my outstretched palm. I could have wept, cursed, *screamed* with embarrassment, all at the same time, but hung on somehow, murmuring, "Thanks." She knew she'd got me rocking. Stella was a clever one alright, if shortish on book-learning; well aware she'd scored... *and* converted. Then came the transition. The lovely big eyes showed a morsel of interest – she spotted the cauliflower ear. But the upstaging had drained my confidence, and caused my boorish attitude.

"You're the boy I sent flying yesterday – aren't you?"

Her voice had a kind of metallic ring – I liked it. She didn't smile.

"Yes," I mumbled, trembling now. The girl was dynamic, the current tangible. She overwhelmed me in that few seconds. I was totally hooked by this close, yet remote creature who rendered me so damned juvenile. Face to face, the world fading to nothing, my five foot-ten put Stella four inches shorter – but it was obvious who called the shots!

"Sorry about that," she said simply, turning away, making for the stables. Dimly I wondered why, seeing they were empty. A second block stood over the road, next to the cottages. I'd seen nags poking their heads out when I came by. She had a long, anxious look in the end stall, leaning right over the half-door: I came to life. Trudging back to the tradesmen's gate, thinking what a prat I'd been, I sensed a vague ripple of alarm. 'How much *more* have I lost? Where did the half-crown *come* from?' I always kept big silver along with the banknotes, in an old cartridge-bag buried beneath the papers. My palms began sweating.

'What if it *isn't* mine – or rather, isn't Jack's? Did she just *guess* I'd dropped it, and did the decent thing?' I dived for my jacket-pocket, groped anxiously – no holes there. Then the other side – likewise nothing. 'It *can't* be mine. I haven't touched my pockets since coming up here. Who's the clown with dosh enough to drop half-crowns?'

Meticulous with the takings, every last farthing went down in my little red book where I'd laboriously drawn verticals criss-crossing the horizontals. Every tuppence, fourpence, sixpence, shilling... sometimes a quid – I did a tally the minute I got home. Discrepancies were rare. This time the pattern varied – two-and-six to the good!

'That proves it – the coin *isn't* mine.' For ages I weighed up the options. 'Do I keep it? Hand it to Jack? Give Mum it? Or... *hell*, return it to where it belongs – the Hall. That *would* kibosh the plot. Insult the girl's honesty, snub her kind intentions, embarrass her. Hang on! What about some brownie-points?'

'No! She'll think me a bigger nerd than she does already. One other option. Tell Mum. Spin her the whole yarn (bar emotional bits) then listen to her canny solution. She's bound to better anything *I* can come up with.' She shouted from the kitchen, tetchy as ever.

"Francis! *Francis!* What the devil are you up to? That wretched bicycle's *broken* again, isn't it? Dinner's ready, come on in or I'll plaster it on the wall."

Alone in the shed, I'd spread the coins over the bench in piles, wedging the notes behind the vice. I swept the lot into the cartridge-bag. I'd deal with it later.

"Coming, Mum. The chain's playing tricks, that's all."

My appetite suffered nothing from the mental acrobatics, and I tried to steer clear of paper-rounds, the Grant-Wiltons, or any talk of windfalls. But Mum, like all women, wanted details. 'Who's ill, who's out, who didn't pay, who hid behind the door, who's doing their washing, whose dog chased you?' My mumbled replies fell a long way short of the folksy tittle-tattle she wanted.

"Have you fixed that wretched bike, then?"

"Yeah... it'll be alright."

"You shouldn't need to fiddle with it *every* day."

"No. It's OK."

"Well, you had it to bits on... Oh, go back to your dreaming."

Her change of tack surprised me. It often did.

Nobody else to turn to, apart from Grandad, and I never liked troubling *him*. 'If I mention it to Jack, he'll say 'stick to it' then dock it from my pay... it'll have to wait.'

Jack kept the grocer's by the green, selling papers as a sideline – most delivered, some over the counter. On the quiet, he sold other extras too – men only! Unlike most folk, I didn't dislike the bloke. He was OK with *me*, going out of his way to praise me at times, like the time I passed off a 'News of the Screws' as more of a 'family' paper to some innocent Baptist, after Jack had cocked up the sorting. On Sundays he masterminded a sizeable operation: eight boys setting out first-thing loaded to the gunwhales with news at twice the price of the dailies, plus 'delivery'.

He was getting on now, into his sixties, but still energetic, still an entrepreneur, nipping around in a grey, ironmonger's smock over a paper-thin pepper-and-salt suit, his head bald as an ice-rink, an artful grin on his weasel-like mug. Half the time he was keeping clear of his warlike wife who dealt him some playful blows when things went wrong however much he pleaded his innocence. She was twice his size, and known, *inter alia*, as 'Winnie Weighfingers'. Shoppers were wary, watching her closely while keeping her at arm's length: her onion-laden breath had been known to cut through fog.

Jack had set out the shop so he could watch the punters using the post-office cum-store across the road, and from his side-window, spot all the foot-traffic to-ing and fro-ing via Jubilee Street. Telling Jack to mind his own business was a waste of breath.

There *was* Uncle Joseph, Dad's young brother. Joe was OK, but Auntie Dora never seemed pleased to see me. With four kids hanging to her arse, and forever nursing a dodgy back, that wasn't to be wondered at. But she never got over

Joseph being denied a chance to take over the saddler's when Dad joined up, which I thought rich seeing the business came to us through Mum's side, and by trade Joseph was a butcher's hacker.

Their council 'semi' was never kept spick and span like our house. The kitchen was blanketed in steam whenever *I* called, as well as knee-deep in dirty washing and crappy nappies. She chucked me a bundle one day, moaning, "Take a look at that bloody lot – *go on* – they won't *bite!*" Gingerly I tried peeling them apart – they stuck like fivers to a bookie's fist. Ugh! Disgusting.

"Why didn't they make shit *WHITE?*" she shrieked. She had a point. I don't remember seeing Auntie Dora without a fag, though she only smoked Woodbines, tuppence for five, in green open-ended packets. For some strange reason she made sure the ash dropped in with the washing – and she could never resist poking the clothes every two minutes, then waving the soap-smoothed stick round her head like a gladiator celebrating victory, sword aloft. Maybe she tried to impress me? Maybe she enjoyed the chaos? Her back-yard looked like a warship dressed with clothes-lines coming at you from every angle, all anchored to the multi-ringed cast-iron brackets, shackled to the wall above the outdoor bog. Not so long ago Dora had been a pretty young woman – she could soon have tarted herself up again... a knowing smile, and a hint of something deeper lurked behind that feisty façade, not unlike Alice Faye's. Of varying talents, she served the community as chief 'layer-out'. The first person called to the death-chamber when church-bells delivered their sombre message. Mary Swanley from the bread-shop helped her out, reassured by Auntie's confident assertion, "Don't worry, Mary. If the body's on the 'high' side I'll hammer the fags and cover you with smoke."

The mock-Oxford loomed, every bit as daunting as the real thing. Just weeks away, I was busy as the devil at school, with

two hours homework at night. It was vital I secure my
'Oxford', and fulfil Mum's undying ambition to land me a
'respectable' job. That half-crown still weighed heavily,
however, whatever the priorities. I wrapped it in a hankie, and
hid it at the bottom of the dressing-table drawer. After all,
whoever owned it, Stella gave me it. It bore her fragrance, her
goodwill – and her awful arrogance. Though it bothered me, it
was by far my favourite treasure.

'I'm being plain stupid! If I return it I'll *see* her again,
speak to her, touch her hand as I pass it over.' The
possibilities were vast – and tempting, but I couldn't bring
myself to risk the humiliation.

'She *didn't* humiliate me. It's just her way. She was kind –
now it turns out it belongs elsewhere. Oh, Sunday's soon
enough. It's mine till then. Unless... unless... she's off
schooling again? But we're into term time... how come she's
still around? Has she *finished* school – for good? Waiting for
college. Off boarding again?' The Hall, minus Estelle, just
another port of call.

Sunday was a long way off, but eventually arrived (it
usually does), and I strode eagerly across the quarter-mile of
paddock, and the sun still shone. In contrast to the week
before, the courtyard bristled with activity. All bustle and
bounce. A recalcitrant nag spun in circles, resisting desperate
attempts by its would-be rider to mount in mid-whirl. A
glance told me it wasn't Estelle. Alarmed, a peacock took off,
screeching like mad as it lumbered towards the vegetable
gardens walled off behind the stables. A second soon followed
suit. Two West Highland Whites fought a 'pretend' battle by
the scullery door refereed by a lofty Red Setter lazily raising
its paw as if in reproof, but enjoying the fun no end.

A uniformed maid, minus bonnet, brushed away
vigorously at nothing in particular, from time to time stopping
to survey the world, brandishing her broom like she was
practising bayonet thrusts, convincing her employers, and

anybody around, of her unflagging devotion to duty; meanwhile Old Sourpuss, the head keeper, cycled majestically down the front drive as if he owned the place, his bike festooned with all the tools of his trade. Snares, nets, canes, string, wire, a ferret-box strapped to the carrier and, of course, the principal weapon in his armoury, a shotgun tied beneath the crossbar. A canvas holdall dangled from his shoulder. Steady as a rock and upright as a Coldstream Guard, he clearly had permission to use the gilded exit. His moleskin breeches looked like they'd last for a thousand years provided he'd plenty of leg-laces.

At the kitchen door, looking in a bit of a tizzy, a biggish lady, bonnet askew and hair hanging loose, beckoned irritably to a slow-moving old character shuffling by the stable-block wearing a blue jacket bleached by the years, grey trousers with knee-straps (rat-repellents), boots with upturned toecaps, and a billycock hat that had begun life as a trilby. He hauled a wicker basket crammed with greens, but I couldn't tell the breed. Brassicas rarely yield in early March. All of a sudden he stopped and, turning his head, gripped his nose between finger and thumb and let go a great trumpet-blast, fortunately diverting the effluent wide of his overloaded trug.

To top it all, hens from over the road were invading the saintly premises in strength. They squawked in terror, leaping like leopards, when a second maid charged in earnest, hustling them raggedly but relentlessly at a hole in the wall, her face pillar-box red. She bristled with indignation, yet was obviously enjoying the razzmatazz.

I took it all in at a glance, for it was incidental to my errand, my one ambition being to catch a glimpse, however fleeting, of the cool and classy Estelle. And I succeeded – albeit in dubious fashion. Cook, growing increasingly impatient, grabbed the papers without taking her eyes off the cumbrous gardener, and I turned away, flat and empty, convinced the week of torment had all been in vain, my emotional energy squandered. The 'coin of remembrance' burned a hole in my back pocket – almost. Retreating to the entrance I turned for a final look, when, surely, *'there's* Estelle peering from that upstairs window. It *must* be her.'

Instantly she flashed like lightning along what I took to be a landing. I watched in awe as she passed window after window, praying she'd at least turn her head, or give some faint signal of recognition. What a state to get into!

'She's obviously seen me, yet pretends she hasn't. Naturally she snubs me. What else can she do? Lady of the Manor... almost – me, a ruddy paper-boy. What crazy dreams!' No point hanging around, and crazy though the dreams were I was so besotted I trudged back to the peak-tuggers' gate with my head in a whirl, though relieved to learn she was still at home; that *had* to be a bonus. And she'd watched me come away – or was she merely weighing up the antics in the yard below? Who knows? Anyway, I'd had my glimpse.

Despite achievements on the school playing-fields, I was never a hundred percent 'action man' but irrevocably given to odd spells of self-doubt and musing, especially after the acquisition of that blessed half-crown. I racked my brains trying to work out where it came from, desperately objective, but couldn't put my finger on a thing, the attempts ever more hopeless – I knew they would be. And nothing could lessen Stella's magic – nor should it. No happening on Planet Earth for the past sixteen years had prepared me for this mental turmoil. A million times I re-lived the moment her hand brushed mine when she passed me the coin. The vision of her charging the ride-gate had become a permanence. The currents of ecstasy coursing non-stop through my gawky frame were as nothing I'd ever known.

The world went up a couple of notches, three perhaps. The sun shone brighter, trees waved their greetings, people became more friendly, Jack bordering on the benign. Girls from the co-ed paled to nonentities: bland, boring, banal even. So did the village belles, and all within pushbike range. Weird spells of discontent were to follow, so alien to my usual outlook I became convinced I was round the twist – or on the way! I'd kick at the poor old sideboard, hating it for its ordinariness, scowl at the dresser in contempt, the stair-carpet looked aged and threadbare, the cottage seemed tiny. All the things I unthinkingly loved and cherished, now ranked second-rate. And I hated myself. I had no understanding of the lovelorn youth of fiction... or of fact. And the world quickly dropped a notch, so soon after its rapid elevation.

Thanks to my youth the moods passed, crystallising into an overwhelming desire to gaze once more upon the beauty of the elusive Miss Grant – if only at a distance. The feeling so overpowered me I jumped aboard the bike when tea was over, ignoring homework, sprinted to Cuckoo Fork, raced across the track to Briarsdale, hurtled down to Bradbury and savoured the delights of Paradise.

Labourers had finished for the day, and I hung around between farmyard and Hall, trying to look both prominent and unobtrusive. Not easy. Desperately I scanned the grounds, praying for a peek, however fleeting, of Miss Wonderful, and hoping *she'd* spot *me*. What a disaster! Not a glimpse on offer – the first night, the second, the third – and by the fourth I'd nearly had a bellyful. I wilted. Then things came right – on the Friday.

Slowing down, almost at the Hall, a thunderous pounding drowned out the universe. With a whoosh of air Stella came scorching by as if Apaches had crossed the ridge. Hair flying wild in the wind, lips parted, bottom raised, she seared my ruddy elbow. Scared half to death, I braked hard, ramming my foot to the road. What a miracle... I'll never forget. She rose in the stirrups, reined in, turned, and trotted back to where I stood, bewildered, using my bike for support. To crown it all she slid from the saddle, standing just yards away, the 'pony', which I now realised was a horse of fifteen hands, blowing like a grampus.

In hopeless confusion I dropped the bike and stood free, shy and awkward, yet almost on fire. *Her* face was red too, with exhilaration – and perhaps (oh hell) irritation? Speechless, I stared open-mouthed at this brand-new vision. Curly copper hair framed the innocent young face, her breasts proud beneath a well-worn jumper matching the ancient jodphurs and the worn-out boots. And the eyes didn't harden. Nor were they soft – somewhere in between – superior, but human.

"Why are you always down here?" she asked, coolly. 'So she *has* spotted me in the evenings.' A flicker of hope.

"I like it this way, Miss." 'There! *Damn!* My ridiculous serfdom again. Calling her 'Miss' just plain stupid.'

"Yes... But *every night* – you must get bored out of your mind."

"No... I'm *never* bored down here. I'd rather be at Bradbury than anywhere."

"How's the ear – better is it? It looks OK to me."

Now she smiled – and I was committed, with scant control over what I said or did. Intoxicated by her magic. Spellbound. Her nearness electrified the world. The transition from hard as nails to near-friendliness was like a wand had been waved. I made no protest nor showed resentment when she powered by – no more than an involuntary jerk – so why the transformation? Why rein in, turn, and jump off? Three bonuses in one.

"It's alright, thanks," I murmured. "I came in the hopes of seeing *you*."

The eyes changed in a flash – to a chilling hostility. They lasered me. Then back to neutral just as fast.

"Whatever for?" she asked, lips taut, her body tense.

"To apologise." What little boldness I'd rustled up, flagged.

"Whatever *for*?" she said, stressing the 'for'.

"I was rude to you. Horribly rude. Something came over me... so sorry."

"I probably deserved it – that's nothing. *I* don't remember, anyway." She burst out laughing. I detected relief. No point now in returning the half-crown, or even mentioning it.

"I wanted to apologise on Sunday, but you vanished – along the landing. You're a great rider – you don't half go at it, Stella!" In a rush I blurted it out, afterthought and all.

"Do you ride?" she asked, quietly.

"A bit." She was suitably impressed.

"Here – have a go then. Come on Maddy, give the boy a ride."

The stirrups looked about right; although shortish, her legs were long, her body small. With no more ado she passed me the reins, I leapt in the saddle, no need for a leg-up.

"Take him to the thicket... let him stretch a bit. He's puffing, though he can't be tired – we've only been out half an hour." Maddy made a kind of huffing noise, giving himself an all-over shake – he wasn't too sure.

She laughed, smacked his rump, sending us off with a cheery, "Hey-Upp!" I sorted the reins, 'collected' him, let him go. He was fast alright, but I wouldn't push him. He had class – I'd never felt power like it between my knees. The ride was a thriller, every stride an experience. We neared the thicket much too soon for my liking. Easing him down, I crossed to the gate, tugging his ears to say 'thank you', then stroked the glossy neck. He panted again. So did I. Soon, however, he relaxed, bending to nibble at the fresh grass beneath the obstacle he'd cleared with such panache a week earlier.

"Good lad. Good lad. There's a good lad." Exhilarated, I talked to him with fondness. Not merely was I on nodding terms with the loveliest creature on Earth, but her horse was mine too – for the moment.

"Well done! You ride well!" I turned in surprise. There was Estelle pedalling along merrily on *my* steed, her face alive with excitement. She looked too good to be true. Reluctantly I jumped down.

"He's great" I enthused. "And so are you."

Out it came – in a rush – the relentless babble of a youth in the first flushes – but I meant it.

"Don't talk rubbish!" she snapped. "I'm horrid – they *all* say so. My temper's frightful! Get the wrong side of me, you'll soon find out!" I thought she'd clout me – she'd hung on to her stick when we changed mounts. We switched again, Stella with Maddy, me with the bike, facing each other by the ride-gate. The silent contest – it *was* a contest – tangible. Then I smiled, reaching out to her. She froze me – easily. I only wanted to touch her. Her eyes went cold as a fish – nob versus yob – the winner already crowned. I reached out again to that wonderful lithe body – she backed off quickly. I was stumped... frustrated.

"I'd love to come again." Taking an extra-deep breath, I somehow got the words out, convinced I'd messed things up.

"Of *course*. Come tomorrow, if you like. I'll be here. Maybe I'll walk up. By the way, you know you're something of a hero? MrGannett's not the most popular of men."

"Eh?"

"The Hunt servants loathe him, and the members had a good laugh when he rolled up riding pillion. He was lucky – he had a change of gear in his box. He's an auctioneer – with Dobbs, Staples and Timms – in Thrapston."

"Oh... objectionable little pig! He was luckier than he *knew*..." She smiled, then with a twist and a wriggle was in the saddle and away. I watched her over the brow of the little hill, and into Bradbury drive. She didn't look round, nor did she wave. In a trance I mounted the Raleigh, pedalling slowly towards Cuckoo-pint, forgetting tomorrow was Saturday, and maybe there'd be a meet somewhere. 'Has she forgotten? Well, it doesn't matter, she's my friend – that's the main thing. Wants to see me again – nothing can change that, even if she chickens out. Boy, what a miracle!'

All the same something kept on nagging. Disturbing, niggling... something significant to the unlikely events that had ended with me, the paper-boy, dating the daughter of the biggest swell in the region, a girl who, even to the short-sighted, was the prettiest on earth.

Here I should point out that although in Farndon parish, the Grants were never looked upon as part of the community. Two miles or so from the church, and the Hall so remote, they had more affinity with Granleigh, and villages south, than with us. None of the housemaids claimed to be a Farndonite, nor did the gardeners, the chauffeur, the groom, the handyman, gamekeepers... not even the labourers were proper locals – they were from Granleigh, or Little Downton.

It seems when they first came to Bradbury the Grant-Wiltons went out of their way to become patricians of the district: friendly and helpful. Locals rejected their overtures with the bloody-mindedness typical of village types – especially worthies edging up the ladder themselves. The 'freshers' from Lancashire reacted accordingly, and went to ground, so to speak, taking damn good care never to surface in Farndon again. They were hurt, humiliated... ostracised for being wealthy. They took revenge in their own sweet way.

And my own attitude? My adulation, my total submission to the charms of the incomparable Miss Grant? 'Do the feelings in some way stem from *who* she is, not what she is? Does her elevated status, and the aura of mystery attaching to the Grant-Wiltons in the fastness of 'Fort Bradbury', free of the common herd (of which I'm an irrevocable slice), somehow spice the conquest? Would I worship the ground the baker's daughter walks on, the milkman's, the coalman's, or...?' A voice tells me, 'No'; but I can live with that – otherwise things are first-rate. As for the mock-Oxford... does it matter? Of course it does! But I had to keep reminding myself, and heed Mum's ceaseless promptings. Not a hope of jumping ship!

Saturday's jobs kept me busy all morning. In turbulent mood after the magic of Friday (I'd skipped homework), duty took priority. Kindling for the week came first. I bashed away in the shed, slicing through the billets like they were butter. Hens to feed and water, garden to dig, and seeds to go in during March. Milk to fetch, the weekly shopping, and for ages Mum had complained of the handgate dropping to pieces, yet it managed to open and close on its one sound hinge. It could wait. I helped shake the mats, empty the grate, find fuel for the copper-fire. Mum never stopped working, though what she did all the time often puzzled me.

"Were the Grant-Wiltons 'out' last week?" she asked suddenly, apropos nothing. We were having dinner ('lunch' if you like). I turned scarlet under her knowing gaze – she frowned.

"Well, the Colonel didn't ride... I don't believe the Lady did either – I'm not sure... *Estelle* did – she's brilliant. You should see her *jump!*"

"Cocky little monkey, I hear, though nobody sees much of her. They tuck themselves away down at Bradbury still. They'll *never* support Farndon. Fêtes, fairs, football, fun-days, whatever... not a sign of 'em. I suppose Rupert's still up at Cambridge... Justin in London – something in the City, they tell me?"

Aliens they *might* be, but Mum knew all there was to know about the Grant-Wiltons, or thought she did...

Chapter Three
Carolean

Five o'clock couldn't come soon enough. Out came the old tin bath and the square of lino. I locked the kitchen door and got down to it, not forgetting ears and elbows. I dashed up the stairs, hooked out my white shirt, tweed (imitation) jacket, Sunday flannels, and prepared to go. Mum nodded approval but didn't comment – indulgence said it all. Behind the dark eyes in the tiny, inquisitive features, I sensed pride in my being big and tall, like my Dad in his army photos. Down went my head, I pedalled hard, whizzing across to the Cuckoo Fork in record time, joining the track to Briarsdale.

'Will she turn up? Am I late? Will she wait? What can we talk about?' Rounding the final bend in that wide landscape of ups and downs (ancient attempts at drainage), workers long since departed, Briarsdale loomed into view, and nailed to an elm by the side of the gate a warning to would-be trespassers that prosecution would follow if they dared to transgress. And alongside the forbidding notice stood Stella.

My heart leapt, I pedalled even harder. Though still, she looked high and mighty. Haughty, contained, in control of the universe – but peering my way. Jumping down, I dumped the bike, striding across the road trying to rival the goddess for coolness. Then she relaxed – a picture of loveliness, smiling, unaffected, eyes soft and gentle, delighted to see me.

"I've brought Adam," she said. "Hope you don't mind?"

"Eh? Who's *Adam?*" I whipped round, surprised.

"Hey! Addy! *Addy!* Where *are* you? He's after rabbits."

She grinned, her eyes wrinkled. Adam was a dog. I wasn't keen to share Stella – with anybody. Leaping from the undergrowth, dancing round the keeper's gibbet came a handsome Red Setter. It looked familiar. It regularly teased the terriers at the Hall. Another touch of class to bolster England's prettiest citizen. Clawing at her legs, tongue flapping, saliva dribbling, tail going like a metronome, he craved attention, but she wanted none of it, controlling him as easily as she did the universe. In a tatty, though top-label jacket, scuffed twills, done-for joddy-boots, her red hair glistened, waltzing round the smooth features and dancing on the resolute shoulders, her eyes bright with humour, lips parted. 'She must be hard up for boyfriends – what can she see in *me*?' Her opening gambit surprised me.

"What do I call you, then?" Face to face, and close up, she posed the intimate question.

"My name's Allner." I replied, with a touch of pride – don't ask me why.

"Is that your first name – or what?" I think she giggled.

"I'm *Francis* – though they call me Frank at school – and in the village."

"Well, you're Franz from here on – I can't stand the name Frank." The simple comment implied a fondness that would last and last. Talk about over the moon.

"OK. Then it's Stella for you, 'less you prefer Miss Grant?" I had an inkling Franz sounded poncey – but what the hell!

"You know all *about* me then, Mister Cauliflower-ear?" Behind the levity I sensed surprise. She wasn't displeased.

"Once seen, never forgotten," I murmured. Corny all right, but it seemed bold at the time, and she knew I was out to please her. Adam vanished again, chasing more bobtails. The keepers wouldn't take kindly to him disturbing the pheasants on the brink of nesting.

"Come on," she said, vaulting the gate like an athlete. "I'm showing you my dolls' house – would you like that?"

Shyly, I replied, "As long as I'm with *you*, I'm happy." I turned to her, beaming adoration. Noses in the air we passed a gibbet loaded with the grisly evidence of the keepers' vigilance. Squirrels, stoats, weasels, jays, jackdaws, crows, magpies... some mere skeletons, rotted to nothing, others but recently slaughtered, the blood still moist, but no longer dripping... At the far end hung a pot-bellied badger – the first I'd seen, and I'd searched the dykes and spinneys enough times. But no FOX! Apart from 'Charlie' anything posing a threat, however remote, to gamebirds was put to the sword without ceremony. Shoot-days were *big* days at Bradbury – big as hunt days.

Happily we bowled along the ride hand in hand. I walked on air – Stella's feet were firmly on the mossy carpet. She looked divine. Not a trace of hardness shaded those big grey eyes – in territory she loved most of all.

The wood narrowed to a bottleneck. Leaving Bluebell Thicket, we crossed into Primrose Holt, the blooms that named it forming a carpet of yellow all along the boundary, as well as brightening the clearings. Pussy-willow and hazel-catkins were approaching their best, with the blackthorn showing off its creamy elegance as the forest awakened from winter slumbers, only the stubborn oak reluctant to join the exhibition, its branches drab and dismal, still shrouded in the cloak of dormancy. Beech sprouted in abundance, though a residue of beechmast from last year's shedding still lay around, proving wild-life hadn't gone hungry through the long, hard winter.

Stella grew more animated the further we walked, her boots growing gooey from odd patches of false ground. We were climbing slightly, heading for the seclusion of Chucklecopse. The woodlands narrowed for fifty or so yards, then opened out again and we were tramping the final sector – the prettiest of the three plantations. Stella grabbed me tighter, hurrying me along. We swung right-handed, passing, to my surprise, belts of rogue privet, the seeds presumably carried from some distant garden by the birds and the wind. All new territory to me. And right on the bend, in a biggish clearing, stood a house so perfect I could only stand and gawp. Seeing might be believing, but it wasn't easy... What a dream of a play-house! Isolated, in pristine state, built wholly of timber with a verandah all round, and shutters to protect the lattice windows.

"Is *this* the dolls's house?" I gasped in wonder. "And it's really yours?"

"Silly! It's the old shooting-lodge, but they never use it now. They come back to the Hall to stuff their ugly faces. Greedy humbugs. Daddy says do whatever I like, as long as it's kept clean, and free of vermin. He means *rats*. My dolls are all up here, so are lots of my books. The keeper lights the fire from time to time, so it's never damp and nasty. So do I. Maddy adores it here. Hitched to the rails on a long rein, he's happy as can be."

I'd noticed the rides and footways browned and scarred, but put it down to the hunt... and I couldn't picture Stella with a doll. 'Addy' and 'Maddy' – I pondered the sameness of the names – Addy, short for Adam. What's Maddy short for? Not Madame?

The lodge was an eye-opener – inside more than out. Stella fetched a key from round the back, told me to close my eyes, grabbed my hand and led me proudly into her ranch-house... typical Bradbury! Green with envy I weighed up the roomy interior. One vast oblong, with cupboards all round, and a giant table up the middle, groaning under the weight of scores of beautifully carved figures as lifelike as you can get. Slowly I recognised it to be a kind of model settlement, each cluster a separate household, with an individual identity and special character. Round the sides forms had been arranged so admirers could squat a while, studying the intricate details at leisure, or, according to status, maybe in time contribute some worthwhile figure themselves, though every inch looked filled.

Dolls, dogs, horses, houses, cows, cribs, cradles, carts, pigs, poultry, lots of differing fence-posts and rails, all chiselled to perfection. At the far end a pair of bench-vices stood out, one wood, one metal, and on the wall behind hung every hand-tool imaginable. Every gadget I'd ever dreamed of, there for the asking. Gauges, squares, clamps, scribers, levels, protractors, fretsaws... you name it, it was there. Everything a boy could wish for. She opened the rest of the shutters.

"Gosh – what a dream of a workshop," I shouted, amazed. Grabbing her hands I examined them closely, nails broken and chewed... turned them over, there lay the evidence, just like mine! And earlier, when she handed me the half-crown, I thought they were fashioned in silk, so soft and gentle they felt. She laughed with delight, happy to lead me around. I was smart enough to keep hold of her hand. Apart from the main 'room' just a store, and a sizeable, though primitive kitchen existed at the back. It bore little evidence of culinary endeavour. In the 'workshop' a motley assortment of armchairs were assembled half-moon fashion round the big open fireplace, where weary 'guns' would slump after a testing drive, and after downing fifty brace of pheasants, then wolfing porkpie, beef, ham, tongue and pickles... all washed down with claret. Evidently, the keepers and beaters troughed their cheese and onions through in the kitchen, with its sparse facilities and scant comfort.

"It's a treat up here Franz... you can't imagine – when things get impossible back *there!*"

I sensed a deep hurt in her insides, her pretty face clouding a jiffy. What could be so disagreeable to a wonderful creature like Stella, prompting her to saddle up and head for Chucklecopse, at times near to despair?

"I suppose the boys started all this, Stella?" She nodded.

"Yes. I thought they were crazy when they raved about what they got up to with their tools and timber. Then I found out. And *we* can enjoy it too Franz, if you're game?"

She squeezed my hands as she turned to me. All at once she was a heavenly young girl, lonely, and desperate for fun which she struggled unsuccessfully to conjure up back at the Hall. It seemed only natural to kiss her on the cheek, which she accepted like we were close and intimate, instead of near-strangers. Silently I praised the Lord, but I didn't ask for the ammunition... *He'd pass that later!*

The time went like mad.

"It'll soon be dark – do you think we should go?" I murmured, knowing it was the last thing I wanted. She ignored the suggestion.

"Do you know what?" she said, suddenly. "Daddy says I'm not going back to Shrewton. I'm lined up for a crammer, the other side of Bedford. After Easter. Then on to college. I don't suppose for one minute I'll make university, but they're set on getting me to Girton – and they'll do their damndest to wangle it, one way, or another. Wealth and influence go a long way... Brains alone won't work the oracle." She gave a wry little smile.

"You're not going away again? I don't believe it!" The thought horrified me, though I knew damn well she wouldn't be schooling locally, anyway.

"It looks like it. We must make the most of what little time we have left." I couldn't believe my ears. Including *me* in her plans – for the immediate future, if no more. I told her about my 'Oxford' but she was too excited to listen – talk of the daunting obstacle fell on deaf ears.

I managed to wrench my gaze from her, looking round the walls again in wonder. Though disturbed by the unwelcome news – especially the hints of unhappiness at home – basically I was ecstatic. Totally hooked by this delightful young creature.

"All right, perhaps we'd better make a move." Something in her voice made me start. It sounded different. I glanced at her quickly, the eyes hard and thoughtful, brow furrowed. 'Have I said something I shouldn't? Dropped a clanger again? I can't have. Is she reluctant to leave home? Thoughts of boarding no longer to her liking? Do *I* figure in the equation? Or is she thinking of the old sepia prints, faded and indistinct, sitting soshways by the door – do they remind her of ghosts from the past? Some less than pleasant family experience? No! She'd have downed them by now – and they're only portraits.'

Adam reappeared by magic, leaping up at *me* this time, then cleared off again, as we set off back, hand in hand. The blues vanished. She laughed and chatted all the way. All too soon we were back at the threatening notice.

"I *am* taking you home tonight, Estelle," I said, trying to sound stern and masterful.

"No!" she said, firmly. "You'd better not!"

She leaned forward, kissed me full on the lips, then turned to go. Adam came bounding up – obviously psychic. This time I'd opened the gate for her.

"What about tomorrow? It's Sunday." I said.

"Don't worry, I'll keep out of the way when you bring the papers. Act normal – if you know how. Be here Monday – unless there's a blizzard, and you can't get through." She smiled, then stuck out her tongue. She knew she could rattle me – easily – and she loved to tease.

"I'll come if there's an earthquake – and pull you from the rubble," I replied cheerfully. She strode out proudly until she reached the drive entrance, with me peering through the gloom like an anxious sea-captain. She didn't turn. I grabbed my bike from the ditch, slightly frustrated. Despite this massive upturn in my fortunes, it was plain nobody from the Hall must learn of our friendship. But I could hardly blame Stella for *that*. 'She'll explain when she's good and ready – and Monday's on the menu.'

"What about your homework?" asked Mum. Monday had arrived – at last. I'd rushed tea, a quick swill, and changed ready to set off.

"Oh, there'll be time when I get home. That's OK. Don't worry."

"Don't start neglecting your studies *now,* young man. There's a girl in this somewhere, isn't there?"

"Yes," was all I said. I felt my face redden. I shuffled awkwardly, embarrassed.

"Ah... I thought as much!" I couldn't read her face, but she meant more than she said.

"Cheerio, Mum." I daren't look her in the eye. Pedalling flat-out, and bouncing in the ruts like riding the cakewalk, I knew heaven lay at journey's end. Then came a smack in the eye. Wallop went my heart. Not a sign of Stella when I rounded the final bend. I scrambled off, dropped the bike, and had a good long look all around. Not a creature to be seen in that vast landscape – but then, there seldom was. A lonely old back-road leading to nowhere, bar a hamlet and one or two farmsteads.

Sunday had passed without incident. Estelle was nowhere around when I took the papers – and despite her warnings, I'd scanned every window. Nonetheless, there was the satisfaction of knowing life was irrevocably linked to the delightful young thing I'd discovered and who lurked somewhere in the corridors of that distinguished edifice.

'But that was yesterday – what about today?'

I stared and stared, until my eyes almost dropped out. Nobody showed – no sign of movement anywhere – apart from sheep in the distance, and a few grazing cattle. The sun dipped lower. I was tempted to bike down to the Hall, but didn't want to annoy Stella, and upset the applecart. I left the bike, wandering towards Bradbury, hands in pockets, flummoxed and forlorn. The Hall was a mammoth magnet, the nonchalance I affected as false as the big white fiver some rotten sod once shunted on to poor old Grandad. Aimlessly I kicked at a verge scarred by a million hoofprints. It was fast growing dark. Crestfallen, I drifted back to a silent Briarsdale, grabbed the bike, when a series of bellows, grunts, bumps, thuds and lurid curses, plus the snarls of a maddened dog, broke the stillness. My hair stood on end, my neck tingled, my buttocks clenched, when blood-curdling roars, and cries of 'help' joined the cacophony coming from the trees... and not far off! I dropped the bike, jumped the gate, heading full belt into the darkened wood, my ticker in overdrive. The rumpus rose to a crescendo. Despite the blackness I had no trouble finding the action. Abe Conway, Sissons's number two, his back to a tree-trunk, had a shotgun pressed to his throat, a man on each end shoving like buggery, trying to choke the poor bastard. His retriever clung desperately to the thug on the barrel, its teeth sunk deep into the reeking, stationmaster coat. Recognition was instant – even from behind – Dick and Clothcap! I waded in, and coming from the rear caught the buggers on the hop. They let go of Abe, dropped the gun, making a dash for the ride, but not before I'd enjoyed the satisfying crunch of knuckle on bone as I fetched Clothcap a beauty across the jaw. They abandoned their bag and I let them go, watching anxiously as Abe coughed his way back to normal. All 'shook up' he was nonetheless in one piece, and when his voice finally returned spent the next ten minutes swearing violently – and I don't recall any repetitions!

"Good on ya, lad. Tom told me the bastards were doin' this end – every other week, but could he as hell peg 'em. Catapult men – from out Granleigh way. Did you twig 'em?"

"I've *seen* them – out hunting – that's all. I don't *know* them, though the tall one's called Dick. Are you alright, Mister Conway?"

"Yeah – thanks to you, lad... and your dukes! You're pretty 'andy with 'em! I was plumb helpless – couldn't do a bloody thing, though I managed a few bellows before they choked me. Tom'll go bonkers..."

"What happened, then?"

"I rumbled the thin 'un some way off – or rather Clover did. She started snufflin'. I told her to sit, then stalked the bastard on me own, thinking he were on 'is tod. I were closing in when that other twat jumped me."

He fondled his neck, his face purple in the gloom, his eyes bloodshot but no longer bulging. At the best of times Abe was no saint – he was a vicious bugger according to Farndon folk, but I guessed how he felt. Late forties, married, three kids, life was no great bonanza. "Here lad, catch hold o' one of these." Groping in Clothcap's sack he came up with a monster, if late-season cock! Thanking him, I dusted myself down, then mixed up, moody, and just about knackered, pedalled through the gloom to the fork, worried as well as disappointed. Even after such short acquaintance I knew Stella wouldn't let me down without good reason! 'Something's wrong! Is she ill? Crikey – I hope not!'

Mum soon spotted the downbeat mood. For a start, I was early. To her eternal credit she didn't grill me. No third degree. Girlfriends weren't even mentioned. Homework enjoyed a more than adequate spell, but my heart wasn't in it, and I knew that whatever I learned wouldn't stick. Bradbury, as it would for always, ruled my world.

The next three nights turned out repeats of Monday. Then the doubts did begin to surface, my faith in Stella tested to the full. But on Friday came a turn for the better. Sitting on the ride-gate, staring gloomily at the tall chimneys of the Hall, as always, a rustle in the undergrowth had me whip round quickly. A deer, maybe? A fox ? More likely rabbits at play. No matter what, it didn't count, for wedged between the gatepost and the top-iron sat a luggage-label of sorts. Reaching cautiously along the rail I carefully lifted the weathered card, unfolding it with great care. My hands were trembling – I knew for sure what it was.

The message read brief and simple, 'Be patient Franz. Will explain.' No name. No signature. No need! Stella must have been desperate to get word to me. Whatever prevented her from keeping our serial rendezvous, hadn't stopped her galloping up in the daytime, but which day I'd no way of knowing? Hastily I groped in my pockets for a pencil. One was in there somewhere – down in the lining. After lots of stretching and squeezing it finally popped out the corner. Carefully, and with much thought, I replied, 'Stella. Will wait for ever. F.'

Folding the label the other way round I shoved it back down the crevice. Bright and breezy I jumped on the Raleigh, tearing home like a dingbat.

I knew she'd be waiting on the Saturday, despite me being early. She'd crossed the road and was heading my way, when I dropped the bike and ran to her. For precious minutes we embraced. I kissed her passionately – and didn't she respond! She clung to me as if I might vanish in clouds of smoke. Finally we relaxed, and set off happily for Chucklecopse. She volunteered nothing, and I kept quiet until she felt free to explain her worrying non-appearance. Half a mile on she stopped all of a sudden, turned to me, and said, "Franz, I've a confession to make! I *saw* you on Sunday! It was horrid – being such a cheat."

"Where were you?" I asked, incredulous.

"In the stables – at the back of Maddy's stall. I had to have a look at you because I knew I couldn't keep our date. Aunt Pen and Cousin Freda turned up late Saturday evening – totally unexpected. Uncle Horace is off abroad, on business, to Switzerland, and Pen said they were lonely. They live near Nottingham."

"Why didn't you shout me?"

"I daren't. Freda had gone looking for the peacocks; she was due back any second. Had she spotted us together she'd have told the whole world. I couldn't bear that Franz – our secret in the open!"

She looked so innocent, so lovely, her eyes so gentle, I'd have forgiven her anything.

"It doesn't matter Stella. I can imagine how difficult it must be, but I've had a rotten week, worried in case you were ill, or in trouble, or something."

"Hmm! You obviously got my love-letter? I put it there Tuesday. Thanks for the answer. I knew there'd be one. It cheered me up no end." She smiled – that delightful smile which always gave me the wobblies. "Freda sticks to me like glue. And Aunt Pen always wants to know where we are, and what we're doing. She thinks we're still infants. Anyway, we've got our own letter-box now – pity it's not waterproof. I thought of sticking a note on the gibbet, Franz, but changed my mind in case Sissons got hold of it, and showed Daddy."

"How did you manage to get away?"

"I made out Maddy was off colour, then brought him up bareback, to try him out, sort of. I found the labels in the kitchen. What about you?"

"Mum's been mystified. Every night, bang on time, I came up praying you'd show, then drifted home early, miserable as the devil. I used the spare time to swot up for next week's 'mock' – but I'm bound to fail, then the fat will be in the fire."

"You'll be alright. You must sit down and forget me. Promise?"

"Out the question! You know it is. You only mean forget you for the week, don't you?"

"Of course I do, Silly!"

"When do the blighters go back?"

"They've gone! This morning, thank goodness, though they're not too bad really, and Mummy comes out of her shell a bit with Aunt Pen there. I don't think Daddy's very fond of them, and I know Miss Barlow isn't."

"Who's Miss Barlow?"

"Er... well. The governess, sort of. You know..."

"Oh," was all I said. And I *didn't* know. For a long time I didn't know.

On the edge of the great wood bluebells were budding, the air sweet with their scent. A few heads were starting to shine blue. Primroses looked a picture, one that would very soon fade however, with the early fern clamouring for supremacy.

We were through the Holt, and well into Chucklecopse, when to my surprise Stella pulled on my arm, taking me on past the shooting-lodge, in a westerly direction – as far as I could tell from the sun.

"Where are we off to?" I asked, happy but puzzled. No reply. On the western boundary we finally emerged, but not right into the open. Half the natural world was on view, not a building in sight. No cowsheds, barns, houses, stables... just gentle undulating territory, mostly pasture, dotted with spinneys, coverts and copses stretching for miles in every direction. No hint of man, or of his machinations.

Away to our left, the face of Chucklecopse curved like a crescent moon, embracing us in its fold, while to the right, leafy inlets and alternating bulges ran down to Primrose Holt, on past the thicket to the highway, hidden though the little winding back-road was. At intervals along the sunlit boundary, mountains of hawthorn, pristine white, proclaimed the true coming of spring. And the two of us were alone together, in an arbour fashioned by nature, unaided by any human. A mediaeval masterpiece of natural trellis, and virgin greenery, with the luxury of a perfectly shaped boulder of oak to squat on, plus a backrest formed by some fallen giant from bygone days.

And the sun! We watched it slowly sink, the sky blood-red beneath a mix of orange, blues and yellows that might have had even Turner struggling. And I had Stella! By the simple medium of a meet of the West Thorncliffe, my world had been transformed – from happy and content, to unimaginable ecstasy.

Further to the right Cuckoo-pint Rise was beginning to settle down for another night. Above us, pigeons cooed happily, diving in to roost with great panache, once they spotted volunteer decoys ensconced in the taller, more attractive, 'sitty' trees. Rooks circled endlessly but, taking few chances, in the end settled away to our left, where huge bundles of sticks signalled the re-construction of some ancient rookery. Pheasants were the noisiest of all, carking like the devil as they rocketed up to their favourite boudoir to spend the night in peace, giving the lie to the old wives' tale, they only sleep upstairs in winter.

The woods I loved so much, though denied to hoi-polloi like me except on bank-holidays and hunt days when some of them were open, were now paradise. Rabbits bobbed from beneath the trees in twos and threes, sussing out verdant spots ready for night-time feeding, getting further and further from the sanctuary of the woodlands in ever bolder spurts of what at first were just tentative hops and skips. We cuddled together all the time, revelling in the incomparable ecstasy of adolescent love. From time to time she'd give a big sigh, absently stroking my hand, as if anxious to tell me something she found impossible to put into words. I prayed for time to stand still.

How long we sat I can't say – little light was left when we at last made a move. "It's wonderful there, Stella," I stammered, as we clung to each other on the way back.

"That's where I always go when I want to be alone – to sit and think. I call it Carolean – King Charles is supposed to have hidden somewhere there... from the beastly Roundheads. Not that it did him much good – they say he hid up an oak tree."

"Probably up a gumtree," I murmured irreverently. I had mixed feelings about the headless monarch. Anyway, Cromwell was a local... but it wouldn't do to argue with Stella!

"You're having an escort tonight, Miss Grant. No way are you going home alone." It took some getting out – but like most bits, emerged in the end.

"Only to the brow of the hill, then. No further!"

"OK. I'll watch you to the drive then go home the other way." On Sundays I delivered Farndon's papers first, joined the Kettering road as far as the Bradbury turn, did the cottages, the Hall, then on to Granleigh and home via Little Downton. Tonight I'd do the circuit in reverse.

"What is it you're afraid of?" Stella looked up at me, her face anxious.

"Afraid something might happen to you. I've dreamed of you since I could walk and talk – now I've found you I'm taking no chances."

"Silly!" was all she said, then kissed me goodnight.

"Until Monday," I whispered. "Pretend Sunday doesn't exist."

"Well, ready for your exams, Francis?" Mum sat by the fire, intent on her complicated embroidery, her brow furrowed studying the intricate patterns she seemed to prefer. A Sunday evening, she was home early from church. The day had passed with nothing to record. I'd used her 'church time' to cram in extra swotting, desperate for success but knowing I hadn't a cat in hell's chance. I couldn't even *think* straight… other than of Bradbury.

I sat at the drop-leaf table, with a good view of Mum's face framed in the copper warming-pan by the fireplace. A masterly, if antiquated barometer graced the side opposite – its claim to fame an uncanny ability to forecast rainfall to the tenth of an inch. The coal suddenly flared high, sending a golden glow across the doll-like features. Despite her age she looked angelic, her head brightly lit in an ethereal setting, floating in a never-never land Italian painters of the sixteenth century captured in such style. An illusion of frightening accuracy I'd always remember.

Life hadn't been kind, but she harboured few grudges. No bitterness. Or if there was she hid it well. I guessed she lived largely through me – boys seem to know. *My* success (if any) would be *her* victory. A life blighted by political oafs going empty-headed, and empty-handed, into war with Germany, then wasting the next twenty years saying 'never again' as they watched, hypnotised, the bizarre behaviour of the punk they called Hitler, convincing themselves this psychopath was just the guy to shield us from the evils of Communism, and preserve indefinitely the 'purity' of the West! That would be after a similar bunch of clowns hitched up their skirts and dashed to Munich to secure 'peace in our time', a promise set in concrete by the signature of the same malign little monster.

Mum was just over forty, nominally the prime of life, with skin smooth as alabaster, dark hair drawn to a bun, parted in the middle, but not flattened so as to make her look severe. She had blackish eyes – sharp, deep and penetrating in turn, with a longish nose above a 'standard' chin. She was wearing her maroon frock with the lace collar which she favoured for church, and special occasions, but I don't suppose she'd have taken off her coat in that frozen temple, where even the flies found survival a problem. Suddenly she looked up.

The gesture shrieked 'watch it!' An opening salvo was about to shatter the peace! She was like that – a feeler, then a launch into serious stuff.

"Who's the lucky girl then, Francis? The young lady controlling your moods, and who lets you down more often than she cheers you up?"

On the rack with a vengeance, instinct told me to sidestep the issue – I'd been dreading it for weeks. Embarrassed to almost tongue-tied, I peered down at the homework, frowning as if stumped by a problem, then grudgingly muttered, "Estelle... from Bradbury Hall."

"What?" Her eyes glazed. She dropped the half-finished linen, sitting, needle poised, turned instantly to stone! Had I said Cleopatra it couldn't have hit harder. For the very first time I saw Mum speechless. Bereft of sound. I heard the wind get up. The fire blazed, the copper pan again reflecting the bizarre patterns dancing around her head. For one terrible second a new vision of Hell crossed the anxious visage. Her jaw dropped, she was a monument of incredulity.

"Estelle Grant-Wilton. She... er... she's my sweetheart," I whispered.

She gave a giant start, gasping for breath, then coughed like a worn-out Tommy-gun. Finally she halted, spluttering.

"Francis! *Francis!* What *are* you talking about? I hope you're not serious... but I can see you are. Don't tell me any more – I don't want to know." That was blatantly untrue – it's just what she did want.

"Well, Mum... you asked, now you know!" I was hurt, embarrassed, angry, indignant – aghast at the frightening reaction.

"Have nothing to do with that family," she blurted, trying desperately to regain her composure. Obviously the news was a shock, but dammit, I was only a schoolboy. She should have laughed it off. But *no*. Much too serious for that... to Mum!

"How did it all come about? How the Dickens did you get in with *her*?" She was hoarse now, her voice barely carried. In a way I sympathised, though stunned by the severity. This was a different Mum.

"Come on, Francis. Out with it. You might as well tell me. Where did you meet that little madam?" Again she fought for breath, panting painfully, clearly anguished. But this wasn't just indignation. More than that. More than disbelief. More than alarm. *Fear* lurked. Naked fear. Why? For Pete's sake, why? What can of worms had I opened?

"When I took the papers," I replied, quietly. "She's nice." I felt guilty all round. To describe Stella in such banal fashion was an insult to so lovely a creature. To evade Mum's thrusts was even more demeaning.

"Well, Francis, I don't know! What a shock!"

"Why, Mum? *Why?*"

"We're working-class, that's why," she retorted hotly, hoarseness gone, her speech clear and fluent again.

"Dad was in business." I didn't like to argue, mad though I was, but jeepers, I must defend Stella! She couldn't help her birth – she didn't choose her parents. Like me, and all the rest, she was a delivery nobody ordered.

"Not *their* class of business," Mum said, calmer now. "They're top-drawer folk. You know as well as I do. They don't come posher than the Grant-Wiltons."

"They're only people, Mum."

"Rubbish! Do you actually know any of 'em?"

"Only Stella. I've seen some of the others – out hunting, but that's about all. I know Cook a bit, and one or two servants, but nobody to talk to."

"Have you seen inside the Hall? Had a look around?"

"Of course not. I've been in the kitchen a few times, but not lately."

"Is the Governess still there? And Mister Stewart – is he still knocking about?"

"The Governess certainly is – I've heard Stella talk about her. I don't know of any Mister Stewart."

"First it's Miss Estelle, then Stella... My word, you're getting well in. You'll be invited to dinner next."

Mum was hurt, as well as shocked – her face scarcely recognisable. I couldn't understand it. She seldom went in for sarcasm, even when rattled. I knew her well enough for that.

"Alright, my boy. If you're friends, so be it. But don't go getting big ideas for heaven's sake. Sorry to get so cross, but I worry – with your exams close."

I knew she didn't throw in the towel that easily, but accepted the armistice for what it was worth, and relaxed. I hated upsetting her; we got on so well. But I knew, for all her apparent concern, my academic hurdles weren't causing the anguish. And I hated to hear Estelle criticised – even in oblique fashion.

She was above that sort of thing. Way, way, *way* above!

Chapter Four

Noel

Aunt Pen's departure heralded a mammoth upturn in affairs. The hunting season ended, putting paid to the nearest serious rival for Stella's attention – though she'd never short-change her beloved Maddy. He figured little after tea-time, anyway. Clocks switched to summer-time, evenings lengthened, the weather pleasant, April showers drying faster than they're supposed to.

We made for the Lodge every day. I watched, fascinated, as she finished off models she'd fashioned from scratch. Sheds, pens, gates, hutches – these were simple, being angular and regular, but she was equally adept at quadrupeds – pigs, sheep, cows, dogs – *they* called for the real skills. She'd obviously kept a sharp eye on Justin and Rupert, helped them as well. It was magic watching her wield fretsaw, file and foot-rule, the pretty face grimacing, lips pursed in concentration, bent over vice and clamp. Nothing less than perfect sufficed, and soon I was coaxed into taking part, keen as mustard on what became *our* model settlement. Now I understood the broken finger-nails, the less than silken hands. The touches of intimacy were as nothing I'd known before. A loaned hanky, a shared apple we'd bite at alternately, the way she'd suddenly reach up to straighten my hair, knock sawdust from my shirt. That's how I'll always think of Estelle. If only she'd never grown up...

Every model she finished to perfection. Nothing was too much trouble, her skills uncanny. I recall how she'd fiddle her way round a pig's tail, a dog's ear, the haunches of a prancing pony, a randy cockerel's comb, the smallest detail observed with stunning accuracy, and reproduced to perfection. Gradually they'd grow from raw chunks of wood to near-masterpieces, then a final grooming before the climax of applying paint to give them the kiss of life, and they'd take their place in the showcase. No humans sullied the results of these long hours of toil – fretting, fluting, filing and finishing – by the Grant boys, and continued so ably by their young sister.

Then the artillery opened up.

After an especially happy weekend, spent mostly in Chucklecopse, the results of the 'mock' were made known. I'd forgotten it. When we traipsed into assembly that morning it felt like any other day, the impending humiliation undreamed of. The savage announcements got me by the short and curlies... my form-master went spare, his cheeks tight as a drum-skin, and nearly as pale. He knew I could *do* it – that's what irked. French, my number one subject, a disaster. Literature, which he'd earmarked for 'distinction', even worse, and anticipated credits in geography, history, and maths, came to nought. Overall, I just about scraped through, and no more. The marks were abysmal. 'Humph' was raw with rage – that's the understatement of the century – and didn't he let me know it.

"So... what's happened to Five 'A's super-scholar then? Where have all the brainwaves gone? What have you been up to lately, Allner – not scanning textbooks, that's for sure. It's your funeral, young man – not mine. All that talent going to waste – for what? You crass idiot. You stupid, stunted, short-sighted, simple-minded skiver. In my study – twelve o'clock sharp. *Be* there!"

"Yes, sir. I don't know, sir. Sorry, sir..." I cringed – effortlessly. Seething, he grabbed up a ten-ton tome and banged it on my head – a right pile-driver!

"I should think so, too... *numbskull!*"

And he let Mum know as well. In black and white. Pen and ink. But where he was stuck for daylight (if not for words), Mum was not! Then *she* let me have it – the full monty – gushes of tears, angry explosions, sighs of disappointment –

and oodles of 'just as I thought' venom. She fixed the blame squarely on Stella. Like mothers the world over she exonerated me, dreaming up ludicrous excuses, like I was a victim – the dupe of some dastardly plot hatched by a coven of witches solely for the downfall of youths with the temerity to fall in love. And I was forced to listen, to defer and, of course, to agree. For Mum was absolutely right – so was Mr Humphreys, but he, poor devil, was puzzled into the bargain... though he'd hinted at womanising!

"We'll have this out later my boy. Don't think for one minute I'm finished. And don't you be late..."

Mum was still shrieking orders as I reached the one-hinged gate. I set off for Briarsdale in sombre mood. Fortunately Stella soon showed, aboard Maddy, as usual. He was panting hard, and Adam, tongue hanging out, eyes eager, ears flapping, lolloped along behind. Stella was on top of the world. After a spin through the woods, then over the meadows to Granleigh, she'd come up the thicket's central ride to join me.

The minute I spotted her the blues vanished, exams dismissed, Mum and the irate Herr Humphreys banished to the back-burner. Maddy's flanks heaved, his nostrils flared. He turned towards me, poking his head over the gate, wanting me to stroke his velvet nose. He'd got over his initial hostility – he hated strangers. For a time he jerked his head up and down in a syncopated rhythm, as if some hidden contrivance might help rid him of the shiny, double-cranked bit, and the heavily-buckled bridle denying him the freedom he felt should be his. The silken mane of bright chestnut glistened like hair on the garish placards advertising fancy shampoos. Maddy was unique... the ham-fisted idiot of a vet who gelded him made a balls-up of the job (so to speak), leaving one testicle *in situ* – so Maddy was neither an *entire horse*, nor was he entirely a gelding! No wonder he grew coltish at times, and sometimes showed us five legs.

I opened the gate, asking what she had in mind?

"Oh... I hadn't thought about it," she cried. "It's a lovely evening, let's try Cuckoo-pint, shall we? On your bike, and don't hang about."

Off she galloped across the track I'd just travelled. Dutifully I leapt aboard, pedalling like the clappers, but Maddy's rump and Stella's bottom vanished into the distance in double-quick time. I could just make them out as they swung left handed at the Fork, then climbed the gradient to Cuckoo-pint. Ten minutes later, breathless but elated, I joined her on the edge of the great circular wood. I had to push my bike up the final slope – push hard too. She'd already slid from the saddle, and Addy lay panting alongside, while Maddy forgot his exertions and bent with gratitude to nibble at the fresh green grass.

"Poor old Franz. Come here, let me give you a big kiss." I let the bike go without a thought, thrilled as ever to wrap my arms around the tiny waist, to feel the thrusting young breasts pressed to my body, her open mouth pressed to mine in a passion heightened to sheer ecstasy by the exhilarating dash from Briarsdale. Not that *my* journey was all that thrilling. Even with Estelle at journey's end, a pushbike's hardly the machine for massaging the senses.

The gorgeous face glowed with pleasure, eyes sparkling from the excitement of the high-speed charge, and the bonus of top-class health. Not a care you'd think ever clouded those innocent young features. Arms linked, hopes high, we gazed down on Farndon, and its surrounds, only half seeing the panorama of meadows, brooks, hedgerows and copses.

"Where exactly do you live, Franz?" she asked, a little later. "Point it out to me, so I can picture you when we're not together." Something about the words, and the way she came out with them, made me want to hug her for ever. 'Where's that horrid creature Mum talks about? How can anybody dislike the delightful Stella Grant? *Anybody!*'

It was simple to show her the cottage, standing half a mile east of the track she'd just travelled at such speed.

"How lovely!" she exclaimed, as she took in the neat little house, rendered white, topped with red pantiles, detached, resting in a more-than-generous garden, enclosed by hedge and shrubs, with a biggish shed, and a hen-house to boot. A similar dwelling, though of red brick, stood west of it, finishing off the lane, and beyond, on the east side, ranged a typical terrace of three up, three down council semis, housing families of Farndonites of long standing. The Carters, the Browns, the Crowsons, the Bradfords, the Cockcrofts...

We stayed long... and late – mother's threats forgotten.

"I'll show you the source of the River Farndon," Stella said, mocking the wretched brook that never failed to flood the village once the rains set in. *We* were lucky. The dwellings in our lane were built on ridges of solid Midlands clay, and we stayed dry.

"You're not your usual cheery self, Franz. Afraid we'll be late? Don't worry. Anyway, I'll get a bigger earful than you, I'll bet."

"No. Not exactly, Stella."

"What is it then? *Something's* wrong – I know it is. What's the matter? Don't you love me any more?"

"'Course I do. That's forever. It's these blooming exams... I made a right mess of the 'mock' – I told you I was on a loser – and all you did was take the mickey." She laughed her head off – and I couldn't help joining in. But I daren't tell her all Mum said.

The unscheduled safari made us later than ever. I'd never been inside Cuckoo-pint, though as a youngster I'd often looked longingly up the distant rides, pondering the secret interior, investing it with all sorts of fairy-tale inhabitants – gnomes, pixies, fairies and the like, but the forbidding notice, a replica of the one protecting Briarsdale, always held me back, as it did all villagers, I suppose. Then there was that miserable sod Tom Sissons to watch out for. He could bob up anywhere, any time, across the wide estate, barking in his gravelly voice, rabidly hostile – or his truculent side-kicks could, which was even worse, according to some who'd had a taste, and got a boot up their arse. Apparently Sissons wasn't *all* bad... and nor was Abe Conway.

"Do you fancy trying Lucans Pond, Franz?" asked Stella, all at once. "There's bags of time yet."

"I'd love to," I replied, thinking she was joking when she mentioned the River Farndon earlier on.

"Come on, then. I'll leave Maddy here; he'll be OK."

She looped the reins over the bottom rail, patted his neck, kissed his nose. We clambered over the gate, she grabbed my hand, and off we went into unknown territory – foreign to me anyhow. I can best describe Cuckoo-pint Rise as volcano-shaped, but well-treed and lush. Situated high on the terrain, for most of its perimeter it sloped down to a crater-like heartland. The remaining segment where we were trekking sat much lower, the deep ditches bordering this extra-wide ride obviously connected to the compulsion of Lucans Pond to regularly overflow, and gush its surplus on to Farndon, and beyond, as it had for the past thousand years.

At first it walked squelchy, and marsh-like, but a well-trodden, half-grouted path had developed up the middle, obviously much used, though by whom I couldn't think – apart, maybe, from estate workers and wood-choppers, plus the industrious, if sadistic, keepers.

Stella's joddy-boots had never been of the brightest – our expeditions told me why! A flame-red jumper, blue and white neckerchief, red hair swirling round her collar as we strode along, with Addy nosing about somewhere behind, is a lasting memory of that safari to Lucans Pond.

As usual, Addy had us fooled. He wasn't behind! Frenzied flutters, and quacking from up ahead, told us exactly where the pond lay – where Addy was too. Ducks lifted in hundreds, alarmed and indignant, wings doing overtime. They climbed rapidly, narrowly dodging the treetops in a bid to flap their way out of danger.

Stella pulled me along faster, and rounding the bend we came face to face with Lucans Pond. I stared in astonishment. I'd always pictured it as the typical farm-pond – fifty yards round, dark and dreary, with the familiar gunge of pond-life slopping round the edges. I never guessed it to be a great shining lake, some two acres about, water blue, yet crystal clear, with fishing-pads, diving points, row-boat, a punt, a child's paddleboat – and a pavilion! I'd heard talk of this 'pond', but had taken little notice. Being out of bounds I'd have dismissed it.

"What do you think to it then, Franz?" shouted Stella, darting smartly to the bank pretending to take a header into the crystal water. More ducks lifted in terror, resenting the further intrusion.

"Do you swim here? I bet you *do!*"

"Not this time of year. I often take a dip in summer – in the altogether... let's try the punt; it's in going gear."

"Watch out, Stella – it looks pretty shaky!" She shaped to jump aboard as I chased after her. Rather than lovers, we were like infants, intoxicated by adventures new. To me, it was a different world, totally transformed by Estelle's presence. With her around I felt a new awareness, life was intense, her every move significant – an impossible fulfilment.

She grabbed the pole, confident as ever, stuck it in the bank and with a mighty heave pushed off. I scrambled in behind, nearly going for a Burton as I struggled to keep what looked a decidedly dodgy craft on a more or less even keel. A coat of tar would have helped inspire more confidence. Don't think I was scared... I wasn't – but I was far from keen to look gauche and primitive, where the 'young madam', as Mum so unkindly called her, was so competent at everything she tried. So confident, so unafraid, but above all so happy.

"Great!" I cried. "How deep is it? Watch out, for Pete's sake – I don't want you impaled over fathoms of aqua, while the punt sails merrily on..."

"Oh, don't worry, I'm used to this caper. I often came fishing with the boys. They made me take a turn, when it was as much as I could do to lift the pole... Rotters, at times, they were, to me."

"Nobody could be rotten to *you* – I don't believe it."

"Huh! Couldn't they just?"

I took for granted she'd take over, like she did everywhere we went, everything we did. *She* made the decisions, she planned the programme, she led the way, yet it all came so naturally. She wasn't at all bossy – in how she spoke, the way she behaved – she was just out to show me, to lead me, to please, to entertain – and Stella did that all right. Nothing of the kind had happened to me before, and I owed everything to this girl with the perfect face. I understood the pride when she demonstrated something – it was all Bradbury's. She was puffing hard now, her face scarlet, but still adamant I shouldn't take over.

"We'll try the pavilion, though I bet it's locked," she yelled. In expert fashion she crossed the pole so we turned through ninety degrees, gliding smoothly to the slatted landing-stage. Jumping out, she chained the punt, tried the pavilion door, but it *was* locked, and Stella hadn't a clue where the keys were hidden. We peeked in the windows, but there was nothing much to see, just bits and bobs, mostly fishing tackle. Nets, rods, and all that, three or four unmatched oars, broken poles, wicker chairs, forms, a ladder (?), and lots and lots of rope – miles of it. A general dogs-breakfast of the odds and sods that are so handy in a multi-featured haven of privilege, peace and privacy like Cuckoo-pint Rise. Right around the lake we walked, arm in arm. Moorhens fled, screeching, from the verdant reeds, desperate for fresh cover, while a pair of lordly swans eyed us with respect, but with the typical aloofness of their kind, cruising back instantly to where they'd been upending.

Not for the first time, I'd clean forgotten the Setter, but he hadn't forgotten us, and, after finishing the trek back where we started, he squeezed his way out of cover, looking the worse for wear, but sublimely happy.

"Old Maddy'll go crazy," laughed Stella. "He'll think we've deserted him. We must hurry!"

"You must tell me more about your brothers, and the rest of the family, Estelle. You never talk about them." A moment's silence then the storm broke! She rounded on me like lightning, the big eyes wide and wild.

"That's none of your damn business!" she snapped, hostile in seconds, like when I first saw her. I faltered, the violent reaction had me reeling. An innocent comment, and those lovely features were contorted – transformed into a mask of something in excess of anger!

"Er... Oh! I only wondered what they did in their spare time, nothing more." I was flummoxed, floored, flattened... Luckily she simmered down, contrite in seconds.

"Franz! *Franz...* I didn't mean to be horrid! Sorry, darling. My poor Franz. I mustn't be nasty to *you.* "We were almost to the gate, with Maddy watching anxiously. Stella put her arm around my neck, pulled me to her, kissed me a dozen times, her eyes again soft and gentle. I hugged her fiercely, telling her it didn't matter a damn. Nothing could change the way I felt. We scrambled over the gate, she untied Maddy and jumped aboard.

"I love you," I murmured. She ruffled my mop, my head resting on her knee. Then she said, "See you tomorrow." She took up the reins, shook them once, turned Maddy towards Briarsdale, and cantered off down the track. I pedalled slowly towards Rose Cottage. It was to be ages before I set eyes on her again.

Weeks of desolation followed that trip to Fairyland, but the resentment at being left in the dark eventually brought me to my senses – though in a way I was lucky – I did learn *something*. On a Sunday following the safari, and after Stella had failed to show any more, I crossed the paddock feeling mixed-up and edgy, wondering if perhaps she was watching from some secret peephole, and maybe other members of the grand establishment were kicking around?

The kitchen door stood open. I could hear the ringing tones of Mrs Thompson as she held forth on what, to her, was obviously a matter of great importance. I cocked my ears, apprehensive, certain it had to do with *me*. Illogical perhaps, but there all the same.

"The next thing I knew she was *gone!* Charles chucked the cases in the back, the Colonel eased himself in, like he does, alongside the Mistress, while the Miss Estelle jumped in the front with Charles. Talk about *angry*... she was redder than a turkey's wotsit!"

I stopped, listening in awe, but well out of sight, determined to hear every word of Cook's vitriolic outburst – presumably to a servant? It didn't take much working out. Stella had been *whisked away* – to *wherever*. To the crammer she talked about, perhaps? They'd be *her* suitcases. From what I could gather only Stella had gone. Charles, the chauffeur-cum-assistant-groom, had brought the Colonel and his lady back later on. And she must have gone without warning or she'd have got me a message – somehow. Our private letter-box hadn't obliged – I checked it every night. That in itself was odd. 'Did they lock her in the cellar prior to hauling her off? No! She'd have found a way out – *easily*. There'd be no end of shopping, of course. Lots of clothes. All sorts of odds and ends for a new school – as well as a fresh uniform.' I emerged quietly from the shadows and handed the papers to Mrs Thompson. She looked at me a bit old-fashioned, but then she frequently wore a strange expression...

later I'd work it out – *much* later! 'Does she *know* about us? Is she suspicious? More like scared I'd overheard her going on about the boss – in less than glowing terms. That must be *it*,' I consoled myself. 'Hell, Stella's sixteen! Me too, almost – our birthdays just weeks apart. And I've bought her nothing – not so much as a card. And certainly nothing'll come my way – not now. We might as well be strangers – from alien cultures.' I lingered a minute longer, watching Madame Thompson fuss over the great big Aga, her face red as beetroot, strands of hair falling loose from her earphones. She looked up again, surprised to see me still around.

I wanted to ask her the truth – but didn't dare. I didn't lack the nerve – I was thinking of Stella. It would be just my luck to put my damn great foot in it again, compromising *her*, after she'd treated me as an equal. Even now it was hard to believe. I couldn't let her down.

Amy, the servant who'd been listening in wonder, bobbed under the worktop, anxious to dispel any notion I might have of conspiracy. She eventually came up with an outsize baking-tin, her face on red alert. She wasn't much older than me, if at all. Both were from Little Downton, though of course, they 'lived in'.

'Dare I ask? No! No!' I turned away, mighty relieved despite the disturbing news, my faith in the girl I worshipped restored at a stroke. She didn't just clear off, leaving me in the dark, to mourn at leisure. The so-and-sos had *Shanghaied* her!

Stella didn't write, but it was confirmed she had gone off to a new school – near Bedford. The Mothers' Union know everything. If they don't, the Women's Institute do. Failing that there's always the Sewing Circle, and the women's branch of the British Legion. Imagine my surprise when I got home, to have *Mum* open the batting.

"I hear the Grant-Wilton girl's been rushed away to Bedford then, Francis?" Never 'Frank' – always 'Francis' – it would never be 'Franz' – only from my Estelle.

"It seems that way, Mum."

"I'll bet it's a funny old household now – without her."

Mum obviously meant more than she suggested. But *what* did she mean? She was smiling... with a hint of triumph, as she leaned on the mantelpiece, pleased, no doubt, that my studies would at last come first, and I'd get down to business for real, attacking the Oxford with vigour, my confidence restored. We were well into summer term – not long to go, the scope for improvement immense. So vast, and the 'mock' such a disaster, things could only get better – that's how I pretended to feel.

"You never go round to your Grandad since you took up with this young woman. He misses you. Anyway, it's time to forget her, and come down to earth. The rector's asking after you. You know you missed confirmation last year – he wants you to take it late – this year, like."

'Oh God – the rector! Not a bad idea, perhaps? He'll know all there is to know about the Grant-Wiltons – nosey old sod – though he never sees them.' My mind went back to last year's classes... ("Bring out the scones, Sunshine, *and* the strawberry jam!")

I had no inclination to be 'confirmed to full participation in church activities', but I was up for anything that would bring news of Stella.

"I'll think about it, Mum," I grunted, knowing jolly well it was an order. But I felt guilty over Grandad. I *had* neglected him, and he was a smashing old guy. Generous, helpful, he knew everything worth knowing about horseflesh, having been 'in the trade' so to speak. That alone made us kindred spirits.

The term passed like lightning. I took every opportunity to stuff my head with facts and figures, even lugging text-books to bed, reading by candlelight, desperate to succeed, but even more desperate to blot out the longing for Stella, the emptiness indescribable. No longer free to gaze upon those gorgeous features, to bask in her spell. '*Why* doesn't she write? She's got a pen... and ink. She's not incarcerated – in a dungeon, in chains, with guards watching over her. No barred windows, no drawbridge. It's only a wretched school, when all's said and done. Ah well! She'll tell me about it... when she's ready – I hope.'

The subjects fell... like driven game birds over waiting guns. First, a distinction – French. Then *five* credits – literature, maths, chemistry, history and geography. Pass in the rest. I'd matriculated. Qualified for university. Had riches been on tap Frank would have been on his way. But they weren't. They never would be. So he wouldn't 'go up to Cambridge'. He'd look for a job – bring home the bacon. He hadn't a clue what to go for – the future hinged on Stella Grant-Wilton... and Missus Allner would be looking for support – though she never complained of going short. She wouldn't. Not the type – too proud by half. The grapevine functioned at last. The Grant girl home for the 'hols' with a couple of school-friends. Not the village grapevine – the shepherd's wife at the cottages. She was bursting with the welcome news. 'How does she know I'm interested?' I bit my tongue – pondered the next move? At the tradesmen's gate I hesitated. 'What if Stella's kicking around in the courtyard with her grand friends? At the stables, maybe – sizing up the gee-gees? What's the best approach?' Propping the trade-bike against the gate, I pulled out the *Observer* and *Country Life* and set off across that familiar track.

Three quarters there I stopped all at once, and listened – a voice rang loud and clear – that *glorious* half-metallic voice! Ticker in overdrive I moved up a gear, at the trot by the time I reached the courtyard. Then I stopped dead... too shattered to move!

Stella was crossing to the stables, while Maddy, ears pricked, watched from over his half-door. And linked to Stella's arm was a male of around twenty. She gazed up at him in the adoring fashion that always made me wobbly. He was a tall chap, almost my height, but heavier built, blond hair curling down his neck, his cheeks rosy. Tatty Oxford Bags with enormous turn-ups, plus a crumpled cream shirt, comprised his rigout. The stamp of an upper-class twit was plain to see – definitely top-drawer.

"Er... Hello," I murmured, coming to life and moving swiftly across the yard.

"Oh! Good morning, Francis! Leave them in the kitchen, will you – the door *is* unlocked. This is Noel, by the way."

Her eyes were glazed and impersonal – I was a *stranger!* Noel nodded briefly, looked past me rather than at me, drawling, "How do." They carried on to the stables. Surprisingly the kitchen was empty. No cook, no servants, no bubbling saucepans, no rising steam, nothing but a void.

Seething with anger I flung the papers at the scrub-top surface, making sure they didn't reach... they skidded untidily across the red-tiled floor, as intended. I turned in disgust, hurrying from the yard without a backward glance. From the corner of my eye I caught a fleeting glimpse of Stella and Noel making a big fuss of Maddy. I prayed the old chap might swing round in a hurry, flattening the blond man's ear like he had mine – or better still, spin half-circle and do the dirty on him! All of a sudden, hurt and outraged, I felt a tug at my elbow. Whipping round fast, whom should I see but an excited Addy begging acknowledgement. Deflated though I was, it was good to know *one* Grant-Wilton still loved me. I steadied up, bent to stroke the silken head – he licked my hand. Exploding with jealousy and resentment, I blessed that faithful hound, promising to see him again and again, until he ended his days where canine saints go to their final rest. He left as suddenly as he'd appeared, bounding back happily to the courtyard, then droopy and dejected, I trudged back to the road, dragged myself over the five-barred gate, lifted the bike, straightened the paper-bag, and pedalled steadily homewards.

The paddock was deserted, not even the ducks deigned to sound off. Their young would be strong and on the wing by now. Perhaps they were on patrol? A potent mix of anger, despair and total disbelief just about gave me the strength to carry on.

Flashman, Stella's old donkey, loose amongst the fruit-trees, let go a series of brittle hee-haws, like a lift-pump crying for oil. That just about summed me up.

Chapter Five

Trespass

Harvest rolled round – time to join Mr Barford's barley brigade. But the thrill of driving his hairy Shires over the bumpy stubbles, up dusty tracks, across rutted pastures, down winding lanes the whole day long, had diminished – in spite of the buckshee pony rides. Stella's betrayal had squashed all interest in ordinary goings-on, leaving me a sparse, sterile agenda. And I had mixed feelings about saying farewell to school, though they gave me the option of returning to join the sixth, should a suitable job not materialise. Six weeks to discover that elusive niche or back to the class-room.

Mum weighed up the pros and cons of chucking harvest-work and hunting for a post, or sticking with Barford's until one reared its head. We weren't that hard up, but harvest-money was always handy. I decided to say nothing about Estelle's whereabouts. We hadn't set eyes on each other since the yard incident, and months were to elapse before I discovered that two pairs of eyes watched our every move on that memorable occasion – human eyes.

Mum knew something was wrong: I mooched around, sullen and bored, without a clue what to go for. That aspect had never bothered me, a confirmed live-by-the-day wallah. Stella's defection had stifled any remaining ambitions. But if the harvest-fields were to win, any remaining hopes of seeing her could be forgotten. Nightfall, when the carts ceased to roll, was near enough bedtime, leaving only Saturday free, from tea-time on. Sunday would always be tricky – Jack's paper-round gobbled up all the morning. And another thing, dammit, I hadn't given Stella a chance to explain. But she *had* the chance – there and then. She knew I'd be calling – and the time, within minutes. 'Ah... did she flaunt the ghastly Noel on purpose – to make me jealous? She couldn't have! And it wasn't jealousy – I was gobsmacked.' I'd had the elbow myself – and dished it out a few times – but nothing to match this. Wallowing in self-pity, I suffered the hell of unrequited love, the agony two-timing brings. It hurts just as much at sixteen.

In the end, as far as job-seeking went, to my surprise Mum gave Barford's the thumbs-down, plumping boldly for 'wait and see'. She was still ignorant of the Noel factor – which was just as well. In the meantime we'd scan the papers, and poke about seeking openings for ambitious ex-grammar types with loads of credentials to support their claim to excellence.

Secretly, I was relieved. No way was I ready to write off the lovely Estelle, treat her as lost. Frank was of sterner stuff than that... 'Maybe she can explain the sickening exhibition? *Maybe?* But the contempt, the arrogance. Ah... somebody pulled the strings – to curb my ardour, and stifle any ideas the young mistress herself might be nursing? But who? The answer was plain – Mummy. It *has* to be Lydia!'

Holidays duly arrived. I'd grab the papers, with Mum at my shoulder, turn swiftly to 'vacancies', at the same time nursing vague hopes of something out of the blue – though jobs rarely jump up and beg. A disappointed Mr Barford had listened patiently to my apologies, sorry I'd not be joining him to 'gather the yield'. "Sorry, sir, it's time I faced the future." (I'd read that in an Ethel M Dell on Mum's dressing-table.) But deep down I'd miss those swaggering Shires, with their bold pouting chests and feet the size of chopping-blocks.

One day, biking through Farndon, passing the village-green, with Rowells' store on the corner, my ticker did a rollover – the first time in months. There stood Maddy, stamping impatiently, jerking his head in frustration, tethered to the hitching-rail at our old saddlers' shop. Braking instantly, I turned into the lay-by where the modern vans parked after they replaced the horse-drawn wagons that had brought the bread, milk, fruit, vegetables, vinegar, paraffin, soap and soda to our doors. I darted in amongst them, too excited to go and look in the shop door. Any minute and the saintly Estelle would appear... and I'd surprise her!

What a let-down! I could have torn out my hair. Waddling down the cobbled path, lugging saddle and bridle, came the squat, stubby figure of the ageing Charles, makeshift chauffeur to the Grants. He half-turned, shouting cheerio to Dad's successor, then, after struggling to get mounted and haul up his burden, trotted off down the street, his feet sticking out above the stirrup-leathers like grass-cutter blades. He was too lumbered to even notice me, leaving poor old Maddy with thirteen stone to hump, that's without the tack, and the further he went the more he looked like Humpty-Dumpty on a bad day. I should have helped him aboard.

Seeing Maddy brought it all back. Not that I'd forgotten – I half-wished I had. Momentarily the magic of life with Estelle came to mock me. So did the salutary smack-in-the-face ending. Thoughts of Noel Fawcett, with his cocky manner and fancy accent, pawing my Stella like he owned her, made me want to vomit.

But I learned a lot more from, of all places, the rectory, being into what Mum was so set on – preparing for the Bishop to 'confirm' me. And the rectory *was* just another gossip-shop, after all. The Fawcetts *were* close friends of the Grant-Wiltons. Sir Martin had been George's commander in France, with the local infantry, after horses were made redundant, and later, in the tank regiment. They'd served together for years. Now he spent his time 'working' in his Midlands constituency, gracing the bright green benches of the Commons, along with his blood-brothers, the Tories. Daughter Sara was at the crammer to which they'd so cursorily bundled Estelle, with Noel reading modern history at Cambridge – at Magdalene – according to Charles. They'd long been guests at Bradbury.

At first I was relieved. So Blondie wasn't the latest in a long line of admirers, but a family friend, naturally close to Estelle. I felt a surge of affection for Reverend Jackson for divulging this priceless information. He didn't tell *me* – he told a newcomer filling in on local colour to keep abreast of us oiks. It wasn't often I felt so well disposed towards the holy man. Neither a lovable nor lovely creature, his great domed head innocent of all but the most meagre whisps of hair above the ears, red sweaty face, and piggy eyes were hardly features to inspire reverence, let alone affection. Beads of perspiration dripped periodically from his top lip to the little black bib tucked into the dark grey suit preacher-men tend to adopt. He was a dead ringer for the guy I pictured when pondering Billy Bunter's father – gross, and not especially devoted to personal hygiene. He was fifty-five and a bit... so Mum said. From time to time, when giving his flock the benefits of his learning, he'd run his finger round the inside of his off-white collar as if afraid it might suddenly contract and choke him. And I could never quite grab that crap about 'filling the hungry with good things, and sending the rich empty away'. The buggers never *looked* hungry... *or* empty!

My affection for the Rev Jackson faded fast. Whether or not Noel, of the blond curls and rosy cheeks, was a family friend, Stella had snubbed me. Treated me like the serf I was – and rubbed it in. *Francis* indeed! 'Hello Francis – leave the papers in the kitchen.' Time after time the ugly phrase pounded through my cranium. She'd dismissed me in seconds like I was never other than an adjunct of big-wigs, sent on to Planet Earth for the sole purpose of brown-nosing the likes of the Grants, the Fawcetts, and the Fanshawes – sorry, the Featherstonehaughs. I spat clinker. A million times I re-lived those nauseating seconds when she looked at me as if I'd come up a manhole. 'This is Noel.' SOD Noel! And what about sister Sara? Why does *she* not charge around, flaunting her bits and pieces? The truth is, neither Sara, nor the rest care to hang about round the servants' quarters. They prefer frolicking at the front, where the grounds are really elegant, albeit screened with box and sixty-foot evergreens, like Hampton Court Maze (according to my Encyclopaedia), or down the sides, tuning up at croquet, and bashing tennis-balls at the twelve-foot wire mesh.

How many were in residence was always a mystery. The rear of the great pile didn't give away secrets. Mention of the family was taboo, even with Stella fairly oozing charm. Mum brushed aside 'that lot' with a contempt I never understood. But it was more than the ritual clash of plutocrat and peasant prompting the acid side-swipes.

At last I shook myself into life – showed a bit of gumption. 'So Briarsdale's Verboten? So what? The surrounds aren't no-man's-land. There won't be a welcome in the meadows, but nor will there be firing-squads, or man-traps consigning intruders to the dungeons.'

Scorning caution I opted for the bold approach. Biking to the north-west corner of Bluebell Thicket – well away from 'our' gate – and after a despairing peek in the letter-box, I dumped the much-abused Raleigh in the ditch, crossed to Tate's Meadow, clambered over the stile and set off smartly, hugging the forest edge – no point in inviting trouble. Bluebells were a memory, the primroses, oxlips, early-flowering anemones long since gone and forgotten, though a handful of purple cuckoo-pints lingered on, livening up the fading greenery. Not that I had flowers in mind.

Soon I was striding out with confidence, passing the stretch where the thicket joins Primrose Holt, stepping up the pace and before long reaching the bottleneck leading to Chucklecopse. Hopes rose in ratio to my rapid progress. Soon I'd be back at our haven. Back at 'Carolean' where all was bliss and sunlight. Where, with Stella at my side, the world could go to hell, like on the day she first took me. Was there half a chance she'd be there? Wild and woolly fancies like that helped ease an underlying wariness of hostile keepers, warlike servants of the Grant-Wiltons, sullen estate-workers cutting out fence-posts, sawing logs, harvesting the coppice yields, fashioning hurdles with which to pen the flocks and keep the boundaries secure.

Luck was with me – nobody in sight. I ran the last fifty yards. Despite foliage still clinging on, I spotted the hidden arbour. An elm stood sentry at the magic retreat.

Puffing hard, I rounded the mighty tree... then stopped dead, just staring! All hopes plummeted. Nobody had sat there for years. Mountains of growth had encroached on to the love-nest, writhing, twisting, turning, and clawing its way to where Stella and I had once sat huddled, kissing passionately beneath a canopy of briar, elder, creeper and honeysuckle that was then just pushing out tentacles. The hideaway wasn't so much derelict, as buried – under a camouflage of every climber in the book. Looking along the choked-up path beyond the arbour into the heart of Chucklecopse, I could just make out the Lodge roof through the yellowing leaves.

The miserable anti-climax had me stumped. It was a crazy mission from the start. Plain daft. I knew she wouldn't be there – why should she be? The girl wasn't psychic. But I had to try *something!*. Now the maddest thing of all came to mind. Why not a rapid sortie to the workshop? I knew where the key lay – Stella showed me last time we went. Something came over me. Somebody rubbed the lamp. Ditching the doubts, I squeezed past the arbour, dashing full pelt up the roughened track, swerving between humps and hollows resulting from disuse, and from the excavations of a million amorous, if ravenous, rabbits. Rounding the lodge, I grabbed the key from beneath the gintrap, jumped on to the verandah, unlocked the door, and eased it ajar. It squawked like a stoat on heat. Why the caution? Trespass – that's why. What a liberty... I'd no right in the woods, let alone the Lodge.

By the time my grade-three brain clicked into gear, it was too late. A drumming of hoofs, then footsteps clonked on the verandah. I'd left the door open so I could at least see something. Nowhere to run to – windows closed – and shuttered. I was cradling a model – the Hereford bull, chiselled to perfection, painted with the flair of a Leonardo. And that's how she caught me! Thank God it *was* Stella – silhouetted in the half-light of the doorway.

"There you are Franz! Oh Franz – I miss you so much!"

She ran to me, arms outstretched. I caught her, held her, kissed her a thousand times, fiddling to put down the model without breaking it. It's impossible to describe the way I felt. Filled with wonder... yet puzzled.

"How did you know I was here, darling?" I whispered, at last. "How did you *know* ?"

"That's easy. I was out for a spin, that's all, with no intention of coming up here. I passed 'our,' gate, carrying on to the far corner, when I spotted your bike. What a shock. I guessed straight away where you'd be – more or less. I turned, belted back to the gate, told Maddy to step on it, and here I am. Oh Franz, it's wonderful to see you."

"Are you home for long Stella? I heard you'd gone to that school you were dreading – you didn't tell me. I suppose you told Noel." I piled on the agony. She ignored it.

"No... back tomorrow. This is very much a buckshee break. Rupert rang me at school, from Magdalene, promising to pick me up. Good of him, wasn't it, diverting to Lode's just for my benefit. Showing off his new motor – that's the long and short of it – cocky hound. I wish it was mine. I can't stay long – too many questions – from too many people. I'm still a baby to them."

"Does Rupert do as he likes at University, then?" I asked, in surprise.

"More or less, I reckon," she answered off-handedly, grimacing.

"Stella... Estelle... I know you hate third-degree, but... I'm going to ask you this – do you still love me – like that day at Carolean, and at Lucans Pond? Well... *do* you?" I'd hung on to her hands. I squeezed them hard. "And why didn't you tell me you were going away? I nearly went potty."

"Yes, yes, yes – of course I do. More than ever. Noel's an old friend – so is Sara. She's in a higher grade than me – that's why they bunged me there – because of Sara. Sorry about the breakdown in communications – that's another story – a long one." By her manner I knew no explanation was forthcoming – not then. I was too ecstatic to care.

"Aren't you going to crown me for breaking in? Some unknown force drew me here. I had to touch something you had touched – helpless, I was. And that's the truth."

"Silly," she said, her eyes big and gentle, lips soft as silk. "You poor Franz. You make me feel so guilty."

"Life's dead without you, Stella. One day I'll marry you, so we're never apart."

"That would be nice. Oh, you're such a dear. Come and enjoy the place whenever you like – but don't let Sissons catch you – or Daddy. I must say goodbye; they'll wonder where I've got to." I clung to her ages, finally seeing her aboard Maddy, then she galloped off like a bat out of hell. I sighed, locked the door, and put the key back.

I'd asked her little about school, and she'd volunteered nothing. She was like that. She so overpowered me; her agenda came first. Only when she'd gone did I think of all the things I wanted to say, but never got around to. Questions I should have asked. And she seldom asked me anything. Not important things – about life, and money. Our affair was outside convention – apparently. The everyday ceased to exist. We didn't have stars in our eyes, it just felt that way. It was unique.

I went home elated, though disgusted I wouldn't see her again before Christmas, nor hear a word. 'But she knows where I live! Why doesn't she write?' It never occurred to me *I* might write to her. You don't pen letters to a goddess... What an ignorant young prig I'd become. It never occurred to me that such a gorgeous creature as Estelle could be seriously unhappy. She'd hinted enough times of hostility at home. The signs were all too plain – looking back!

I found Mum in a rare state of excitement. The afternoon post had brought news of tremendous significance – a foretaste of the big wide world of business I hovered on the brink of. An invitation for Francis Allner to be interviewed for the 'interesting and promising' opening as junior assistant, and later, articled clerk, at the chambers of the distinguished, highly respected law-firm of Sangster and Sangster.

Switching attention from the thrills of life with Estelle to the mundane processes of pushing around reams of bumph at a desk in Peterborough wasn't easy, but it was essential I do something rewarding, waving goodbye to the carefree days of romance and adventure. Staying focussed was essential to bring in the lolly that would keep Stella in the 'circumstances to which she's accustomed'. I'd never make a fortune with Sangster and Sangster... the name was too ridiculous to start with. And I'd no inclination to dabble in matters legal – though I was certainly due to earn some corn, and give Mum a boost after the long, lean years. For the life of me I didn't dare tell her I intended marrying into the Grant-Wiltons – I'd need stacks of dough for that. And she'd go through the roof if I so much as mentioned such an absurd idea, though I couldn't see why, beyond the perceived incongruity of the union. The caste system went unchallenged in those days, and few from the lower order bridged the chasm with honours. Admittedly, a handful of flouncy females 'did well for themselves', making a 'good catch', but so bizarre a union seldom lasted, and there's nothing more painful than a return-ticket to the upper reaches.

In collar and tie, new serge suit, with a waistcoat ('vest' the man in Foster's called it), clutching a folder filled with testimonies to my learning ability, I crossed Cathedral Square in a state of 'hope-I-do-well', but half-hoping I wouldn't, hurrying to keep up with a Mum done up to the nines – I felt proud to have such an attractive parent. She insisted she accompany me on this milestone mission, and I was glad of that – but didn't say so.

As we sat in reception, at what seemed an exceptionally fusty establishment, I found it hard to shake off the feeling I was in church. Maybe it had to do with the tall ceiling and the whispered exchanges which passed for conversation between nervous, hesitant visitors and the sour-looking man behind the sliding window. From the start he put me off, waving us vaguely to a faded settee when Mum announced our arrival... albeit twenty minutes early!

In wonder I studied the oak-panelled walls, where certificates of testimony to the academic excellence of the 'inmates' had aged to the colour of wrapping-paper, the frames filled with long dead midges, and here and there even the remains of a housefly. The names were recorded in immaculate script, relating to one Sangster or another, going back an awful lot of years. The waxen seals were being slowly eroded by stray shafts of sunlight filtering in by the side of the Cathedral tower.

We'll gloss over the rest. Within a week I was a cog in the legal process, under the wing of a non-legal incumbent, Stanley Forest, the 'managing clerk'. A high-flown title, but one he merited, for whereas experts deliberated on weightier issues, he kept the show on the road, knitting together diverse and unlikely briefs until a vein of coherence emerged from the solemn process.

To Mum's delight I was deemed ideal for assistant to the sainted 'Sherwood', as he was inevitably known, by greater and lesser mortals alike. In other words I was earmarked as his dogsbody. There was more than enough on the man's plate, and the solution to his cries for help were well affordable by this aloof and discreet organisation. He drummed into me that at all times, theirs was a 'Secret Service!' Nothing I heard, saw, read, or suspected, must leave the sanctity of those four walls. To me there looked to be more like four *hundred* walls in the labyrinth of private bolt-holes closeting the scores of po-faced 'lawyers'. It took a week to find my way around, for I wasn't desk-bound as anticipated, but a messenger, in permanent demand. Fortunately, it didn't extend to tea-boy: a mature female attended to that vital side. I learned to live in a world of claims and counter-claims, fraud and embezzlement, plaintiffs and defendants, summonses and dismissals, courts and contestants – Sherwood proved an astonishing encyclopaedia of all-round knowledge and expertise.

A small man, with sharp features and a brillianteened head of dark hair, parted in the middle, he sported large horn-rimmed glasses, giving the impression of a character of inexhaustible knowledge, and unrelieved suspicion. He was forty-five.

Much of the time I spent tidying the strong-room. Sangsters' strong-room really was strong: no outside walls. An inner lining of metal made it look like a safe-deposit. That's what it was... I suppose. An inside door of green baize rested behind the main portal of steel, opened by means of a massive crank-handle like the ones on nineteenth-century railway carriages. The 'dugout' was about thirty foot long and fifteen foot wide, shelved all round, with trestles in the middle and stools scattered about at random. Naked, low-power bulbs dangled from the ceiling – handy retreats for all breeds of spiders. Documents were stored in hundreds of metal bins, foolscap size, with lift-up lids. Alphabetical order was obligatory, bins being arranged under subject headings, beginning with 'Arson' on the left as you went in, and 'Zoo' on the left coming out, though what caged animals had to do with the law and its clutches, I never found out. Officially, these fireproof containers were top secret, but you'd never know from the way the legal types treated them. That's how I came to spend so much time in this windowless dungeon – re-filing dog-eared documents, re-tying ragged lace-files which the frowning beavers grabbed so readily, skipped through, then, contrary to requests, half-heartedly rammed back into the open-mouthed containers, regardless of place and propriety. Subconciously they knew Joe Muggins would put the files to bed – eventually – that's why the clowns were so bloody slipshod! Often I was tempted to scatter the lot in all directions – then had second thoughts. At first it was exciting to handle such sensitive bumph, but it soon became an unwelcome chore, eating into the time I could better spend learning the real tricks of the trade. Nevertheless, it was in this airless, chilly, featureless, impersonal retreat, I first learned of the misdeeds of the Grant-Wiltons.

What an eye-opener! Of all things, the Colonel had contested a paternity suit – back in the Twenties. With trembling hands, I studied the file in wonder, trying hard to make sense of it. All legal jargon, puncuated with 'in-so-fars', 'whereases', and 'aforementioneds'.

Careful not to be spotted ogling this white-hot history of Bradbury, I learned with dismay the gallant tank-captain had been charged with siring the child of an eighteen-year old from Little Downton, who 'lived in' at the Hall. George St John Grant-Wilton hotly denied such nonsense, but was subsequently 'convicted' on the evidence of the girl's parents, and a blood test. Not only did the revelations make me sit up and gasp, they swept aside the cocoon of new interests that life with Sangsters had weaved. My mind went back to Estelle, back to Bradbury, with a vengeance. My first thoughts were irreverent. 'So the old boy's spinal problems don't stunt his bed-performance. Or is it the kitchen-table?' The more I thought about it the worse it seemed, the possibilities mind-boggling. Could this be the reason Farndon folk didn't love the owners of Bradbury Hall? Did it explain Mum's hints. The shivers of disgust, repugnance, hostility, or whatever, any time the family was mentioned? Did it point to further kicks at convention? 'Crikey, this is the secret of the strange, unhappy household Stella hints at, but suggests more by evasion than by anything positive. And this affair... with Sophie Johnson – the tip of an iceberg?' Now seventeen, I knew full well George's wife would never have thrown in the towel over what, to them, was such a minor peccadillo. Maybe he'd fathered scores of little bastards? Standard practice amongst blue-bloods. Tupping serving wenches integral to life in the sticks with the well-to-do. They boast of their prowess when the port flows, and when it doesn't. If only Stella were here. But she wasn't, and she wouldn't be. She didn't write, and as the weeks went by I slowly but surely, meshed in as a worthwhile cog in the wheeling and dealing that went to make Sangster and Sangster function in such masterly and rewarding fashion. Soon I'd adopt a stiff collar... Sherwood confided I'd go on from articled clerk to become a proper solicitor – which he, alas, could never be. I didn't breathe a word of my discovery to Mum, for despite holding a driving licence, and the proud owner of a perky little BSA, I was decidedly uneasy when matters of a sexual nature cropped up. Thankfully she didn't dwell on them, but being female it was inevitable she now and then touched on the disagreeable subject.

Chapter Six

Captured

Mum must have shed, or shared her hang-ups at the WI, the Mothers' Union, or with neighbours. Her sexual attractiveness meant nothing to me. I knew she was pretty, and a snappy dresser, that's all. I never thought of her as a target for horny men. Had we been closer we'd have sidestepped lots of aggravation. Or had I been female... Ah! And had she made a worthwhile effort to meet me halfway. I guess it was hard for her too.

The significance of that wretched eye-opener really got to me. Nothing else mattered, not even the dollops of bumph dropping on to Sangsters' mat every morning. I longed for Estelle – to confide in – though she hardly fitted this bill! I was disgusted, revolted even, but nobody cared.

How did the Grants hush up a scandal this nasty? All Farndon would know, and half the county. How many more lassies bit the dust? My head filled with crazy notions. 'Maybe the haughty Lydia isn't all she might be? And Alan Stewart – what's *he* doing at the Hall? The Agent, Henry Railton – what about him – he lives in? The governess, the housekeeper, the guests, the never-ending visitors, big in everything they do... besides fox-hunting. What about them? And what about those strangers?'

I overlooked one vital factor – the period in question. Aftermath of a long, dirty war. Euphoria, thanksgiving, celebration the orders of the day.

Heroes returning. Villains too. Up went the birth-rate like mercury up a tube. Flu swept the land, victims dropping faster than on the Somme. Two whole years slipped by before any semblance of normality returned. Funny things were happening all across the land – funnier than the odd case of cross-breeding... How do nations manage without men?

Young men. Virile men. For four long years. Not just in Britain. In France, Belgium, Germany, Italy, America, Turkey... War-weary peoples desperate to blank out memories of the frightful butchery – make something of the mess left behind. The 'scars' were bad enough, but the real sadness lay buried – in the hearts of the bereaved and in foreign fields. Folk hide their anguish, set aside the misery, gloss over the beastliness. Being a boy, only the vaguest rumblings reached my ears. Never the details. Never the anger. Never the disgust at gormless politicians, inept commanders, myopic glory-seekers. Congenital idiots who even denigrated the war-poets, yet these scribes saw the picture with frightening clarity. Sassoon, Graves, Owen... dismissed as whingeing nutcases by smart-arse journalists hell-bent on advertising their own skill with a pen, bouncing on to the page with their latest buzz-words and puny puns, doing handsprings down the column.

And I lost my Dad! Mum protected me from all that.

Some gut instinct warned me not to mention the Colonel's antics in front of Mum; she'd obviously know. With her relentless antipathy to the Bradbury tribe, it surely made sense? For all that, at the slightest chance I'd find myself rootling around for more pointers – to more Sophie Johnsons. It's not easy re-living the emotions of a virginal adolescent. I even went the length of perusing church registers, going early to confirmation class just for a snout – I found nothing.

But my interest was no longer neutral. Whether I hoped to find more Grant-Wilton scandal I can't be sure – but something kept me burrowing. And being on Sangsters' payroll opened doors to fascinating establishments, not the least being the domains of the local papers.

On the pretext of seeking a record of some mythical happening from the past, I'd quickly flip back to wartime, and the troubled Twenties. But it wouldn't do to waste too much of the law-firm's time, so I'd pose as extra diligent, wading through *The Gazette* archives in dinner-break. Harry Paten, guardian of records, got to know me through my legitimate visits, and was happy to leave me to it. Mostly alone, the exercise gave my life a much needed burst of oomph – livening up a spartan routine. Maybe I'm nosey? Often I'd be sidetracked, diving into some spicy item foreign to my 'research'. But in time, even that began to pall. About to give it all a rest, I hit the jackpot. Three big, juicy, tongue-tingling lemons. The name Grant-Wilton leapt from the script like a pop-up page from a picture-book. Not headlined – a modest half-column down the side – but it scorched my eyebrows. 'Landowner sues for libel'. And the defendant was none other than *The Gazette*'s great rival – *The Herald*. Heart thumping, I dug into the details with relish. Depressing it might be to find more scandal to taint Stella's family, I pressed on regardless, like watching a horror movie – scared to look away. A driven urge to solve the mystery of the sinister redoubt known as Bradbury Hall. It seemed *The Herald* had hinted at 'unhealthy' goings-on, when bouts of revelry consigned convention to the rubbish-tip, round about Remembrance Day. High-jinks lasted a week.

Excesses common to Hunt Ball evenings paled by comparison. Claims were made of not merely dubious behaviour, but that the whirligigs were designed solely with erotica in mind. This was *before* 'Sophie Johnson'. Why the Colonel reacted with such vigour as to sue, took some figuring out, unless... ah... unless the raves had been *outside his ken?* Maybe he'd lingered abroad longer than was thought, though he'd hardly stay on in the army with *his* injuries. Besides, the war was over. Anyhow, guesswork solves little, but the man had to convalesce somewhere.

In the event, Grant-Wilton won the day. No firm evidence surfaced to support *The Herald*'s innuendoes, and at the time, scurrilous tabloids had no place on the racks. Undisclosed damages were awarded the plaintiff – but the affair left a nasty taste. Not that I heard of it – then.

For the rest of the week I was stuck with the oldest adage – about smoke and fire. My mind went pear-shaped pondering Bradbury's shenanigans. And that wasn't all. Uglier thoughts intruded, some so wild I began to wish I'd never delved into the bloody archives. Never short on imagination, visions of nightmarish deviation haunted me, inspired by earthy Spanish artists who hit the art world with force back in the nineteenth century. Also, I'd tentatively tried reading Oscar Wilde, and this affair was distinctly 'Dorian Gray-ish'. But most frightening of all was that which hovered on the fringes. I thought of the lovely Estelle – and the day she was born! Not an anniversary – the day she first saw daylight – part way through the war – same as me, 1917. Was there any significance? On the face of it – no. But the Colonel's tours of duty were unknown – to me – France, Belgium, Holland, Gallipoli, Egypt... or wherever? They *would* be, wouldn't they? Unless, perhaps, I took a closer look at Alan Stewart's chronicles?

In time the fascination faded; the exercise tiresome, it began to get on my wick. That wretched column in *The Gazette* had sown seeds that could only flourish – and the contradictions were awesome, the doubts uncomfortably real. They concerned all Bradbury's cranky inmates, not Estelle alone. Something must prompt the weird regime, though I had little to go on, no hard evidence, nothing concrete to justify the crazy notions – apart from things Stella *didn't* say. A sort of negative indicator. Like all worries, the shadowy do the damage, finally leading to total unreason. As I put pen to paper I'm ashamed of the idiocies of my youth. I could have done with the steadying influence of siblings. Somebody to turn to, confide in, lean on, kick me up the doughnut now and then, and bolster my confidence – or maybe to shatter it.

Mum was out the question – as confidante – in matters like this. But it was imperative I talk to somebody, which left only Grandad. He'd know... and he wasn't old, like most grandads.

Only mid-sixties. He showed his delight the minute I went in –me, his only grandchild. Out rolled the usual tit-bits.

"My, you're looking well. Don't you grow! You'll be bigger than your Dad. You should come more often, it's too far for me to walk – with this blessed leg. Have a toffee." He nodded to the dresser – I knew the tin well. When I was smaller it was the first thing I made for. Granny used to fill it, then. It wasn't hard to see where Mum got her good looks. I never knew my Dad's Dad. For that matter, I never knew *my* Dad.

"How are you, Grandad?"

"Fine, my boy. What brings you round here? Something's on your mind, I can see that."

"I don't know where to start – it seems so daft."

"Try the beginning."

"Well... there isn't one, really."

"Give us a clue, then."

Not merely did I oblige – I gave him an almighty shock.

"The Grant-Wiltons... er... Well... are they *alright,* Grandad?"

The minute I said it I knew I'd dropped a clanger. His face changed in seconds, from gentle *bonhomie* to a bleak neutrality. For what seemed an age he stared unseeing at the wall. He couldn't meet my astonished gaze. I'd offended him, and I wouldn't do that for worlds. To make matters worse, I tried unscrambling the egg.

"It doesn't matter," I stammered. "It's nothing – nothing that can't wait."

"They're far too grand for the likes of us, Frank lad. But then, you'll know that already. Anyway, you're unlikely to come up against them, so it makes little difference what they're like. How's the job going – getting to like it, are you?"

"Yes, thanks. Nothing like as bad as expected. I always thought work was drudgery – too much Dickens, no doubt."

"So it can be, boy. So it can be." Evidently, he thought repetition added weight. He'd blatantly changed the subject, and I was never slow on the uptake – not in that line of country. Bradbury's challenge would have to wait. We chatted a while, he offered to brew up, but I declined. I never liked seeing him hobble about, though I'm certain he'd have been glad to. Granny had died some years earlier, but Grandad coped well, considering his disabilities. Foolishly he'd insisted on trying out a new type of saddle which he'd had a hand in designing. One with a pommel, like the cowboys use, but with the back-end flattened out. 'Foolishly' because he tried it on a horse he'd never ridden. Whether the saddle felt strange to the nag, and didn't sit right, nobody knows, but the animal dumped Grandad in seconds, and effectively ended his working life. His knee was shattered. In Irish parlance he was 'kneecapped', his left arm broken, on top of which he put his shoulder out. Dad took on the workload, under Grandad's guidance, and they managed fairly well, I gathered, until the Kaiser's rotten ambitions mucked things up. Fortunately, the enterprise sold for more than expected, leaving both Mum and Grandad clear of the breadline, if not exactly dripping with diamonds. The saddle went on to be a great success – it's called the Sandon Seesaw.

No bitterness stemmed from the calamitous blows, and Grandad found plenty to amuse him in his garden and his greenhouses, struggling with only half the working limbs of normal folk. His greying hair, goatee beard, and unblemished features, gave him something of the appearance of an academic. Only when he moved did his deficiencies show. The benign expression seldom changed – unless he was seriously disturbed. And he'd suffered some savage blows... terminally crippled, business lost, son-in-law killed, his beloved Amy gone.

Life is essentially sad... and cruel, though people get on with it. Few wear their hearts on their sleeve – rich, poor, or in-between. I feel sure seeing Mum widowed saddened him most of all. As I got up to leave, Grandad had second thoughts. It was painful watching him grab at the wall for support, edging his way to the door – he was better at leaning on a spade.

"I say, Frank. Did you have a special reason for querying the Bradbury folk?"

I didn't like to lie, but remembering his face earlier, I'd no wish to rattle him further. In any case, his manner said it all – without a word being said. A brush-off's a brush-off, even when applied with tact... "No... Nothing that matters, Grandad. It'll sort itself out – I suppose."

I came away puzzled... and peeved. But the more I thought of his reactions, so I came to realise it wasn't a brush-off at all. He'd answered in definitive style, though avoiding the actual words. 'NO! The Grant-Wiltons are *not* alright.' That's plainly what Grandad meant! Not a casual observation, palpably a warning, though he'd hardly guess my reason for asking. Somehow, this made me bristle. Enough obstacles faced me at the Hall without my family muddying the waters. One thing stuck out a mile – pursuing Estelle would never be a straightforward pastime, but nothing would ever stop me.

On the short trip home I punished the motorbike in anger. It always copped the rough end of my volatile moods, but as ever, responded nobly.

"How's Grandad then, Francis? Pleased to see you, I'll warrant."

"Oh, he's fine Mum." Then, angered by thoughts of *more* guarded exchanges, I flew off the handle, and started to talk turkey. "What makes everybody so damned hostile to the Bradbury crowd? *One* innocent comment, and the world clams up."

I never used what Mum disparagingly called 'foul language' in house, but I was heading that way. As she went to sit down she looked like she was parking on a land-mine. I squatted opposite, gingerly, and the anger bubbled up. I was spoiling for a dust-up – with *anybody.*

"I hope you haven't gone upsetting Grandad. What have you been saying – you, and your big ideas?"

"What big ideas? I've done nothing. I've said nothing – to be ashamed of – and I certainly don't have big ideas. Be fair Mum, for goodness sake. Tell the truth, do. It's all to do with the Grant-Wiltons – that's plain. What is it, Mum? For Pete's sake get it off your chest. Somebody'll talk, if you don't. It's to do with Estelle in particular, isn't it – and with the *war.*" For a long time Mum said nothing, then tears began to trickle – she did nothing to hide them.

"Everybody dislikes them, Francis. Not just us. I can't explain, and it's no good keep going on about it. I'll tell you one thing, though – I've no intention of sitting back watching you get hurt just to satisfy the whims of that little Madam. She's out of the way – for God's sake forget her?"

There's no answer to an attitude like that, so I kept quiet, but the injustice hurt – deep down. Mum didn't know Estelle – but *I* did, and I loved her. But I felt the same (if different) about Mum, so we called a truce – in silence. Somehow we got through the evening without crossing swords, and secretly I think we were both glad of that. But I couldn't sleep that night – a new experience. And as I tossed and turned, so my anger returned. Boiling with indignation, and fancied victimisation, I racked my brain to make sense of the enigma I'd become a part of. I was angry because I'd nothing to feel guilty about. Yet even from my favourite persons, Mum and Grandad, accusatory rhetoric was levelled my way. Mum's regular digs plainly stemmed from my tenuous links with Estelle. *Why?* Why erupt over such a natural development? And I was convinced I was causing parallel trouble down at Bradbury, though it was stretching things to liken Mum's anxiety to the Grants' ostracism of Stella. But in that mood, I wasn't prepared to play down facets of the affair that had come to light at home. As for the Grant-Wiltons...

Next day was Saturday, chores back on the agenda, last night's animosity forgotten. Mum was her usual self, chivvying as ever, but in reasonable humour, and I was of that age when domestic conflict rarely merits a carry-over. The day went well. One of those sunny mornings when there's a nip in the air saying winter's on the way, while summer still clings on. I played football after dinner, and called at the local in the evening, where the match was given such a going-over I was glad when I'd had enough... I went home early. Mum sat reading, her embroidery dumped on the sofa. The wireless was going too, but I couldn't decide which item enjoyed her attention? I slumped on the sofa, picked up a magazine, flicking through the pages without seeing them. A thumping on the front door made both of us jump – we were supping our nightcap – tea. I downed the dregs and dashed for the door, only to see a frustrated Jack Rowell, of all people, going round in circles, breathing fire, stamping his feet, clenching his fists, and consigning the world to the Hothouse. Even in the gloom it was clear he was in a right old stew – we didn't have a lantern over the door then... his van rested soshways by the gate.

"Ah! Ah! *Frank*... Thank God you're home!"

"Why, Mister Rowell? Whatever's wrong?"

"Everything! Every bloody thing!"

"Such as?"

"Those two little buggers have let me down proper. Supposed to be ill, they are! They're off to the bloody seaside, to Skeggy, on that bus trip. I know for sure!"

"Who do you mean?"

"You *know* who I'm on about... Sid and Stan... the little sods!"

"Don't tell me you're stuck?" I knew what was coming.

"Help me out, Frank. Go on, PLEASE! Surely I can count on *you*?"

"How?" I was far from keen. Sundays free was the main perk of working for a living.

"Do your old round for me Frank, there's a good lad – I'll make right with you. What about an extra bob?" He actually cringed.

'Blimey – Five bob!' I hesitated a minute, amused at his discomfort. He rubbed his shiny head in mock despair – or was it real? I let him sweat a bit longer, then nodded.

"OK, Mister Rowell. Yes... I'll do it. See you at the usual time, then."

"Bless your heart, lad. Bless your heart. That's the worst off me back. I knew I could count on *you*." I was scared he'd kiss me.

He ran to his van like a ferret let loose, pleased as Punch, off to press-gang some other dubious substitute into service. Mum laughed her head off when I told her.

"I thought somehow that was Jack's voice. Doesn't he get in a state? A wonder he didn't shout something rude through to me. You won't regret helping the man out."

For ever I'd remember that simple comment. For ever the consequences would haunt me.

Sunday... the day I met Lydia Beamish – Stella's mother. I'd toyed with the idea of doing the round by motorbike, but it just wasn't on. I couldn't kick-start the old girl a thousand times – anyway, the load was too heavy. Jack's trade-bike was the only answer. I'd packed up delivering papers when I went in for 'law', and surprised myself by being glad to see my erstwhile customers – and vice versa, I believe. Nothing had changed, though the heaps of soot, tea-leaves and ashes, stacked neatly on their back gardens had grown considerably. And the stench persisted. That sour, gut-churning stench of poverty. Unmistakeable. Inimitable. Poverty – with a bloody great P! Whatever the house, whoever the people, young, old or in between, the smell *never changed*. It was *always there...* God, I don't need reminding!

The change of routine so captured my attention I thought little of Bradbury until I reached the gate, striding briskly across the paddock to where I'd lost my heart. But I had a premonition something was wrong. I can't explain, and I hadn't a clue what the trouble might be, but something new.

The doors were closed, and I was about to poke the papers through the letter-box, when some imp suggested I try the kitchen door. My nose again. But after all, I did have vested interests. The girl I was to marry lived here... some of the time. The door jerked open like magic.

"What do *you* want?"

"Eh? Er... Sorry... The papers, Miss... Er..."

I was expecting Sadie, of the hooded eyes, tight lips and strained expression. What a turn-up. But for the flimsiest of gowns, a naked lady!

Her bouncy bosoms struggled to break free, the gown open from the waist down. She fumbled about as if trying to tie the girdle – without much luck. Her feet were bare, the toenails painted pearly pink. But the face was the thing!

Honey-coloured hair protruded from just about everywhere... eyes, nose, ears, mouth. Oh, from the head as well! The eyebrows were in sharp contrast, darkish and pencilled in, horseshoe shape; big blue eyes compounded the look of permanent surprise the brows suggested; the mouth full and pouting, like it had suffered a thousand bee-stings, the smudged lipstick giving it an artificial twist. She was laughing and sneering at the same time. Yet overall the lady had class – that stood out a mile! That she was Stella's mother was also agonisingly clear. The knowledge brought little comfort, though it's fair to say she had the shapeliest legs in the business – yet she had to be fifty – at least. The few statistics I'd squeezed from Estelle told me that.

"Thanks," she snarled, with such condescension I could have dropped dead there and then!

"Just a minute! Hang on... Come in... Let me have a good look at you! *You* must be Franz!"

The rider was a sort of afterthought. She dragged a pack of Senior Service from the gown pocket, at the same time grabbing matches from the window-sill, poking the fags vaguely in my direction, drawling, "Take one. Put it behind your ear, if you like." I'd never smoked, but I felt a bit of a prig as I shook my head. She lit up, blowing the smoke ceilingwards, and dropped on to Mrs Thompson's stool. The inevitable happened – the gown fell apart as she languidly crossed the exquisite *jambes*. I must have been pillar-box red at the flash of pubic hair. She took not a jot of notice. I turned away fast. For the first time ever flesh (almost) mesmerised me. She'd forgotten I was *there*. Coolly she surveyed the ceiling, watching spirals of smoke float gently towards the open window.

'Where the devil is Cook? Where're all the servants? Where's everybody *got to?*' The mind plays tricks in bizarre situations like this. 'Hurry back... *please*. Save me from surrender.' The pleas didn't help at all: nor did the 'please'. 'Come on Frank, pull your socks up, mate! Be a man – you're pushing eighteen!'

"So you're the boy who insists he's in love with Estelle? My word, you are a big one. Good-looking too. *My*, no wonder she's smitten. Have you slept with her yet?"

She stared at me with contempt, her gaze hard and unwavering, pale eyes icy, her sensuous mouth straight – and something else too ? And I knew for sure she wouldn't give a damn whether I answered yes or no. But the question shook me to the core – a blatant insult.

'Stella's *pure*. It'll be ages before sex ruins our affair,' so I reasoned in my country-boy way of thinking. The question had stung me, and my hackles were up.

"No, I haven't! I love Estelle. I wouldn't dream of that."

"Isn't that the whole idea? Oh, I say, turn your back on that sort of thing, do you? Surely you must be tempted – sometimes?" She lost some of her archness. I think she smiled. I realised how handsome she must be – when she was properly done up.

"She's a virgin. I *know* she is. She's saving herself for me. She loves me. We never discuss that sort of thing." It was a case of full cry now, shyness shelved, inhibitions kicked to one side. I fought to convince this brazen hussy I was worthy of her daughter.

"Come here!" she said. "Come over here. I want a proper look at you. That's right! You're a virgin too, are you Franz?"

I stood facing her – trembling. She turned her face up to mine, smiling now. In wonder I stared down her cleavage. It looked warm, wobbly and welcoming... all at once she stretched out her hand – and fondled me. It was a toss-up whether I'd swoon or explode? She kept on smiling. Her hands were warm, gentle and soothing, even through the cheapest flannel... She undid the buttons in seconds, yanking the flies apart, breathing heavily, then began to caress my manhood... it was rock-hard! And Lydia was mustard hot! It happened so *fast* – the whisk to madness so sudden, in the great magic mansion that was Bradbury.

"We'll have to do something about this, *won't we, Franz...*" I bent, kissing her lips, helpless, horny, hungry... Lydia was firing on all six, the transition from 'normal' breathtaking. She darted her tongue into my mouth, sending it writhing on a circuit of exploration. I thought she'd *eat* me...

"Come," she whispered, urgently. "Don't worry..."

She slid from the stool, slipped through to the great wide hall leading to the back stairway. 'It must be the servants' quarters', I remember thinking. Up the stairs, along a galleried landing, she swept like a wraith. Glancing down, I saw two heads disappearing through a door in the south-facing wall.

Thankfully, they didn't turn – I could hear their chatter – their voices carried as if in an echo-chamber. Both female, in outdoor gear: I didn't recognise them. We quickened. At the far end she undid the last of many doors, pulled me inside fast and turned the key.

We were in some sort of windowless ante-room. She opened a door to the right and pushed me in. It smelt like an opium-den, but was essentially a female retreat. Yet this couldn't be Lydia's boudoir – nowhere near grand enough! But it had *something*. There wasn't time to ponder. She stubbed her fag into a powder-bowl wilting under a thousand lipsticked butts – gave a sensuous wriggle, shed the flimsy gown, flashed me a seductive smile, then started to undress *me* – it didn't take long.

Ten minutes later she turned away, groped on the floor for the fallen garment, recovered her fags and puffed away hungrily. I could tell she was disappointed. She murmured, "Well done," however, as we disentangled, and lay appraising each other's nakedness. She soon ditched the ciggy, turned towards me again, stroking my neck like a cat licks its kittens, smiling benevolently, her eyes filled with heady anticipation of joys still to come. Gently I lifted her arms, wrapped them around me, wallowing in the warmth of her body. Nothing to match this had ever happened before, though I'd often wondered. Her eyes were like dancing bluebells, mouth puckered and hungry, her breasts firmer than her buttocks. Soon she began to fidget, shuffling impatiently. Once more she commanded attendance, passion re-awakened. This time I didn't fail. Finally, with eyes closed, her neck arched, she shuddered in great sighs of ecstasy, sinking slowly to the crumpled bedding, smiling up at me as if I'd worked a miracle. Perhaps I had? Maybe her orgasms were rare?

"Where are the servants?" I managed to ask.

"Halloween holiday – they always take the following Sunday off – don't ask me why." A shiver of irritation accompanied her explanation of the peculiar ritual.

"Where's everybody else?"

"Oh, they find *somewhere* to go and eat. Chores have no place in my itinerary!" Even her whispers were in a posh accent.

"Come on, Franz. You must go. Let me help dress you. These bags look dreadful. They're not fit to house such equipment."

She had a fair sense of humour... I laughed.

"Are you alone, Mrs... er... Gr... Grant?"

"Good gracious, no! They don't all clear off – worse luck. Bless you, my darling boy. Estelle's off to Rome for Christmas, by the way. I suppose she'll come home first."

"What about your...?"

"I never make plans – not of this nature. Away you go. You know the way. If you meet anybody, say you heard fire-bells."

Like a shot I dived for the ante-room, grabbed the nearest handle, and went in. I nearly collapsed. I was in a strange apartment – I'd got the wrong door! The room looked sparse and bleak, walls painted white, matching the ceiling. Just a single bed, a small wooden cabinet by the side, two kitchen chairs and a waste-bin comprised the furnishings, although the curtains looked pretty, fanning out in the room on a lively breeze. A jar crammed with chrysanthemums rested on the bedside cabinet.

Lying face up on the covers, her skin so white it matched the walls, was what I took to be a corpse – until the eyes opened slightly. Apart from opening and closing her fists, she didn't move. She wore just a black slip, her legs bare, long and slender. She looked twenty-ish, but it wasn't easy to tell. Her face was framed in long tresses of dark hair, damp and matted above the brows. I'd barely taken this in when I suddenly heard footsteps – the door opposite stood ajar. I caught sight of a white coat... Waiting no longer I jumped for the ante-room. This time I got it right. Sighing with relief I dashed along the landing, down the stairway, through the hallway, the kitchen, and out. Still nobody around. I didn't stop to investigate...

I'd crossed the paddock on previous occasions in something of a daze, but never as bad as this. Ashamed of my third-rate trousers, fuddled from Lydia's ministrations, stunned to think Stella wouldn't be home for Christmas, and bemused by the 'body on the bed'. On top of which, in some strange way, a part of me had gone for good – left behind at the Hall.

In a dream, I pedalled up to Briarsdale – not even pondering its wonderful memories – on to Little Downton, delivered the last of the papers, then biked steadily home.

Chapter Seven

Ascot

Angst and anger followed my five-bob excursion to rescue Jack Rowell from depression. Silent, moody and subdued, I had Mum guessing, though she wasn't slow to hint at likely causes, albeit not reaching third-degree, and I volunteered nothing. In time the guilt wore off but I had doubts about facing Stella, having bedded her mother (so to speak), losing my innocence in the process. These gloomy reflections weren't helped by knowing she wouldn't be putting in an appearance until New Year at the very earliest. She'd miss the best of the hunting, and chances of re-kindling that magic flame were less than zero. The misery persisted, the only relief being hard work and, when possible, delving deeper into the history of the Grant-Wiltons. 'Them Grants' as they were known locally.

What I'd done was far more important than what I'd managed to ferret out. It didn't sink in I might have solved the Hall's biggest riddle – for the *third* time. For a while I kidded myself I was some sort of charmer. I ignored Lydia's raunchiness... typical male, trying to normalise the more bizarre aspects of existence.

But I wasn't that young... and I wasn't that stupid. 'The woman's a nympho!' Nothing less would persuade a lady like Lydia to coax the paper-boy to bed. It stuck out a mile – plain as could be. 'That's what hogties the Grants. That's what they're desperate to hide. That's what triggers their life-style. That's why they fled Lancashire.'

But the theory was never more than naff! It held up for four to five days. 'What about George's war-wounds – do they prompt the wildness? Do *they* put the mockers on domestic harmony? Put Lydia at odds with convention?'

'Well, whatever, at least I'm getting to grips – though it hardly explains Mum's fears, nor does it nail Grandad's alarm whenever Bradbury gets a mention. And it's imperative I stay focused on the legal niceties of Sangsters' emporium – it's their brass keeping me afloat!'

Stella didn't come home for Christmas, she went straight to Rome, as Lydia had indicated. I was careful to steer clear of Madame Bedworthy. No word of Stella, though I picked up some scraps in the village – no excuse now to hang about near the Hall, and Jack had got his rebellious seasiders back into line – he hadn't boned me as stand-in since their unauthorised dash for the coast – the infamous trip that resulted in me losing my virginity. He'd have got a lovely big earful had he tried.

I was due a change of luck – and sure enough, a slice of the best landed smack in my lap. Charles, the Grant-Wiltons' chauffeur, took a shine to Farndon's favourite tavern – the Blindon Arms.

Now eighteen, bitter the poison, pocket-money dictating gallonage, I was fast approaching manhood. The coming of Charles proved a mammoth, if unusual, bonus. At first his calls were infrequent, and with me just a weekender I had to grab every chance to bend the man's ear. It was a relief to learn he was ignorant of my links with Estelle – I could tell. That's the way it must stay. He was easy to pump once he'd downed a few 'Exports'.

Thanks to an innocent and wholly unsuspecting Charles, tit-bits began to come my way as routine – the juiciest morsels mere throwaways – to him. I learned of Stella's movements – disappointing though they were – and listened to fascinating recitals of the kitchen gossip: the pronounced wisdom of Mrs Thompson and her minions. Who came a callin', who went where, who was locked out, who was locked in, which lass due the chop, which one up the duff, who half-inched the game-pie. I found these diverse fragments fascinating once I got them into some sort of order – every story paints a picture.

But never a whisper on the Sleeping Beauty. The memory of that sad, slender, silent, semi-conscious stripling still sent shivers down my spine.

Henry, the estate agent, early forties and single, was something of a recluse. Alan Stewart, another 'live in', somewhat older, mid-fifties... same as the Colonel. He was a military historian of sorts, with several manuals to his credit, and forever researching his next tome. A wiseacre of eternal enthusiasm, he'd forged significant links with the Imperial War Museum. I wondered if perhaps a military connection explained the closeness of the tricky trio – Stewart, Grant-Wilton and Sir Martin? After all, Fawcett and Grant-Wilton had fought side by side in France. Incidentally, George was 'only' *Lieutenant*-Colonel – Charles wasn't short on facts. But it was time I faced up to the conundrums.

'Does Stella know Mummy's a nympho? Do the others know? Are the servants suspicious? Particularly the servants. The Colonel? *He* knows. Bet your life all the men have her taped. Men are men in any situation. Perhaps they all amuse Lovely Lydia? A right old bunch of studs... sure as hell they're not gigolos... and if not, what are they doing there? How do they pass the time? Don't they socialise outside Bradbury?' But the riddles were only sidelines. Estelle's vagaries hogged the attention.

'Not a hope of furthering our affair unless I shape up better and pay Lode's a visit. Not far, fifty miles maybe, but motorbikes are dodgy animals – forever conking out. Fifty miles without touching a spanner, a biking miracle. And what of the reception? Not just from Stella – from anybody. Trespass at a school exclusive to offspring of top-brass, begging the whereabouts of one Estelle Grant-Wilton? They'd laugh me out of court. Do me for aggravated entry. I can just hear the judge, "Take him down." The porters would crucify me – and revel in it. Ah, I know. Pose as a tradesman. Plumber, painter, candlestick maker.'

'Forget it. No dice. It's crazy – too big a pipe-dream. But it needn't prevent me from writing. She's free to receive mail. The post isn't censored – like in a prison-camp. They're strict alright, the routine spartan at these highfalutin joints, but there has to be a limit. All the same it would be daft to go stirring up the smelly, making Stella the focus of unsavoury probing.'

And there were plenty more posers to deal with.

'Did the Grants rig my downfall? They couldn't have... Lydia was hostile. Indignant.'

"What do *you* want?" she'd snarled. They couldn't have fixed it – but hard to believe it spontaneous. Unless... Ah! Unless... I remind her of earlier frolics? God, she's past all that. Has to be. And the boudoir? No marital chamber, that's for sure. But what else... ponced up with fripperies and fancies, yet buried in dust, dog-ends and talcum, and doused in evil-smelling perfume? Only on screen does such frivolous 'luxury' exist. In the madness of mating I'd glanced in the long triple mirror – seeing more than even Hollywood dare reveal – hints, however broad, at the limit of the censor's indulgence. He'd never have OK'd my behaviour, or rubber-stamped the nakedness. Very Valentino... Very Bankhead...

The weeks slipped by, the guilt gradually faded. The emptiness generated by Stella's vanishing tricks I must learn to live with. I buried my head deeper into matters legal, devouring costly correspondence courses arranged by Sherwood (at Sangsters' expense). They had more faith in my potential as a lawman than I had.

Mum carried on in her quiet though sometimes mysterious way, seemingly content to abide the constraints of a colourless existence, throwing her energies into an ambitious mix of local activities, mostly offshoots of the workings of the church. I was too self-centred to even think of the emptiness she managed to hide so cleverly. I never sat back to appreciate the kindness, the understanding, the generosity. The selfishness of youth is hard to comprehend... and harder to forgive.

Hunting finished for the season. The endless prattle about clobbering an April fox, like so much else in that realm, no more than hot air. Easter came and went, with little to record, but it gave me a chance to plant the garden as dictated by the calendar. In went the peas and beans, carrots and spuds, radish and onions, lettuce and leeks. An essential warm-up duty in order to enjoy the gastronomic joys of summer, of autumn, of winter. Yields from the garden ranked high in the list of seasonal pleasures, bringing a satisfaction I'd never lose. A procedure vital to a countryman's economy – and to his sanity.

One May evening, all jobs dealt with, I sat with Mum as she worked her way through yet another square of unbleached linen, her brow furrowed in concentration, figuring out what the eventual result might look like. Idly, I picked up the paper, *The Gazette*, where they always greeted me with such civility. A gentle tap on the door surprised us both. It was latish for callers – apart from Jack Rowell – though still bags of daylight to come. We knew it wasn't Jack's knock. I got up to answer, frowning, wondering who the devil it could be? Slowly I opened the door – the surprise floored me. I was steam-rollered. I just stood and gawped.

There was Estelle, prettier than ever, and ten times more grown-up. She smiled – that wonderful smile – revelling in my confusion – and my delight.

"Who is it, Francis?" Mum called, sitting with her back to the door to catch the light as she bent to the intricate stitches. My lengthy silence had her puzzled – as did the caller's.

"It's... um... er... Miss Grant-Wilton," I finally stammered, reaching for Stella's hand, dragging her into the living-room. We had no hallway.

"This is my mother, Stella," I said, as I sat her in the chair I'd just left. A useless comment, but I had to say something. Mum's face alternated between all the colours of the spectrum, finally settling to a warm pink. Valiantly she battled to greet Stella with her customary, ladylike demeanour, and with the friendliness she exuded on special occasions. Stella beamed her delight. She was more beautiful than ever, curls hanging in glory around the perfect face, eyes wide and gentle, lips parted, as if life was just a carnival after all.

"I love your cottage Mrs Allner. What an absolute joy to live here." She glanced swiftly round the attractive, spotless domain, where everything polishable shone brightly, reflecting not just the bits and pieces, but the deep devotion of its keeper.

"This is an honour, Miss Estelle. My, you're a handsome one – so like your mother – if you don't mind my saying." Mum smiled benevolently as she delivered these gracious comments, cool and collected now.

"Small wonder Francis can't wait to get to Bradbury when you're at home. I don't think I've seen you close up since you were a child – you grow up so quickly."

I noticed Mum spoke in the semi-posh accent she reserved for nobs, or those of 'higher station', yet somehow it suited her, and seemed to come naturally.

"It's so long since I saw Franz. I'm a terrible one for writing, or for not writing. I hate letters, they're such a chore, and I can never get down on paper what I really want to say. Besides, I've always wanted to see your cottage – I've looked down on it enough times, from Cuckoo-pint."

"You haven't walked Stella, and there's no sign of Maddy – so how did you come?"

She grinned as I chipped in excitedly. She was in a pink dress and white cardigan, bare legs and plimsolls. Spartan apparel for a goddess – as usual.

"I pinched Cook's bike! Didn't you see it on the fence?"

"How could I look at anything but you? Are you home for long?" As I asked the all-important question Mum winced, terrified she'd hear a 'yes'.

"No! Back in the morning. Rupert picked me up again. Handy arrangement, that."

For half an hour we chatted about nothing in particular. Mum unearthed her best china, to 'take tea and biscuits'. She kept up a steady flow of trivia, with Stella giving due attention, adding her own two-penn'orth in bright, breezy style, as if she'd known Mum for years. I was proud of them both – and mighty relieved. All too soon it was time for her to go. Mum grabbed her by the arm and insisted on walking her to the gate. I snatched my bike from the shed, then we set off for the Hall in high spirits. Stella turned to wave – a rare concession. Mum responded with panache.

For the first half-mile we were like saucepans on the boil – bubbling until the news ran out – though mine amounted to little. Reaching Briarsdale an arresting hook reached out. For ages we clung to one another, loath to break free. In a fever of passion (and frustration) we kissed a million times. The doubts vanished. I cursed the churlish suspicions I'd nursed since the day she went away, fears that almost convinced me our affair was nothing more than a childish game practised by adolescents the world over. To know she still loved me, as I loved her, soon put paid to the anxiety. 'That romp with Lydia meant nothing. Estelle's mine – for ever. I'll wait a lifetime if necessary.' We came close to consummating our great longing for each other. I realised later that's what she had in mind all along, but I was too green to see in the resurrected delights of togetherness. Maybe our love surpassed the mere physical, putting her mother's caresses in the shade.

The next time I met Estelle she smiled at me from the centrefold of *The Times*!

This violent kick-up-the-arse caught me bending at the office. 'Better' papers were ordered routinely, for official use, and it was my duty to flick through the august pages, looking for anything special in the legal section. Reports I thought noteworthy I referred to Sherwood – a vital part of my training, expanding my insight into law and order. On this particular morning I wasn't even aware Royal Ascot had started, despite a fast-developing love of racing.

'Sir Martin greets his champion'. The headline hit me. 'Fairline takes the Charnwood'. The usual journalistic tags accompanied pictures of an unconcerned thoroughbred chewing on his foam-flecked bit, wondering what the fuss was all about. The Colonel's former commander wore the benign look of a man who knows his onions, and never doubted he'd scoop the prestigious trophy. The all-seeing eyes were temporarily hooded. And smack in the middle of the exultant group, clinging to Noel Fawcett's arm, gazing up at him in worship, stood a very adult-looking Stella Grant-Wilton. Poised as a princess, wearing an ultra-smart suit, extremely high heels, garden party hat with lots of trimmings, and that unmistakeable air of 'belonging'. From beneath his topper Noel's blond locks suggested a trip to the barber was overdue. I suspected he was horribly hot – I hoped so. The joy of clobbering the spoils in such a prime set-to, and the burden of a heavy morning-suit, with obligatory bits and pieces *de rigueur* for royal occasions, doubtless contributed to the overheating. It looked to be a family affair, for Sara was there too, chatting to a delighted trainer, but hanging tight to the Hon. Aubrey Griggs-Downley. Of Lady Fawcett there was no sign – which wasn't surprising, seeing she had died six years earlier... so I learned. The captions identified the 'unknowns'.

So soon after Stella's surprise visit – just weeks – an overwhelming sense of inadequacy swamped me. Seldom had I felt so minute, so out-of-it, so ridiculously small-time, and a sinking feeling soon kiboshed the renewed interest in a job at which I was doing pretty well. The correspondence courses had proved a great help in resurrecting my ambitions: the kindness of clever Mr Forest, invaluable.

I quickly snatched up the other rags, turned to the racing pages, and sure enough the pictures figured in them all. The jottings varied, but half the world would be admiring my Stella on that far from memorable morning – which just happened to be Hunt Cup day. Bitterness choked me. I could have reneged on my promises to Estelle. I wanted to curse Bradbury and all it stood for. The only thing missing from those bloody photos was the Royal Family... As usual I was unfair. This wasn't the Bradbury crowd – it was essentially a Fawcett fandango, supported by 'extras'. Being a Member, such achievements were the elixir of life for the gallant, garrulous, greedy, gimlet-eyed Sir Martin, who, amongst his knick-knacks, sported a DSO, an MC and one or two civilian gongs.

It was the way Stella looked at Noel that got up my nose. The next move would obviously be a smother of kisses, and that wasn't imagination. Then I was rattled further – if at something of a tangent.

'What if Mum spots the pictures? What will she make of 'em? Is there a chance she'll miss out? It'll make life easier if she does. Highly unlikely – *The Express* is the Allner bible – they're in that too. She'll see them alright, then jump on me the minute I go in.'

"Francis!" (here it comes!). "You've seen the papers I suppose? My word – Ascot of all places – ROYAL Ascot. Your friend'll figure in the glossies. We must tighten our belts and buy one – we can frame the pictures."

She rarely resorted to sarcasm, not with me. Outbursts like this were rare. The stance didn't suit her. It didn't suit me.

"Yes," I said, slowly, affecting nonchalance. "I didn't realise it was the Fawcetts until the headline hit me. Stella's leading a double life – I hope her headmistress doesn't spot the report. She'll go spare – in term time too."

"Never mind her wretched teacher – what about you? Do *you* approve?"

"Not my business, Mum. A wonder her mother wasn't there."

"She'd be there, bet your life. She just didn't catch the camera's eye." Mum was like a stranger – I'd never seen her so venomous.

"Oh." There was little I could say. It griped like hell, Stella having made such an impression on Mum. Swept her off her feet, pretty well. Now savage anti-climax. I guessed how she must feel – I knew how I felt. And the questions raised were endless. 'Is this a one-off or part of a pattern? Do they do Epsom together? Regulars at Newmarket, perhaps – just a stone's throw away? So swanky, superior, show-off bloody Noel's following in father's footsteps. Race-days in his diary, I'll bet. And what man with lead in his pencil, could resist having Estelle on his arm?'

Mum was unusually quiet once the sparring died down. Something was troubling her, over and above Stella's top-billing. I ignored her, burying my head in a text-book – but my heart was a long way from matters legal, and something was about to break – I'd no idea what, but crisis loomed.

"Francis, come and sit by the fire," (here goes!). She wriggled her shoulders about until she was comfortable, albeit as good as upright. I just slumped. "You're going on nineteen, and there's one or two things you ought to know. Things you have a right to know!"

She was so intense the alarms started clanging. I straightened up, staring at her, surprised. She was reasonably composed, but with a determined look signalling the matter 'important!' It'd pay me to take note... then pray. I did just that (minus the prayer). The light from the window fell across my mug leaving Mum's face fully shadowed.

"This is not easy, and by no means pleasant, but I wouldn't want you hearing it elsewhere – you'd worry yourself stiff."

"It's to do with Bradbury, isn't it?" That didn't take a lot of working out – the same old wavelength.

"Yes. Partly. It's hard to know where to start... You always thought the Grant-Wiltons came to Farndon around the time you were born, didn't you?" I nodded in silence. It seemed of little import.

"Well, they arrived much earlier than that – before the war. And they didn't come here just to cut a dash, as folk imagine. George, that's the Colonel, was banished from the family home in Morecambe, and told in no uncertain terms to get out of the cotton business, and start life afresh, as far away as possible."

"Oh! How strange." I was baffled, but there was more to come. 'What's it to do with me?'

"It seems he got tangled up with some woman who didn't come up to scratch. The family didn't approve. Daughter of the mill foreman at Rochdale, a flighty piece called Beamish – *Lydia* Beamish. *Old* George, that's the Colonel's father, went barmy. He forbade closer ties – until they found the woman was pregnant. They were dignitaries of the church, elders of society, a proud and generous family, the backbone of local enterprises – you know the sort of thing. So George found himself first ostracised, then wedded to the extrovert Lydia, and, eventually, the reluctant Master of Bradbury Estate. Most would think it a move in the right direction. A shrewd investment, and only the cotton fortune made it possible – but young George *didn't,* though he tried playing the country gent as well as he could, lumbered with a man-mad wife to embarrass him at every turn. Not that she had much scope to kick her heels in this turgid backwater – in any case Rupert came along, not that far behind Justin, so in spite of the nannies and nursemaids, for a long time Lydia found herself fenced in."

"How do you know all this, Mum? And what's it to do with me?" I was genuinely puzzled, and so far, unimpressed – in spite of that milestone romp.

"We'll come to that in good time. And don't think it's common knowledge – it isn't! Not even the old-timers know. Anyway, to go on, the war drew closer, when the world finally went mad. Men disappeared... coming back in uniform, then off again, then home on leave, or injured, or sick, or released on compassionate grounds. Some vanished for ever. It was a time of constant comings and goings, of tightened belts, self-denial, especially with the working-class."

"I still don't see what you're getting at, Mum."

She leaned forward, turning slightly. The light just caught her, revealing more of her features. She was still reasonably calm, and not all that worried, though there was a moistness about the eyes. She'd done away with her old-fashioned hair-do, the earphones gone, the bun a memory, as was the middle parting, her hair now bobbed and waved, full and bouncy. It glistened in the half-light.

I butted in again, puzzled, but impatient now. A bombshell was on the way – or some hidden fantasy. But above all I sensed her unwavering affection for me. That didn't change.

"That's all very well, Mum, but I'm not terribly interested in the cotton industry, or in a potted history of the war. I've had a bellyful ever since I was a nipper." That jarred. I regretted the interruption, but she got my drift and, I believe, saw my point.

"Be patient, boy! Though you're not a boy any more – you're the man of the house – have been for years. You've done a good job." She smiled slightly then leaned back, carrying on. "Well, George was one who disappeared fast."

"Do you mean the Colonel? Why do you call him George?"

"That's his name, for heaven's sake!"

"Oh, all right..."

"Naturally, he was commissioned right away, and somehow wangled into Fawcett's command – the local lot. There was some link between them, even then. In no time at all he had three pips. Captain Grant-Wilton. Then came the Military Cross – it was all in the papers, naturally. Mind you, so was plenty more war news."

"When did Dad go?" My interest soared. "And how the Dickens do you know so much? You weren't that old yourself!"

"Old enough!" she snapped. "Old enough. And married!"

"Did he join Fawcett's mob?"

"Yes... later on."

"Why wasn't he an officer?"

"Not the right background, Francis. You're judged on status – and money, of course. You could buy a commission, though in the infantry you only bought yourself a cross!"

A bitterness had crept into Mum's voice, at first barely noticeable, and a hurt so deep it made me wish she'd veer off the wretched war altogether. But for all that, I was hooked. I still wanted to know.

"I thought it was the cavalry," I spluttered.

"So it was, after he'd settled in. That is, until they realised horses wouldn't win a war of that sort. Later on, it was all about tanks. Damn things!"

'Get to the point Mum, though I can guess how you feel about the war.'

"Dad got into that side through his saddlery experience, I suppose? He'd know all there was to know about horses. Not many could match his skills, I'll bet."

"No," she muttered shortly. I waited for her to elaborate, but nothing came.

"Anyway," she went on. "Back to the Grants." She often dropped the 'Wilton' bit – too big a mouthful. A new solemnity crept in. Mum looked different – and sounded more mysterious, more remote – as if she'd gone into a convent to address the nuns.

"Lydia was in the family way again... and from what I gather, the dates didn't tie up!"

"Didn't tie up what Mum?" She looked at me with pity. 'Did she have to spell it out?'

"George hadn't been on leave for ages. He certainly wasn't home when Lydia fell for Estelle. Only the family, and a few close to knew the facts, but anything like that spreads fast."

"You mean?"

"Yes. That's exactly what I mean! Estelle's not a Grant-Wilton! Maybe she knows. Maybe she doesn't. In any case I felt it only right you should know."

"It doesn't matter now, does it Mum?" The indifference startled her – though it wasn't easy to tell – and I was a long time answering. In fact the news shook me rigid. It never left me. It came to mock whenever I put aside my law-books, or eased up at Sangster's.

'Did that cause Stella's rebellious nature? Was that the reason for the chips on her shoulder?'

The weeks rolled by, then the months, and still no word – apart from morsels I gleaned from Charles. But rather than open up, seeing our familiarity, he'd developed a new caution – I couldn't fathom why? However, I found she did well at Lode's, fulfilling Daddy's ambition to get her to Girton. Stella had mentioned that goal a million times. She was well into first year, close to home, but apparently they saw less of her than ever. Charles couldn't remember when she last came to Bradbury. Sometimes I'd wonder if the family treated her as badly as she made out? 'They must – that's why she keeps her distance. She'll live out next year, in the town – come and go as she pleases, lectures permitting. That'll help a bit.'

One thing struck me as odd. In a welter of doubts, and in the worst of moods, Stella seldom complained of Daddy. Come to think of it, she rarely condemned Mummy – not in specifics. It was more a case of being 'out of it', whatever the 'it' happened to be, in a crowded, complex world of parents, friends, relations, near-relations, and grisly hangers-on. And another thing – she never ever mentioned Sara Fawcett. Yet they were schoolmates at Lode's, met at the Hall sometimes, but never rode together, bashed tennis-balls at each other, competed at croquet, explored the estate holding hands – nothing to suggest affection.

Inevitably, these jumbled theories and cranky suspicions centred around George St John Grant-Wilton – when Stella could be forgotten for a moment. What exactly were his injuries? The man looked more or less normal. An odd straightness of the back, sometimes a hesitancy when he walked, otherwise an impressive exemplar of the archetypal war hero. He'd more than repaid his debt to society for straying from what proles call the 'straight and narrow'. It seemed 'life' reserved to itself the right to sit in judgement, deliver a verdict, then dish out punishment. Judge, jury, plus executioner. A concept so alien, yet sufficiently commonplace as to be unworthy of civilised humanity, with its Christian beliefs. But was George still a MAN? That question was crucial. ''Course he was – or there'd have been no Sophie Johnson – and no 'others'. Then again, who'd need affairs hitched to the raunchy Lydia?'

The more I kicked it about, the dafter it seemed. The theories so contradictory they made me dizzy, but a solution was vital if I were to stand any chance of 'conquest' at Bradbury Hall – and no amount of gossip, scandal or 'I told you so' smugness would prevent me from trying. Whatever Stella did, or didn't do, however much she ignored me, for however long she kept up the torture of 'no contact', nothing would change my feelings. There'd be other loves, other entanglements, other passions, other pursuits, but they'd all rate second-best. Estelle would forever rule; command a union so strong it was inviolate. I knew the real Stella... the rest of the world was blind – and stupid!

Chapter Eight

The Party

The disclosure so rattled me, I'd got Bradbury on the brain. But I must watch my step: to the outside world the tribe hadn't changed – still top-dogs, cocooned in privilege, cornerstones of the county set, renowned hosts. The generosity of the controversial bunch, whether to casuals, regulars or dyed-in-the-wool scroungers, was never doubted. The servants were loyalty made human. The legendary Sissons had patrolled the woods since George first came to Farndon; 'Sadie' was part of the fittings, though something *about* Sadie always puzzled me; a couple of maids cocked a snook at marriage (if not their amours); and the grizzled, bent-over walnut-skinned labourers working the land, in their winceyette shirts and corduroy London-Yorkers, were as durable as the marble war memorial welcoming visitors to the village at the corner of Church Lane. How harmony ever prevailed, slaving for such non-conformists, foxed the most ardent of observers. Something special must prompt the devotion, and threads of gold must have run through the sack-cloth, George being the weaver.

Henry Railton, the little-seen but able estate agent, an impressive individual – albeit flogging a long-dead horse – forty, ex-Oundle, a cricketer of some eminence in the amateur ranks, dark, good-looking, with the presence of a somebody, and a confidence more common to crooks. The full moustache and the polished finish, made him film-starry enough to turn ladies' heads. Then came Alan Stewart, a bachelor... so they said. Nobody seemed sure who he lived in with... he was also distinctive, but nothing stage-like about him; fifty-five and ginger, he sported the complexion of one who's spent his life in steamier climes, with ready access to a bottle. A big man, shaggy and untidy, he wore the same suit every day, and spent more time plodding round the estate with a gun under his arm, than with pen and ink, though his books graced library shelves in every town in the land. Occasionally, Rupert from Cambridge, and Justin out of the City, were home together bringing friends, mostly male. Next came Noel, and sister Sara. With his eyes on my Estelle the blond bomber took full advantage of the obliging set-up. Plus George himself, who entertained sparingly, but never guests from his native Lancashire.

Martin Fawcett had long figured amongst the regulars. He confessed he'd be delighted to make Bradbury his principal residence – Charles heard him. But on looks alone he was off-putting – too smooth by half. Eyes over-hard... mean, menacing, malignant, when viewed close up. On top of which he was a toffee-nosed bugger: how he ever persuaded folk to vote for him only he (or maybe his agent) had any idea.

That the overheads of the grand establishment would break any bank was agonisingly clear, and seeing the downturn in farming it would have taken a goldmine to ensure survival. On the female side, a bigger tribe still. Mrs Thompson ruled like an adjutant controlled other ranks, hiring and firing at will, apart from the select few outside her jurisdiction. There *was* something funny about Sadie, as Stewart called her. Superficially the cook of legend – rosy-cheeked and amiable – but at times palpably not so. The pale eyes would narrow to cat-slits, the lips twist to a sneer, as she weighed up a world she didn't much like the look of. Maybe the lady feared her own Reverend Davidson would show up one day? Or maybe she feared he wouldn't? I'd find out soon enough... without the assistance of Mister Maugham.

Finding fresh girls was dead easy – families were all skint, as well as over-populated. Miss Barlow, 'Miss Ada' to most, was officially 'governess', slotting somewhere into the upper echelons, though exactly where was far from clear. A carry-over from early days, nobody questioned her status, nor was it ever defined. Fair, handsome, intelligent, she cut her own track through the Bradbury jungle, aloof yet friendly, superior though equal, *prima inter pares*. No credible role existed with the kids grown up and gone. She could have had lovers by the score – had she wished – and have passed for thirty in any company, in spite of admitting to forty. Ada would remain an enigma, coveted by males, respected by females, admired by all. Today she'd be pilloried as Lesbo – mistakenly.

Lydia... *Lydia*... was just... well, LYDIA! A butterfly settling where she liked, when she liked, yet in some strange way contriving a permanence few could have predicted. How she entertained so lavishly, albeit with Ada's help, and organised such a hostelry, defied imagination – and that's apart from funding. And who was it constantly waging war on Stella? From her bitterness, just about everybody! 'What else can explain the vanishing-tricks, the acid indictments? What prompts her to slam doors, saddle up, and gallop off on her beloved Maddy, with the equally adored Addy upsides? Why bother with an oik like *me*?' Other leeches, too numerous to catalogue, too anonymous to analyse, stretched still further the overheads of the palace they called Bradbury. Whether George *was* the philanderer history suggested I couldn't be sure. Somehow he and Lydia contrived to live beneath the same roof, albeit one of some size.

Deep into a tricky case of arson, head buried in bumph, Sherwood called across the office, "Frank, there's a call for you. Personal. A lady! Take it in the post-room, if you like."

I looked up, surprised. Not often the phone rang for *me* at the office – not personal anyway, and certainly not female. 'Mum's in trouble' – the first thing to cross my mind. I jumped up and dashed next door – instantly apprehensive.

"Hello... *Franz*? Is that *you*?" A half-familiar voice greeted me. '*Franz*?' Only *two* ladies called me Franz – and this wasn't Stella.'

"Ye-e-e-ss? Hello... Er... Mrs Grant-Wilton?" Astonished, I nearly said 'Lydia'. I disguised my disappointment at not hearing Stella's voice, relieved it wasn't Mum in trouble.

"Would you like to come to the Garden Party? It's our turn, this year." The bizarre invitation shook me – the outdoor Hunt Ball! The season's highlight. The West Thorncliffe summer bash!

"Well... Er... is it formal or what, Mrs...?" I started sweating blood... my palms were sticky, I trawled for an escape-route...

"Of *course* not... casual!" I wriggled – like a stoat on a pitchfork, impaled, helpless, yet flattered by the startling attention. I stalled a little longer, trying to visualise the 'do'. 'Who can I latch on to?'

"When... er... mm... when is it?"

"Saturday. Don't bother with a ticket – there'll be one at the gate. Just ask the stewards."

"I shan't know anybody – I'll be out of place... lost!"

"Rubbish! You know me, Franz." It wasn't a giggle, more a gurgle. My temperature spun off the dial.

"Thanks! Yes... I'd love to come." A blatant lie – politeness posing as pleasure.

"We'll see you, then – any time that suits. I'm just ringing round. Bye Franz – be good." Bang went the arson folio!

'Go for him Towser – grab his goolies!' They'd set the dog on me. They'd cornered me.

"Not bad news, Frank?" Sherwood looked concerned. In spite of his sharp appearance he was essentially a kind man. Lydia's lilting tones had startled him as much as they had me.

"No... on the contrary, Mr Forest."

"Good! Chuck me that file when you're done."

"Certainly..."

'Farndon's turn to host the biggest rave of summer. Only for nobs! No hoi-polloi. Bradbury the perfect setting – where else? Not exactly Farndon, but near enough. The Grant-

Wiltons at play again, the 'do' raising oodles for the Master, easing the onerous burden of running a bitch pack as well as the dogs. And I'd be there – but not Estelle. The thought sobered me. Why wouldn't she be there? Why? Her bizarre pattern of behaviour had me groping again – sufficiently erratic to make me ponder the worst... Trouble was I'd grown used to it – took it for granted. The little time she had for Bradbury and its people didn't surprise me any more. Yet she loved the woods. Revelled in screaming up the rides on Maddy. Proud as Punch of her dolls' house. Adored 'Carolean'... And *me?* I give up!'

The party was a case of wait and see, but the prospects were as daunting as they were tempting. With Stella not there, who the hell could I talk to, and mix with? Dancing would be out of the question.

Saturday rolled round, the weather at its kindest. The sort of balmy warmth that lasts all day, and lingers on into darkness, suggesting a night beneath the stars might have its moments. I decided to go late, so festivities would be well underway. Easier to mingle in the dusk un-noticed. After deliberating on what to wear, though not over-spoilt for choice, and Lydia had stressed 'casual', I settled for blazer and Oxford bags, then, after more deliberation, opted for a tie – old-school variety. Telling Mum I'd be late, then telling her the venue, was the hardest bit of all.

With no mention of Estelle for what seemed ages, Mum must have thought our affair had fizzled out, especially with the swotting I crammed in, seldom going out, apart from Friday's trip to the pub, where I'd become expert at pumping Charles. Her face fell a mile. First disbelief, then flagrant disapproval.

"How much are the tickets?" She demanded, breathing fire.

"Five guineas," I muttered, defensively. I turned to the mirror over the fireplace, pretending to straighten my collar.

"What! That's a month's pay – for a *worker*!" She had me by the jugular. For the life of me I daren't tell her my invitation was personal – from the Lady herself. I'd go in for free. Either way, five guineas or five bob, the do was nothing less than scandalous – in Mum's eyes. My face paled. Angry and resentful, I started to lash out – verbally, anyway! To glares of disapproval and gestures of disgust, I muttered "Cheerio," barged through the door, grabbed the bike, and let it have the rough end of my mood. Letting go a stream of obscenities, I kicked savagely at the starter, turned the throttle to flat-out, and shot up to the Blindon Arms.

"The usual, Frank?" The barman gave me a questioning glance. I looked like a wolf – on the wild side! I could see a little in the mirrors over the optics.

"Er... No! Something a bit stronger, Bill."

Bill's eyebrows lifted... slightly. He turned to the spirits, proffering a balloon.

"No! No! not *that* Bill... for Christ's sake, no!"

"Ah... OK. I know, Frank."

After two Four X's in as many minutes, I simmered down to near normal, contemplating the knees-up with something approaching equanimity – provided Estelle didn't come, and stoke the boiler. I wanted her both there and not there. A third quickie had me in total command – and the fourth helped. Within minutes of shouting 'so long' to Bill as he trundled a tray of barrelled-magic from the ground-level 'cellar', and lurching across to the BSA I turned into Bradbury paddock, windswept and warm.

Parking the bike by the bottom hedge, I stared in wonder at what looked to be an upper-class Butlins. The whole world had turned out for the party, the paddock bulging with cars, all big and expensive-looking. Avenues of rustic poles yoked to a lattice framework, carried ropes bedecked with multi-coloured lanterns, fairyland fashion, in a run-up to the courtyard where a handful of latecomers were jostling to get in. Their ladies were the last word in elegance, 'casual' or not; the splendour of the great Hall enhanced by the stunning, yet tasteful disposition of floodlights; the gardens and lawns aglow with fairy lamps and exploding stars. Generators were pounding away somewhere to my left, pumping out the extra power needed to light the extravaganza in such lavish fashion.

As Lydia promised, Charles was on the lookout, with a colleague sitting alongside, beneath clusters of twinkling bulbs suspended from a weeping willow. The two were minding a jumbo cashbox, and a basketful of buttonholes. Charles's swarthy features twisted to a cynical grin when he spotted me. His face was sort of flattish, as if the midwife had picked him up the minute he was born, smacked his arse, then pressed him to the wall, face first, until he stopped howling. Grunting, he groped beneath the baize-topped table, coming up with the most ornate ticket imaginable. In script across the gilded left-hand top corner, were the words 'for Francis Allner'. His sidekick gave me a sly, though drawn-out smile, then winked ostentatiously at Charles. The reinforcement of several strong ales saved my blushes. The stables had been emptied for the evening, though the horses were mostly out to grass anyway.

Happy bursts of laughter drifted under a tranquil sky, as the orchestra took a brief rest.

I pushed my way through the merry crowd. On the far side a temporary dance-floor had been laid – bigger than the one at the village hall. The eight-piece orchestra got ready to blast our eardrums.

They performed on a makeshift platform, belting out 'Ramona' in tremendous style, with all the enthusiasm of well-oiled instrumentalists. Down the sides of this arena, bars and refreshment tents, in green and white stripes, like Lyons lay on for royal garden parties, were jammed to bursting with excited revellers, while plenty more strutted their stuff on (and around) the improvised dance floor. What they lacked in finesse the males made up for in energy. They reminded me of pictures I'd seen at school of the ancient art of trampling corn, all in the best of spirits. Everything went with a whoosh.

Knots of over-the-top youths, unquestionably public-school, lurched around wearing truculent expressions, threatening to sweep the lassies off their feet, then persuade them on to their backs on the verdant turf away behind the scarlet dogwood... the girls looked sufficiently agreeable to suggest they'd welcome macho attention.

Eats were on the house, drinks, unfortunately, were not. I forgot my inhibitions, grabbed a chicken-leg, and a jar of ale, determined to go for it, and have a whale of a time. The interval over, from hereon all would be action. Fillies by the dozen still kicked around loose, so to speak, while the booze tents were bursting with baying males, keen to drink each other under the table. Barmen worked like galley-slaves, heaving crate after crate of Griggs and Downleys bottled dynamite on to the groaning trestles, and whipping off the tops like circus clowns juggling their balls. I tried sorting out the faces, to see if, perhaps, I knew anyone, apart from the Finmore sisters who looked to be propping each other up over by the bandstand after giving the thumbs-down to a polka! Our hosts were nowhere to be seen – certainly not performing on the dance-floor. Suddenly my head started to spin – and spin in earnest! A timely reminder I was a long, long way from sober. So what!

Then it happened. Wiping my paws to divest them of chicken-fat, a hand grabbed my beer-mug, dumped it on the trestles, caught me by the ear, dragging me protesting to the illuminated arena. In a crazy whirl I found myself dancing the foxtrot in overdrive, with the prettiest girl in creation, showing off the smartest frock you ever saw.

Fair hair bouncing, blue eyes sparkling, cheeks on fire, radiant from the healthy exertion, revelling in the merriment, through a beery haze she looked like an early delivery from heaven. Without second thoughts, as the band halted, I carried on dancing. I spun her round like a top, kissed her on the lips, clinging to her lissome chassis as if I'd known her from day one. She responded with fervour, until, to my horror, I realised we were the last couple on the floor... dancing *'sans musica'*! About to flee in terror, or die of shame, a shattering burst of applause rang out, like we were a pair of clowns doing a warm-up act for a stand-up funny-man. She threw back her head, laughing even louder, grabbed me again and prepared to smother me with kisses. A mammoth boost to my vanity. In seconds the lot went belly-up.

"You dance like Astaire, Franz," she murmured. "Come on!"

The trumpets blared, she spun in ecstasy, I caught her by the shoulder, then just as we'd performed a second nifty pirouette, and preparing for a third, she grew over-ambitious on the smooth surface. *She* went one way, her legs the other, and over she spun like a supercharged augur. I followed suit, in a mad, mad flurry of twists and turns, trying desperately, but unavailingly to catch her and keep her vertical. We crashed to the boards together, albeit ten yards apart!

The orchestra boomed, onlookers roared. Her dress rode high above the waist, revealing the shapeliest bare bum ever seen at a country knees-up. Horrified, but horizontal, I clawed my way anxiously towards her, throwing my blazer over the lily-white flesh, pulled myself to half-sitting, and somehow scrambled upright, hauling her to her feet. The doll was still laughing. And finally I realised who she was. *SARA FAWCETT!* I'd never seen her in the flesh – just in the papers.

A deathly hush fell over the roisterous mob. From the French windows a lady emerged, descending the marble steps with great dignity. The crowd parted like magic, anxious to let her pass. She was in black – in full-length regalia designed for evening revelry. At her throat a triple string of pearls gave her a queenly appearance, her copper hair drawn tight in attempts to control the curls. The huge grey eyes were at their iciest. She passed me without a second glance, strode up to Sara, froze her with contempt, then smacked her across the mouth with her evening gloves. Not in a million years could I have imagined *my* Estelle in such cold, outraged fury. For five seconds more she lasered her indignation on the uncomprehending Miss Fawcett, then spat out her soundbite, "Take *that,* you cheap little show-off!" She turned abruptly, making her way back to the Hall. You could hear a feather drop. Fortunately, the band-leader was on the ball. He struck up an extra-loud version of Colonel Bogey, and sanity slowly returned. Crowds surged to the dance-floor, anxious to blot out the unsavoury incident. Probably they did – but *I* didn't! The shock of learning Estelle was there, and knowing she'd witnessed my inglorious exhibition, sobered me in seconds. I turned to Sara, expecting to find her in tears. Instead, she was laughing again – louder than before.

"That's ruined *her* evening – get lost, Madame Frost!" she hissed.

Her eyes were a wicked mix of mirth, envy, hatred and calculated rudeness.

"She's jealous, stupid bitch," she grunted, then followed Stella across the lawns, up the steps, and out of sight. Apart from praying the ground would open, I was a bundle of confusion. Sara must have planned this little episode, with the sole purpose of putting one over on Stella.

'But Stella can't love me enough to react like that – or *can* she?' It was ages since I'd seen her, or heard a word, yet here she was at Bradbury, got up like some bloody duchess, waiting to join me. Lydia must have told her I'd be there, and Sara obviously got wind of it. What to do next? The ground didn't open, and my mind was made up for me.

"That was all very embarrassing, young man. Don't worry. You're Francis Allner, aren't you? Come and have a drink."

"Er... Thank you, sir." I looked in awe at the immaculate Master of Bradbury. He was relaxed and smiling, wearing a cream linen suit from which a red silk handkerchief dangled in elegance. I dusted myself down, and straightened my collar. He was so unobtrusive, so natural, my anxieties evaporated, though by now I was dead cold sober. He must have had a good idea how I felt – his kindness so genuine as to put me instantly at ease.

"So you want to be a lawyer, do you?" He had a twinkle in his eye as he made the disarming comment. The change of tack surprised me – a clever manoeuvre.

"Well... I hope so."

We sat in what seemed to be a snug, next to the gunroom. I'd liked to have looked in the gunroom any normal time, but it was obviously bolted and barred. Anything can happen when hunting-men are arseholed.

"What made you go in for that line of country?"

"I didn't, sir. It was a case of doing *something* – my mother picked the vacancy. It's quite interesting."

"Here – you look as if you could do with a proper pick-me-up." He poured two glasses from a decanter resting on the plain little table. The curtains were drawn. I didn't know which way the room faced, but had an idea we were somewhere at the rear of the mansion, the orchestra sounding muffled and distant. When I'd followed him through the labyrinth of passages at varying levels, fortunately there was no sign of Lydia's love-nest. The thought of it made me shudder. Sweat too, like the memory of that staircase! Gingerly, I sipped the potion he handed me. It was my first taste of brandy. He was right – it did liven me up. After the trauma of the last half-hour it was more than welcome.

"Sangsters speak well of you. Claud is my solicitor. Do you see much of him?"

"Oh no, sir. Hardly ever. He's managing director. He's rarely at the office. They talk about him a lot." My brain was

121

back in overdrive. Frightening clarity succeeded the muddled thinking of minutes before. Hilarity vanished. The significance of the Colonel's drift penetrated like the east wind. He'd known of me for *some time.* (Claud Sangster was 'God' at the office.) He knew I was mad on his daughter. She must have mentioned me after all, so why all the secrecy? Why was I kept hidden? Who was I hidden from? Not *Lydia!* And the Fawcetts had me weighed up, at least Sara did, or she could never have staged the humiliation of Estelle – or of me. I kept up a suitable deference to the Colonel, as masses of disturbing and contradictory thoughts rambled in my head. I liked the man. The austere and distant character of my imagination faded. How could I ever have thought him a buffoon? His fine looking face, dark hair, neat moustache, hardly reflected the agonies he'd suffered, and the frustration of his shortcomings as the years rolled by.

When he entertained the Hunt, granting them the freedom of his broad acres and use of the great twin woods of Briarsdale and Cuckoo-pint Rise, he must have raged at his own inability to take part: been envious... and resentful. Or was he above all that?

"Why has Stella gone away, sir? I know she wanted Girton. I know that was your big ambition – but she never comes home, and I never see her, or hear anything, and I'm going to marry her one day."

The clarity clouded. I couldn't believe it was me talking. 'What am I saying? Has he put gunpowder in that decanter? Crikey, I've only had two swigs.' But my tail was up, and the truth surged from my mouth in volumes. Colonel Grant-Wilton listened patiently, and as far as I could tell, with sympathy – and with *something else!*

"You'll have to hurry," he said finally, in a much changed tone from his earlier chatter.

"Why?" I asked. His new voice surprised me... and shocked me!

"Didn't you know?" he asked, then cleared his throat, putting on an even sterner manner.

"*Know?* Know *what,* sir? Is it Estelle?"

"She's become engaged – to Noel. They were to make the announcement this evening – until the unfortunate contretemps on the dance floor caused a postponement."

Unbelieving, I stared at him in silence. 'So I'm just a pawn! This whole thing stage-managed. That's why they invited me – to witness the announcement. My final humiliation. A blatant kick in the balls for having the temerity to fall in love with a Grant-Wilton. Lydia *planned* it – so I'd never want to go near Bradbury Hall again.' The audacity, the cruelty, the sheer cynicism, turned my guts to ice. 'Why would they do this to me? Apart from the obvious... and Stella? This explains everything. The long absences, lack of contact, contradictory emotions... she's twenty now. No longer a child. She didn't *look* like a child when she whacked Sara Fawcett across the gob. She's adult all right. And there was me imagining she'd turned out solely for *my* benefit. Thought she was jealous of Sara, when all that happened was in pursuit of some long-standing feud in which I didn't even figure.' Absently I surveyed the snug. The green leather-topped desk, waste bin, pipe-rack, dog-basket, filing cabinet, fireplace laid ready for lighting, chest of drawers that looked mahogany, well-worn armchairs, battered *pouffe*, a telephone. Around the walls large-scale maps of the estate hung between sporting prints as unoriginal as the (known) pursuits of the occupants. I remained silent – nothing to say. Nothing I *could* say. I felt cold and empty. The brandy-charged boldness had vanished. The Colonel suddenly coughed loudly, reached for his pipe, stoked it, then had second thoughts, put it back on the rack with strands of tobacco dangling from the bowl. A passing thought struck me. I'd never imagined that one day I'd have the pleasure (?) of seeing the Master of Bradbury shuffling uncomfortably in *my* presence. A satiric reversal of the norm – but it brought little satisfaction. His next announcement had me stunned.

"Would you like to *talk* to Estelle? I'll get her – if you wish. Sit still, young man. Help yourself to the decanter." He could have called a servant – plenty were on hand. Probably he was glad to disappear. The last thing I needed was more firewater... I sat perfectly still, seeing nothing. The clouds up ahead were awesome. A quiet tap on the door and there, in all her finery, stood Estelle. Still I didn't move. Dazed and dejected I looked at her with stark indifference. The queenly apparel clung as if part of her. She *was* from another planet – I realised now!

"Franz... you wanted to see me? How *are* you? It's been a long time – *too* long." The lovely grey eyes looked me up and down as I got slowly to my feet.

"You're growing still. You're bigger than a policeman. Come here. Kiss me! Kiss me like you used to! Don't you *love* me any more?"

"Stella... *Stella!* Darling Stella. I love you so *much*. You know I do." I swung round angrily, giving the door a vicious kick... it slammed with a bang, then I took her in my arms as of old, clinging to her until scared she'd collapse. She was so worked up breaking free wasn't easy. Nothing lurked beneath the silken gown, her bosoms exploding, the nipples rock-hard... proud, inviting. She pressed closer, we merged to a single entity.

"Oh, *Franz,* isn't it *awful!* I *want* you – want you NOW!"

"*Estelle!* Be sensible, for God's sake!" Knowing I must reject her, I yet clung to her as she pleaded. It wasn't right to take her like this...

But I'd dreamed of it all along – being young, healthy, and normal. I went on, "What about Daddy? *What if he comes barging in?* We'll be up the creek... paddle or no paddle. What if...?"

"For God's sake lock it then. Bolt it as well. If *you* won't, *I* will! To hell with the lot of 'em. *They're* not ME!" She dragged me to the rug, releasing her gown-clips as she sank to the floor, shedding the garment in a single sensuous wriggle. Her curls hung free, tumbling about her shoulders as that wonderful alabaster body writhed like a python... impatient, urgent, *demanding!*

Finally we came together in the all-out passion of young love. She swooned in the joys of fulfilment, sobbed aloud, but smiled up at me as if the world had ceased turning. 'If *only!* If only it *would* stop. Stop for ever. No complications. No more barriers. No living apart. Stella belongs to *me* – as surely as the sun rises – and sets.'

"Franz... Oh, Franz, why can't things be different? Why isn't life straightforward?" She sat beside me on the arm of the big old chair, re-fixing her hair to the austere style she'd adopted earlier on. Her face had never looked lovelier... gentle, vulnerable, humble. Then she held my hand as if she meant to keep it.

"Where's Noel?" At last I managed to speak normally.

"Gone out to the guests. Daddy took him. They're presenting some point-to-point awards. They won't be back yet."

"Is it *true*, Stella? Is it? Are you going to marry him? You might as well shoot me *now*. I don't understand. He doesn't love you. You don't love him! You're mine. You're *mad*."

"No, I don't love him, Franz, darling. But yes – I am going to marry him. It's more or less been arranged for years."

"You're old enough to do as you wish. And what about me?"

"You'll get over it. You'll forget me. It makes sense. Martin's a baronet, you see. They like that, Mummy and Daddy."

"So?" I grunted.

"The title's hereditary. It'll be 'Sir' Noel Fawcett. Don't you see, Franz? I can't give all that up – it's a way of life. I just *can't*..."

"We can run away?" The offer carried little conviction.

"Where to, darling? Where on earth to? You'll never have money. You'll never have the... the... the background." What Stella said made sense. Too much sense. If ever an arranged marriage had been properly laid on, this one had.

"You've known for years, haven't you, Stella?"

"More or less. That's why I'm a rebel. But it does have its points, darling. You know life's all about being practical. Pragmatism rules – so Daddy says – and he should know."

The remark puzzled me at the time but, sunk in misery, I'd no desire to pursue that line of talk. And something else struck me – she hadn't 'saved herself' for me, like she'd always promised. I'd never doubted her before. But I'd no desire to dwell on that either. My features must have darkened – with her devastating insight she read my thoughts. That was something else I couldn't change.

"*Should* he?" I muttered, not sure what I was on about. Moving to safer territory I said, "I see now why you had to hide me, Stella. I think I understand a lot more after tonight. Whatever you do, wherever you go, for however long I have to wait, you'll come back to me one day. I *know* you will. If you need me in the meantime..."

"I *know*." She stood up and left. Three weeks later *The Times* announced the engagement.

Chapter Nine

Interview

Yawning, I jerked the bedroom curtains open and looked over to Cuckoo-pint Rise. A month had passed since the garden party fiasco. Gazing uninterested at the morning sky, memories of Lucans Pond drifted back. How rapidly things change. That magic day we found heaven wasn't light-years away.

'Nothing on the menu now. Stella gone – for good – there's little good in it! The Rise forbidden territory – Sissons, plus Abe and company, will take care of that. No more links with Bradbury to spur me to action. The thicket alien territory, Chucklecopse a dream, Carolean, like the Dolls' House, a piece of history.' But mourning the demise of the bright side wouldn't help, nor would it disguise the facts – Estelle had transformed existence – introduced me to new horizons. She *was* life – one that had never seemed possible – here on earth.

In typical style Mum put paid to the daydreaming, screaming up the staircase, doing her nut: "Are you ever coming down? Breakfast's ready. *Come on* – Beautiful Dreamer."

"Sorry," I muttered, lurching down the stairs, shirt in hand, edging smartly through to the kitchen. "Won't be a minute – I'll shave later... sorry."

A splash, and back into the living room. Frowning, she lifted the plate from the hob, gripping it gingerly with the bottom of her pinny, and plonked it on the table; it bubbled fiercely at the edges. Traditional fare – egg (with eyelid), and a rasher of home-cured bacon. For paupers we ate pretty well. At least, *I* did. Toast and marmalade tided Mum over, provided the grate was in the mood to brown the bread. Always a tricky fireplace, it performed according to which way the wind blew. A westerly, and you could sit bare-arsed on it without burning up. An easterly, or north-easterly, had it tear through a bucket of coal in minutes, turning all fare to cinders – sausages became fossilised dog turds.

"It's no use mooning over Bradbury all the time, Francis... forget the damned place! Forget Stella too. And the woods. Forget Charles. Wave goodbye to the lot of 'em. The Grants aren't the begin-all and end-all of life, you know. Get out more, not just cricket and football. You're luckier than most, a job to go to... then there's your motorbike. How's that nice Mr Forest you talk about? Glad you passed your courses, I'll bet. When do you start the next?"

"Oh, in about a month, I believe. He's OK. He keeps me at it now I'm better qualified. A junior does the running about – that makes a change."

Telling me to avoid the Grants was like advising a eunuch to cut out crumpet. 'Thank God nobody's mentioned the party shenanigans, or the gist of George's announcement. But she'll see the engagement in the papers! It'll be a shock – but a *pleasant* one!'

I lacked the bottle to tell her myself. The name Noel stuck in my throat like cotton wool. Thoughts of that smooth red face, curly locks, cocky manner, had me spitting toenails. I thought of the day I first saw him – when he looked right through me like I wasn't there. And a part of me could understand Stella's dilemma that rotten morning. I remembered, too, the magic half-crown – I'd still got it.

"You're mooning again," snapped Mum. "Finish your breakfast, do, and get off to work."

I smiled, trying to reassure her, then as something to say, I volunteered: "Looks like there's another war on the way, Mum." She stopped dead, looking at me in horror. Her face had never changed so fast – over one simple comment. The papers were for ever banging on about Europe, and the seething unrest prevailing. She must have had some inkling things weren't looking good – Spain's civil war hogged the ruddy wireless.

On the way to work Mum's angst-ridden face came to haunt me. 'Tactless bugger. But she's heard the broadcasts, seen the papers. Hearing it from someone close – that's what put the wind up her. You know what she's like when the war crops up, and mention the Grants, in any context, and her brain's straight into overdrive, going over and over the ghastly set-to that robbed the West of its most able citizens.

'And Estelle – who is Estelle? According to Mum, nobody knows! Balderdash! LYDIA knows! She knows who laid her. And another thing... George St John would be only too aware she'd cheated on him – despite the fuss he made of his new 'daughter'. Which led to more mental acrobatics, for though Stella had forsaken the stage, Bradbury still entertained the gods.

By chance I popped into the city library that week, to kill lunch hour, and found myself browsing through the military section, when I spotted a familiar name – etched in gold, on a red spine – Alan Stewart. At least a dozen volumes, ranging from China's troubles early in the nineteenth century, past milestones like the Indian Mutiny, the siege of Lucknow, the relief of Ladysmith, Rorke's Drift – episodes I'd covered at school – through to the Great War itself, which I hadn't – then 'finis'.

Little had happened on the battlefields since, as far as I could recall, bar Spain's internal bust-up, and Mussolini's ambitious swoop on to Abyssinia.

'So Big Alan doesn't just amble around with a gun, after all... he does tote a pen!'

I turned to the days of our 'contemptible' little army in France, working through to the advent of something revolutionary on the Western Front – the ubiquitous tank. That's when I spotted a familiar face – by the side of what looked to be a metal garden-shed on tracks.

Major Grant-Wilton, wearing the ribbon of his first

Military Cross, didn't look that different from the man whose brandy I'd supped so recently. Apart from the posture. Here he was undoubtedly a Warrior. Peering closer to read the caption, I jumped a mile. Three soldiers stood at the major's side – and the middle one was MY DAD! Through the years I'd looked at his photos so many times he lived in my mind. No date was mentioned, nor the location, or names of 'other ranks', just hints on the period, around the middle of the war, to my mind before the tank was in general use, though I wasn't too sure about that. Later I found they were tried out in numbers at Flers.

No chance of borrowing the book – not from the reference section – but I thought it strange we didn't have a copy at home? Mum would have pounced on something like this especially being written at Farndon – or Bradbury, to be exact.

I found myself thinking of the lurid tales I'd heard about Martin Fawcett, the Brigade Commander, George's overseer. Where did *he* fit in? I knew where his son figured – only too well!

The book left me uneasy. I had strange premonitions. I was tempted to tackle Mum – right away – but decided against it. Why not bone the Colonel? He'd know – know it all.'

For the first time ever I felt uneasy about confiding in my mother. The past hurt her so much. She'd shrug, screw up her mouth, chunter, "No point raking over the ashes of war," and confirm to anybody in earshot, "It brings nowt but sadness – best forgotten." Though, totally out of character, she had come up with the startling news of Estelle's arrival on earth... for my benefit, no doubt.

Much as she'd taken to Stella on her surprise visits, she was adamant no future for me existed in that direction, citing the inevitable class-barriers, yet hinting at something darker; a sure way to set me puzzling. And she refused point-blank to enlarge. 'Maybe there is no mystery – bar Lydia's sallies into erotica – which are no longer a mystery, nor are they any of my business. But Mum's antipathy to Bradbury has to be rooted in some colossal wrong-doing.'

She seldom nursed grudges – nor was she that class-conscious – or easily overawed, despite her constant reminders of the chasm separating the Grants and the Allners. 'And another thing – only since Estelle 'appeared' have the riddles seemed significant – which is only natural... I suppose. Or is it just me – growing up?' Well, whatever – I couldn't escape the conviction that the past would for ever rule my future – and I didn't like that – I didn't like it one little bit.

I kept the misgivings to myself. The following Saturday, on an especially foul morning, I said I'd be gone some time, but would make it home for dinner. By the long way round I drove down to Bradbury, stopped by the traders' gate and lugged the bike up on to its awkward little stand, crossing the familiar paddock for once without newsprint, my coat collar up round my ears, cap pulled low, heading full on into a storm raging from the north. Loping quickly across the courtyard, I rapped on the kitchen door, praying the servants were in!

Contrary to forecasts the rain still sheeted down, bouncing off the concrete six or more inches, sending rivers of foam gushing past the stable-block, carrying a dirty frothy mix of twirling twigs, yellowed leaves, 'dog-bones', and the usual tit-bits of domestic rubbish. A typical late-summer 'soaker' to gladden the hearts of enthusiastic gardeners.

The dire elements meant nothing to Addy. As usual he appeared from nowhere, tail going, head cocked in lordly fashion, tongue flickering a welcome. He'd remembered again.

"Oh! Hello, Frank – you've brought a rum old morning with you. You're not doing Saturday's papers now, are you?" A surprised Mrs Thompson greeted me, her hair in its usual state of disarray, her face like cherry-blossom. She was in the early throes of preparing lunch, judging by the half-peeled spuds, un-scraped parsnips, raw onions, and the pots and pans standing empty on the crowded worktops. She was alone – unusual.

"I'd like to see the Colonel, Mrs Thompson. Will you let him know I'm here, please. I've come to the wrong door, I suppose?" I shook the rain from my cap, then whacked it across my knees to stop it dripping.

"That's alright, lad. You'd only have got *me* if you'd knocked on them all. The maids are round the other side. The Finmores are supposed to be looking round the gardens, then taking coffee on the slabs. They've probably dived into the conservatory." I took it she meant coffee on the patio. She was in one of her 'open' moods.

"The Colonel's not with them, is he?" I asked, anxiously.

"Oh, no. Miss Barlow's got that job. I don't envy her." She laughed, slightly, but like most people had a grudging admiration for Emma and Elsie. I wondered for a moment how they looked with their feet on the ground – they weren't quite themselves at the party – nor were their feet on terra firma all the time.

"I'll just go and see – hang on a sec, I believe he's in the gunroom. You'd better hang your coat by the stove – you'll find plenty of hooks." Within minutes she was shouting, "Come on through," from somewhere beyond the kitchen. My face went hot, partly from thoughts of facing the Colonel, without a clue what to say now it had come to it, and partly from the memory of earlier excursions into the mansion's roomy interior – especially when Lydia beckoned.

"This way!" Cook called. I slipped quickly past the turn to what looked like *that* staircase, wiping the rain from my face, and posing as a butter-wouldn't-melt-in-his-mouth type, anything to look above board! Whether I succeeded I wouldn't know. And it makes no difference.

"Ah... Come in. You're lucky – ten minutes later I'd have been gone."

"Good-morning, sir. Er... don't let me hold you up." We

were back in the snug.

"No. It doesn't matter. I was only driving up to Briarsdale for a quick look around. It can wait, and maybe this storm will have passed. Now, I take it this is important?"

I went completely crazy. A hotchpotch of questions I'd worked on the night before went sailing out of the window, forgotten.

"Whatever you do, whatever you say Colonel, I love Estelle. and she loves me! She can't marry Noel Fawcett. I'll put a stop to it somehow – you see."

"Is that what you came for Master Allner?" he said, after a lengthy pause. Shaken slightly, he fussed with the phone-cable, twisting it round and round his little finger, then sat up straight, his eyes troubled, but nothing like as angry as I feared. The features were unchanged, though his mouth had hardened somewhat, and his moustache was quivering.

'Will he kick me out? What a clown, messing things up like this!' But even at such a touchy moment I felt drawn to the man. Maybe it was the calm demeanour, the poise, the general upper-class stance? Whatever it was, we were certainly poles apart – in everything – especially status.

"No, I didn't, sir. I apologise. Whatever came over me?"

"Hmm," was all he said. He waited for me to pull myself together. I continued.

"You knew my dad – that's why I'm here. Were you with him when they killed him? Did you *see* him die, sir? You were in command – in Colonel Fawcett's outfit. What happened?"

"What's brought this on all at once?" He sounded friendly, but defensive. "It's a long story my boy, and I don't think I'm the right one to tell it. Have you talked to your mother? Found out what she has to say?"

"Everybody shies away when the war crops up. Even Grandad refuses to discuss it. Uncle Joseph's nearly as bad. It seems so daft. Surely I've a right to know what went on. If people behaved like grown-ups there'd be no cause to worry – but they don't, and it gets me down. You must know, sir! If *you* don't know, then nobody does! Don't tell me he went down with VD – like most of 'em – according to old Bill Langton. *He* copped a packet, so he says, but got over it alright. They doused him in gentian-violet – all round his privates and over his backside."

The Colonel nearly coughed up his tonsils, his face danger-lamp red. He also went boss-eyed.

"And another thing, while we're on the subject. Why do the locals avoid you Bradbury crowd like the plague? What makes you so unpopular? That's to do with the war as well... isn't it? If it were not for the Hunt, they wouldn't know you exist. Then they only come for a snout around, and to drink free beer... it's like another world to 'em, and they don't come near the Hall proper. Estelle opened my eyes – she's so *kind...*"

I faltered, courage flagging, the outburst floundered. I'd hit deep water... and I'd been as rude as the devil – like I was telling the gardener where to stick his celery.

"Well, that's quite a grown-up speech, young Allner. I admire your spirit but you'll have to wait a bit for some of the answers."

"Why is that, sir? Surely you can tell me the way he died?"

"German bullets finished him. *Machine-gun* bullets. *Christ...* but there's more to it than that – a hell of a lot more, and I'm not prepared to go into it... not now, for your sake as much as mine. It's a long story, and you'd never forgive me if I left half of it out. It's more complicated than you imagine. And lots of people whom you know well are involved – most of them unwillingly. There's such a thing as loyalty, you know. Not only to King and Country, all sorts of loyalty – to your family above all. Some things aren't for the public to pick over – and it's by no means best for everybody to know everything about those around them. At times it's better they don't! The truth can be wounding, my boy – I don't mean in your case, necessarily... I mean, in general. Nothing's simple.

"My own family's had more than its share of upheavals, but we get by, and none of us can change the way we are – however hard we try. Nor can we put the clock back. It's not just keeping up appearances – deeper than that. Much deeper. I do my best by them all – even with this bloody back to cripple me. It's murder at times, but I suppose I'm lucky to be here at all, when I think about it."

I looked at him with even more respect, though the 'necessarily' didn't sound promising! The coughing had dried up, his colour back to near-normal. To open up to me – him a distinguished, much decorated soldier – must have cost him a hell of an effort. We were on different planes, family wise, breeding wise, status wise, every wise. You can't *get* further apart, unless, ah unless... I stifled my febrile imagination. But it was more than imagination! We both knew that. At least, I think we did.

"Look, Francis. We'll leave it at that for the moment, if you don't mind. We'll talk another time. How about that? Will that suit you? Give me a chance to dig out all the facts, and put them in some sort of... er... order."

"Yes... Yes, of course, sir. Whenever's convenient – but soon. *Please* put a stop to the marriage."

"That won't be easy – Estelle's her own mistress, I'm afraid."

"She says it was all arranged – years ago!"

"Not in the way you think – or Estelle thinks. There's more to it than you know."

"She doesn't love him – I know that much!"

"In which case we must all be sorry. That's all."

When I weighed it up I wasn't a lot wiser, but at least I'd breached the silence, chipped at the granite a little – that had to be a plus. As for the wedding – lots still to be done, and not much time left.

Cook muttered, 'Good-day,' as I went back to the kitchen, collected my dried-out cap and coat, and stepped out to the courtyard. I noticed she was in 'slitty-eyed' mode now – had she listened at the door? The storm had about blown itself out. Maddy cocked his ears as he watched from the door of his stall, but I was too mixed up to go and talk to him. He knew he'd carted me around a few times, and he watched me out of sight – I remember turning to check. The ducks were quacking like billy-ho, but I was in no mood to appreciate them either. Reluctantly, I kicked the BSA into life, dried the saddle with my cap, then turned, and went home via Briarsdale, the track across the fields now bordered by furrowed, bumpy, straw-strewn, weed-infested stubble – the sheaves up in stooks, in theory drying out, ready for carting to the stack yard and, in due course, dealing with by the threshing-tackle. Up ahead, Cuckoo-pint Rise crouched on the hilltop like a big brooding monster silhouetted against the dull grey skies. I was in bags of time for dinner.

'Chores can wait.' Cricket had tailed off to friendlies, football not yet into serious stuff. In spite of my ambitious sortie I hadn't solved many riddles, but the headway was encouraging. I'd formed a bridgehead – and that couldn't be bad. A definite link between the Master of Bradbury and Master Allner!

'Get ready for fireworks... But the Colonel implied there might already be some affinity. If there is, it has me foxed – unless it's financial?'

Although poor, we were far from the breadline, which is more than you could say for most of Farndon's flock. They were firmly anchored at the bread-and-marge, suet-pudding line, with jam on Sundays – with luck. Surely selling the saddlery didn't produce rhino enough to keep both us and Grandad going for ever – especially having splashed out on Rose Cottage? And as articled clerk my income counted for little, though taking it all round things could have been worse

– and many like me had to *pay* for the privilege of studying Law.

But one giant drawback blighted any optimism. Mention Dad, and the world still clammed up. My slice of it, anyway...

Killed in action – a euphemism for thousands of poor buggers who had died in mysterious circumstances, some guilty of no more than blotting their bloody copy-books!

But it wasn't so strange, when you thought about it. Hundreds vanished without trace, and without a sniff of evidence – some in action, some out of it. The stretcher-wallahs seldom recovered *all* the dog-tags. It made things easier that way... Then there were the ones shot for cowardice – or desertion – albeit the poor sods were suffering shellshock! Not a pretty war at all. They never are – but we don't get to hear all that nor do we learn of the wagonloads down with VD. That sort of mishap doesn't set the presses rolling either.

'I wonder why the Colonel turned scarlet, nearly choking, when I touched on the revolting subject?'

Nothing of substance ever came my way – that was the trouble. Lack of facts could only suggest a cover-up of sorts. But why a cover-up? Dad had his army pals. Colleagues, company personnel – they wouldn't all be wiped out. Plenty must have come back – eager to tell the tale, or at least contribute some worthwhile tit-bits on what the action was all about. Locations, dates, weather conditions – that sort of thing. They'd talk about *that!*

'Old so-and-so died at Arras you know' – or wherever – was the commonest of comments in post-war years. Only the details varied. Fragments of fallout from the unholy conflict the peoples of Europe prayed would never happen again.

Around this time I realised just how badly I missed Estelle – if only to think about. The emptiness of my agenda griped, and so many facets of the Estate's goings-on didn't tie up. I felt it time to start life afresh.

Sissons struggled to promote the shooting, working his balls off, keen to make it as popular as the fox-hunting, like it used to be. God knows, the man showed enough birds – but the odds against him were daunting. George was adamant hunting would always take priority, which left the two 'sports' in permanent conflict. It's no easy matter to present high-flying pheasants over ambitious, experienced guns, in regulated waves, two days after seventeen and a half couple of foxhounds, and a hundred horses, have thundered up and down the rides for hours on end, ravaging the birds' hideaways – on top of being invaded by hordes of slavering foot-followers.

Charles confided that George and Tom Sissons had never seen eye to eye on the controversial issue – though Sissons, as far as the shooting went, was obviously right! One day they nearly got to blows, until George told the keeper in no uncertain manner, "Mind your own f...... business, Tom – do as I say, or there'll *be* no bloody shootin'!"

Yet George was an expert shot – with or without his bad back. And since he could no longer ride in comfort (not horses, anyway), it seemed a strange stance for him to adopt. I could imagine the righteous indignation of Sissons and his cohorts when hounds were heading for territory where the men had worked like slaves to nourish the birds in breeding season, sussing out their nests, gathering the brown speckled eggs and slipping them gently beneath the warm feathered bellies of Rhode Island Reds in the rearing-pens back near the farm. A similar situation to that of autumn, when part-fledged, multi-coloured screamers were aching to test their wings against the biting winds and the barrage of gunfire their elder brethren had told them to watch out for!

Small wonder the grim-faced Sissons had little cause for celebration – yet was apparently the most faithful servant of them all.

Just like Stella – loyal to a fault – or so it looked to

outsiders!

But maybe George had a point? Shooting was more of a private affair. Only the guns and the beaters knew what really went on – only they knew the size of the 'bag' at the end of the day, whereas fox-hunting welcomed guests, going so far as to wine and dine them, and begging them to come back for more.

In those days hunting didn't have 'antis' to contend with. What the nobs did in their spare time was very much their own affair. And I never met a homo sapien keen to sample the flavour of the vulpine population, whereas everything the keepers nourished became targets for hungry, ill-fed peasants, for whom cheese and fat bacon formed the only backup to spuds and dry bread. Poachers weren't just the subjects of sentimental ditties, or characters in Christmas tales – they were essentially earthy individuals. They were *real*. And *hostile*. And *ornery!* And keepering could be a dangerous occupation – in the middle of the night, in a wide landscape of darkened woods, deep ditches, uncut hedgerows and impenetrable shades. It wasn't unknown for the snares set with such skill by Sissons and his sidekicks at dusk, to be emptied by dawn, the nooses re-set into 'strangle' position by crafty, aggressive raiders with too many mouths to feed... and rabbits weren't the only target. Pheasants at roost were easy prey for a stout heart, a good eye, one smooth stone, and a 'London-made' catapult.

Chapter Ten

Casualty

First thing Monday a worried looking Sherwood came pattering up to my desk, shuffled uncomfortably, his dapper little figure looking sharper than ever in a blue pinstripe suit polished by years of loyal service to Sangsters.

"Er... Frank – the boss wants you." He was half-scared to tell me.

"Eh? Who, Gosling?"

"No. The *big* man – he's here! I saw him come. Alice says he wants you – right away!"

"Oh... I'd better get along there – fast." I hoped I looked better than I felt. Claud could be terrifying – but human when he liked. 'Which mode's he in?' I straightened my jacket, pulled at my mop, then grimacing, tacked along the corridor to where His Nibs would be waiting. Gently I opened Alice Roberts' door. Thirtyish and single, she was the archetypal secretary of the Thirties. Plain, diligent, conscientious, and competent, she bore the fixed notion the sun shone permanently from her barn-door bum. I think she fancied me – she always preened before speaking. Now she nodded with indulgence, as if bestowing great benefits upon me, peering over her half-moons, intoning in a half-throttled diction, "Go on in, Francis, he's waiting." She smiled, cautiously, hiding her near-horizontal teeth, her features expanding beneath the quivering earphones – the epitome of patronage. The one person at Sangsters who refused to call me Frank. I crossed to the door of the inner sanctum, tapped, and waited, ignoring her suggestion I go bowling in.

"Alright! Come in Allner. Don't stand on ceremony." They must have heard him in Bombay.

Smoke filled an office big and ostentatious as he puffed hungrily on a mansize cigar. His waistcoat sat smothered in

140

ash. Irritably he knocked the stuff off as another dollop descended to the same spot. His belly was the trouble – the ash couldn't miss. He was in traditional costume for his calling, and for the period – black jacket, waistcoat, and trousers with bold white stripes. He looked like a great big hippo, with horn-rimmed glasses, lots of oiled grey hair, clean shaven, but sporting a permanent shadow – they're called designer-beards now... Sixty-two and a half he was – according to Stanley. The wide-open eyes and the full lips suggested a blandness that had fooled a thousand clients, as well as a million opponents!

Instantly I twigged him to be in reasonable humour. He waved me to the obvious seat, a sit-up-and-beg opposite his swivel armchair, across a mahogany desk typical of company chairmen, the 'in' tray bare, the 'out' tray full. The one wall visible sported oak panelling, the rest shelved, and filled to the ceiling with leather-bound volumes of varied hues. I wondered if he ever looked at them, or knew they were there?

"Thank you, sir." I settled gingerly, wondering what the devil it was all about?

"George Grant's been talking to me, Allner. Seems you're busy researching the war?"

"Well... not exactly, sir. But I'm twenty now – it's time I got a picture of my Dad. I know he wasn't decorated, or anything like that, but he *was* a staff-sergeant, in the Colonel's Company much of the time. I'd like to know more about his army days. Mother knows little – she keeps it to herself."

"I see," he replied evenly.

"Did you *know* my Dad then, Mister Sangster?"

"Yes. I met him several times, on business you understand? They used us when the saddlers' concern went on the market – before he joined up."

"Is that all?" I felt slightly let down, or the ungracious comment would never have slipped out.

"No. That's by the way." He leaned back, starting to talk straight, after telling Alice on the 'internal', "No interruptions." I felt edgy – certain she'd hear every word – all confidential. Then, I could hardly re-arrange the offices! Nor could I tell Claud not to shout.

I listened, spellbound. At last a voice of authority.

"Trouble began at Bradbury towards the middle of the war, when casualties at the Front hit the ceiling – exceeding the fears of even the biggest of pessimists. Something radical was called for – and *fast*. Hospitals were crammed to bursting, staff woefully inadequate, and still the ships kept coming. Leave from France became a dream, every inch of shipping turned over to the wounded and the shell-shocked. And all had to be housed *somewhere* – preferably out in the country. First they explored the South, then the Home Counties, creeping inexorably up to the Midlands, East Anglia, the North, and finally Scotland. Every manor house, mansion and building of size was targeted for emergencies, routine treatment, but most of all for convalescence.

"The whole kingdom became a land of Red Cross districts, peopled by females from all walks, and of every age. And Bradbury Hall, inevitably, became a prime target. Lydia went berserk! With George abroad in the thick of things, Rupert and Justin on her hands, to lose her home was too much to even contemplate. Patriotic as the rest, she drew a line at giving up stone and mortar, and making a tail-between-her-legs exit to she knew not where. Not even a suggestion the family retain one wing of the Hall found favour, and moves to requisition the place soon reached an advanced stage, so much so that Lydia Grant *did* appear to lose her marbles. Their secrets were in jeopardy.

"In desperation she called on George to come home and sort things out. But the Major, as he then was, couldn't down tools and oblige, any more than could thousands of other poor sods bogged down at the Front, where the touch-and-go struggle looked destined to go on for ever, or until the canon fodder ran out. And George had good reason to side with his missus. In this he supported her – to the hilt. It was plain Lydia alone wouldn't pull any rabbits from the hat – the Home Office isn't that stupid.

"A substantial 'defence' was imperative if the mansion were to remain private. In those days there were fewer hangers-on at the Hall, but the agent had too much on his plate to fight the estate's corner properly, struggling to respond to endless calls of 'dig for victory'. George wasn't blind, and far from daft. He knew that to stand any chance of hanging on in there he must come up with alternatives – and luckily he still had Groby Manor, the one mansion on the estate with comparative amenities.

"'Why couldn't they pick on that?' It had stood empty for ages, but needed little to knock it into shape. The reason was obvious. It lay off the beaten track, whereas Bradbury's road and rail links to London and the Channel Ports rendered it ideal. But the Major could only lend his mind to these matters at intervals – when fighting permitted!

"Nonetheless he found time for a brainwave – a deputy could do the business. Leave being out of the question, apart from breaks to what were euphemistically referred to as 'rest areas' back behind the lines, it would have to be a casualty – and where would he find a fit 'casualty'?

"In addition to combat duties (laughingly called 'routine') George was deep into secret training, attempting to master the intricacies of the metal-clad monster that would end the war in a hurry, bringing victory in its wake – the ubiquitous Tank.

"A solution stared him in the face. Send Allner – a fellow Farndonite. Somebody he knew and could trust. In peacetime he looked after the tack for Bradbury's horses; supplied and repaired the wide range of gear used by both the Shires and the hunters. A man of stature, moral as well as physical. Smart, willing, efficient – already a staff-sergeant, despite the demise of the cavalry he'd first joined, seconded to the Infantry until the revolutionary tank found its way to the Front.

"First George must consult his commander – Colonel Fawcett. Fawcett knew everything. If he didn't he soon found out. Martin agreed right away. No point seeking a half-fit casualty – turn Allner into one! A word in the MO's ear, hints of something not right on the inside, and they hastily booked the staff-sergeant on the long journey home, in space reserved for casualties, but not before a detailed briefing by the Master of Bradbury on the task facing him. Top priority – 'engage Sangster and Sangster the minute you land, then convince Lydia, Lady of the Manor, everything's under control'.

"They came up with two portfolios, courtesy of the Adjutant – one for Lydia, the other for Claud Sangster – ME! Robert Allner must guard them with his life – if necessary. He also received a formal 'authority to act' along with a forged sick-pass – 'severe enteritis, burns and blisters over all the body'.

"They moved him to the clearing station, where he suffered the indignity of superfluous injections and vaccinations, and eventually loaded him on to a Red Cross train to base hospital, along with hundreds of other 'victims', then over the Channel, on to Victoria, and finally to Bedford General. An endorsement of tremendous significance was etched in code on his sick-pass. Twenty-four hours after reaching hospital they sent him home by ambulance, with orders to rest up and report for duty in four weeks time. When Agnes saw him arrive, unannounced, she knew he was in trouble. He wasn't! That would come later."

Mister Sangster paused, lit another cigar. I sat entranced by the story. It sounded more like a John Buchan, than a resumé of Father's exploits. It came fresh as paint, and the big man seemed as enthralled as me. His not unpleasant voice, now suitably modulated, delivered this incredible story with neither notes, nor reminders. Far from terrifying, he was almost benign. Alice did her stuff – no interruptions. Claud continued...

"The hardest part of all now confronted Mister Allner. First, he must concoct a cover story plausible enough to satisfy Missus Allner, and sufficiently authentic to deflect the attention of Nosey Parkers in Farndon, as well as satisfy genuine sympathisers, of which there'd be plenty; then he could get down to business. Fortunately, he'd already met Missus Grant-Wilton through his saddlery and harness work. Lydia, like the rest, was an accomplished horsewoman, taking a keen interest in the stables. It was mostly Lydia's enthusiasm that turned Estelle into such a first-rate rider, as much as George's tuition. She could be a friendly person away from the limelight, or, paradoxically, when talking business. Her working-class background in no way inhibited her from fraternising with the varied layers of society that graced the horse world – certainly not with the less distinguished."

All of a sudden Mister Sangster halted his oration, descending to a personal level.

"You know, Allner, the next part's going to be difficult..."

"Why is that, sir?"

I sensed something special about to break. Something I *had* to know, but more than likely preferred not to hear. A new awareness had me wriggling – but still fascinated.

"To this day, only your mother knows how much of the truth Robert told her. Nobody else! There'd be his constant visits to the Hall to explain away, plus, of course, the time he spent here with us. It would be simple to just dismiss it as 'estate business', but she's far too intelligent to be fooled by half a yarn. She'd know he was fighting fit, so she'd know too he was home under false pretences. Scrounging, if you like. On top of which she'd know damn well the Colonel hadn't the authority to shuffle men over to Blighty as and when he pleased. Every man was needed out there to help shred the Kaiser's army!"

"Oh, crikey! I see what you mean, sir."

'No wonder Mum has so little time for Bradbury and its residents!' I trembled at the thought. Sangster carried on.

"It was a hell of a task your father took on, you know – posing all the time as a casualty. At least he was protected by his sick-pass from any suggestion of desertion. But if he uttered so much as a single word out of turn, they'd clap George in irons so fast his feet wouldn't touch the ground.

"This is all confidential, Allner – you understand that? The Colonel thinks you have a right to know. And I agree. He has a high opinion of you, my boy. Of course, you're twenty now." I'd told Claud that – at first.

"Yes, that's right sir." Already I had Dad down in my book as some sort of Scarlet Pimpernel. And Mum hadn't breathed a word about knowing Sangsters when she put me forward as a recruit to their legal battalions. The governor went on...

"The battle for Bradbury began – and ended – abruptly. It lost its attraction as a mini-hospital, whereas Groby Manor fitted the bill to a T. The powers that be settled amicably for the change, Lydia breathed again, and things returned to normal – *for a time.*

"Then once more it was stalemate at the Front, and George was awarded leave. He arrived in Farndon with a bar to his Military Cross, promoted Lieutenant Colonel, to find Bradbury had got its reprieve, and Lydia had got morning sickness... she was pregnant!"

For the first time Sangster faltered... he knocked more ash from his waistcoat.

I stared at him, open-mouthed. Speechless! He didn't leave much to the imagination. Then, he was only telling the tale. Just the narrator. But he'd turned my world upside down. The message could hardly have been clearer. Impossible to digest, the implications diabolical.

At the very place I'd lost my innocence, Dad had sampled the fare first! Did Mum know? *Did* she? She'd surely suspect – or was it typical – wife the last to find out – if she finds out at all.

Or was it all imagination? Did guilt generate the horrible conclusion – just because Lydia had seduced *me*... Of course it did.

Knowing Lydia, not just by reputation, any one of a hundred, a *thousand* men, could have put her up the duff. And how much of this nonsense had Estelle been forced to suffer? What if there was a *sequel* – involving Dad and the Colonel? Would George have spotted the link... had there been one? How would it have affected their relationship – as soldiers – later on? After all, Dad was killed in action... Grant-Wilton crippled for life. A hell of a lot still to be clarified.

I forgot Claud Sangster was *there*. For ages he sat back, allowing it all to sink in. He knew how I must feel. His razor-sharp mind, honed from years of sorting the unsortable, fixing the impossible, turning black white, would latch on with ease.

"Is that all, sir?" I just about got the words out. I was deflated, downcast, ashamed of my stupid assumptions. BUT... Estelle's dubious pedigree wasn't fancy!

"Yes, I'm afraid so. What happened later isn't within my remit. I just don't know. Now don't go jumping to conclusions – you could be miles wide of the mark. And for goodness sake don't go upsetting Mrs Allner. Think about it. Oh... you may take the day off – I'll get Miss Roberts to let Forest know."

"Thank you, sir. Thank you for... everything."

I reached the bike before the penny dropped – the biggest penny of all!

'Christ... Stella's my sister! Well... *half*-sister.'

When I'd driven to work first thing I never guessed my world was soon to be in turmoil. The news was unbelievable. A monstrous kick in the guts. And not a soul to turn to. Mum, or Grandad? Out the question! And Stella? Even were Stella here I could hardly involve her.

'Mustn't be home early – Mum'll have kittens – she's jumpy enough as it is.' Slowly I climbed on the bike, kicked the starter, and just drove. Aimlessly I cruised the countryside without a worthwhile thought in my head. My sandwiches I'd left in the desk – not that I felt like troughing. After miles of going nowhere I pulled in at a pub near Melton, ordered bitter, and sat by the tiny lattice windows staring unseeing at the Mecca of fox-hunting. A handful of round-hatted locals puffed on their pipes, without a care in the world – so I imagined. At the dark-stained table an animated foursome were trying to outsmart each other at dominoes, giving the bods alongside plenty to amuse them – from the sound of it.

Where did everything go belly-up? What was the big blunder? All I did was fall in love five years earlier, with a girl I prayed would be mine, but never could be – now!

As I supped the ale, trying to come to terms with the savage revelation, my mind inevitably settled on Martin Fawcett.

What was his role in the audacious bid to hang on to Bradbury Hall? Christ, he's the guy who started the trouble. He figures big in everything – Mister Sangster said so. Fawcett masterminded Dad's sick-pass. If Dad hadn't crossed to England to do Grant-Wilton's dirty work he'd be alive today – not buried in some bloody wasteland across the water, reduced to a sodding statistic. A man. An honest man. And what about ME? What about Francis Allner? Well... I wouldn't be around – would I?'

I shook myself out of the nightmare, decided I'd give Sir Martin a bit of third-degree. But the idea faded. It was only the beer... on overtime. Nonetheless, the name 'Fawcett' stuck in my gullet. Not only Sir Bloody Martin, but ghastly Blondie as well. Then there's pretty Sara...

I drank up, called for another (no bag to blow in, in the far-off Thirties). When I eventually said good-day to the landlord, I was more confused than ever – and the bike wouldn't start. It was empty, which somehow seemed significant... Luckily a one-pump, lean-to garage stood a hundred yards up the road. Three gallons filled her, then mixed-up and muzzy I kicked her into life and set off home, dawdling to fill in time. I'd hang about in a gateway if necessary. Never had I felt so horribly alone, so marginalised, in a world forever changing.

Mum's staid existence hadn't even crossed my mind. Getting home (sober), diplomacy won the day – as usual. I remained silent. The sheer absurdity of the fears I was nursing at last filtered through. They were irrational, preposterous, pure poppycock.

Hunting proper got back to full swing, cubbing over and forgotten. Bradbury's first full meet was scheduled for Saturday. The thought turned my stomach, yet I was drawn inexorably to where life began in earnest, and ended in such a bloody mess. Bradbury *was* life! I went solely in the hopes of seeing Stella. The blond bomber might dance, or ride attendance, even both, but I was determined to have a look at what went on.

My contempt for Noel was total – and I didn't know the man. I didn't want to know him. That Sunday had told me enough – or had it? Ninety per cent jealousy would be nearer the mark.

A cloudy, albeit fine, morning set the tone for the day. The sparkle was gone. Where once I'd thrilled to the colourful cavalcade, longing to be a part of it, so a new awareness came about. A new cynicism, as I studied the thin-lipped, purple-visaged emptiness of men with minds as dim as a recalcitrant sun that refused to even take a peep, let alone shine.

The women on board were all of a breed too, their rear-ends designed only for a saddle, hips not moulded for child-bearing, feet purpose-built for stirrups. This jaundiced view

149

persisted until the Field thrust deep into Briarsdale, hounds busy, but mute. The familiar smell of mouldering earth, nourishing peat, thriving woodland, failed to lift my spirits, when all of a sudden horn-blasts rent the air, clear and strident, hounds started yelping ('speaking' if you're fussy), men bellowed, women shrieked, hoofs thundered, divots flew, and off they hurtled westwards, over the meadows to Granleigh, the meadows I'd sat and enjoyed when Estelle first showed me Carolean. Slowly my senses returned. I ran for the bike, kicked it into life, and went rattling round the backroads, keen once more to savour the joys of the chase, desperate to be in at the kill. A 'shrink', however clever, would have been pushed to weigh me up that morning.

Estelle didn't show. Nor did her fiancé, thank goodness. But Sir Martin paraded himself – so did Sara, pretty as a picture, dangerous as a viper, galloping over mound and furrow by her father's side, forever crowding the hounds in their nose-down pursuit of 'Charlie'. I doubt 'Cocky' Gannett would have guts enough to swear at them like he did at the rest of us?

The Finmores were showing their age, but still mustard-keen, scrubbing along with unflagging zeal, in sure and certain faith that they knew where the fox would make for. At the meet I'd deliberately steered clear of the Colonel (which wasn't difficult) as he stalked around in customary style, amusing his bunch of sycophants, the grisly hangers-on cashing in on his unfailing generosity, and on his anxiety to play host in established style. Rupert and Justin, still unhitched, had made a special effort to be there, and Lydia wouldn't have missed it for worlds. She was aboard Maddy. I choked for a minute when I spotted her. From the back she didn't look that much different from Stella! For that matter, nor did she from the front, except that...

This time 'Charlie' went to earth. Earth-fillers had sold the hunt short. Hurriedly they pressed the terrier-man into service, his trade-bike loaded with spades, a fork, wire, string, and a blood-stained sack, but I hadn't the stomach to watch them dig out the poor little bugger. I turned, tramped back across the early plough to the road, climbed on the BSA and drove slowly in Briarsdale direction. I'd asked Mum to forget dinner, but to save me something for tea. I was in no hurry. Pulling up short of the thicket, I parked the bike, and squatted my arse on the familiar stile leading to Tate's Meadow. It brought back memories – most of them happy. Then suddenly I twigged voices, their owners obviously on horseback. I could hear every word – clear as a bell. The horses were walking – slowly.

"I'm surprised Estelle didn't come. I suppose she's up to her neck preparing for the big day, though I haven't heard when it is – have you?" Henry sounded puzzled. Ada answered, "No," then added, "*I* don't believe it'll come off." Evidently they'd pulled on to the verge by the thicket gate, to work out where the hounds had gone. Latecomers were by no means rare, if frowned upon. They wouldn't have a clue I was listening. Not a snooper by nature, I was never averse to titbits coming my way by accident. The road curved through ninety degrees at the northern end of the thicket, so, like them from me, I was hidden. It was seldom the ladylike Ada held forth – unless she and Henry were...

"At times I feel sorry for the girl. She's nothing like the monster they make out – she goes out of her way to be kind to the servants. It was her, remember, who got Daisy off the hook when that money went missing. Estelle made up the shortage. The fuss the Old Man made! And she's for ever looking after the shepherd's kids. Takes them for walks. Remembers their birthdays. Buys them Christmas presents. Keeps them well stocked with fruit – from the orchards. You can often see her at the cottage – makes herself at home. That's all in the past, though. What do you think stops her from coming home now, Henry?"

"Search me," replied Railton, in his deep voice and 'frightfully' accent. Very public school.

He continued, "Maybe it's her love-life? They're both in Cambridge."

I cocked up my ears, cursed inwardly – still as jealous as ever – still resentful. Hooked like I always would be. It wasn't news they were sprouting – just baleful, if unwitting reminders. I realised too how little I knew of the real goings-on at the Hall. All *I* got to hear was surface gloss, in spite of Charles's contributions. And I remembered Stella talking of Mummy coming out of her shell when Aunt Pen and Freda came to stay. It wasn't easy to picture Lydia *in* a shell – let alone coming out. And, somehow, it was difficult to think of the Colonel doing his nut over a handful of missing shekels.

"Didn't you ever fancy her, Henry? You must have – you're quite the ladies' man, yet you manage to keep out of trouble. Perhaps you've got your eye on Sara? Or *Lydia*? Don't tell me you're playing celibate you horny old devil."

"Now, now, Miss Barlow. Don't get excited, we're not in bed now, you know. And some things are sacred – even in pillow-talk."

Ada gurgled with amusement. Anything seemed to go with this pair! Then she coyly said, "Come up and see me some time."

Henry whooped with laughter, the morsel of Mae West apparently new to him.

'Gosh! Does Ada entertain the punters, as well as Lydia? I wonder?'

"Be serious, Henry. What's the latest on George, by the way?"

"Latest what?"

"About his... you know... damage."

"Oh... *that!* Not good I'm afraid. And not much chance of improvement."

"No!" Ada must have sat up quickly.

"Yes. He's finished. He's had problems for some time – now the old devil's impotent. They told him he would be – just a matter of time. And the time's up."

"Oh shit! Poor old sod!"

"You mean you didn't know? Come, come, Ada. *You'd* know – if anybody!"

"Oh, go to hell, you saucy sod."

"Well... you're the hidden force running Bradbury, aren't you Ada?"

"The army specialists said it would lead to that – when they finally let him go. George didn't believe them. He had a good splash around to find out. There was little wrong in that area through the Twenties. Ask Sophie Johnson... amongst others."

My head spun. My neck tingled. My hair stood on end. My buttocks clenched – I think. In an innocent five minutes I'd learned more about the Grants than I'd gleaned in the last five years. But the best – the worst – was to come.

"Things have never been the same since Lydia ravished the paper-boy. He must have something special... I wonder if Estelle found out? That silly hound Sissons didn't help matters – spying on them when she took the lad to the Lodge. Looks like Lovely Lydia was jealous of her own daughter – and that takes little working out."

"Stop it, Henry. That's enough. Come on... let's get a move on. We'll head for Little Downton. They're bound to draw Temple Gorse before doing the embankment..."

I dropped from the stile, diving headlong into the undergrowth, desperate they shouldn't spot me as they rounded the bend on their way up to Hookers Hill. They'd see the motor-bike, that's all. Any thoughts of re-joining the chase evaporated, leaving me to absorb the dynamite in solitude. Like every household, only more so, the Hall *was* then just another gossip-shop – scandal concocted to order. Oddly, it was the prod-nosed Sissons who angered me most – at first.

'He would have to poke and pry when Estelle first took me to Chucklecopse and showed me the Lodge. He'd suspect the worst. Probably prime his sidekicks to keep their eyes skinned.'

The trouble was, I was naive. I lived only for Estelle. Closed my eyes and ears to others. I never imagined my modest exploits could be of interest to anybody else. The truth dawned slowly – the richer the folk, the richer the scandal. The wealthy have all the time in the world. It's always at 'the manor' rumours are made facts, in every village, every hamlet. That's where they garnish and varnish the tit-bits!

But what I'd been listening to was more than mere chit-chat. More than rotten gossip. This was nitty-gritty – with bells on. I thought of Estelle's pedigree. Sangsters clearly believed Dad had sired her. Since the morning Claud filled me in I'd tried stifling the ugly conclusion. Argued vehemently with myself there was no way me and Stella could be siblings. But Mum evidently thought so – why else the warnings to steer clear of the Grants – and she should know. No wonder she's wary of Estelle.

Yet, knowing Lydia, I was hesitant to condemn my father. Men would be clay in her hands (as they say), and in her bed. He wouldn't stand an earthly... back from France, back from the trenches, difficult to weigh up, honest as they come, patriotic to a fault, yet fighting for the Hall's independence? Leading an arrogant, ill-judged attempt to deny the nation space it needed so desperately for its cripples. Men lacking legs, without arms, minus eyes, their minds gone. Mission contemptible.

Claud's warning drifted back – 'Don't go upsetting Mrs Allner'. Oh my God! What a bloody admonition... like telling a snail to get cracking. And Dad paid his forfeit. Made the ultimate sacrifice. Laid down his life – for ENGLAND – as they trot out at Armistice time. The ramblings wouldn't stop bugging me. Hard as I tried to laugh it off, Henry's babble had shaken me to the marrow. So had the crazy tittle-tattle of high-flying Ada Barlow.

I forgot the hounds, though I could taste blood – my forehead was torn and bleeding, my *good* ear in ribbons – the undergrowth was denser than I thought.

'And where does the money come from to fund the Bradbury lifestyle? Take the two I've just been listening to. What's the big secret? *Why* couldn't the place have been a hospital?'

On top of the conundrums I finally realised hopes of marrying Estelle were nowt but moonshine. The riddles needed a new approach. 'Somebody knows the score – apart from the louche, yet strangely loyal, Lydia. There's Fawcett! What about him? Is the loaded Sir Martin supplying the lolly? Does *he* work the puppets? You couldn't put a figure on his racing investments. He'd know the way Dad died. And another thing... why would a senior politician spend so much time in another constituency? It sticks out a mile – he *is* the guy with the dosh. He *is* the man playing it big. Family friend, he covets the Hall. Can't keep away. Practically lives there.

'Sir Martin looms in a new light. Things don't *begin* to add up. I don't know the man. How would I? Is he approachable? Estelle could tell me. I can't ask the Colonel.' Hindsight confirms I scored little for intuition.

Fawcett figured in everything. If he didn't, then Noel did, his son and heir. They were close to taking over the reins at Bradbury, with Martin riding shotgun – though not overly bossy – at first. Blondie would soon be calling Lydia 'Mummy'. Which left only bubbly Sara to tie up the loose ends... Ah, she could get her claws into Rupert... or Justin.

'Whoa, boy! Whoa!' I slapped on the anchors – chilled out a while – cooled my fevered brow – dismissed the ramblings as rubbish. But I had to wonder why the Bradbury crowd couldn't sense the threat? I released the brakes... 'Only the Colonel, only George, stands in the way of a takeover. And he grows frailer by the minute – poor sod. What will the robin do then, poor thing?' My brain spewed out the ancient ditty – Lydia's bosom turned crimson.

'That explains the tenacity. Her loyalty – to a cripple. An impotent cripple. Lydia a well-known... it fits. That *has* to be it! What started out a jumble no more than a kid's jigsaw.'

And Frank worked it all out. Who said I was barmy? Imagination or not, the future looked ominous. The Grant-Wiltons ousted – or 'absorbed' – the Fawcetts triumphant. I didn't like the taste – I didn't like it one little bit! And every bit stemmed from seeking the truth of Dad's last days.

The Fawcetts hailed from Market Harborough – at least the family pile stood there – that's all I knew of their background. I'd never seen the place, and I hadn't a clue where their wealth originated. Like the Grant-Wiltons of Lancashire, they had to be big in something – apart from the turf. I might have guessed, being Leicesterites, it would be to do with more horseflesh. Come to think of it, Martin looked slightly equine. Once on track things began to falls into place.

He was the proud owner of two Studs. One where he stood his four-legged aristocrats of the Flat, the other designed to meet the more humble ambitions of National Hunt buffs. Amongst his Flat stallions the Classics hero, Monarchs Choice, took pride of place, well over twenty years old, yet still going strong. Martin had married into the Griggs-Downleys – and everybody in the horse-world knew them. So did everyone else within a hundred miles. The name rang a bell. The Hon Aubrey figured in those notorious pictures in *The Times*, presenting Estelle to the world of racing – and to the world at large. There were few in the Midlands who hadn't tasted Griggs-Downley ales – the biggest brewers outside Burton, the name a byword for bitter.

'No wonder Martin's knee-deep in dosh. Not surprising he's four-square behind the Tories. *He's* from the county set too. "Fawcett flour – famed for fineness." Harry, at *The*

Gazette, proved a mighty encyclopaedia of knowledge in the relentless search for facts. Little Harry! *He* liked the gee-gees too. Knew the names that mattered, human *and* equine, and their pedigree. He reckoned Martin was called 'Foreskin Fawcett' at school. He couldn't tell me why... Harry was no Uppingham man. A story did the rounds saying Martin took the Sporting Chronicle to bed every night, and wiped his arse on it every morning. Harry expanded: "By the way, Frank – you heard about Martin's sister, I suppose?"

"Sister? *What* sister, Harry?"

"Isabel... his twin. She was engaged to Grant-Wilton when he misjudged his timing and put Lydia in the puddin' club! George and Martin schooled together – at Uppingham. Not in the same form, naturally. Anyway, George spent all his holidays at Harborough."

"What happened to her then, for Pete's sake?"

"She vanished." Harry's voice dropped to a whisper.

"*Vanished?* Where from?"

"Hong Kong apparently – for a start. She was into missionary work. At the last sighting she was heading for mainland China. Never heard of again!"

"*Crikey...*" 'Keep the tit-bits coming Harry, I'll need more than *one* leg to stand on when I tackle Fawcett.'

Often I'd wish I'd gone for journalism rather than law. A passport to people who matter. 'Nonetheless, men of rank are usually approachable – that's more than you can say for subalterns. Let's hope Sir Martin is one such!'

By an odd stroke of luck, Martin came to *me*. Not personally – to Sangsters. And I was lucky enough to greet him, and talk a while, before Gosling butted in. The clipped diction, the educated vowels, were true army, yet he bore the unmistakeable look of an Ascot steward. A natural for the Jockey Club. Loden suit, jacket brushing his knees, trousers half-mast with sixteen-inch bottoms, and marks on his lapels where he pinned his badges. His tie doubled for a scarf. I'd seen pictures of him in *The Field.*

But as he passed 'reception' a chill wind swept through the elaborate foyer. The temperature dropped. I shivered. I don't know why. It seemed he'd brought the Arctic Circle with him.

"Why, it's young Allner, isn't it?"

('Of *course* it bloody is!')

"Yes. That's right, sir. Mister Gosling sends his apologies – he won't be a moment. The Lord Lieutenant has just called."

"Ah! Very well. I'll wait. What *is* it Allner?" With his piercing eyes, bushy brows, leathery hide, and outsize ears, he was more elephant than horse – and he did have a prominent hooter. Snow-white hair, long, and curling down his neck, he no longer *looked* army. Overall though he had charisma – I can't say why – you never can. The eyes were shrouded. He was round about sixty.

"I understand you knew my father, sir?"

"Fine man! Fine man! Haa! I *knew* him alright!"

"Who killed him?"

"Eh? *Killed* him?" Fawcett jumped a mile. "The Bosche! The bloody Bosche killed him, of course. Hosed him down with machine-guns. Should have been decorated. I pushed it. Pushed it hard. Some swine down the line scuppered it. Never knew who – couldn't find out. Never knew *why.* Fine man! Plenty more bought it that day. Hmm! Hmm! Bad time! Bad time! Cavalry, you know... Tanks later on. Infantry in between. Remarkable. They called us all-rounders."

"How was my Dad killed, sir?"

"Cutting wire. In *daylight.* Cutting wire... with the sun up! Foolhardy... should have gone earlier. Much earlier. Madness! Crazy! Stupid! Saved many lives, mind you. Preserved the battalion. Had to be done – must clear your own wire... if you can't the enemy's. For the push, you know. Right tactics – wrong timing."

"What went wrong, sir?" I could tell he was back in Belgium.

"Orders! Bloody orders! You cut wire at night – or early dawn. Never at sun-up! Pooh!"

"Were you *there* then, sir? Did you see what happened?"

"Goodness, no, boy! Goodness, no! There – but not in the bloody line."

"Was the Colonel? Was Mister Grant-Wilton there?"

"He was stood down – sleeping. Been on all night. Bowers took over, but didn't go. Bloody idiot! George went mad – when they told him. Too late! Too bloody late!"

"How big was the wire-party sir? Was my Dad in charge?"

"Randall took four with him – Allner took three. Two got back – out of nine! Other seven – whoomph! Curtains! Madness!"

We ignored old Gosling. He stood in the doorway, listening, uncomprehending. I reckon he was peeved. It wasn't my job to chat to distinguished visitors.

"I must talk to you when I have more time, Allner. Hmm!"

"Thank you, sir." I slipped away before Gosling lost his rag and butted in. I didn't know what to think. Fawcett might sound like a twit, but for all that I got the impression he could tell butter from marge. And what more could he tell me? Nothing. If Dad 'bought it' cutting wire in no-mans' land, then that was that! Maybe Bowers *was* at fault? Maybe Grant-Wilton would have done different – so what? It's over now. Been over a long time. But the doubts lingered on. They wouldn't go away. Stuck in the deeper recesses was a distinct suspicion that somewhere along the line there'd been dirty work. Something fishy, after the Colonel found Lydia pregnant. And since discovering for myself what a playful creature she could be, it seemed certain Dad fell for her charms – that's why she liked the look of me! And George would hardly see the joke. He'd want revenge. The humiliation of being cuckolded by a ranker was enough to drive any officer up the wall. And it was near as dammit cuckolding. It wasn't just fancy... Dad *was* Estelle's *père*. He had to be.

Mum's hints, Grandad's anguish, Lydia's passion – rekindled via me. The ostracism by the villagers of Bradbury's cosmopolitan crowd. The wild carryings-on substituting for merriment. The insatiable craving for 'fun' generated by a lady whose life lay in ruins, who suffered agonies from the snubs of the locals but was determined it shouldn't show. Who said Lydia was a nympho? People only talk – they don't *know*. Her love-nest? Possibly a refuge... Maybe she fell in love? Perhaps Dad did? War plays funny tricks – weirder tricks than that! Naturally it hurt Mum – terribly. Maybe it hurt Dad too? For a time I was swamped with crazy, contradictory images of gothic proportions.

A wronged Major rising up in wrath to strike down his treacherous servant – then making sure his erring lady paid for her sins – to her dying day. Greek Tragedy – almost.

But speculation must end. Only action solves problems. In no uncertain fashion I'd told the Colonel I'd put a stop to Stella's wedding. It seemed but days ago I'd made that empty vow. It showed now for what it was – an idle boast. She'd marry whom she liked – *and not a bloody thing I could do about it.*

I thought of doing a Heathcliff: roam the world, make a fortune, return and rescue 'Cathy' from the 'Lintons'. Even *that* was ruled out – I didn't want Stella dying on me.

Chapter Eleven

Together

Charles lost his appetite for Farndon fizz, as well as his taste for the Blindon Arms. Was he on the wagon, was the bike-ride too far? A bit of everything, perhaps, but boozers don't bow to trifles. For weeks he didn't show, then surfaced as if he'd never missed. I tried tapping him on his strange absence, but got nowhere. A casual 'How are things looking at the Hall' had him rear up angrily, refusing to reply. I laughed it off, but it left me intrigued. Then three Exports later, he mellowed. He almost cringed.

"Sorry, Frank. No 'ard feelings, mate. You caught me on the raw, that's all. Bloody lot. I'm thinking of packin' it in. I've had enough. We need more hands, and another groom – now! With the season at full swing the ole man could drive 'isself round the bleedin' estate. They expect me in two places at once. Thank God Stella come home – she helps with anything – 'specially the nags – that frees me for the drivin', like. To be fair though, he's not up to bargin' round them back roads on his own. That ruddy spine..."

"Stell... Estelle *home? When?* When did she come?" I bit my tongue, but fortunately Charles was half-way to being pissed – my gaffe passed him by.

"Last week," he said, grinning like a baboon.

"With Noel?"

"Noel's in the States, so they tell me. Six months at 'arvard. He got a 'First' whatever that might be, from Mordlin'. Cocky bastard. They said summat about going for a 'doctrate'. What's that when it's at 'ome?"

"Drink up, Charles. Have a brandy, mate. A double. Go on!" I pressed him to drink up – I'd gladly have bought him the pub – his query went unanswered. 'Estelle *home.* She oils the world's axis, keeps it turning. Get your skates on Frank.'

Next day was Saturday – chores could go to hell. I tore down to Bradbury junction, did a speedway special at the corner, dropped down to bottom, revved like mad, then sailed past the Hall driveway, honking on the horn like a ship in fog, before cruising on up to Briarsdale. The first time for yonks I sat on the thicket gate. The 'keep out' board looked drab and weathered as if in apology for its salutary warnings, the gibbet chock full, the letter-box bare. The wind started howling for real, as clouds gathered ominously in the west... not the day for sitting about.

But the old 'leather' coat felt warm and comfy – the elements could go to hell too! There was nobody around, though estate men usually worked until twelve on Saturdays. But trivia's trivia – of no import – my mind fixed firmly on more important matters.

The calling-card worked. My heart began to thump. She strode up the road like the Duchess of Dreams. Shoulders back, chest proud, cheeks glowing, pale eyes wide and wonderful, war-paint missing, a raincoat with belt and shoulder straps, like private eyes are supposed to wear, deflecting the elements (which once seldom bothered her). A silk scarf swirled above the rollneck sweater she'd worn since time began. Slacks and flat-heel shoes completed her rig-out. 'Where's Addy... where's Maddy?'

I leapt from the gate like an escapee leaving Strangeways. The empty years rolled away. Nothing had changed – I felt the same. Only one thing to do – and I *did* it. I ran to her – coat flapping, face glowing, and grabbed her tight. 'Biologists can say what they like – she's Stella! Nothing can change that. Never mind the 'sister' nonsense – she can be my ruddy grandmother for all I care – I love her like nobody on earth.' Words were superfluous. I swear she wept – then blamed the wind.

"You'll never change, Franz. Silly! Next you'll tell me you love me..."

I released her an inch, then hugged her tighter. Five years had passed since I first thrilled to that magic presence. When the waist was a shade tinier, the shoulders leaner, the gorgeous face innocent. But the love had endured. I knew it would. I knew too she'd feel the same. *My* Estelle... always *my* Estelle.

"Don't let go of me Franz... ever! Kiss me again."

"This is madness, darling."

"I know it is! Take me to the dolls' house, Franz. Please. *PLEASE. Take me...*"

The irony of *me* leading Stella to her own paradise was lost on the wind. Along the familiar ride we tramped, hand in hand, the trees near leafless, undergrowth scarred and scarce, grass stunted and yellowed. Here and there odd pheasants skulked in resentment at the intrusion, some scuttling for cover, trembling with alarm, leaving their milky-white trademarks on the scarred earth. The migratory pigeon hordes were yet to sweep down from the north, though resident birds, with their parsons' collars, flitted like ghosts between the treetops, wild as hawks now the shooting season was upon us, the rooks nowhere to be seen. But the scenario scarcely registered. Only Estelle counted – nothing else. Happy and unstuffy, face alight, she reverted to girlhood in all its subtle innocence.

"Do you still manage to dodge old Sissons, and come up here, Franz?"

"Haven't been for ages. Since your engagement. Haven't the heart."

We crossed to the Holt, still holding hands. She didn't answer. I didn't expect she would. Finally she turned, and murmured, "Old Silly," between the tears, nostrils flared as she fought to keep the lid on. We lost little time reaching the Lodge. I grabbed the key from beneath the gintrap, and had a quick look around for snoopers. Something moved, over towards the western boundary, but the silence, apart from the defiant rustle of the few leaves still clinging on, told me the wood was empty. Maybe a deer?

Inside, the lodge was surprisingly comfortable. It hadn't been long without a fire. Tom Sissons was far from my favourite character, but he kept the lodge in order all right – for his own comfort, no doubt. A devoted servant, Sissons. Sometimes there seemed more to him than first appeared, and he kept many a poor bugger off the 'starving' list with his rabbits at give-away prices. The only meat they ever tasted – apart from on Christmas Day. And he'd extended this service to Farndon. We frequently enjoyed one... and the occasional pheasant... on the quiet.

The models were dull and dusty – practically mummified – but still there. All present and correct. The delight on Stella's face was alone worth the trek. We talked over old times, old memories, wishing we could turn back the clock, but I couldn't help feeling *this* rendezvous was as false as one could get. She sorted some chisels from the wall, nursed them lovingly, selected her favourite, turning it, twisting it, making sure it responded to her coaxing. Fondly she cradled the carving she'd caught me with the day I had the nerve to trespass – the Hereford bull. She remembered that too. Would she ever forget? After dodging the issue for long enough, I asked her why she came.

"The motor-bike of course! When I heard the honking I knew it was you – aren't I clever? And I knew you'd be waiting. I can read your mind – easy as pie. Luckily I was out in the yard, mooching, fed up being stuck indoors. Their mother's taken the shepherd's kids shopping. I was too lazy to saddle up – and Charles wasn't around to help."

"You mean you wanted to see me?" I snorted. She ignored the taunt, sniffing in contempt.

"Come here! Come on you great big Silly."

Twice we made love in our dream-house – the 'Guns' cushions came in handy. Stella was never more passionate, giving all she had. The real Stella – honest, genuine, totally abandoned. Only I *knew* Stella – nobody else. How we missed each other. How stupid life can get! It was like a dream – lifted from a Thirties movie – the days when Hollywood could make films.

"Estelle... I'll never let you go. You can marry whom you like but he won't love you like *I* do. The first Noel..."

The grey eyes came alive again, the spent emotion ebbed back.

"Don't play games, Franz. My future's firmly fixed."

"And you a rebel?"

"Don't spoil it, darling. Nothing can change. Be here for me – that's all I ask. If you're married, with lots of kids, it makes no difference. As long as you're always *here*."

"How long this time Stella?"

"Two days... maybe three. I'm not sure. Things aren't good at home. Daddy's poorly – in bed much of the time. Mummy fears the worst, but doctor says no, he'll make it alright, he went downhill so fast! Mind you, things carry on as normal – he wants it that way, though it's not cluttered with guests like it used to be. Ada spends lots of time with him. She's ever so good, really – got the patience of a saint. Mummy hardly knows he's there – he's never been one for moaning."

"Who *is* Ada?"

"Ada Barlow, of course. Our old governess."

"No... I mean... Oh, it doesn't matter. Forget it. Are the boys home? Are you missing Noel? Do you usually live with him – in Cambridge?"

"I'm boarded out – with a couple of girls. When he's in residence he's the other end of town. Some weeks I hardly see him. Apparently Rupert was home last week. Justin's a law unto himself. I reckon he forgets where we live – or should live."

"Ugh! You can talk! You're *never* home, and I wouldn't know if you were. Had it not been for Charles I'd be in the dark again this time – it drives me up the wall! It *is* rotten you know, darling."

"Ah well... You know what I am, Franz."

"Is Sir Martin there? And Sarah? How *is* Sarah?"

"Yes. They're both there, as you might guess. I'm always thinking of you, Franz, but never do anything about it. There's not much point... how's Mrs Allner... is she well? I must call and see her again. You're so peaceful there. That lovely cottage. That's what I'd like – and a fortune to go with it. That sounds terrible, I suppose?"

"Don't ever change, Stella. It's corny all right, but it doesn't bother me. You're honest, that's what counts. We can't help the way we are – or how we're raised."

"You sound exactly like Daddy. I do wish he'd pick up – he'll miss the season. So shall *I*. Maddy'll get rusty. I must tell Mummy to keep him on the move."

"Charles tells me you help out with all the horses, Estelle."

"Oh! It's like that, is it! Discuss me with the wretched chauffeur, do you?" Her face changed in seconds. She went berserk. I stared, horrified. I wilted, dropped her hand, nearly knocking a pig for six as I backed off. The change was uncanny... frightening even.

"No, I do not! He was moaning about too much work, what with chauffering, odd-jobbing, mucking-out – said it's time you hired another groom. He paid you a compliment. Called you a brick – I think! Said you help more than the rest put together. It was out the blue – completely. We were at the bar together when he let off steam, that's all. To be honest, he'd had a few. Anybody could have copped his broadside – it happened to be me!"

She softened as fast as she'd bristled. The old chameleon at work. Making up the same old magic. I laughed – when I could breathe.

"Crikey, you terrify me, darling. You're on a short fuse!"

"Silly! Come on Franz, we must go. There!" She kissed me and cuddled up for a minute. We tramped off back, meeting the wind head-on. It roared up the ride, making our eyes stream, our noses blue, and our ears feel like dropping off. The auburn curls bounced up and down the way they used to. Cheeks shining pink, lips parted, the perfect teeth, the proud set of her head – I pictured her in armour. We finally reached the road.

"Bet you daren't get on?" I ventured, climbing on the bike.

"Of course I dare." She giggled, not at all Stella-like, desperate for fun.

"Hang on, then. Hold on tight." I stifled a smirk. We buzzed down to Bradbury as I gave the old bike the office. Yelling 'Christ' she clung to my middle as if afraid we'd take to the air. I grinned with delight. I loved the air blasting my face, the smell of burnt gas.

"*Slow up! Ah-h-h-h-hhh. You stupid sod!*" She screamed. She raged. Another turn on the throttle and we were flat-out, the exhaust roaring in defiance as the pipe glowed red – I felt free as a bird, elated, doing what I do best – acting on impulse. For a welcome change life was complete – complete with Stella. She thumped my neck, bellowing her protest.

"Sto-o-ppp! *Damn you – STOP!*" I slowed as if turning into Bradbury drive, then opened up fast, shooting her half way up my back. Joining the main road I drove hell for leather to anywhere. Being alive, with those arms around me, I went crazy. We were up to sixty – going some, then. The few motors around I passed with contempt, careering wherever the bike cared to take me. Through peaceful villages, dusty little market-towns, over scores of road bridges, river bridges, rail bridges, level-crossings – all at full bore, the engine roaring appreciation at the clear-out of carbon. The 'pillion' went completely quiet, the grip loosened. Eventually, I'd had enough. I throttled back, cruised for a while, then raised my goggles and drew up near to a narrow-looking bridge. One of the many tributaries of the River Nene flowed serenely below.

"Franz, you swine! You *pig!* You *bastard!* I'll get you for this – you wait. Damn and bugger you, you great big clodhopping oaf!"

"Sit down! And shut up!"

"*Where? Where* can I sit?"

"On your bum!"

Too late I ducked! Smack on the chin she caught me – with a haymaker, Dempsey fashion. She was barking mad. I scrambled up, all twelve stone of me, grabbed her wrists, held them vice-like as she strained and struggled. The bike subsided to the verge, then twisting her first one way then the other I worked her down to the river bank in a series of smart, if reckless, manoeuvres, until she wondered where the hell she was, blinded by the mists of outrage. I'd never seen the lovely face so contorted – that face I adored. Short of the water by inches, I eased off. Released her. I laughed until I thought I'd pee my pants. Then she *did* go mad. 'Crikey, I hope she's not hurt!'

I clawed the old coat off, spread it on the ground, careful to dodge the cowpats, and forced her down to it. If looks could kill I'd be dead.

"Take me home!" she growled, eventually. "And *damn* you! You've got a bloody nerve! *Nobody* does that to me – and gets away with it."

"You're divine when you're mad, darling. Did you know – my Lady of Bradbury? You're beautiful – and I worship you."

Slowly, very, very slowly, she stretched flat out on the cuddly coat, unwinding in a series of spasmodic twitches, until finally settled. I edged towards her, looking down on her, slightly apprehensive. Part mollified, she managed the faintest of smiles. I kissed her a thousand times.

The wind blew harder, the waves went rippling downriver. Then, surprisingly, a dim autumn sun peeped from behind the threatening clouds. It glinted on the turbulent river, playing tricks with the weird reflections sun, wind and water can conjure up between them. A skinny-looking heron uncoiled its snake-like neck, lifted from the opposite bank, rose leisurely above the bridge parapet, and made off up-river with slow measured flaps of his great barndoor wings, seeking a more peaceful spot to spear fish.

I pulled Stella to her feet, turned to get the coat, when she curled her foot swiftly round my ankles, gave my bum a great shove, and sent me hurtling head-first into the swirling waters. Breathless, and spouting fountains, I struggled against the chill water, grabbing desperately for the rust-coloured reeds at the riverside – they proved weaker than they looked! In the end I managed to grab an old pollard willow, and inch by inch, my chin clipping the surface, battled towards the bridge where the banks were less precipitous. Heaving with exhaustion and mighty relieved, I clawed my way ashore and lay panting for ages, spewing weeds and water. Eventually I mustered the strength to look up, only to see Miss Grant-Wilton doubled up with laughter, not prepared to even give me a helping hand. I struggled up the slope like a drowned rat, stumbled over to the motor-bike, pulled it upright, then slumped in the saddle, feeling for the controls like somebody blind. Estelle clambered up behind. Without a word I set off home, river-water pissing from my laceholes.

Even today it's hard to think Stella could practice such double standards. She was all mine when home. Away, she must metamorphose to a stranger. Jeckyll and Hyde in drag.

But it went deeper than that. I was a sort of life-raft, a crag of safety, a refuge to run to and mend her bruises. She needed me – as much as I needed her. Whether that's love I wouldn't know. I have an idea it must be. And Stella was due to melt away again any time now. In the meantime she'd curse me, vent her anger, display her arrogance and generally demean me. The first time I'd challenged her dominance – she'd want revenge.

Meanwhile, things in general looked shaky. Mum tried making out all was beer and skittles, but it was only a pose – for my benefit. She knew I was in up to my neck at Bradbury but even *she* didn't guess there was no bottom... Had she known half we'd have sailed for Australia next boat.

Life at Sangsters' carried on with its ups and downs but my own riddles hogged the frame.

What brought Martin Fawcett to the office that day? What was he after? Stanley would know. I had a go at picking his brains – a rare exercise.

"What did he want Mr Forest? You can find out from Gosling, unless you already know?"

Stanley lifted his head, glared, sniffed, snorted, shrugged, then turned back to his desk as if I'd never spoken. I got the message all right and backed off. It was strange nonetheless. Sangsters, on behalf of Fawcett, controlled the operation when Dad saw off Bradbury's requisitioners. The firm masterminded the whole shooting-match. Fawcett organised Dad's sick-pass so he could come home and 'act'. Dad *died* under Fawcett's command. Now Fawcett's close to taking over the works at Bradbury. And the Colonel's days are numbered... where will Lady Lydia figure then? Or *Ada?* Fawcett a widower – he'll need a consort – and since George didn't sire Estelle, who the hell did – unless it *was* my Dad?'

One of the drabbest winters on record followed this unholy spell. Stella did disappear – for final year at Girton. Noel's spot of 'polishing' at Harvard ended. The big spring meet had to be cancelled, despite George's pleas it go ahead as normal. He still clung on, but spent more and more time resting. According to Charles he remained perfectly lucid, and occasionally took the passenger-seat for a ride round the estate in the Alvis, well rugged up, and bolstered with cuddly hot-water bottles. He wasn't fussy which way the car pointed – he left Charles to pick the route, but he enjoyed the outings immensely.

It was about this time a shock brought the Hall to a halt. Justin found himself a bride. In the *City*. *From* the City. A Windmill hoofer. He married her at Chelsea Registry Office – without informing his kin – or his distant relatives. Just *friends* signed the Register. Just friends, presumably, attended the service. The ensuing high jinks didn't reach the ears of Bradbury clientele. He didn't even bring her to the Hall, and had few regrets at shaking the dust of Farndon from his itchy feet – what little clung. One more headache for Lovely Lydia, though she'd seen little of him since London reached out and clawed him to its bosom. Maybe Justin had doubts about his brand-new bride being safe at Bradbury?

I grew convinced of what daily became more obvious. Dad *did* sire Estelle. Mum knew he did. But I could hardly broach the subject. Had he confessed to her? Admitted the betrayal? And Grandad? He'd know. Mum would have to tell him. And another thing – *I'd* be on the way when Lydia was expecting Stella... the thought made me shudder – on Mum's behalf. A double whammy for Dad.

Time passed – party politics loomed. Fawcett made the King's honours list – 'for public and political service' O.B.E. "Other buggers' efforts," as Harry called it. Quite what he did all the time was a mystery. I'd no idea how often he frequented 'The House' or the time he spent in his constituency. As for Shining Sara – she'd long been a fixture at the Hall when free of university. That had to be the reason for Stella keeping her distance.

Sara intrigued me more than a little. Bouncy, bubbly... so pretty – yet *so* disliked. What could be prompting the relentless feuding of the pair – the spats almost tangible. I'm not certain if they came to blows... Party-night still haunted me. Never had I felt such a prat – with half the sporting Midlands looking on. Being tanked up didn't help. Stella's exhibition was bad enough – yet it somehow had class. Sara's was unforgivable – if partly my fault. She did do it to embarrass Stella – I was sure of that now. But why? It's common for fillies closeted close to kick out – but not to flaunt their enmity. After all, Sara was free to clear off any time she liked – nobody shackled her to the Hall – her choice.

Sometimes I'd wonder how Lydia ever reconciled her status as Matriarch with such a trigger-happy tribe? To cap everything, Aunt Pen and Freda turned up, as usual out of the blue, to announce 'Uncle' had hopped it to Switzerland again, and was likely to remain there for the foreseeable future.

Charles remained true to his re-awakened love affair with the Blindon Arms. Facts and figures flowed freely – unless I pushed too hard. He kept talking about George – which always sent my mind flying to Lydia! I confess to sometimes feeling pity for her. The underlying resentment wasn't for her seduction of me – it still takes two to tango – but for the way she must have lured Dad. The naivety persisted – and it all stemmed from conjecture. 'Meet the King of the Charlies...'

Sir Martin filled *The Gazette* – *The Herald* too... His military exploits, his gongs, his political nous, gave him the aura of a man the common herd loves to lionise. And he wasn't even our MP – he belonged next door. But the boundaries were common, so his constituency at least ran us close, and the interest it generated was natural. Papers can't look a gift-horse in the mouth, especially local rags. Any news better than no news at all.

But my mistrust of the Fawcetts kept growing. They were parasites – on a grand scale.

They'd got the Grants by the short and curlies, and against the odds their grip tightened. And poor George weakened... not swiftly, but sure as hell. The fear of Fawcett becoming O.C. Briarsdale, boss of Lucans Pond, Master of Bradbury, gave me nightmares, though why I can't rightly explain.

In the end, shelving my better judgement, I decided to turn to Mum. At least she wouldn't laugh at me. And I was a voter now. A man. A big man... in inches.

"You're getting fanciful Francis. Anyway, why should you care who inherits the wretched estate? And there's plenty come before Martin Fawcett! The boys, for a start, as well as that young madam, when the Colonel goes. By the way, have you heard when the wedding is? It can't be long... they were saying only last week at the WI."

"They would be. Right up their bloody street – other folks' business. Nosey sods." The bitterness choked me. Mum adopted a stance of mental agony.

"You can cut out that language," she snapped, her lips invisible. But it took more than that to upset her. I was bursting to talk about Stella – but not in this vein.

'How long can she keep up the farce? Go on ignoring the obvious? Dad must have betrayed her. And it was Mum who told me Estelle was a cuckoo. And everybody knows there's a mystery-man funding Bradbury... if not Fawcett who the hell can it be?'

She was of no help on that score.

For the first time ever I really thought I saw daylight – 'There's a military explanation!' Farming in the doldrums, returns reducing daily, Farndon's farmers, like the rest, facing ruin. Only the Big would survive, looking to alternative ventures to bolster the slender rewards – stock-farming, breeding, weaning, fattening, forestry, butchery – they have the space to diversify – and the cash. In time they'll take over the stragglers – and all will end up in the pockets of the few. Then *they'll* struggle.

'Where can I lay hands on wartime data?' Sherwood couldn't help. Too obscure for Harry to assist – archives don't run to that. And not only Fawcett affluence, Fawcett influence.

'But Sangsters would know! *Claud* Sangster... not of the military, but the one common denominator. The thread running through the lot – Fawcetts, Grants, Sangsters... and the *Allners*. Somewhere the gen is on paper... where else but at Sangsters? On the spot, where I live my life every day. So why didn't Claud finish his story? Ah... he couldn't – not with the Colonel still alive! Nor, for that matter, as long as Fawcett retained his crown!' I'd long since concluded that when the truth came out few would smell of roses. It was that kind of mystery. All because I fell for Estelle – and Estelle loves me'.

Sometimes I'd go up to Carolean. Not via the woods – through Tate's Meadow. I no longer had the neck to venture to the lodge. Sourpuss Sissons might be on the downward slope, but he still packed a punch – and a shotgun! Big as I was, and handy with my dukes, I had no desire to tangle with *him!*

I'd fiddle with the entrance, plait the fibres, re-arrange the canopy, pull out the dross, fashion the creepers so the arbour took shape again – and often I'd just sit and think. If the sun shone I'd sit for hours, asking the same old question – was I on a loser all along?"

And Estelle always appeared. Running, riding, walking, talking, laughing, crying. She'd call me 'Franz', tease me, bully me, mock me, ruffle my hair, rumple my shirt... then she'd smile, that wonderful smile, the world fading to nothing – all I'd see were those big eyes of grey, beckoning me to where the skies never darkened – all silk and sunlight. I'd pinch myself awake, I'd shiver, and look around me – she was so real. I could feel her presence – alive, electric, galvanic. But above all, loving. Always loving...

Chapter Twelve

At the Front

I got down to work for real after my twenty-first. Sangsters told Mum I'd make the grade alright, and go on to become a fully-fledged team member, so long as I kept my mind connected, and my nose clean. I'd survived two hurdles, the 'preliminaries', but still plenty to master before I could stand up and plead in court. The idea didn't thrill me – if anything, it terrified me. But I'd get my name on the staff board – letters after it, too. Gold on teak. Often, though, I'd be haunted by the wildest thoughts – light-years away from the dry, pedantic clack-clack-clack of matters legal.

I'd corner Claud, tell him to reach for the sky, then screw him for the Grants' secrets. Mesmerise Alice, tease her, tickle her – then raid the den myself. If only the *Internet*...

I overlooked the likeliest source! 'What about Alan Stewart? What about the shaggy historian? On the spot, at the hub. He'd be wised-up. Know everything.'

But he hadn't committed it to paper – as far as I could make out. Then, he wouldn't, not for the benefit of nosey sods like me. And another thing – we bow to these historians – treat them as gods – yet they only poach their material – from earlier beavers, many of them nutcases. At times the anomalies of life, the perceived unfairness, the contradictions, drove me to the edge – the 'no father' syndrome. And I could never easily make friends, despite the Stella connection. As far as self-assessment went, I sidestepped my own parasitic leanings, my grabs at the social ladder, deliberate or not! Anyway, Stewart wouldn't have catalogued Lydia's love-life. Or *would* he?'

The shock of finding Lydia pregnant when he got back to Blighty, seeing she caused the family bust-up in the first place, kick-starting the exodus that sent them scuttling to the

Midlands like herded sheep, drove George right up the wall. Following that convincing victory in the 'Battle for Bradbury', the bold, if unpatriotic fight to repel invaders, the sackcloth must have come like a shit-cart from hell, just as he'd declared Sergeant Allner a man for all seasons. And not a thing he could do about it.

Backstreet abortions weren't unique, but there wasn't the time – nor was it the occasion, with Lydia in that mood... The flagrant betrayal by both wife *and* servant, the sheer cruelty of such treachery, had George running for cover. And Lydia suffered agonies of remorse, as well as the pain of rejection, but was left to grin and bear it. She was powerless to brighten up his leave, even had she felt that way.

Bit by bit the agony eased, and George made man-sized efforts to face the music, dragging himself up by the bootlaces – but the bitterness proved too much. He'd suffered the ultimate ignominy for a homecoming warrior. The horrors of the trenches receded; he'd learned to live with the shells, the shit, and the snipers, but this was different, impossible to shoulder. Old as the hills, common as time, a hurt endured by thousands and thousands still to come. But that didn't help.

Seven days and George had had enough. Fourteen days and it was back to the mud and mayhem of the Line, with murder in mind, and hatred in his heart.

He'd behaved like a pig at home – a wounded pig. His sons had seen nothing of him, nor he of them. It felt like they'd gone from his life for ever. Squeezed out of existence. Somehow he'd clung to a morsel of self-control, but Satan hogged the passenger seat. The vast estates lost their attraction. The great woods, and the rolling acres, left him cold. Even the Hall in all its magnificence turned chill and cheerless, the once-splendid rooms ceased to sparkle, the ornate gardens a wilderness to his jaundiced eyes. The battle for Bradbury was over – but victory was a bloody nightmare!

Lydia suffered agonies of remorse, her life blighted. Who dare judge the temptations loneliness brings. Not for *days*.. for weeks, for months, for *years!* Years of hand-wringing, when any day could bring the news mothers, wives, and sweethearts learned to dread. To an uncaring world woman attracts her own woes. It was ever thus...

Meanwhile, away on the continent, the Push is imminent. One *more* major onslaught. The push to end all pushes. The final heave-ho to secure that vital breakthrough. Then, and only then, can come the all-conquering surge across the Low Countries into Germany's heartland. That vital onslaught to settle for all time the ugly, senseless, ongoing madness gripping the Western World. Few knew exactly *when* – apart from a few red-tabbed, red-faced, red-eyed moustachioed supermen back at base: they'd know! But even to the men at the sharp end signs were plain.

Fresh fodder fed forward every day. Raw protagonists shagged almost senseless by the slog up to what passed for a 'line'. Green young men slotting uneasily into the messy, complicated twisting network of rat-infested trenches where so many before had awaited their own final push. And still the new-fangled mobile strongpoint, the answer to war's problems, the TANK, months away from general use despite a try-out at Flers.

Once more the guns would lay down their fearsome barrage of fire. Once more the hopes of millions would rest on the Poor Bloody Infantry. Yet again the blunderbuss approach for that ever elusive crack in Germany's wall.

Unless, and until, somebody cut the wire, progress could be forgotten. Major Grant-Wilton worked like stink, pepping up his men, telling them *this* time they were on to a winner. A revitalised Grant-Wilton – stern, severe and soldier-like. As he ploughed along the sloping, sour-smelling, slimy, six-foot stretches of shit and slush, men lolled on the sides like dolls on a toyshop shelf in recumbent attitudes of mute resignation, puffing endlessly on their cheap cigarettes, eyeing any officer with a degree of cynicism. But the haunted look was always there – the eyes told the tale! When they poked their heads above the parapet, snipers sent swift reminders. Sandbags are poor companions, albeit the last bastions when your number's up.

Across this desolate landscape fighting raged non-stop: the awesome, ferocious clash of warring factions, their desperate efforts laughingly referred to by the *cognoscente* as 'static warfare!' The murderous concentration of artillery fire, the relentless plop-plop of mortars, the never-ending sweep of the machine-guns... against a backdrop of unimagined ugliness, the like of which had never before been seen.

Tangled wire, battered tree-stumps, shredded tunics, busted helmets, burnt-out boots, bloodied blankets, warped webbing, weeping water-bottles... all strewn at random across the bloody, muddy, grassless wasteland pock-marked by craters five foot and more deep.

At the limit of his sector, where C Company took over the line, George Grant turned, making his way back along the treacly, glutinous cuttings, as shells continued to drop, mostly off target, but subscribing massively to an air of chaos and confusion. His heavy trench-coat protected his battle-gear, *and* disguised his majority. By the time he finally ducked into the tiny dugout serving as headquarters, he was plastered head to foot in brown, clinging slime, his boots double their normal size. He found Captain Greeley and Lieutenant Randall squatted on battered fish-crates, rubbing their legs in vain attempts to keep out the chill, their faces solemn, shadowed beneath the stuttering storm-lantern. By supreme self-control they maintained an air of studied nonchalance, like convicts on Death Row.

A plan had formed in the Major's mind. He'd do his duty, *and* rid the world of the treacherous swine who defiled his lady – as long as the Hun played his part. Meanwhile he'd wait, and wait, and wait... until Redtabs decided the time was right to get up and go. For any move to stand a chance, the masses of barbed-wire guarding blue (George's) sector, must be breached. In darkness, a fearsome challenge – in daylight, suicide. So he'd try a flanker. Send *two* parties – just before dawn. A better chance – if a bigger risk!

Randall first – Allner ten minutes later. Each with a handful of picked men – four at most. The first lot centre-left, the second lot, right. All they'd wait for was the signal 'GO!' *Few would come back.*

And back in Britain the armchair brigade would bend over crumpled maps, work out tactics, pick the route, decide on timing, then hail the success of yet another 'final assault!' The Big Breakthrough – at last! 'BERLIN here we come...' Ha! Ha! Ha!... Ha bloody Ha! Ha bloody *bloody* Ha!

George suffered two long, anxious, days – *and* nights. Then a third. And a fourth! 'Is the moon in the right quarter?' Nagging away every minute, every second, a voice prompted him to go on and finish his grisly business – until Allner was dead, his ghost well and truly laid. But the doubts were never far off. Doubts forever questioning the justice of his ugly solution. Slowly, but surely, sanity began to ebb back. That once fair and orderly mind had second thoughts. 'After all, Allner was sorely tempted – like hordes before him – and hordes still to come. Stronger men than him lost their way in the darkness of war. Bigger men than him bit the dust. What sort of build-up led to the cheating? Only Lydia knows that – and she isn't talking – not yet. Not to *Me!*'

Yet, paradoxically, George had a scintilla of sympathy for Lydia in that sentimental way of his – a pillar of magnanimity. For George was a *good* man – until the madness got him! Now the sheer evil of his plan at last filtered through the detritus. For the first time he recognised the enormity of his lust for vengeance. Wire-cutting was an awesome enough task without a murderer loose, waiting to kick your arse before stabbing you in the back.

By the time Fawcett came forward with orders for The Advance, and a briefing for Company Commanders, George had regained a measure of stability. He'd banished Satan from the driving seat, and thought up a feasible alternative – he'd take the first wire-party himself, Randall the second, leaving Greeley in command until the job was done – the prelude to action proper. Keep Allner on ice.

But the best laid schemes of mice and men... the foray went according to Sod's law!

The ghostly light of dawn flickered wanly over the shell-torn, cratered wilderness that was no-man's land. Any hint of movement and the Hun raked the spot with fire – so intense it shredded everything in range – sometimes ripping the very wire the suicide squads were after destroying. He was more than ready – he lay waiting.

Just *two* made it back – seven would never move again – until somebody stretchered their remains. The two were really just one and a half. With superhuman effort, helped by a reserve who selflessly abandoned his trench to face the fearsome fusillade full on, the Major dragged in a casualty under cover of blistering return-fire that at last kept the Hun in check. George escaped unscathed – the only charmed life he'd ever know, the future a closed book – fortunately for him.

Allner had been spared the sally – and Grant-Wilton was glad about that. Saved for a later skirmish, when he'd take his chance with the rest. The very next assault, as things turned out, with Satan at the helm. For the push was launched as 'planned' – wire or no bloody wire. Five hundred yards from his own lines, up to the balls like all the rest, in coils of uncut wire, Robert Allner's days ended. Nothing spectacular, nothing heroic... just good, old-fashioned guts. Routine obedience. 'Orders is orders.' The natural extension to the familiar old-fashioned ineptitude of politicians out of their depth. A standard exercise in disaster. Another chapter in the besmirched book of botched, blind, boneheaded bloody balls-ups. Only Grant-Wilton knew the pain of remorse after the Hun killed Robert Allner. Pain he'd never conquer. A nasty cocktail of shame, guilt, and pity, for one more man among the hundreds thrown to the wolves in yet another ill-judged attempt to break a line that didn't so much as budge in three days of non-stop man-to-man stuff never before experienced in that bloodied wilderness. A brush with Fritz that earned not a single mention in the official record of that God-forsaken sector through the deadly dangers of a winter that lasted a thousand years.

The will to fight on, that crucial element in any man's make-up, stood the test well in Grant-Wilton's battle with himself. The lapse brought on by Lydia's treachery was consigned bit by bit to the bin of experience. Luck, and a new *laissez-faire* attitude, played their part in his revival. Then the day came, near the end of the whole bloody conflict, when at last George drew the short straw.

Back where he belonged – with the cavalry – albeit motorised, the Germans blew his tank to smithereens, and George would never walk again – not like he did before. An inch from paralysis, he was lucky to recover at all – but the shell did its deadly work.

George went crazy. For long spells he was held in a nursing home, away in Marseilles. He refused repatriation, determined to surmount the damage, mental more than physical, before going home. He was luckier than the medicine men prophesied. He finally began to 'walk' again – unaided. And as his body mended so his mind began to straighten out. In the meantime, the Great War drew to a close. From then on his progress was rapid, until a surprise visit from his erstwhile Commander brought recovery to a juddering halt! The Brigadier regaled George with details of his earlier visits to the sanatorium, when the Colonel was undeniably off his rocker. He told of the nauseating babble he'd been forced to listen to, when George insisted on confessing his sins. When he boasted of his audacious plan to rid both himself, and the world, of that traitorous wretch, Sergeant Allner.

Fawcett professed horror at learning the details of George's scheming, and finding what George had in mind for Allner once the attack went in. And he was a long way from happy. George strenuously denied the accusations. Denied involvement in Allner's death. Pleaded insanity for any rubbish he might have spouted in his highly-charged state.

But it didn't wash! Fawcett refused to believe that George had a change of heart. That he dropped his plan for the hideous finale he had in mind for his staff-sergeant. That his conscience was clear.

Fawcett wouldn't listen to the truth. Didn't want to know about George's second thoughts. Didn't believe George took the suicide party himself. Refused to believe Allner was spared George's vengeance.

'And after all he'd done for Grant-Wilton – on top of negotiating the sick-pass. Put his neck on the line for that!' Impasse. But being a 'gentleman' Fawcett declared George's secrets safe in his hands – and in his head. Swore to keep it that way.

Time passed, with nothing more said. George continued to convalesce. When he finally returned to England, promoted and decorated, apart from a certain stiffness in the joints he presented a well-nigh familiar figure to family and friends. The pain was mostly internal... But he promptly fell in love with his new 'daughter'. The affection, deep and sincere, helped form a new, if uneasy relationship with Lydia. To help things along he gave tacit approval to the wild, rebellious behaviour for which Bradbury had become a symbol.

The establishment became, in part, open-house to an even wider, though still select crowd, behaving with an abandon never before witnessed. And drifters were quick to catch on. Once a week, at least, was party time. Wine flowed like the sea at flood-tide as a feverish dash for gaiety succeeded the stringent regime of ration and restraint that characterised the years of conflict.

Hall and gardens rang to the happy sounds of laughter and indulgence, in an upbeat atmosphere of 'bugger the expense, pass the champers'. All was whoomph and whoosh. And Lydia valiantly played her part with extravagant, extrovert enthusiasm. If anything, she grew prettier as the years rolled by, her voluptuous figure back to near-normal despite the delivery of three healthy children.

This brief account of the salient points of the war years, and their aftermath, as relating to my tale, are, of course, a compilation of reports, and research from the most reliable sources I could penetrate. All has been edited, and confirmed where possible, and I can vouch for the general accuracy.

But *some* episodes, as you'll have spotted, leave yawning gaps and giant question-marks. For a start, and most important, they make complete hogwash of Fawcett's account of the day my Dad got the chop. Why pump me full of bullshit on that chance encounter at Sangsters? If it *was* a chance meeting? Did the man not *know* what took place? Had he based his account solely on the fevered ramblings he'd been forced to listen to in Marseilles? He *must* have known George didn't go through with his murderous plot, that he took the wire-party himself! If he didn't know – then why not? And what about sister Isabel?

As you'd expect Mum and Grandad figure high, as do Grant-Wilton, Fawcett, Lydia, Claud Sangster, Noel, Sara, Mrs Thompson, Ada, Charles... not, of course, forgetting Stella. To those I've omitted, I offer my apologies.

But I can't allow modesty to cloud the truth. It owes more to my own diligence and intuition, than to the efforts of the rest put together – including Claud. I've left out rumours and hearsay.

Sara came down from Girton with a Second, and promptly installed herself at Bradbury as if she'd never been away, with not the slightest idea what to do with her life, and not a care in the world. Her father was, of all places, in his constituency, presumably at home, in Market Harborough. I'd often wonder what sort of residence it was, and who kept it going, though doubtless he'd have an army of servants, plus a battalion of grooms (and a batman), for he liked his horses home when the 'flat' finished, a firm believer that a change of scenery does as much for the equine population as for humans. Sara had me puzzled. Prettier than ever, fit as a fiddle, wild as a hawk, yet rarely seen – like some rare bird whose habits fool the most dedicated of twitchers. A mammoth magnet for horny men. But none seemed to stay the course.

In spite of her antipathy to Estelle, I could never dislike Sara. Maybe the sight of her shapely butt in all its awesome splendour had some bearing on this affection. Lydia must have liked her a lot to welcome her to Bradbury so readily. She treated Sara like an extra daughter – only better.

Whether the rivalry between Stella and Sara still featured I'd no way of knowing, though with Stella so often absent the question was hardly relevant. Not once did Stella write. Her wedding arrangements would be well in hand by now. Autumn of 'thirty-seven would see her finished at Cambridge, though Noel took on for two more years, to go for his doctorate. I pictured him in print – Noel Fawcett PhD, MA (Hons), BP (Blond Prat!) How childish.

Purely by chance I bumped into Sara one day as I was leaving the office for lunch-break. She was hurrying towards the city centre in the smartest of navy suits, glossy high-heels, and a cheeky little hat, known then, as now, as a pill-box. She fairly radiated health and *bonhomie*, though only after she recognised me. She wasn't in the 'glad-eye' mode to interest casual punters. Way above that sort of caper... Daughter of a politician – a *Baronet!*

Lots of make-up adorned the pretty features. Cupid's-bow mouth bright red, fair hair waved and collar-length, the brightest of blue eyes, oval face, delicately powdered and perfumed, designed to drive men wild. She deliberately set out to overwhelm me. She succeeded with ease, then threw back her head, laughing, showing the even teeth that snapped now and then but seldom bothered to bite. The handbag matched the beautifully cut knee-length suit. She carried two parcels, shoebox size, and a fancy-looking brolly.

"Hello Fred," she cooed. "Been dancing lately?"

"Sara... Oh *Sara.* Don't remind me. You make me blush. What a night *that* was. You dance beautifully... pity we got carried away." I leaned forward to give her a peck on the cheek, then thought better of it.

"Go on!" she said. "I'm available." Meekly I complied, thinking of envious passers-by.

"I... I didn't realise you were so pretty. Where are you off to?"

"Meeting Lydia, for a bite at Bennetts, then Charles is picking us up."

"What do you do with all that spare time you have, Sara? You hide yourself away still. But then, you always did – whenever *I* called at the Hall. Well out of Stella's way too!"

"Call her 'Stella' do you? My, that's a fancy handle. Asking me for a date, are you Mr Allner? Or are you just being polite?" She flirted outrageously, eyes laughing, taunting, teasing. I can't describe my feelings – in a way I was floored. Daughter of Sir Martin...

"I'm a peasant, Miss Fawcett. You've better things to do than fraternise with Farndon oiks. Not long since you graced the lordly pages of *The Times*, is it?"

"We're democrats down at Bradbury. I thought you'd know that by now, Mr Allner!"

She poked out her tongue – just the tip, following the catty dig, then laughed again. Could it be she wasn't being ironic? When I looked into her eyes I couldn't read them. She had me confused, attracted, and more than a little embarrassed.

"Yes," I said, with conviction. "I *am* asking you out, but I've no idea where to take you."

"Fetch me on that motorbike..."

"When?"

"Saturday... around ten."

"Put on some old clothes then, and wrap up well. You'll want an extra warm coat!"

"OK."

I watched her wriggle across The Square. She had the poise of a supermodel and the dignity of a lady. She left me feeling limp and inadequate, but bucked up by the surprise date. A stupid thing I'd done, but what the hell! I couldn't be faithful to a dream. In no time at all Estelle would be Mrs Fawcett, later on, Lady Fawcett. Sara wasn't scared of recalling our crash to the boards or she wouldn't have called me Astaire. Well... Fred.

My stupid impulses only led to trouble. Always would. 'She spoke because she couldn't ignore me. Nothing more.' The doubts bubbled up – as usual. 'What a clot – to snap at the bait like that! She'll have her fling, then flush me down the drain... where the Dickens can I take her? And at the very least, it means a run down to Bradbury!'

I decided not to tell Mum. I knew damn well she'd fly off the handle if I so much as mentioned 'that lot'. I'm sure she offered thanks to the Almighty for Estelle's engagement. I'd kicked lots of my habits, and adjusted Saturdays to more in keeping with my uneventful existence. The chores got dealt with when I felt like it, though I was careful Mum didn't suffer. Neither football nor cricket any longer hogged the afternoons, and foxhunting failed to beckon.

Chapter Thirteen

Towcester

For a change I undid the gate, revved on the twist-grip, and charged flat-out across the paddock, legs dangling like a grass-tracker's. It didn't please the ducks. Kicking up hell, they lifted hurriedly, whacking the water, their wings going like clapperboards. I swung into the courtyard, shut off, propped the bike by Maddy's stall, and thumped on the scullery door. Another 'nobody about' day, typical of Bradbury, not even Sadie of the apple-red face and whistling thighs was on show. Beneath those great folds of black the tops of her legs must have been like tree-trunks or they'd never have rubbed together like they did, when she walked. Call me daft, call me what you like, but I was staggered to see *Lydia* open the door. *She* wouldn't tend the stove? Were the servants enjoying *another* special day off?

"Oh, it's you" she muttered, looking neither glad nor sorry. Somehow, seeing *me* had her stumped. Unusual to see Lydia toppled by a mere boy – even yours truly. She quickly turned on the treacle, coy as ever, and on this occasion had the merit (?) of being adequately attired.

"You're at the wrong door, Franz. *Why?*" The sarcasm sizzled.

"I don't really know Mrs... er... er... I'm in a dream."

"Not on that blessed thing!" She gave the BSA a dubious glare, contriving the faintest of smiles. Addy squeezed between her legs, tail wagging, eyes alight, tongue flickering – he'd twigged my voice. He remained my surest ally in this sprawling edifice – he trusted me. Lydia was only part dressed – no shoes, no stockings – her face daubed in war-paint, hair shining like morning dew on pampas, the curls more numerous than ever – and not a trace of grey!

"Where are the maids?" I asked, rudely.

"Oh... they're somewhere around," she replied, as if she couldn't care less. "It's early, you know. We're going over to Rushmore – to the meet. Just there and back. We're not riding."

"How is the Colonel, Mrs...?"

"He's coming with us. Do him good. About the same, thanks. Some days better than others. Come in... or did you want something?"

"I've come for Sara."

"*Sara?*" Had I said 'Cleopatra' she couldn't have been more put out.

"Oh! Oh!... Ah! Just a minute. Hang on..."

A grudging response, like she was reluctant to rustle up the Fawcett girl – and her so fond of sparkling Sara?

"She's busy typing – for Alan, I believe. She helps him a lot, you know." As she turned to go and look, Sara came bursting through, laughing apologies for her tardiness.

"Oh, you're there," Lydia cried. "I was just..."

"Won't be a sec Mr Allner. Just grab my coat..." She ignored Lydia completely.

"*And* hat, *and* scarf, *and* gloves – wrap up warm!" I shouted. Bright and breezy, she was in a long, loose sweater, over slacks in a houndstooth check, tight as if they were painted on. I was enveloped in imitation leather, peaked cap, and goggles. Sara stuck out in all the right places, eyes alert, face alive with humour. Lydia looked on, puzzled, and faintly amused, though for some reason not over-pleased. This seemed strange, but knowing her not altogether surprising.

"I suppose Charles is taking you, is he... er, Missus Grant-Wilton?"

"Naturally," she snapped. "I'd rather be riding, but there we are. I don't need the exercise."

"No!" I grinned cheekily, looking her up and down. It was hard to know what to say – contradictory emotions flitting about inside me, not the least being resentment.

"Come on then, Fred, let's go." Sara pulled on a white bobble-hat and a tartan scarf; a giant furry coat brushed her ankles. Turning, she picked up some gauntlets big enough for Charles's stonefork mitts.

"Hang on tight! If I'm going too hard bite my ear, and keep that coat out of the wheel. Don't burn your legs – the exhaust gets to roasting – watch it."

"OK. Chocks away," she shouted, cheerfully. Lydia waved briefly as we took off. The stables were empty, horses across the other side. We wobbled across to the gate then I let her rip.

"Where are we off to? You haven't said – I look like nothing on earth." Her screech just about carried above the engine's roar.

"The *races*," I shouted, turning my head.

"Oh Christ, not *Towcester? Hell!* They'll think I've escaped from Whipsnade."

"You look great – better than you did at Ascot!"

"They all know me, Franz. I can't go there." She shrieked even louder.

"They know you everywhere – what's the difference?" I bellowed.

"Oh God! OK! Towcester, here we come!" She laughed approval. I told her she looked like Amy Johnson – she had my spare goggles on. The journey was uneventful, if on the fast side. She was near-ecstatic at what was apparently a new experience. We cruised into the car-park where the attendant recognised her instantly, despite the unorthodox rig. He pointed us to a prime spot. She fluffed up her hair, painted on more lipstick, shaking herself vigorously into shape. I fumbled for dosh but the gate-man on 'Members' quickly ushered us in, waving aside my offer with disdain, then bent so low his bloody bowler fell off! With relief, I slid the cash back into my pocket. Sara grabbed me by the arm as if she owned me, and we set out to give the bookies a trimming.

She had the luck of the Devil – four winners out of six – first three on the trot. Buffs treated her with spontaneous, if deferential, gaiety. Proof they'd heard of, maybe even witnessed, the indecent exposure that sent her rocketing up the ratings. Her flamboyant garb lent a roisterous air to goings on, shocking traditionalists into disapproving shakes of the head. In the Members' bar she held court to a clutch of young, and middle-aged admirers, anxious to learn the secrets of her punting success. After her third coup she caused an even bigger stir, offering to mark their cards at a quid a go, and she got plenty of takers at that. All the time she chatted about nothing in particular, ensuring I wasn't left out of things, and making plain my position as chaperone went unchallenged. She handed me a fistful of notes 'for the next stake'. I wasn't broke, but welcomed the added security.

Sara was that odd creation, on the face of it loud and ostentatious, yet at the end of the day giving far more pleasure than offence. She was several inches shorter than me, as were most women, and had to look up all the time as she waffled on. I was well over six foot now, but mercifully, at my peak.

Comparison with Estelle was inevitable. Most of the girls I mixed with were what we call ordinary, so to date *two* denizens of Bradbury Hall (three counting Lydia), was an 'exclusive'. Both from the privileged class, yet totally, bewilderingly, different, Estelle deep as the ocean, Sara light as thistledown. She was terrific fun, enthusing about all that went on in that plain, homely enclosure, where the real stars had four legs! 'I should do this more often! You clot, you can't find a Sara under any old stone. It'll be the rubbish-tip for you tomorrow.' Certainly her presence made the day. Delicious icing on an otherwise ordinary cake.

Memory of the garden party came back to haunt me. 'Where's the spite that fairly sizzled that night? The jealousy, the rivalry, the provocation – the nastiness? The ebullience still shows. So does the wit and warmth.' I felt guilty as hell.

My biased views of that disastrous evening sat awkwardly. But nothing would alter my love for Estelle, though I couldn't see Sara trading in the man she loved just to enhance her status. Light-headed – we'd downed several Griggs-Downley specials – I concluded Sara passed the judge with her nose just in front.

All too soon the day ended. We clung to each other as we weaved our way back to the bike. She climbed up behind, bouncing on the pillion to soften it up. She waved gaily to fellow race-goers who were busy tearing up their losing tickets as they drifted back to the car parks seeking their chariots, and ruefully counting the cost. We circled the perimeter then turned and headed for Northampton, happy as pigs in you-know-what. The excursion had been a huge success. BUT – Francis must watch his step. The intimacy of both girls was wholly fortuitous – so, in a way, was the 'link' with Lydia.

'Daft ideas' as Mum regularly warned, 'lead to trouble!'

The constraints of a rural existence are well chronicled, characterised by an absence of transport. In the Thirties, it was impossible to be other than parochial, even owning a motorbike. And strange things happen. Class barriers do collapse, from time to time. Woman meets man, and man must have his mate... mind you, darkness helps!

"I had you down as a dull dog, Frank," Sara whispered. She'd dropped the Franz. "Sorry, old chap!" She kissed my ear, twice, then bit me on the neck. I'd pulled in the entrance to Bradbury drive. Swift and sure she ran her febrile hands over every inch of my bundled-up torso, lingering at vital venues, before clambering down.

"My legs are burning. Switch her off, do." I obeyed, closed the throttle, raised my goggles, pulled the bike on to its stand, then thanked her for a grand day out.

"My pleasure," she giggled, as I stretched my legs to restore the circulation. It was just about dark. She tugged off her hat, bent over, shook her head from side to side half a dozen times, her hair falling loose around the waist.

"Am I allowed to kiss you?" I asked, teasingly.

"You certainly are – I'll debag you if you don't." She opened her coat wide – roomy as a chief's wigwam. Her bosoms rose rapidly, making the shaggy old jumper quiver.

"Estelle would have a fit if she could see us!" She laughed, a brittle hee-haw, pulling me inwards, grabbing my neck like she did on the dance-floor, hanging on in a kiss that had me struggling to measure up.

"Would she?" I replied, absently. Stella was worlds away. Sara was *here,* alive, warm, and willing.

"Why do you hate Estelle?" I whispered, afterwards. I eased my grip, kissed her eyelids.

"You would too if only you knew! If you knew *half.*" Try as I would to wangle more out of her, she refused to enlarge on the cryptic, even sinister, remark. She didn't give a hint of what she was getting at, but the remark would stick!

"Well, what about Noel? What about him? Have you warned him? It's Noel she's marrying – not me, Sara."

"A thousand times... Oh, change the subject, Tallboy!"

"Sorry... I want to see you again, Sara. You're great fun. What's more, you're extremely pretty!"

"Well, of all the stilted, sickly-sweet, snivelling suckers, you take the bloody biscuit! Extremely pretty, am I? Tell me you love me, tell me I'm fab, tell me I'm mustard, but Jesus, don't tell me crap like that! Just as I'd decided you ain't such a dreary after all!"

"Come to Poppa, darling! You're the bees-knees, the cat's whiskers, you're every cliché in the book, and I love you. Does it make your eyes water?"

"That's better... much better." She clung to me, eager, abandoned, crazed with passion again, thrusting her body to mine, enveloping us in that great rug of a coat that would have shrouded Mont Blanc. Words were superflous.

"I'd better be off, Sara. Thanks for a wonderful day. We must do it again sometime. And, at the risk of more insults... you're most kind!"

"Kind, nothing! I'm a bitch. All women are bitches... and some bite more than others! Don't worry, I'll not bite you." Upon which odd note she rocked with laughter. She was in top form, but disappointed at 'breaking up early'. I walked her up the long, impressive drive, where lofty cypress trees stood sentry the whole way. The Hall looked different from this angle, against the heavy, clouded sky.

"Till soon, then. Goodbye, Sara."

"Farewell, Tallboy." She went through the white door in the south-facing wall, turned and waved, once. It was as good as dark. I stood for a minute taking in the massive outline, and the tall chimneys. To me, architecture is a closed book, so I can only tell you roughly how the place looked (and felt), on that unique occasion. I didn't expect Count Dracula, then again, nor did I count on Miss Earnshaw... that's the kind of edifice it was, not creepy, but awe-inspiring, and solid, and real. I was too taken with Sara to dwell on all she'd told me, but her opinion of Estelle was scarcely reassuring. I dismissed it for the time being, murmuring to myself 'they're all barmy down here, and I'm as bad!'

I wondered how Lydia had fared at Rushmore? Had the Colonel enjoyed his outing? I hoped so. Were Aunt Pen and Freda still on the scrounge?

As I kicked the starter and turned for home, a flock of birds passed silently across the dim horizon to the west, headed in Cuckoo-pint direction, but not to roost for they were plovers. When plovers fly late they're the last birds you'll see that night. They eventually sleep on the ground.

Being five quid to the good gave me a warm, satisfied feeling.

Where earlier the keys to Bradbury's secrets lay with the vagaries of wartime, so now my thoughts did a switch. There was nothing in Sara's manner to suggest venom when she touched on Estelle's 'oddness'. She only skimmed the defects, glad to give the subject a rest. Yet... they were undeniably enemies. Ponder though I did, no explanation presented itself, the speculation fruitless. But this was no mere difference of opinion between two opposites. It went deeper than that. If Estelle was around, Sara wasn't. Yet they lived beneath the same roof – *Estelle's* roof! But only at holiday time. Estelle's disdain for Sara was total. Something big must trigger the antipathy.

By degrees, Bradbury cooled off. No longer crammed with 'guests' like an Open House of elegance and fashion, its people were aging. Not markedly, but inexorably, the years took their toll. With George sidelined, though still hopping around, confounding his medicine man, Lydia suffering that 'awkward' age, the steam to generate the whirligig of earlier years had evaporated. Estelle gone, Justin a memory, Noel deep into study, Rupert rarely on display, Martin 'working' for a change, or busy at the Sales, looking for yearlings and broodmares in his ever more determined, if vastly expensive pursuit of the jewel of racing – the Derby. Aunt Pen and Freda had gone back to minister to the demands of Uncle Horace, fresh from his latest junkets in Switzerland... Or was it just a quiet spell? Lydia couldn't live without spice! And, luckily for me, Charles couldn't live without beer!

The magic of Bradbury would never lessen for me, but, like the rest, I grew older. And I worked harder, determined to be a credit to a profession I'd begun to enjoy, though adamant I'd never wear a wig.

Sometimes I'd wonder if Mum might marry again? She didn't age! Maybe the emptiness of her staid existence was imagination? Life didn't look much of a carousel, but more and more she took over the flower garden, indulging her fancies with inspired taste and at the end of the day with immense satisfaction as well.

194

Ours became the chocolate-box cottage of a townie's dream. Roses round the door, and all that. Mistletoe in the apple-trees, honeysuckle crawling over the hedgerows. She seldom mentioned the Grant-Wiltons these days. My diligence at Sangsters must have given her great satisfaction. Her chief moan was how little I saw of Grandad – but she was round there most mornings herself, weather permitting, so she kept me in the picture on his aches and pains, and on his own horticultural achievements. For a time I was tempted to mention Sara, but resisted the urge, and I wasn't expecting a saga! Sara could never take Stella's place, however low she set her sights. But where had all the punters gone? Were they sleeping – or blind?

Then doubts would arise. All the 'what-ifs' of a callow youth, franchised or otherwise. And Sara had me by the unmentionables. 'She's bound to boast of conquering the paper-boy the minute Estelle turns up. And Lovely Lydia – *she* knows I'm infatuated. Whose side's she on? Whose indeed?' The uneasy, if big-headed suspicion that Lydia might fancy more fun and games confused things further. I'd never face the truth of Estelle's betrothal to nauseating Noel Fawcett. And he was Sara's brother...

When I looked in the mirror at a face fast maturing, though growing no prettier, not that good a replica of either parent, I'd put on a stern expression and ask myself, 'Where's the bloke who boasted of putting paid to Stella's wedding? What's happened to him? Lost his bottle? The will to win? Was it only infatuation after all? The love of a headstrong misfit?'

"YAH... No guts! Loser! *Loser!*"

I'd shake my head in disgust, kid myself it was all a dream – it brought little comfort. Then suddenly they ran up the flag! Estelle was back at Bradbury. Minus Fawcett the younger. Minus friends. Minus relations. Minus everybody. The noble Charles came across with the welcome news, and the crafty old devil had known all along why I plied him with so much beer. Aware I was irrevocably hooked at the Hall. How could he not – seeing I was a 'guest' at odd times? He was the soul of discretion... I was seriously indebted to the man.

It must have seemed quiet for Stella, with not just the regulars thinned out, but friends and hangers-on as well, though the place was by no means empty. Henry soldiered on, doing his best to turn things around and square the accounts, though quite what he did, apart from that, nobody knew. Ada continued to oil the wheels, now the proud owner of a Morris Eight. Only a week earlier she'd fetched her ageing mother from Kettering station, for a 'short stay'. Alan Stewart – the man with a gun – continued to peg away at his chronicles of large-scale warfare – presumably. He'd taken on a female researcher, also 'living in'. George kept mostly to the gunroom, or his beloved snug, though he'd take a turn in the paddock, weather permitting, or potter about the stables and the gardens – but never at the front. When the pain got to be too much he crawled to bed.

If jollity beckoned, the younger element were still sharp enough to rustle up a handful of playful makeweights – so long as they weren't Farndonites! Cupboard love endureth.

Not merely did Stella come to Bradbury – she came to Rose Cottage as well! Mum was at morning service – leaving Francis to watch the (anticipated) dinner. The first I knew was the unmistakeable clip-clop of hoofs. By the time Maddy juddered to a halt, stretching his neck to nibble at the hedge, I'd caught Stella, jumping down. I held her tight, squeezed her half to death – pure magic.

"Franz... Ooh! Please! Let go, you fool, you'll crush me!" She looped the reins over the gate, patted Maddy's quarters, pulled off her gloves, as I hauled her down the path to where the roses rambled. I'd left the door open. Strangely hesitant, she crossed the threshold and stood with her bum to the fireplace, tapping her boots in equestrian fashion, eyes scanning a room where everything glittered though little was made of gold.

"Well! You're taller than ever! Is that supposed to be a moustache? Franz! It's horrid! Shave it off at once, or don't come near me." She dropped the stick, held out her arms, smiling. I kissed her hungrily. She clung tight, the lost hours forgotten, the lost years...

"Darling, I love you so much – where's Noel? What would he say?"

Cautiously we eyed each other. I stifled my surprise. She looked older, the face narrower, the jawline more pronounced. 'Of course! It's the hair!' She'd left it on some stylist's floor in Cambridge. But the eyes shone... large and luminous. The magic hadn't changed. No longer a handsome teenager, here was a beautiful woman. Stella had grown up. I felt more of an oik than ever. Like a budding painter seeing his first Augustus John. Sophisticates didn't figure on my list of friends – even in jumper and joddies. As so often, I was unfair to Estelle. She was totally unstuffy. Natural as a landscape, the poise ready-made. That's why I loved her.

"Stay to... er... lunch. Go on. Will you... *please?*"

"Where's Mrs Allner?"

"Church. She'll be home soon."

"Do you think she'll mind?"

"She'll be delighted... I promise... Estelle." I heard Mum's footsteps on the path.

"*Mum!! Mu-u-u-m...* Estelle's staying for dinner." Mum was 'prepared'. She'd spotted Maddy when she turned the street corner. I'd staked him out over the road, the verge being wide and grassy, taken off his tack and trundled him buckets of water the minute Stella said she'd consider staying. He was grazing quietly. Mum had time to gather her wits before coming in. She'd be glad Stella hadn't 'caught her in her rags'.

She carefully arranged her hymn-book in the sideboard drawer, unpinned her hat, eyeing our guest warily, doubts wrinkling her brow – but the handshake was warm and welcoming if proffered with surprise. Two pretty women – I loved them both. Mum nipped upstairs to change her Sunday best while I set the table for what promised to be the most romantic feast Rose Cottage had ever hosted.

"You must be excited by now, young lady – over the wedding?" Mum put out a feeler – but Stella didn't enthuse – or enlarge. She shrugged, implying a degree of indifference.

"I suppose I should be, Mrs Allner," was all she said, though an odd sort of grin twisted the pretty mouth, followed by a grimace.

"Come, come. It can't be as bad as all that!" Mum took the bull by the horns, it seemed to me. *I* daren't have asked.

"Of course not..." Stella murmured. "Life's life." With which cryptic utterance she dropped the subject. From then on things went with a swing. As ever, on the rare occasions guests were present, the food proved excellent, the joint, from a local-bred Lincoln Red, done to a turn (thanks to my attention and the indulgence of the Almighty who controlled the wind). Beef was half as dear as pork – lamb cost the earth – out of the question. Stella relaxed, and for her was almost garrulous. Mum was on a new plane! She fetched a bottle of her very best wine, elderberry, I remember, which Estelle supped with relish – so did I. As I look back on that simple, yet significant meal, I wonder why we aim for hurdles rather than settle for the level? Life's a mystery – it deepens with age. Odd snatches of the friendly exchanges I remember well, even Stella prodding and probing – a new act for her.

"How was I doing at Sangsters? Where did Mum pick up her ideas for the garden? Had I been to Lucans Pond any more? Did Sissons still guard the woods? Was Charles still a regular at the 'Blindon Arms'?" Then, strangest of all, "Had

Mum ever seen inside the Hall?" And the faltering response that had me flabbergasted – "On many occasions!"

I kept my cool, and I wasn't as startled as Estelle! She murmured, "Oh, good!" What she meant I've no idea... and I don't think *she* had. She rapidly changed the subject, albeit with aplomb. Mum had never mentioned that! Had she *worked* there? She couldn't have... Her people were business people. In trade!

"Will you live this way, afterwards, Estelle?" Again Mum shook me with her directness. It never occurred to me Stella would live other than at the Hall – which was daft, really.

"It depends. Depends on Martin. It seems he's expecting Noel to take over at Harborough – but where *he'll* live is anybody's guess – Bradbury, no doubt. It's closer to Headquarters – Newmarket. And further from his politics."

"Would you like that, Dear?" Mum's tone was silky.

"I'm easy," murmured Stella. "This pie is delicious."

'Dammit, Mum, lay off the bloody wedding!' The thought rankled. Telepathy did the rest. We moved to safer territory. I found myself staring at the engagement ring. Whether it was good, medium or Woolworth's, I'd no idea. I just knew it glittered!

I wanted to rip the damn thing off and flush it down the drain. We emptied the wine, and things ended on a happy note as Mum regaled us with plans for the Institute's summer fete. Stella had never looked lovelier – nor had my mother.

She stayed until tea, then, with reluctance, I geared up Maddy, and gave her a leg aboard. She looked down at me like she used to. I knew the love was still there. 'If only!'

"Thanks for everything Mrs Allner. See you tomorrow Franz. After tea... you know where. Bye." She squeezed her knees, and Maddy cantered off with relief.

"Don't forget to shave!" she cried, as she rode out of earshot. We walked slowly back indoors. It felt as if the sun had gone in. But tomorrow beckoned. Mum glowed with pride at the success of her efforts to 'do things right' – without any warning. Nothing was said, but I could tell she'd had a change of heart. How could she not love Estelle?

Next evening Stella *walked* up to Briarsdale. I was doubtful whether she'd turn up at all. It was ages since I'd had the pleasure of seeing her two days running. She pecked me on the cheek, then said, "Where shall we go?"

"*You* choose," I replied. She was charming, but cool.

"Alright – to Carolean then. Come on; through Tate's Meadow."

"Fine!"

We walked hand-in-hand along the thicket's northern edge, climbed the well-worn stile, wading through the long grass, careful to keep close to the boundary. All at once Stella turned and said, "You didn't tell me about *Sara Fawcett,* Franz! How long's this been going on? I'll be damned! I can't believe it..."

"Nothing's going on!" I protested. "I took her to the races, that's all. To Towcester. WHY?"

"I never thought..."

"That's your trouble – you never do!" I flamed.

"I'm jealous, blast it! Did she wear any knickers? I'm furious! I nearly didn't come. After *yesterday.* You promised you'd always be here for me. I *love* you, Franz. Always will. *Sara Fawcett...* and YOU!"

"You're impossible, Stella. I am human you know – it's years since I saw you. And you're spoken for – another man's prize – if you can call him a man."

I knew something was wrong when she came. Cool and sniffy, she had me thinking some clot at the Hall had upset her!

"Franz, you're the one person I've ever loved, including parents, relations, and all the rest. Don't go spoiling it. I can't help the way it's turned out. There are things I have to do, and I'll do them. I only feel natural when you're around. You understand me. Accept me for what I am, not what I ought to be. Can't you see – I don't have to *pretend* with you. Anyway, you'd hate me too if I had a face like a boot."

"There's no answer to that, darling. Sara's not as bad as they make out. She's great fun. Anyway, our trip was a spur-of-the-minute thing. And *she'll* marry some blessed Lord, so it's not important. Me? I'll stay a bachelor." My voice was quiet and even.

"Sorry... but I was upset. Mummy wasn't slow putting me in the picture, as you can imagine. They think I don't have feelings. When I'm here, with you, I feel so free. It's hard to explain. The world stops hustling."

"I can't see *you* leading a peaceful life – with anybody!"

"I was reared on conflict! Born to it – that's me. It's still the same, cant and can't, the story of my life!"

"WHY? For goodness sake, Stella. It's been like that ever since we met! Why, why, *why?*"

"I'm one of the great unwashed Franz – I think that's how they put it – I *wasn't wanted!* Now you know!" We were passing Primrose Holt, the bushes bursting out, borders lush with new greenery, hazel forming, chestnuts too, soon there'd be acorns, and beechmast.

I stopped dead, caught her arm, held it tight, stared into those great big eyes, shouting, "WHAT?"

"They didn't want me, Franz. I'm a *mistake* – on legs!"

The blood flooded my head. My ears buzzed. I began to sizzle. How *much* did she know? Was the truth about Dad coming out? It couldn't be! They wouldn't sink that low.

"How... er... how do you know, Estelle? *Tell me*, for God's sake."

"There's not much to tell, really. Kids always know when they're not wanted!"

"You mean they don't love you? Is that what you're saying? *Is* it? *Is* it? *That's* why you loathe Bradbury, then? Hate the goings-on? Despise the others? Oh *Estelle... Darling.*

No wonder you're bitter! *That's* why you're marrying Noel Fawcett... isn't it? *Isn't it?*"

"That's right! Swapping dependence for a new dependence," she said, wryly, following the comment with a cynical cackle.

"It torpedoed the family – *my* arrival! Sent them off course with a bang! Triggered the wildness, the jollity, frivolity, partying, the madness – all a front, Franz! Mummy apparently went loony, but I blamed the war when I was old enough to think. And you can guess the shape *Daddy* was in. He didn't come home until long after Armistice, then he was only half-fit. But somehow they made a go of things, though no little sisters came along!"

It didn't sound like Estelle talking. The jarring mix of sarcasm and sadness was like a stranger holding forth. *But she didn't mention my Dad.* She didn't question her pedigree. She didn't know THE WORST. What a relief! A glimmer of light on a far from sunny day. And she'd lived with the ugly revelations since she was old enough to comprehend. The moment she could walk and talk, the clouds descended. There was no doubt she was telling the truth – as she saw it – which amounts to the same thing as far as cause and effect go.

Yet in a way, sad though it was, I was glad it was out – provided the deadliest bit of all stayed buried. How she'd missed out on *that* I couldn't begin to guess. The gods *were* kind, after all...

There, beside the great woods we both loved, I took her in my arms and held her tight, determined never to let go; but she was undaunted. The shoulders didn't sag, tears didn't roll, the chin still firm and jaunty. Her courage made me want to bow and scrape, then wage war on the culprits. A handful of cogent comments had wiped out doubts that had haunted me for years. Her resilience was uncanny. We carried on to Carolean in good spirits. She didn't refer to Sara Fawcett once! I took care to avoid thorny issues – with Stella around, the world could get stuffed.

But I was far from the street-wise character my scribblings might suggest. Thoughts of Noel *making love* to Stella wrenched my guts from their moorings! I tried to blank out the scenario. Tried to be a smoothie – cool, broad-minded – but to fool oneself is bloody hard. The thoughts were unbearable when I held her close. I understood why men commit murder – and *hara kiri*!

But I kept the darkness at bay. The pleasure of Carolean, though buried under mountains of greenery, and the joy of being together at the Lodge, worked their magic as always, and somehow I stifled my anxiety to learn when the darkest day would dawn – wedding-day! But the target date was vital if I were to fulfil my arrogant ultimatum!

Chapter Fourteen

The Legacy

With Stella gone I felt it time to pay Lydia a visit. Nothing to lose now. Nothing the Grants said or did could mess up my life as much as the forthcoming wedding. I'd catch her on the hop, and this time, *I'd* call the tune – I was man enough now to get down to nitty-gritty. Common sense told me things were more complicated than she made out, a lengthy agenda on the cards. I was so maddened by Stella's revelations nothing else mattered – 'outlawing' her topped the bill, wedding-date next.

Lydia was surprisingly civil, and that steadied me. Shooing me to the conservatory she confided, "The nosey devils won't see us here." She flashed me that wicked smile – same old Lydia – in a red, figure-hugging dress but little else apart from make-up. Nodding me to a wicker chair, she hitched up the dress as if scared she'd explode, and spread herself the other side of the little cast-iron table, legs apart, her face expectant. We overlooked the immaculate south-facing gardens.

"Well... none of the horny stuff this time, Franz."

I coughed, and went red. A Saturday afternoon, I'd cried off cricket. Her saucy gambit struck an awkward note, but I stuck to my guns.

"It's personal, Mrs Grant-Wil... er... Mrs... You know I *love* Estelle! Worship her. I intend marrying her – one day." She nodded. She didn't bother to answer, nor did she protest. That made it harder. She could at least have mentioned Sara...

"Well... go on, then," she murmured, frowning, the bright blue eyes losing their brilliance.

"Stella's not a Grant-Wilton at all, is she?" I blurted, John Blunt style. The lady winced, squirmed a little. The seductive features darkened.

"No... She's not! But you already know that, don't you?"

"Yes, but..."

"But what?" Her eyes widened, the sensuous lips quivered, the woman was palpably afraid and to me that was uncanny. The last thing expected. I was embarrassed. I hesitated, but carried on, "You seduced my father – like you did *me*... didn't you? A ghastly silence followed the bald indictment. Taking time to collect herself, she drew up her legs, rested her elbows on the tiny table, pushed the curls to one side, stared me straight in the face and spelt out with great deliberation.

"He *raped* me – the bastard! He was crazy! *Barking mad...*"

"Oh... Oh, God. Hell... You're lying. *You must* be. You *are*... No... you're not!"

She *wasn't*. What she said was gospel. At times you know! And nobody could lie like this! I believed her – absolutely. He did rape her – Stella was the fallout! No wonder her arrival was anti-climax. That's why it signalled battle stations. You could hardly blame the Grants! I could have wept – and me a man. Not wept for Lydia – for *Stella*, for myself, for Mum, for... yes, for Dad as well. 'How many know the truth? Just who does know?' My head spun... nobody answered.

"He was a pig, Franz. You're nothing like him – don't worry." She got up, edged round the tiny table, stroked my neck, cooing gently, then bent and held me tight. Somehow I got to my feet, welcoming the embrace. My shame was total. Pride in Dad shattered. 'He was dirt. A right turd.'

"You want the full story I suppose, though there's not much to tell – thank goodness." She tightened her hold, stroked my mop. Despite the bombshell I began sweating.

"Please..." I muttered. 'I must tough it out. No point papering over the cracks – not now.'

She went back to her chair – that surprised me. I pulled myself together as best I could – after the worst broadside ever – bar Stella's engagement. Right out of the blue. Undreamed of. Talk about a knockout...

She stretched across the table with surprising kindness, held my hands, her face a mix of emotions, the lipstick smudged, making her look almost childlike.

"Don't upset yourself, Franz. It's better you know – you can judge for yourself. He buggered-up everybody's life..."

"Tell me... tell me everything." I rubbed my eyes, sat up straight, looking at her with the next best thing to craven humility.

"I already knew your father, of course, from looking after our tack – for the hunters as well as the Shires. I liked him. We all did. He was an excellent craftsman – his work top-class. Anyway, you've heard about Bradbury, and the threats to turn it into a hospital, I'm sure?" I nodded.

"After frantic appeals to George, poor devil, to come home and sort things out, to my surprise Mr Allner turned up, got in touch with Sangsters, came to see me several times, and between us we worked a miracle. Don't ask for details – I just don't know. The Ministry finally settled for Groby Manor, run down as it was, provided we did some improvements. God, were we relieved!" She brushed away a tear, bit her lip.

"I'll bet you were!"

"The last time he called, the night before he was due to sail, everything changed. Early evening, I was alone, in the drawing-room. As usual, I invited him through. When he sat beside me I didn't give it a second's thought. We had a drink, we talked, I thanked him for his efforts, and wished him well. Everything was normal.

Then it all went wrong. It happened – suddenly. No warning. He was vile – but sober. An *animal!* Crazed. I fought and fought... I screamed. Nobody came... it's a big place. He even rested, taunted me, ridiculed me – then raped me again. He showed no mercy. No feeling. Just lust. He had no excuse. A lovely wife – your mother – nothing to justify his bestial assault – nothing! Had he been drunk I might have understood. I'm *glad* he died – so was George when he learned the truth. I never got over it. Life was a nightmare... I know what it means to live on the edge. I'm not proud of my record – I'm not ashamed either. *Something* messed up my hormones – you understand? You *know* me Franz... don't you?"

I forced a smile. She had the guts to grin back.

"Yes," I said, "I *know you.*"

"You're a handsome young devil – so was Robert."

"People aren't kind to you, Mrs Grant. They're unfair – I was. They don't know the truth – apart from a handful here, in the Hall? They know – I suppose?"

"*Some* do. Some *don't.*" She shook her head, dismissed it, discussion too painful. At odd moments, especially when she looked down, she was so like Estelle I felt awkward, confused – and guilty as hell. I thought of Stella's pedigree. By Robert Allner out of Lydia Beamish! 'No wonder she's complicated. Schizophrenic, almost. But brave, lovable, compassionate... on the flipside.'

"I suppose you didn't... you hadn't... you hadn't kind of *led him on?*" I had to be doubly sure she didn't trap him, despite the protests, and the grieving. The complications were awful – 'give a dog a bad name...' And Lydia's name stank. She was scarlet from the day she arrived... *some* knew. Part of the baggage, and she'd suffered ever since. Pillorying Lydia came naturally.

I pictured myself in the Colonel's shoes when she told him Dad raped her. Staff-Sergeant Allner – his trusted aide, who led the fight to keep Bradbury independent. George's career lay in Allner's hands. His credibility as Officer and Gentleman rested on Allner's discretion. 'An NCO of the highest standard – Robert Allner. Rape Lydia? Not on your life. He couldn't have...'

"I wouldn't lie to *you*, Franz – on something this delicate. No, there was never a question of encouraging him. Nothing like that ever came up. Until that night I had him down as straightforward... and trustworthy. The bloody war warped his mind – it warped everybody's mind. Don't dwell on it, and don't go telling your mother. Let sleeping dogs lie. Poor devil, he paid his debt to society, if not to me!"

"You didn't mind me coming? I'm sorry. If only... nothing like that crossed my mind. Dad's always been my hero. Mum's done her best to keep up the pretence... that's if she knows?"

"She knows alright, I assure you. George'll confirm that. Glad to, I'll bet."

"How is the Colonel, Mrs Grant? I like him."

"Oh, he copes fairly well. Some days better than others, but altogether he's not that bad. Ada thinks he's improved – so does Doctor French, and he's the one who counts. We just keep hoping..."

"Oh. That's good. Some day, when he's better, I'm going to have another talk with him – he asked me to – any time."

"He'd like to see you, I'm sure – let us know when you're coming, to be on the safe side, eh?"

Steam-rollered, I left Bradbury Hall knowing things couldn't get worse. The warnings, the orders, to shun the now-sombre pile with its cranky 'inmates' returned to mock me with relentless malice. For years I'd been tied, one way or another, to this Gothic giant. Come to love it, hate it, to mistrust it, and I'd never free myself of its baleful influence, nor from the dubious bent of its non-conformist, if colourful inmates. Mum's words of long ago drifted back, "Steer clear of that lot down there!"

Who was right – Mum or the Bradbury clique? Maybe guilt on both sides? I cursed my impotence. My failure to cut the mustard, and get to grips with the sinister, yet magnetic lure of the impenetrable set-up. In reality though, what were the ties? Were they imagined? A case of scotched ambition? So Sparkling Sara was a dainty dish to set before anybody, let alone a king... but more likely to end up a Griggs-Downley than an Allner! Not that I nursed marital ambitions in that direction. And Stella could never be mine – unless, maybe, second-hand?

Beyond these two attractive, confident young women, my links were really slight, and both would end up with a guy sporting a handle, not wed to an erstwhile paper-boy. But I'd entered this fantasy world with eyes wide open. It was *always* fairyland. My own bloody fault. Nobody begged me to fall for Estelle! Fortunately, the damage wasn't irrevocable – or so I imagined.

But the bloody place did for my Dad!

For ages I re-lived the horror of Lydia's revelations. I thought of little else. Nobody to turn to, on this, the most serious challenge of my sheltered, and to onlookers, uneventful existence.

I don't need to spell out the gravity. 'If Mum knows, she's lived with the knowledge for years. If she doesn't, the subject is obviously taboo. To think, on occasions, I'd carped at Stella's quirky behaviour. Baulked at the swing-high, swing-low moods punctuating our affair. Behind that confident exterior raged a spirit plagued with doubt – no wonder she means to marry young Fawcett. I assumed normal offspring don't derive from the crime we call rape. What a prat.'

When I turn and read what I have already set down, it's hard to believe these happenings were mere sidelines in my daily grind to become a law-man. I worked damned hard, ploughing through correspondence courses, beavering away at the 'tech' every night, determined to gain more stars, taking on ever more important briefs, gaining the confidence I'd need, and the knowledge to go with it. No short cuts. Academic achievement alone works the oracle – intuition just helps. Sherwood made sure I kept plugging, though there were times when he must have despaired of me, and my inclination to woooden-headedness, when my mind could only wander.

But work's a great healer. It keeps your mind on the road – and clear of the potholes.

For a time I gave up nosing about for Bradbury tit-bits, content to let *them* come to *me*. Thoughts of rifling Claud's den died down, and Alice had gone off me completely – thank goodness. I thought of the characters who'd offered me 'second hearings'. Claud, for a start... then Sir Martin – *he* said he'd talk to me later, in this very office, but hadn't obliged. More to the point the Colonel's deterioration had denied me that vital avenue. 'Could it be there's nothing to discover? Is that the answer?' I'd long since realised Mum was right – delving into the past brings nowt but sadness... and disillusion. Are there no joyful secrets? Ah... they wouldn't be secrets unless... and cupboards wouldn't shelter skeletons!

People nod sagely, tell you to 'live your own life', but nothing of the sort comes about. Life just travels alongside, designed mostly by others. We might organise the odd thrill – but that's about all. We spot the pitfalls too late.

An inspired spell followed. I stood back and took a long look at things – with an (almost) open mind. What a bloody young fool I'd become. When deciding the eternal enigma had military connotations, I'd overlooked the obvious. Bradbury's secrets were *already there – before the war began!* When Dad was in civvy street, George a Territorial, Fawcett a 'Reserve' and MP ordinaire, with Sangsters doing the business.

Gosling earmarked me as his next assistant, should my latest results 'prove pleasing'. Sherwood whispered this tit-bit soon after Lydia's 'confessional'. I should have been delighted – in a way, I was. For a change, something good to tell Mum. I'd hidden my dismay at Dad's defection pretty well... from Mum. She'd got her burden. I was tempted to try Grandad again, but inevitably it would get back to Mum; so pointless. I'd seen nothing more of the mercurial Sara... but I wouldn't, unless I woke up. Somehow, though, I felt it time Bradbury took a back seat – unless the wedding loomed.

Every morning I'd scan *The Times*, going straight for forthcoming marriages. The legal stuff had to come second. No way would the wedding go ahead without lashings of publicity – not with the Fawcetts involved. Third, I'd squint at the racing, to see the latest bauble Sir Martin had picked up on his costly, and highly optimistic route to the turf's Blue Ribbon. Then one miserable day I happened on Charles again – at Jack Rowell's shop. He looked more melancholy than usual, and he hadn't shaved. The gloomy news emerged. George St John Grant-Wilton had taken a turn for the worse. Confined to bed, receiving no visitors. Doctor French had made it clear it was only a matter of time, but hadn't told *George,* and hadn't said *how much time!*

Bang went the hopes of seeing him, discussing Stella's future, taking a peep at her past?

Boxing-Day 1938, George departed this earth, peacefully, in his sleep – as they say. He was sixty-two. Ada alone was at his bedside.

By some perverse decision, he was to be buried in the local churchyard – 29 December – in *Farndon* – where the Grant-Wiltons hardly dared to tread. The church was packed. With typical hypocrisy the locals filled the pews to overflowing. Dozens took up standing room at the back, crowding the vestry and propping up the font, in their anxiety to miss not so much as a single tear, or a troubled grimace, for an able and largely amiable man, whose lot was never easy, however good it looked.

I sat with Mum at the sad ceremony. Watched from the corner of my eye as the bereaved filed quietly into the jammed house of prayer, shuffling like disorganised geese as the coffin came to rest, and they sought their places. The ushers looked more bewildered than the mourners. I took in most of the relations, and the Bradbury regulars, but really I only had eyes for Estelle. She ignored the arm of Noel Fawcett, maintaining a stance of independence, until finally guided to the family seats, five pews ahead of Mum and me. Then, with great deliberation, she turned, eyeing the congregation with calculated coolness, until finally resting her gaze on me. She smiled wanly – that beautiful smile she reserved for special occasions. So I believed! Black suited her. So did every other colour... The solemnity of it all got to me that day. Somehow I felt involved, yet strangely remote. Mother was even worse, treating the whole business as a national tragedy – like the monarch had passed on.

It was rare to see a composed character like Mum fold – but sadness is contagious where the masses are concerned. After an uninspired address by the unlovely James Jackson, we stood, with due respect, until relations evacuated their ringside seats, then we ambled after them with that peculiar gait reserved for funerals, and shuffled to a vantage point to watch the interment, until the lead-players were back in their limousines, when we advanced in single file to take a peep at the lowered coffin. An irreverent thought crossed my mind '*My* Dad didn't get a fancy send-off like this! *He* got buried in a bloody sack!' The guilt that usually ensues after kicks at convention came over me. 'Ah well...' And Dad still comes top on the moss-covered memorial at the entrance to the village.

The minute I sat down next morning Stanley told me Claud Sangster was not merely present, but awaiting my pleasure. I came down to earth with a wallop.

"Go on in Francis – he's waiting." Alice, as usual, nodded her head, as women do, towards Claud's door, like she was showing me the Taj Mahal.

"Mornin', young Allner," he growled, in ultra-serious fashion, as he put a match to his large cigar.

"Er... Good-morning, sir." I was uneasy, my palms sticky, I wriggled uncomfortably on the edge of the leather-padded chair.

"This is private business. It has fallen to me to pass on to you, as soon as is reasonably convenient, which means now, this package relating to the estate of the late George St John Grant-Wilton."

With a touch of importance he slid the package across the oversized desk. It wasn't a parcel as such, but a business envelope, signed across the flap, sealed and dated. It screamed VI. The front bore the simple legend, 'For Francis Allner'.

"Find somewhere quiet, shut yourself in, and read every word. I'll give you an hour, then come back here." I gave the Hippo a nod.

"Yes, sir. Thank you."

Apart from the strong-room, where people were always in and out, and the post-room, which suffered the same shortcomings, I was stuck. I knew it was vital to be alone... Claud's manner told me the package was dynamite. *Bradbury* dynamite. What the hell could it be? I solved the first puzzle in seconds, scooting round to *The Gazette*, a quick word in Harry Paten's ear, then I dived into their archives. Two empty rooms, two empty desks. With shaky hands I broke the seal, and snatched out the contents. The document was typed – well, the text was. Names, subject matter, date, and all the rest were in Indian ink. I reproduce the details below:

Bradbury Hall
Farndon
Northants

2 December 1938
For Francis Allner.
Francis
    My MO, the esteemed Doctor French, makes it abundantly clear my days are numbered.

Before I go it is essential that what you are about to learn is conveyed in conventional manner, by *me*, and *only* by me.

Your love for Estelle is well known, so it will come as a relief, or *something* of a relief, to know she is neither your sister, nor your half-sister. That sounds strange, but has the merit of plainness.

She results from a liasion between Robert Allner and Lydia Grant-Wilton (*née* Beamish).

But something of which you are totally unaware, follows. Brace yourself, young man, for *your* paternity is a matter in which I understand your mind has never been exercised. Get ready...

You are the result of a brief affair between myself, George, and your mother, Agnes. I beg of you, do not judge your mother harshly, do not condemn her, do not sit in judgement *at all!* You will for ever regret your actions if you do.

Think of the trauma when she discovered her much-loved husband had violated my wife, Lydia. *Not* from provocation, but in unforgivable, brute fashion.

You, my boy, are turning out a son I could have loved, had circumstances been different. I leave your judgement of *me* to be mulled over at leisure. When I found Lydia pregnant, by *your* 'father', when I came on leave (the dates you will be aware of), on top of the rumpus about 'the Hall' becoming a hospital, for a while I was out of my mind. But it was left to me, and me alone, to acquaint your mother with the gruesome details. For obvious reasons, secrecy was of the essence.

You will understand from this statement, there is no legal barrier, nor for that matter, a barrier of any kind, to prevent a marriage between yourself and

Estelle. On this issue you must fight you own battles, although I concede the odds are heavily in favour of Noel Fawcett. At this stage I am too weary to go into detail about the Fawcett links to Bradbury. Doubtless you will find out. By the way, I'm aware you have *always* fought your own battles, ably seconded by a wonderful mother.

Now we come to the meaty bit. I am by no means a wealthy man, but funds are always available to live in some style, and keep the flag flying, for which I confess I owe a good deal to my erstwhile Commander, Martin Fawcett.

It is my dearest wish to provide for *you,* somehow. Your mother is secure, if not in cash, in kind. Your love for my estates is borne in mind, and I leave part of the woodlands to *you,* in perpetuity. Funds are provided for them to be managed as you see fit. This is all confirmed in the official will, and you will become the sole owner of three areas, Bluebell Thicket, Primrose Holt and Chucklecopse, which together comprise Briarsdale. It is up to you whom you chose to share them with!

Affectionately yours

George Grant-Wilton

Witnessed by me – Ada Barlow. 2 December 1938.

The fine-quality parchment was crumpled and sticky, where I'd clutched it in horror, indignation, astonishment... and thanksgiving. I trembled as I wrestled to take it all in, the conflict of emotions indescribable. But towering above all was Stella's pedigree. The Colonel, I felt sure, had done his best to give me a chance to run Noel Fawcett close.

But *Mum* must be faced. And Lydia. For now it was back to Claud Sangster – within the hour. And *he* knew what this incredible document contained – better than *I* did. *He* drew it up. He supplied the words. But the Colonel formulated the substance! Colonel George St John Grant-Wilton of Bradbury Hall. *MY FATHER!*

I rubbed my eyes hard. They must have been bloodshot. Somehow I forced the envelope into my inside pocket, shouted "Thanks" to Harry, making sure he didn't get a good look at me, then shot back to the office.

Claud was indulgent. He smiled benignly as I settled on the hot-seat.

"Read it then, Allner? Take it in? Well... What do you think?"

"I... I really don't know, sir. Is it real? Is it as straight-forward as it looks? *Am* I his son? *Am* I a landowner? Is mother... Is my mother... Is she? *What* is she?"

"It's all real. It's all true. I can vouch for that. Go home and think about it, lad. And jolly good luck to you. I suppose I'll lose you?"

"Er... I don't know about that, Mr Sangster. Thank you. In time I'll take it all in."

I beat it home fast, my head spinning, ticker in overdrive. But deep down I knew I'd never look Mum in the eye. 'Would she look *me* in the eye?'

At full-throttle I concentrated on driving, but Mum's early warnings kept on coming back. "Steer clear of Bradbury." And I marvelled at the simplicity with which the Colonel had set out his bequest – not like the double-Dutch we used in the office. No legal wizardry, no 'last will and testament' gobbledegook! 'Anyway, this isn't a will – it's *my inheritance.*'

No point hanging around, I went straight home. As usual Mum was through in the kitchen, ironing on the edge of the scrubtop table, the connecting door open.

"What's wrong?" She looked up, surprised, first at me – then at my face.

"*This* Mum," I said, quietly, putting the package on the drop-leaf table. She stood the iron on end, came up the step to the living-room, gingerly picked up the envelope, eyeing the broken seal with suspicion.

"What is it?" she whispered, her eyes guarded; she wiped her hands on her pinafore. "What is it?" she asked again.

"Have a look, Mum," I murmured – stuck for something more adequate.

"Some of it's news to you – some isn't." I couldn't resist the snidery, and despite the warnings I could hardly shrug off a landmine.

"You'd better sit down. It's not all pleasant. It's new to me."

"To do with the Colonel, is it Francis?"

"Yeah."

"Oh..." She sat down, took out the document and read it through without comment. Not once did she look up. I sat opposite – not staring, just gazing. I'd remembered every word – I could read it upside down. There hadn't been time to ponder the likely impact on Mum – anyway, it had to come out, and it wasn't all bad, not by a long chalk.

"Well?" Slowly she raised her head after the perusal, looking at me with a cool detachment that not only surprised me, but relieved me too. Her eyes were neutral. "It's all true... is it Mum?"

"It's true, Francis. I prayed you'd never find out, but I suppose it was inevitable so long as we lived around here. I've done wrong but I've had your well-being in mind ever since!"

"Why do you hate Estelle? It doesn't make sense!"

"Robert disgusted me. He destroyed my life – life as I knew it. I'm a hundred per cent prejudiced. Biased beyond hope. How do you expect me to treat the results of a union like that? It's brought nothing but misery. The girl's beginnings began a landslide."

On the verge of the biggest slanging match in history Mum kept her cool, and I kept my temper. It wasn't easy, and it wasn't pleasant.

When George first forced from Lydia the facts of her pregnancy, he swiftly sought out Mum. She knew something was sadly wrong when Dad cleared off in such a hurry, but put it down to the army, and his peculiar mission. He'd told her nothing – and his odd behaviour, on top of the clandestine excursions, hurt her as much as they'd bemused her. And Lydia's claim that he raped her was the last straw, leaving her in tatters. Like George, she was convinced Satan *had* taken over. Even the war lost centre stage. George insisted Mum accompany him to the Hall to hear Lydia's claims for herself. From the start it was clear she wasn't lying, though Dad's behaviour had been so out of character as to bring his sanity into question, but Mum had to agree that despite the contradictions, and his strange itinerary, his behaviour while home was never that of a nutter...

Naturally the rape wrote him off in Mum's eyes, leaving two bewildered, betrayed, individuals. They sought comfort in each other, leaving Lydia to suffer in isolation – for a time. 'No wonder Mum knows Bradbury Hall – from the inside!'

"So you didn't try to find out what sent Dad up the wall? You accepted Lydia's version – and that was that! But then, so did I... er... I mean..."

"Of course I queried it. I was always asking myself 'why?'; it's no clearer now than it was then!"

"Couldn't the Colonel explain it? Was Lydia alright with you? Didn't she have any idea what set him alight?"

"Do you think I haven't gone over it a million times, and from every angle? Even now a day seldom passes without asking myself the same old questions."

"You say Dad was the same as always – *until that night?*"

"Well, more or less – yes! I knew something was on his mind – over and above the war, and he made no attempt to explain his visits to town or wherever – he caught the carriers' cart mostly. For the life of me I daren't tackle him. It obviously had to do with the Hall becoming a hospital because he was so often there – beyond that, nothing!"

"What did Grandad think to it all?"

"Same as me – he couldn't make head nor tail of it. Without his support I wouldn't be alive today. He was a brick – I'll never forget. As for George, he wasn't here long. I didn't see him again until well after Armistice, then only rarely, and despite looking reasonable, he was in no great shape underneath I can tell you!"

Mum remained unmoved. She was as composed as if talking village tittle-tattle. She'd learned the secrets of serenity. Not at all ratty, she threw the discussion wide open, determined everything come out. Yet there was something in her stillness? I shivered.

"Well... didn't you *ask* the Grants why they wouldn't give up the Hall and help the war effort? Dad must have wondered after he got here – do you reckon he found out and wasn't happy? He'd detest any lack of patriotism, selfish sods, having been in the line himself, along with the Colonel. You're sure George didn't confide in you?"

"Francis... nobody came up with a new slant! The questions had all been asked – and answered."

"Maybe they had, but not by the right people! That was vital if you were to even *suspect* his motives? You must have known something extraordinary set him alight – especially being sober – they drank lemon squash, for God sake! I asked! Dad didn't chase women... did he Mum?"

She smiled, the crowsfeet appeared, the dark eyes narrowed, little lines channelled around her mouth. She was genuinely amused, didn't bother answering, just shook her head as if I'd asked if he was a Mormon? For two pins she'd have exploded, despite the sombre situation. She'd known all right what she was talking about.

"Well, Mum, for all these years I reckon you and Grandad, and all the others, have sold Dad short! I tell you what... my opinion hasn't changed – no one iota! It did – for a time – when Missus Grant first told me!"

"Told *YOU?* She told *YOU? WHEN?*" Mum's composure went flying. Evidently she misheard my earlier admission. She sat open-mouthed. Her shoulders tightened, the guiders in her neck began quivering, her Adam's-apple shot up and down, the black eyes registered horror.

"A few weeks back. I don't remember – exactly."

"And you kept quiet?"

"I could hardly tackle *you* – or Grandad! Who else can I confide in? Tell me! Go on – tell me!" The bitterness surfaced at last – I was merciless.

A long silence followed... I went on, "So you still hate him, do you? I suppose you didn't even mourn when he got the chop? Did you *ever* love him?" Sick with rage, crazy, caustic, my attack was unjust, and unfair, but fairness didn't figure... at the time.

"Who knows what love is, Francis?" She'd simmered down. Once more cool and rational. She continued, "I've never taken a lover since. Since, you know... I've always had *you,* and I've done everything possible to keep your father's memory alive and untainted. I owed you that. I owed it to Robert as well. Once he was a good man, Francis – kind, generous, and honest, until... I've been foolish. I should have moved away years ago – but there was always Grandad. I couldn't leave him, and he'll never desert Farndon – his roots are too deep. But I wish to God I could have spared you the curse of Bradbury."

Chapter Fifteen

Skelmoor

Crisis time! Everybody I knew, everybody I loved, everything I cherished, had turned out flawed. Mum with feet of clay, Dad a lecher, Grandad a weakling – after all. And Estelle... well, *what* was she? They shoot deserters... in the army.

I ignored the pluses. The Colonel's generosity, Sangsters' support, Sherwood's kindness, Sara's affection, Charles's tit-bits (ignoring that six-month gap). Only the downside got a hammering – marrying Estelle mere fantasy.

'Which heads the list? Easy... Dad's performance. Unforgivable. Life's meaningless until that's sorted. With the Colonel gone, now's the time to give it a go. Chance, luck, fortune, call it what you like, solves most problems.' But the pointer registered nothing. Of all people, Grandad showed the way, an unwitting, unlikely informant. *He* raised the veil.

On a rare visit, I got him talking old times (he didn't need much persuading) – before the fall crippled him. We got around to his ancient craft, when he practiced his wide-ranging skills, with Dad just a learner. We roamed from stately establishments where hunting outshone all else, with stables holding pride of place, to more humble set-ups with no more than a couple of hacks of dubious pedigree. Cart horses didn't figure, they were commonplace. Sizeable farms like Barford's fitted somewhere in between. The more lucrative venues were given a proper going over.

Inevitably, Bradbury got more than a mention – and with it the Mistress – Lydia Beamish. He noted, albeit with some reluctance, how knowledgeable she was on veterinary matters, and how gifted at 'nursing'. Her mother was renowned for midwifery and had served as District Nurse for many years in a market-town near Rochdale. Lydia kind of grew up in the healing business. The fact didn't make an impression at the time, and was to Grandad a mere throwaway.

We sat in number one greenhouse, on a plank lodged between two chunks of tree-trunk, the ideal height for messing about with pot plants, cuttings, seedlings, *et al*, and for getting up and down without it giving him hell. There wasn't an inch to spare across the generous decking. He wore the same benign, if scholarly look, as when he talked football and cricket. Eyes bland and indulgent, cheeks smooth and baby-pink, iron-grey beard trimmed wedge-shape, he never lost his distinguished appearance – nor did he lose his grey hair. He prefaced his shrewd observations with an endearing, "I was reading only the other day..." Through the glass I could see raspberry-canes thriving, black currants and red currants budding, goosegogs starting to prosper, the fruit swelling, some colouring up. I'd planted most of them myself – under Grandad's guidance. He grew red-currants solely for the birds – it put them off raiding the black ones.

At times like this I tried to stifle my resentment at his jaundiced views on Bradbury. He wore the same leather apron, over the same checked trousers he'd worn when in going gear (so he said), and more than likely the same linen jacket. Somehow I felt a part of him – so relaxed conversation came easy, not like with strangers. Two days later I was mulling over some of his chatter when the word 'midwife' struck me. It had no special significance, yet it stuck like a song sticks in your head and nothing you do dislodges it.

That's when a link between midwifery and abortion began to form. An unlikely pairing maybe, but real – very real! I guessed what lurked – the Lydia connection. What else? Why didn't she turn to *Mummy* – get shot of her encumbrance? A wild, unlikely theory, but there nonetheless. And at the time it didn't seem *all that wild!* Birth, contraception, abortion – they share the same prelude – *SEX*.

The suspicions were so vivid, so compelling, the thoughts so convincing, I shook off a fast-developing lethargy, and started a crusade that would trigger events so bizarre as to revolutionise my life – and that of one or two others.

On the improbable pretext of going up to Manchester to see Lancashire play the Aussies, I convinced Mum I had nothing but cricket in mind – at least I believe so!

No mention of Rochdale – or of Skelmoor. On my first day free after deciding to go ahead I took the bus to town, picked up a train at Peterborough North, and by a deuce of a circuitous route finally steamed into a Crewe station rank with the stench of sulphur, pickled-onions and rotten eggs – the notorious junction where the whole world changes trains, or loses itself trying. Mum had whittled on at breakfast about missing my connections but luck was with me – I succeeded. I half wished I *was* off to Old Trafford – but cricket must take a back seat on this occasion though I was canny enough to study the teams, and soak up the comments of the pundits on the journey up. A credible alibi was essential... I'd felt devilishly guilty when Mum suggested Grandad might enjoy the trip – and I disagreed.

The journey was eminently forgettable on a dull, dreary day, but the forecast proved accurate, and by mid-morning a watery looking sun broke through – the match would at least get under way and give me some talking points – so long as I remembered the evening paper – that would be vital. I must make it home that night!

It was my first trip solo to the North West. When changing trains earlier, at a dismal, depressing 'New Street' station in Birmingham, I'd felt ridiculously young, unworldly and vulnerable, despite being six-foot and tipping the scales at twelve stone. I thought what a prat I was to embark on such a split-arse mission. The only sleuths I'd heard of were Sherlock Holmes and Bulldog Drummond; I couldn't see myself as either. What little confidence I'd drummed up sagged to rock-bottom. For two pins I'd have abandoned the whole ridiculous escapade, and buggered off home.

But I didn't – and the pale sun helped, though from Brum it was smoke all the way, and after gladly bidding farewell to Crewe what little optimism remained vanished in minutes. Rochdale did nothing to boost my confidence. The same dreary, back-to-back council semis bordering the track. The same tall, stark, sprawling, scab-walled factories where workers were no more than slaves. Drab, run-down, public baths stood out bleakly against the grey backdrop as if to suggest a wash would answer all the ills of man, whether he be on the dole or 'on the parish'. The sidings were clogged with the usual flotsam of the railways. The Lowry-like figures ploughing their weary way to wherever failed to inspire, and thoughts of the talented Miss Fields gracing the town brought little cheer. The station itself wasn't exactly inspirational.

I waited impatiently for the bus out to Skelmoor, pulling my coat tight, and tugging at the latest in a long line of cloth caps. Hardly the day for *cricket.* The egg-sandwiches Mum packed were a godsend. I wolfed them standing at the bus-stop.

After all the anxiety, and the many doubts, the venture proved easier than falling in the canal. The first pub I tried, on the first grubby little cobbled side-street, after clambering down from an old rattletrap of a bus, a dingy dive called 'The Square Bolt' told me all I needed to know. In an enormous smoke-filled, brick-floored, brick-walled, all-in-one public bar, smothered in gaudy posters for Bass and Worthington, Gold Flake, Shag, Park Drive and St Julien, I managed at last to park my arse on half an inch of Rexine settle, down a couple of pints of cheap, but first-rate bitter, and in time, join in some of the animated chatter. Fortunately, in here, and through a pink-tinted haze that only beer can conjure up, poverty looked far, far away – so did hunger.

All Skelmoor knew Connie Beamish! All *Lancashire!* Well... all the ones over sixty. And Connie was long dead. In her day she'd been 'Queen of the Pokers'. Her backstreet proddings elicited more gratitude and admiration than did all those years of unstinting, blue-bonneted service as 'The District'.

She'd saved girls by the score from poverty and shame, and had few scruples where she pursued her vital, if dubious sideline. It occurred to me the authorities wouldn't be too bothered about her ministrations. More likely glad of her clandestine visits to the mean cobbled streets, with her assortment of knitting-needles, crochet hooks and cotton wool, where infant survival at best was hit and miss, and the pleasures of youth were minimal.

But it wasn't for me to moralise, though I did go to the trouble of finding the cemetery and gazing at Connie's grave. Buried alongside husband, Cecil, she'd died in the late Twenties. 'So she was in going gear when Estelle was conceived! *Why didn't she rush down to Farndon?* Or, better still, *why didn't Lydia make a beeline for Skelmoor?* That would have made more sense. And why, for Pete's sake, didn't George orchestrate a move? Still time to abort the 'child' when he first learned the facts.'

I was so cock-a-hoop at apparent confirmation of my slender theory, the penny didn't drop – until later. Far from solving all mysteries I'd added to the list!

That fateful night in 'sixteen... a crazed, animal-like Robert Allner – a shrinking, half-terrified Lydia Grant-Wilton – the seed of an 'unwanted' Estelle. Yet *no abortion...*

'Why NOT? For Christ's sake *WHY NOT?*'

A death-sentence for Dad, the next-best thing for Grant-Wilton... nothing more to be learned.

By evening I was back in Rochdale. Taking no chances I grabbed a couple of evening papers at the station kiosk, and when the train steamed in was lucky enough to bag a compartment to myself. Pleased, and smug as buggery, I flung my cap on the seat opposite, put my feet on it too, then sat back and enjoyed the rare luxury of just letting my thoughts ramble. Things had gone well. I opened the *Echo* first and made a meal of the cricket, the scores, comments, averages, state of the pitch, and all the rest, until I could talk about the game with certainty, just as if I'd been there. Then I pondered what I'd *really* achieved? I hardly noticed the dismal countryside, and couldn't be bothered to even pull down the blinds as darkness fell.

I hadn't solved a lot – but I'd confirmed most of my suppositions. I tried picturing the days before I existed. Struggled to make sense of what could have gone on in that drawing-room of Lydia's. There was little scope for mental manoeuvre. The facts had been laid on the table a million times – though never by my *Dad.*

I thought about Lydia's early days. Took for granted there'd have been no inclination to 'get rid' of Justin! Connie would have been sufficiently shrewd to recognise a passport to the Grant-Wilton dynasty, even if it involved persuasion... And *Old* George would have seen to that! 'Goodness Me! Must do the right thing... Yes! Yes!'

But Estelle in foetus form, was altogether different! *So why no steps to terminate?* I was no further forward when we at last drew into Peterborough North. The case would have to stew... turning my collar up I pulled the cap to a more jaunty angle, hurried to the depot, and caught the last bus out to Farndon.

Around nine in growing dusk the next Friday evening I took my ritual stroll to the Blindon Arms. The motor-bike had done its day's work. I ambled past the village green, where geese were still waddling aimlessly, honking and hissing at imaginary foes, past the council school, the butcher's, where Uncle Joseph worked, the baker's, Jack Rowell's, the post office, then our old saddler's place, turning right at the corner.

My pub, one of Farndon's five, stood halfway down Jubilee Street. Facing on to the road, it had little or no frontage, but bags of space round the back, where a gravelled yard led to what were laughingly referred to as 'the gardens' – a stretch of unattended wasteland, owned by nobody, tended by nobody, wanted by nobody. Today it commands six-figure sums per plot on which to build 'five-bed, superior, executive-style dwellings!' 'Blindon' was the family name of some ancient squirearchy which once ruled the district in return for favours to the monarch, like mustering troops for battles with other get-rich-quick geezers, keeping potential trouble-makers at heel. The face staring down from the creaking sign looked like a Mexican bandit, with long mustachios, sideburns down below the chin, eyes filled with a burning contempt for all things human and humble. The pub's gone now.

I ducked, lifting the latch to go in, when I jumped a mile. Some clot blasting on his horn! I whipped round angrily, only to see Charles driving the family limousine, with Ada by his side. Screeching to a halt he lowered the window, waving like mad, summoning me over to the motor. About to dish out a rollicking, I saw the poor sod was worried sick. Ada was nearly as bad, drawn and anxious, her insouciance absent for once.

"Have you seen a loose woman, or *girl*, rather – running around in a nightgown, Frank?"

"We don't *have* loose women in Farndon, Charles," I grinned, derisively.

"He means a woman *loose*, Frank," Miss Barlow swiftly intervened. "She isn't well. She's *escaped!*"

Then Charles found his voice again, "She must 'ave come this way. They spotted 'er down your end twenty minutes back. Fred Dark, your neighbour, saw 'er race by the end of the road. Jump in, will you."

"What's it all about, then? Where's she escaped *from*, Charles?"

"I'll let ya know later. She ain't well – that's the main thing." He spat out his answer. I scrambled into the back.

"*There she goes!*" shrieked Ada, pointing up ahead. Through the gloom we could just make out the road end, where a right-hand bend leads to the village centre, while a left fork takes you to the church. Charles banged his foot down – we leapt forward. We reached the junction in seconds, overtaking the girl as she made a despairing dash for Church Lane. She looked a forlorn figure, in just a white shift and plimsolls, hair hanging loose, wet and matted from the exertion and what looked to me like terror. Her face was putty-coloured, the eyes wide with fear.

With astonishing alacrity Ada jumped out and ran to her, putting her arms round the shaking shoulders, coaxing her firmly to the limousine, then pushing her in beside *me*. Charles had the door open ready – I'd never seen him so agile! Ada scrambled in after her, as the girl flopped her head on my shoulder, moaning, bleating, and weeping in distress. When she eased off a second she drooled the same few words non-stop... "I want my *baby*, I want my *baby*, I want my *baby*...*"

"You shall have it, Miss Rebecca. There, there... calm down, dear. Everything's taken care of. All in order."

Gradually the girl simmered down, the shaking abated. Charles turned the motor round and headed back, dropping me at the pub, shouting he'd tell me the story later. I went in the door more than ready for a stiffener, ready for several, and more than a little intrigued by what chunk Charles might eventually choose to reveal – instinct told me I'd be lucky to hear the full story! I don't remember much more.

Monday arrived – a Monday more dismal than usual.

Sherwood knocked and came in – to my private bolthole. I found I worked better alone. The door bore a brass nameplate – FRANK ALLNER. No letters after it – yet.

"Christ... Seen a ghost, Frank?"

I'd barely looked up. I gripped *The Times* like it was magnetic, eyes glued to the 'social' columns. At last – the announcement I was dreading.

"Something like that... Only *worse!*"

"What is it – business? Let me see."

He leaned over, grabbed the paper from my sticky fingers, turning it to see what I was gawping at. He stood opposite.

"Forthcoming marriages... Is that it, Frank? Can't be. Oh... I get it. The Fawcetts kicking their heels – with the Grant-Wiltons. *Estelle* Grant-Wilton. I wondered what had come of the romance – they splashed the engagement enough. Are you concerned?"

"Sort of, Mister Forest. You know..."

"I guessed something like that! I'm not a thicko, you know, Frank – though you're good at hiding your feelings. I thought you were getting in deep, but hoped you weren't – for *your* sake. There were whispers you'd be leaving us – I didn't take them seriously. Supposed to have come from the mighty Claud. I put two and two together, but never got other than five.

"Sounds stupid, doesn't it? We *were* close – believe it or not. My one hope was to do well here, and earn a decent income – give myself at least half a chance. I never said anything, naturally."

"Naturally, no, 'course not. I'm sorry. I heard about the garden party, you know. After her mother rang – remember?"

"Can I ever forget?" I managed a sickly grin. Behind the glasses Sherwood's eyes betrayed a kindly interest. He was more than human, but rarely showed it – to anybody. For a manager in a legal concern to have a heart was like finding a duck pond in the desert. The cynicism of legal types always bugged me.

"Ah... don't let it get you down, lad." He turned to go.

"Sorry... did you want something, Mr Forest?"

"Er, no. Another time, Frank. Another time. You've plenty on your plate."

I sighed as he closed the door, picked up the paper to re-study the depressing announcement. It was unusual to give so much notice – two months. They do things differently now. And the ceremony, unlike the funeral, would be at Melton – *why?* On second thoughts, the reason for giving Farndon the elbow was clear. They had little to thank the locals for, and they weren't the most popular of dynasties.

The three giant mountains in my brief lifespan came to haunt me. The mystery of 'Miss Rebecca', the wedding I'd vowed to scupper, and Dad's good name. 'At twenty-two, and alone, for all practical purposes, what's the best weapon? Hatred's a poor tool, jealousy even worse, violence not on, unless... I shirked putting the obstacles in order. But something must be done – *fast* – otherwise I'd drift with the tide and end up on the rocks.

'Since it's all linked to Bradbury, that's the place to start.' I still couldn't quite picture Lydia a rape victim... why hadn't she tried the 'needle'?

Inhibitions shelved, stakes too high for modesty to intervene, I made for the Hall, confident the 'Lady' would see me. I got shock number one! A horribly disfigured Missus Thompson, her face bruised, eyes buried, lips twisted to a sneer, a yard-brush hair-do, greeted me, snarling, like she was about to tell me 'sod off!'

"What do *you* want?" Traditional back-door welcome – served this time with vitriol.

"I want to speak to Missus Grant, please." I puffed myself up with a false confidence, pretending I hadn't noticed the battle-wounds. (Rebecca couldn't have been *that* violent – unless she was drugged to the eyeballs?)

"*Daisy*... Go and tell the Mistress Mister Allner's called."

'Why does a Cook act as doorman?' I never found out – nosiness, probably. 'Why on earth call me Mister?' I waded through the labyrinth of halls and passages – Daisy said Lydia was in the Master's snug and I was welcome to go through. With a little prompting I found my way back to where it once all happened. Shock number two! Lydia wasn't damaged – like Cook, but a long, long way from 'Lydia!' Make-up missing, no big hairdo, no smile, no interest. She sat, listless, writing wearily in what looked to be a foolscap, page-a-day desk-diary. She barely bothered looking up.

"Yes?" she asked, muted, and matter-of-fact, going on, "Don't think you can drop in here whenever you feel like it – because you can't!"

"I want to clear up one or two points – now the cat's out the bag... er... Missus Grant."

"Oh, Christ... What points? *What* bloody cat?"

"You know what about!"

"You can't stop the wedding, Franz – you must make the best of it – you don't stand an earthly. It's got to be over and done with before we come to court, anyway! They might want to turn the Hall into a gaol. A step up from abortion clinic cum knocking-shop! Can you picture *me*, Franz, peering from prison bars?"

The cultured voice was gone, the modulated delivery supplanted by a jarring mix of Lancashire and the flat, ugly vowels of the Midlands. The bitterness, the contempt, the indignation, the rage, as I went to sit down – uninvited – was breathtaking. *And I thought she was listless?*

The word 'clinic' linked to 'abortion', plus the rest, shook me more than I dare admit.

'Lydia's got her wires crossed. She knows I helped capture the Rebecca girl, and assumes I know the full story. Thinks it's been broadcast. Public knowledge!'

SO IT HAD. The Hon Rebecca Manton spread the word *before* Charles and Ada (and me) caught up with her. She'd bumped into Jack Rowell fiddling about round his shop earlier on. Staggered him with a gabbled yarn about being pregnant, and they were trying to take away her baby down at the Bradbury Rest Home. She'd escaped just in time. The girl was obviously free longer than thought. When Jack dashed in to phone the cops Rebecca did a runner. Him the biggest PR man in the business; the word got around fast... but *I* wasn't there to hear it.

"Christo... Will it come to that?"

"We don't know anything – for sure. It's up to Claud... And Martin! They're pretty big wheels – and Martin's got the ear of the Minister – that's one thing in our favour. If there's any way out he'll find it. Anyway, all we do is obey doctor's orders. Give a service. To wives and lady friends of big-wigs – not poor little buggers like *Mum* used to see to. And sometimes I entertain their escorts..."

For the first time Lydia wilted – not half as tough as she made out. She looked her years. Wearied, anxious, almost human. And despite the startling confession, I couldn't quite *hate* her – though I wanted to.

"Come on then, Franz – out with it. I'm up to my neck – as you can see. There can't be much else."

"I want the truth about my Dad. I believe you when you say he raped you – now I want to know why? Anyway, knowing *you*, it couldn't have been much of a shock... not like with a *stranger*?"

"You cheeky young sod..."

"Well, it's true. You're hardly lily-white... are you? Was it the *first* time?"

"If you start..."

"*Tell* me, then! Tell me what set him alight. What did you *say – or do?* Something got him going. It'll cost you nothing. You obviously said something. Own up. I have to know! Don't worry, I can do nothing about it. Nothing I want to do – as long as I know. *Please* Missus Grant..." Lydia's eyes softened a mite – I spotted a hint of compassion. My heart leapt. Frank was on target.

"Well, it..."

"Go on! *Please!* He found you out, didn't he? That's it... isn't it? Discovered your little game, didn't he? Threatened to expose you, DIDN'T HE?" An inspired guess, in spite of the pointers... a shot in the half-light. And lo, Bullseye! Right on the button. Lydia was down and as good as out. Deflated, defeated, done for... But the clues were *there – all the time!* The ever-changing guests, the upper-class if cosmopolitan clientele, the girl in the 'white room', when Lydia seduced me. Estelle's contempt for the whole set-up, the oddness of the 'regulars', the mysterious role of Ada Barlow. Henry's status, Sara's fizzy attempts to 'normalise' life at the Hall... But something else troubled Lydia. Her head fell forward, hair brushing the pages of the giant diary. She clutched at her throat... a touch of theatre? Then she started crying in earnest.

"Yes..." She was barely audible. It didn't matter. The battle was over, and I'd *won.* And all I could feel was pity... Pity... and a dreadful emptiness like I was on a boat going nowhere, and life just one big let-down.

"How?"

"I *told* him. He... He... He kept on asking. The same old questions, 'Why could we *not* convert to a hospital? Did we need all this room? Why the extravagant greed?' He was so insistent! He went on and on – in the end I weakened, tried to explain. After all – he'd be gone by morning. Told him we were committed to the clinic – for always. Our sole income – we couldn't exist without it. But we could hardly publicise the fact.

"I thought he'd see reason... *Did he hell?! Did he bloody hell?!* He went bonkers! Right off his bloody trolley! He raged, stamped, swore... started wrecking the place. And nobody heard him.

"They're dropping in droves over there – and you're killing babies over here! *Now you've made me a part of it!* You selfish pigs!'

"RIGHT, he bellowed, thrusting his face to mine... here's something else you can play with. Then it happened – like I told you. Vile, it was. Horrible. I'll never forget."

I sat paralysed, the relief indescribable, impossible to put into words. Dad lived again! For one mad moment I overlooked the enormity of his action, kidded myself it was justified, put him back on his pedestal. That's all I cared about... I wanted to sing, to shout, to celebrate. I didn't give a damn about anything else – certainly not Lydia. She didn't bother me, sobbing like a child. Rough justice, maybe – but the scales tilted Dad's way at last. The first time in years. And he died an outcast! A pariah, *in his family's eyes! And* in Grant-Wilton's... I'd never wipe the slate clean, and it was a cruel thing he did, but hearing the full story I could almost see his point.

Dare I push it further? "Lydia... er... Mrs Grant, why didn't you abort the child?" My voice was low and even now, the irony lost on Lydia. Anyway, it was a ludicrous question. It made me sound like a numbskull – but I had to ask.

She stared at me long and hard – her face told me nothing. Finally she mumbled, "I daren't! Too many of me Mum's efforts went down the bloody plug-hole – called in too late as a rule. The heartbreak was terrible – put the wind up me for life – I grew up that way. OH GOD! *And* there's been others. I know it sounds daft."

"Oh!" Short, straight, simple, the explanation. Yet I'd puzzled over it ever since Mum told me Estelle's pedigree – or lack of it... I never thought of *that!*

"Franz... don't hate me. Please. You see now why I had to keep quiet. War plays funny tricks. Life's been a bloody roller-coaster – you've no idea..."

"*I* don't hate you, but I'm going to have to tell Mum – and Grandad. They've been merciless in condemning Dad. They reckon he deserved German bullets, though to be fair, they hid it from *me*." Suddenly I was closer to Dad than ever. I left quietly, found my way to a side exit – the door Sara used after Towcester. I didn't want to bump into Sadie again.

The set-up at Bradbury, masterly in conception, miraculously executed, was staggering in sheer audacity. Ostensibly a secret, exclusive, before-its-time health farm; in reality an abortion clinic and luxury convalescent home, offering extras. A miracle-cure, for wives, daughters, and mistresses of 'gentlemen' and the odd showbiz chick who'd cocked a snook at convention once too often! Remember, it wasn't the Swinging Sixties, nor the Naughty Nineties.

A clever plan they hatched, masterminded by Connie Beamish, funded by Martin Fawcett, with Sangsters handling the 'legals'. Denied family support – capital, revenue or any other handouts – George found it impossible to make the estate pay. Farming in recession, the territory largely pasture, with acres of unrewarding woodland, survival was never an option. Fine for hunting and shooting, but hopeless for arable ventures, finding a solution became vital. They laid their heads together, raked in Doctor French, listened to Claud, and came up with the idea of a state-of-the-art abortion clinic.

'Connections' weren't hard to find... once they'd decided. Society screamed for such a service – like today it howls for brothels. Fees were phenomenal, but to the 'afflicted' money mattered little. Every case a Harley Street referral – for the great and the good... Ada became top-dog... poached from Princess Mary's Nursing Service at RAF Halton, where only the cream deigned to practise. She knew it all, including midwifery (which few flyers required), and Lydia herself was no mug at medicine. Ada masterminded the whole scheme with her usual aplomb. Doctor French was a bonus, succumbing to the lure of unforeseen riches with ease, and he enjoyed further claims to fame including an uncanny resemblance to the first Lon Chaney. Sangsters would pinpoint likely pitfalls, and warn of ugly situations where professional cover-up would be essential, confidentiality at a premium. Railton 'kept the books'.

Chapter Sixteen

The Fallout

The Hall's north wing was essentially a fortress. Architectural gimmicks known to a chosen few transformed that section of the great Hall into a retreat for the 'afflicted', notable for its austerity. Few in number, select in pedigree, patients convalesced in isolation, house rules dictating each was accompanied by a chaperone – spouse, guardian, parent – never by a lover. Motor-cars were taboo... they'd have raised too many eyebrows, putting the nosey on red alert. 'Patients' were collected from nearby stations – Kettering, Peterborough and Huntingdon, by Ada and Henry – sometimes Charles was raked in, though he remained in ignorance of the true purpose of the clandestine visits. The irony for poor George, having faced the courts over Sophie Johnson, and suffered opprobrium for 'others', was enough to brain damage a zombie. Salvation at hand yet its use strictly *verboten* for Sophie and all the rest... including Lydia! The ultimate irony for having ignored that succinct motto 'never foul your own doorstep'.

Some staff members knew the score, some were suspicious, but to most the 'guests' were females from the upper echelons struggling to combat the despised, downmarket disease affecting thousands through the depressed Thirties – the nervous breakdown. They call it stress today. None were beyond rescue – their bellies weren't sufficiently distended for them to swan around baying 'join the club' and give the game away... the few who were genuinely seeking rest from busy, dizzy lifestyles were miles apart, enjoying the unhindered freedom of all the establishment.

Bradbury domestics gleefully lined their pockets, trousering huge rewards way, way, way above their station for sticking rigidly to orders, keeping Mum, and never ever socialising close to home. Similar, if more refined, constraints kept Henry and Ada in check – if only to the outside world. The status (if any) of Alan Stewart, remained shadowy. Feverish high-jinks, especially in early days, were salutes to triumphant 'operations' when defeat looked to be odds-on. While George acquiesced – he had little option – his need for dosh having created the clinic – he distanced himself from the more meaty issues, and he failed completely to grasp the threat inherent in Fawcett's every move; didn't recognise the remorseless grip on the Estate's goings-on which his guide and mentor so cleverly developed. He mostly amused himself, out of harm's way, making a big play of the fox-hunting and linked pursuits like pointing and showing – handy camouflage for fooling the plebs, the proles and the playboys.

When Ada first took up the lucrative post of governess to Grant-Wilton's kids, with a string of diplomas a mile long, she could never have foreseen a future so deep, so dark, so illegal, so contrary to her vows, yet so rewarding – in terms of finance. But *some* carrots were dangled or they'd never have lured her from that prestigious niche. Fawcett and Connie, as well as Sangsters, were right on cue when they selected Ada Barlow. Lydia *raved* about her. Said she looked a million in her scarlet and black, but didn't bother to mention that the girl's arm was half-way up her back when she finally nodded agreement... The true purpose of her engagement would be leaked to her later – in snatches. Her mother thought the girl was 'doing well'. Medicine man Lon deserved credit for unearthing such a treasure, through the elite, if universal freemasonry of England's self-regarding quacks.

The scheme they hatched was diabolically clever, and the Grants' self-imposed isolation turned out a blessing – just what the doctor ordered!

The revelations knocked me for six. Which way to jump? I'd known the place held secrets – they'd prompted enough speculation – but no answers had ever surfaced. *All* the people, *all* the time had been hoodwinked with ease.

My relief at discovering the true reason for Dad's assault on Lovely Lydia was instantly negated by an urgent need to address the present, never mind the future. The ramifications were frightening. Everybody seemed tainted – most by intent. Mum, Grandad, Sangsters, the Fawcetts, Grant-Wiltons, Ada, Henry, Sadie, Charles – above all, STELLA!

The 'rest home' ceased to function. The due processes of law and order finally got under way. And that wedding loomed...

The Foreign Legion didn't beckon, nor did the Seven Seas, and I could never quite see myself submitting to facial surgery, though I did have lighter moments! Anyway, soon I'd be a bona fide landowner, with concrete links to Bradbury. First though, there were scores to settle – with *Mum*... and Grandad.

They didn't give Dad much of a chance – condemned him out of hand. Didn't try to understand. Mum lived with him, for Pete's sake... for years. She knew him. You can't be closer than wife.

Was it like the aftermath of every bloody war? Forget the details. Pretend it didn't happen. Leave it to historians, they'll do the business... if it must be remembered.

The Hall's secrets spread like wildfire, though little changed on the outside, and locally they made surprisingly little impact. Sneers and sniggers were frequent, but not much else, apart from Charles deserting the boozer. In any case Bradbury figured little in village life – apart from fox-hunting.

My complex links with Lydia remained my own little secret, like the truth of Dad's plunge to ignominy I'd squeezed from her. The abortions outraged Mum, but I held back from telling even *her* the full story. Anyway a showdown was due, when all would be revealed. Cruel maybe, but I didn't fancy *more* complications with the wedding so close.

Would it come off? Lydia had said, "Get it out of the way before we're locked up." Was she joking? She might have been! After all Bradbury had some pretty big wheels going for it, Sir Martin, Claud Sangster, the Colonel... maybe 'porridge' was still some way off? Bedford Jail could relax... Holloway as well.

Then Stella turned up.

Turned up at *our* house. Said she was staying at the Hall until her 'big day'. Come to put me in the picture so to speak. A different Estelle. One look told me plenty. She'd learned of the miserable exposé – and she knew *I* knew. That deflated her – above everything.

Aboard Maddy, she was in summer top and slacks. Mum was out, which was just as well. I was messing around at Saturday's chores – clipping the hedge out front, when I heard the sound of hoofs on tarmac. I didn't bother looking up. Horses weren't rare down our lane now. It was a short cut to the blacksmith's since they built the last batch of council houses, bringing with them a service-road.

"Hello!" she cried. "How about a haircut, Franz?" She leaned from the saddle, proffering her re-grown curls, playing the light-hearted role – I bet it took some effort. I pretended to oblige, joining in the playful cameo, thrusting the clippers towards her head. She beamed her delight, swung from the saddle, leapt down, held out her arms.

"Stella... Estelle... Er... Um... *Darling!*"

"*Franz... OH, FRANZ!*"

Dropping the shears I caught her, held her, kissed her – gripped her tight. Nothing had changed. Gently I eased her away – stood back a pace, studying the once-gorgeous face. The flush faded, leaving her strangely pale. The face had changed. Thinner – more finely etched – gaunt almost, compared to early Estelle. I forgot Maddy, until he muzzled me in the back with a, '*What about me?*'

"Hello, old chap... go and chomp the grass... you're losing weight... like your mistress.

"What's this in aid of, eh?"

"I've had it all out with Mummy! You have *too*... she tells me. I'm stumped. I *had* to see you darling – there's so much to do."

"You knew all along... didn't you, Stella? You knew *everything*. Yet you stayed loyal – kept your lips buttoned-up."

"For everybody's sake, really... I had to. Though Sara didn't believe in keeping quiet, silly ass – apart from with strangers – and she'd *used* the service, for goodness sake – in her teens! What do you think to *that?* The only one to sidestep the rules – her name tells you why. Mind you, not for the termination – that had to be Harley Street: just for the prelims. That's why she hates me, Franz. She does all she can to blacken my name. Her rotten conscience. And in time I grew to hate her. Not at first... but making a play of being pregnant... well! Thank God old Martin *was* around – he got her to see sense – keep it from the big wide world. And I *didn't* know everything – though I do now. I'd no idea how it was set up – or who was involved, beyond the family. Nor did Noel."

I winced at the name – visibly, deliberately – put my nose in the air.

She laughed. "Silly..." she murmured. "Still jealous?"

"'*Course* I'm bloody jealous. I'll never be otherwise. It gets worse not better. Still prepared to pay the price then, are you Stella?"

"I'm part of the deal Daddy struck. A vital part – if a bit late. Bradbury still has to be baled out, you know. Everything's arranged, and its not all one-sided."

"It doesn't help *me!*"

"You don't understand, Franz..."

"What do you mean... don't understand?!"

"Noel's not... well... he's not... *I don't know how to put it.*
He's not *NORMAL*... He's... kind of... like his namesake, that
Coward man. He's *homosexual* – that's what they call it –
isn't it?"

"Oh! Jesus! Oh Estelle!... *Estelle!... NO!*"

"YES! A wife gives him *status.* The status he craves! The
status Martin craves *for* him! A façade – a sham – a lie – so he
can live on equal terms."

"At *my* expense... more so, at *yours!*"

"We've had this out before, dammit! I prayed you'd
understand when you heard the full story. You know I'll
always love you, darling. And if things work out *my* way for a
change, we'll hardly be apart. Come here, Silly."

She led me up my own staircase. A novel experience. I
hoped Mothers' Union would last all day. It didn't – but long
enough.

Amongst the gruesome revelations one tiny spot of light
still glimmered. So far, it seemed, Lydia had kept quiet about
Stella's own lineage. Though why, I couldn't fathom. Not
from kindness.

I considered putting my cards on the table – having it out
with Mum – that same night. The full Monty. The truth of that
infamous evening in 'sixteen – the real reason Dad lost his
cool, going balls-out for Lydia. But I had second thoughts –
let it rest a bit. Anyway, I doubted if any explanation would
change Mum's views – *or* Grandad's. They'd lived with the
ugly knowledge for years. And plenty was going on to keep
my brainbox busy.

Martin Fawcett's machinations really stunned me. Evil
beyond belief. Alright, so he never got over George dumping
sister Isabel – it's cruel when your twin is unhorsed – but even
revenge must have its limits.

She went out to Hong Kong on missionary work, but
knowing the blinkered views of *old* George, the Colonel
would have had no option but to ditch the girl and marry

Lydia. And maybe, in the end, Isabel was better off peddling Christianity to foreigners, than climbing into bed with a stud like George? I wasn't aware she subsequently expanded her Ministry, crossed into mainland China, disappeared somewhere into that vast interior, and was never heard of again. What, if any, attempts were made to find the jilted lady, I never found out.

But to agree later on to throw his own daughter into the Bradbury deal didn't do George's reputation any good. 'Then, she *isn't* George's daughter – she's my Dad's child!'

What really got to me was Martin posturing as an eminent MP. Under-secretary at the Home Office, ostensibly of impeccable pedigree. Officer and Gentleman. What a bloody mockery. In chilling reality a different kind of being altogether.

A scheming, lying, manipulative bastard of unparalleled greed – a forerunner of the sleaze-merchants of Westminster we saw in the Nineties. His ambitions on the turf were down to nothing more than greed – and envy. But compared to the way he'd treated George, these were minor blemishes.

As he painstakingly did the spadework for easing Bradbury Estate into his own dirty paws, he worked on George *in person*. Did his damnedest to drive the man mad – starting all those years ago when George was at his most vulnerable, held in a Marseilles nursing home, verging on outright lunacy. Even in *that* situation the vindictive swine tried to convince the sick man that his (George's) memories of wartime were flawed.

Deception like that defies explanation, merits no possible excuse. And when he arranged the sick-pass for Dad to come home and 'save' the Hall, in which he himself had vested interests, it tightened still further his grip on George Grant-Wilton. Emotional blackmail of incredible dimensions.

And Fawcett never eased the pressure for a second. Relentlessly he kept up the torture until George at last cracked. It had long since destroyed any hopes of recovery. The day came when George at last cried *finis*. The obliging Doctor French took pity on him – helped him on his way. After all, Lon himself would be signing the death certificate.

As Stella galloped off, clouds gathered rapidly, *real* clouds, up above, up in the sky. It started to rain. I watched her as far as the Fork. She turned Maddy towards Briarsdale. I looked in wonder at the contours of that superb chassis silhouetted against the pale skyline south of Cuckoo-pint Rise. Suddenly she worked a strange manoeuvre. She stood high in the stirrups, reaching for the sky, clutching what looked like a hankie? Anyway, something white... she waved it twice, then dipped it thrice, and went galloping off into the teeth of the oncoming storm. The signals had me puzzled. They were reminiscent of an isolated fort in the Deep South, with Confederate soldiers surrendering to the Goddam Yankees: 'B' movie material. 'What the hell can she *mean?* Who's giving in to whom? There's a message there somewhere!'

I turned away – went in from the rain. The starkness of the future hit me for the first time, the realities awesome. I'd always seen me and Stella as the victims of circumstances. The truth was very different. Couples fight *side by side* when the going gets rough: counter the thrusts, refute the allegations, challenge the hostility of biased parents of whichever clan.

'But in this I'm single-handed. Alone. Isolated. Everybody scuttles my ambitions. Mum, Grandad, Lydia... most of all *Estelle*. She's all for *marrying* Noel – has been all along. She wants it that way. Wants the ultimate in life: 'Lady Fawcett'. Status. So she can throw her weight around – hire secretaries, servants, chauffeurs, slaves, shit-shovellers, grooms – ride with the Quorn... everything she covets!

'And *ME?* Well, I'm just a handy stallion. A stud – for when she feels like it. Discreet, deferential, dutiful. Don't they call 'em gigolos?

'Christ... Stella *is* the opposition. She's the one throwing the spanners. With her on *my* side there'd be no problems – just hiccups. And *I'm* the child of the Master of Bradbury – *she* isn't! She's just a tramp. The fallout... from a rape. *I* should hold all the aces. ME. Why didn't I see it before; it's plain enough?

'Fit me with a bridle, Charles. Lodge me at the stables. Plait my tail with red ribbon (I'll be a kicker!). Tie up my mane. Fill the manger. Keep me free – and in the pink, ready to perform... Any time, any day, any year. Plenty of oats.

'BAH! Bloody hell! What a prat! What a blind bloody prat.'

Mum came home to find me slumped on the sofa, staring moodily into the back garden, where the hens were chasing imaginary flies, pecking at each other's feathers, jumping up and down as if on springs, squawking their heads off, then scuttling for cover when the ever-ready cockerel approaches, hoping to catch them in receptive mood... ready for treading.

Full of beans, Mum was... Wearily I listened to a blow-by-blow account of the debates in which she'd shown them all what she was made of, and she revealed the exciting ambitions of that praiseworthy body to set the village alight through another long hot summer. Myself... I felt like torching the whole bloody country! 'Where has all the promise gone?'

I told her Stella had called, but she showed little interest, despite the surprised twitch. She gave me a searching glare like she knew we'd been to bed – that's all. She was full of her meeting, but seeing I was in no mood for cookery, took herself off to the kitchen to practise some new recipe she'd heard of. I was completely lost. Big, broad, strong though I was, my 'opponent' had no weaknesses. I hadn't a clue how to cope... though wise enough to know that Estelle's resolve was unshakeable – the wedding would go ahead – as planned.

'So blond, baby-face Noel's nothing but a bloody poofter after all – not that it makes much difference – just tightens the screws.'

I pondered selling off Briarsdale the minute I got the nod from Sangsters, but it wouldn't yield dosh enough to support the young Madam Grant-Wilton for fifty years. 'Anyway, *I* can't give her a title – not the sort she wants.'

I remember thinking Noel didn't look like a ponce – not from the way he walked. But evidently he was, and what's the point gearing up for battle without a gladiator to get the better of? Bugger that for a lark.

Dreamer I might be, but no philosopher. I'd developed a lot since joining Sangsters, but I'd taken too long to see daylight. 'I can never be anything to Stella – nothing that really matters. Her course is clear – the one she's chosen – albeit with persuasion.' It wasn't so much throwing in the towel, as wiping away the mist. I could see my future now – with frightening clarity. The Goddess didn't even figure!

For the first time I made an effort to accept the inevitable and get on with life as best I could. Better for Mum, for Grandad, for everybody. I said nothing to Mum, nor she to me, though I'm sure she guessed. The bitter consequences of being born the wrong side of the track, whoever the sire, hit me with a wallop. But seeing didn't solve the problem and I wasn't in the mood for martyrdom, just moot acceptance of a situation that could hardly grow more sombre. And the self-knowledge came fast – in the end. The Foreign Legion did beckon.

Folk rave about ideals, claim they outdo illusions. Rubbish! Nothing comes close to even matching illusions. Illusion propels youth to the only paradise it'll ever know – if life lasts a billion years.

I thought of Rochester... and Jane. They made it alright. But he was no peasant. She was the poor one – not him. That magical difference... and Rochester couldn't even see!

'Ah, well...'

Chapter Seventeen

1946

Nobody came to trial – they don't barbecue nobles. Henry's register would have torpedoed the Establishment had it seen daylight. On occasions, even Bradbury wasn't privy to the identity of its wayward clients. The egregious Fawcett held too many aces for plebs to be more than an irritant – and too many jokers up his sleeve. Claud, in his inimitable style, master-minded the wriggle from retribution.

And soon all was forgotten. World War Two intervened.

A brief resumé of events during my absence follows. Any desire to dwell on that six years of madness evaporated long ago.

Fifty million dead. The Atom Bomb. The Holocaust. The Rockets. The skeletal prisoners of Japanese camps... I leave it to historians. Humanity perished – all but.

In spite of being part of a kingsize air-base comprising East Anglia and chunks of the Midlands, Farndon escaped annihilation, and its few citizens who joined the Forces were mostly spared too. Lots of locals were anchored in 'reserved occupations' – railways, brickyards, farming and the like. Room still remained on our Kaiser memorial to accommodate Hitler's list. The doughty souls who arranged its erection were obviously prophets.

Bradbury functioned (breathe in) as a hospital. Noel spent the war years at Bletchley Park, helping the Intelligence Services decode German signals. Uncle Joseph joined the 'War-Ag', reclaiming hundreds of non-productive acres, turning them to arable with help from Italian prisoners and English Landgirls. Sara signed up for the Wrens, suffered a torrid time when Jerry blitzed Southampton, graduated to the comparative calm of the Clyde after marrying a much-decorated submariner called Alastair Broadhurst, while Ada

Barlow returned to her first love, Halton, and Princess Mary's Nursing Service. Ada remained an enigma, her true relationship with George still mostly guesswork.

The district was invaded by thousands of American airmen and hordes of Landgirls, many of whom lost their hearts (amongst other things), never returning to their native Lancashire. Nor, for that matter, did thousands of the Yanks go home. They lie in state in Madingley Cemetery, close to the University city of Cambridge... well, their *remains* do! RIP.

Being a member of that cheerful bunch who embarked on the renowned Cooks Tour of the Middle East and Europe, all for free, perambulating from the shadow of Table Mountain via the Pyramids, the Western Desert, Malta, Sicily, Cassino, the Apennines, to the awesome splendour of the Alps, attached to Eighth Army as a signaller until time ran out, I wasn't around to savour the thrills and spills of wartime East Anglia... Letters, records, gossip, hearsay, and sheaves of yellowed papers helped fill the gaps.

Estelle found time for *that* wedding, then did an 'Edith Cavell' in bomb-battered Malta, where she performed until the Mediterranean was freed, ending her war in Gibraltar, in one piece, thanks to His forbearance, and my prayers. Ada's medical expertise (and Lydia's know-how) had apparently inspired the Goddess.

Grandad, sadly, had died – all of a sudden – on VE day. Mum found him slumped lifeless in his favourite greenhouse, clutching a tomato-plant.

Life didn't change much for Mum, though like the rest she kept herself busy raising funds for the Forces, sending food-parcels half-way round the globe – though few found their way to the Desert. Sir Martin scuttled off to Harborough for the 'duration', taking Lovely Lydia with him. Sadie was kept on as 'assistant' at the Hall, where they also found room for my old friend, informant, and fellow-toper, Charles, as odd-jobber and occasional ambulance driver.

Rupert and Justin joined the Royal Air Force – Rupert survived... Henry found a niche in the Home Guard – though I could never picture that sleek and elegant individual wielding a pitchfork or a Boer War rifle – at the same time achieving miracles turning the Estate into a viable entity – with War-Ag co-operation.

Jack Rowell was as lively as ever, though his vitriolic better-half was beginning to sprout warts, if little reduced in girth. I noticed she was still adept at including her paw ounces when dispensing groceries – not for nothing did they call her Winnie Weigh-fingers.

Sangsters had kept my post open, though the offices looked filled with strangers when I first went back. Like me, survivors had aged through those interminable six years. Dear old Sherwood still steered the ship – from below deck – and wore the same suit, so it seemed. Maybe he had several the same?

Claud continued to preside, with Alice still pounding the typewriter. I suspect she kidded herself she'd become some sort of legal mega-star in that stronghold of learned men.

For the uninitiated, life returned to normal – or near normal. My inheritance had become reality – Briarsdale belonged to me. Henry had done the gentlemanly thing all along, ordering Sissons to extend his ministry to my holdings until I returned, and was in shape to take over. Quite how to set out my stall I'd decide later.

Anyway, a fresh start was imperative, but first I must sort the conundrums, preferably one at a time. What riddles they turned out.

The reserve between me and Mum – the awkwardness, the embarrassment, that hidden mother-and-son something, had been supplanted by a new accommodation – so I thought!

I remember the date – twelfth October. The Allies were still sorting out Berlin, and carving up adjacent territory of the defunct Third Reich. The Japs were on their knees, praying for forgiveness, licking arseholes for a change.

The evening was chilly, though still daylight. The fire burned bright in the black-leaded range, the wind at its most co-operative.

"Mum... I never really understood the lengths you went to to keep me away from the Bradbury crowd? You knew I was bound to find out some day – about my Dad – my real Dad, I mean. You knew damn well Stella and I were not brother and sister."

"Trust you to get it all mixed up, Francis. You're barking up the wrong tree – as usual."

"*Eh?*"

We sat either side of the fireplace – in the same old armchairs. Mum looked the way she'd always looked – hardly a day older. No grey hair (but in a roll now), no wrinkles, still pretty, still immaculate, though by no means dolled-up and not a hint of war-paint.

"I said, you're on the wrong track again," she replied quietly. The extra-low key caused me a frisson of anxiety.

"*Where* am I wrong? Tell me."

"I did everything possible to keep you from Bradbury Hall – and from its people – Estelle included – terrified they'd recognise you. The bigger you grew the more obvious it became and ever more dangerous."

"*What?*"

"You've got *my* features – rather like Grandad's, but from behind you're the *dead spit* of your father. Your walk, those great big shoulders, the tilt of your head, the mannerisms – even the way you hold yourself upright. Him all over again."

"You've lost me! *What the hell are you talking about?*" I was hoarse, my throat like sandpaper. Desperately I struggled to make sense of the rubbish she was spouting. But I couldn't.

"I beat the devils in the end... Come on, Francis – you didn't *seriously* believe that twaddle about me and George – did you? You don't *really* imagine you're a Grant-Wilton – do you? Some hopes! But *George* thought so – and as far as I'm concerned, that's all that matters! And by God, we've done well out of the deal, haven't we? Financed by George for all these years, now *you* own half the woodlands."

I stared at her, open-mouthed. From what little I could see – her face mostly in shadow – the eyes were gloating, dismissive, evil... her mouth twisted all shapes... derisive, contemptuous. She oozed triumphalism. She threatened to spit in celebration, tilting her head towards Bradbury. I thought she was aiming at *me*... She swayed on her chair.

"Them bloody GRANTS..." she spluttered. *"That'll larn the devils!"*

"What the Dickens do you mean? Have you gone stark staring mad? *Who* am I then, for God's sake?"

"You be a *SISSONS*, laddie... One of old *TOM'S*." She had the gall to mimic the old bugger's way of talking.

"And it makes not a jot of difference – to anything – or anybody. Especially not to *you*."

The fire died down, the darkness seemed to take us up and wrap us in its folds. Mortified, I stared at the dimly lit mask I'd always called Mum. Seeing me stuck for words she stoked the furnace.

"I first got friendly with Tom when he began bringing his rabbits along this lane. They were so cheap... and so good. He'd always skin mine for me. Later on there got to be the odd pheasant, a brace of partridge, sometimes a woodcock. I'm talking about *after* Robert joined the army, you understand? Times were bad, Francis. Nobody knows. I'm not making excuses – just telling you the story. We couldn't afford meat – that's if there *was* any. Grandad earned nothing, and the shop lingered on the market for ages – you must have heard... and what little *I* brought in hardly paid the milkman.

"Well... when Robert came to England on that foolhardy mission, playing Sir Galahad to the wretched Grants, he was more of a stranger than a husband. You've no *idea*... Then, after raping Big-Tits at the Hall, he just vanished. The errand was too much for him – so was the sequel."

She carried on with this ridiculous nonsense in a measured, matter-of-fact manner – but the swank was there alright.

"Yes, I *did* entertain George – the only one I ever liked from that miserable ménage. And all the time I was acutely aware of something evil going on down there. It's hard to spell out – but more than a hunch – like I told you, years ago. But no way did George father YOU! And I should know! Gracious, my periods were regular as clockwork – to the minute – that's *after* the few nights he spent here with me. You're man enough now to hear the sordid details. And it was later on Tom started calling on a regular basis."

As far as I could tell she didn't look repentant, ashamed, or even apologetic.

"Did he bring you a bunny every time he came – or just its foot – for luck?"

I belched out the sarcasm, insensate with rage, trembling with disbelief. '*Somehow* I'd shake this composed little being. Bring the smug recital to a halt. Wipe the sneers from the cocky little face.' Without warning she'd put me in the biggest spin of all time – including army set-tos. She knew damn well she was spouting dynamite. She *intended* to blow me out the water. All along she'd done her best to ruin my affair with Stella – keep me from the Hall. And all that time she'd pulled the wool over poor old Grandad's eyes as well. Made sure he detested the Grants. Maybe this little monster organised Stella's vanishing-tricks? Threatened her – "Keep away from Francis!" The thoughts had me gnawing the woodwork, like the memory of those two-faced displays when Stella called at Rose Cottage. I tried working out the sheer villainy of a character who could spin such a web of deceit – starting before I was born. I could now understand the complicated embroidery.

When she'd comforted George in the depths of his misery, she hadn't given the future much thought. But when *I* was on the way she very soon spotted what Lydia's mother, Connie, came to recognise all those years ago – a *passport* – a passport to Grant-Wilton riches. A chance, too, to wreak vengeance on Bradbury, its 'inmates', and everything it stood for. On principle alone, she loathed them all (bar George), despised every facet of their existence. And, like me, she'd never quite believed Robert had descended to rape, whatever the provocation. On that score Lydia was a liar... She'd obviously coerced him to save herself from a savage beating. And in his rage he'd fallen for her blandishments. In mother's defence (though I hesitate), the vileness that was Bradbury had finished Robert Allner as surely as if they'd put a gun to his head – and pulled six times on the trigger – a bullet in every chamber.

That hazardous, cockeyed crusade to preserve the Grant-Wilton lifestyle, cling on to the luxury doss-house and all its sidelines, set in motion an avalanche that was to bring life crashing about her head. Destroy her very existence. Finish off her beloved husband. At least, that's how she'd *see it*.

And what a brilliant actress. What a loss to the stage. Compared to Mum, Sarah Bernhard was just an extra. And the way she'd kept her chin up through the prolonged ordeal defied all logic – even allowing for her scheming.

And George Grant-Wilton would have had *no reason at all to doubt the veracity of her claims to my being his child.*

That's when she developed the bitterness she was never to lose – cleverly though she disguised it. To her, the Curse of Bradbury was only too real.

To be fair (which isn't easy), she'd been the victim of a catalogue of terrible disasters, while bastards like the Fawcetts had gone unscathed, growing richer by the minute... Father crippled in a fall – just doing his job. The business lost after Robert joined the army – a volunteer. The untimely death of her mother. Robert's tragic end. And finally the incredible smack-in-the-face when she saw her only child being sucked into the Bradbury vortex.

The shock of the century when I told her Stella and I were sweethearts! (Never mind the brother and sister nonsense.) And an undreamed-of threat to ever reaping the benefits of her evil scheming, straightforward though her plans appeared. The *last* thing she needed was me being a 'regular' at Bradbury Hall. In her imagination they'd undoubtedly recognise me as a Sissons – especially from behind. Even Tom himself might twig the likeness? He, fortunately, remained ignorant of the 'development', strange though it seems. Doubtless he served scores of lonely women with rabbits at give-away prices... then forgot all about them!

George didn't exactly pay Mum off, but he made sure we didn't go hungry, nor want for a bob through the long, lean years... using borrowed money – *Fawcett's money!*

"What do you want me to say?" After a lengthy, agonising silence, I muttered the only thing I could think of – bland and banal though it was. It was as good as dark, the fire low and fretful. I couldn't be bothered to get up and light the Aladdin.

"We must get down to planning the *future* now," she said, cool as you like.

"You plan whatever you wish – there's nothing here for me any more. The sooner I'm on my way the better. And you can rot in hell for all I care. All along you knew the one big risk to your scheming was George seeing Sissons in *me*. When I was young it didn't show, but as I grew bigger so did the risk become agonisingly real. And what did you do? *I'll tell you what you did!* You made me believe I was George's son. Not in so many words! Oh no! But with non-stop hints and innuendo, and denigration of all the Hall's other characters.

You *wanted* me to believe you'd told George the truth, after I found my real Dad hadn't figured..."

"Well... yes, that's more or less..."

"Don't interrupt! You went to any lengths to keep me from Estelle. Your scheming was so blatant it had exactly the result you intended – convincing me that Colonel Grant-Wilton was *really my father*, making Stella my half-sister. You cleverly got Claud Sangster, and others with a bit of clout, thinking along the same lines, confirming George's 'guilt', though admittedly you had a hell of a strong case. That's on top of George's 'confession' in his bequest to me. You played it mighty cool when I came home from the office with the news of George's 'arrangement' – *didn't you?*"

"Well, it was no surprise to *me*."

"Of course it wasn't. That's exactly what I'm saying... And you were totally unmoved when I thought I'd been clever reading between the lines. That's what you WANTED me to do!"

"One day you'll thank me, Francis. I've always been ambitious for you." She sounded more or less normal as she mouthed the nauseating platitude. It was dark now – the atmosphere in the living-room stifling and oppressive – I couldn't see her face – only as a blur – and part of me wanted to look into those eyes.

"No wonder the funeral had you wriggling. With George dead, all fears of him learning the truth were gone; a truth that would have done you out of the returns on all that scheming and would have properly killed your pig.

Chapter Eighteen

1952

Things have moved on since my earlier jottings, though the basics are little changed. I'm still at Sangsters', a qualified solicitor, but now living at Granleigh in a rented cottage. The extra miles to work are negligible and I'm near enough Briarsdale to enjoy my strange inheritance, even if in muted style.

As intended Noel and Estelle took over Melton, with Fawcett in the driving seat at Bradbury, his ambitions fulfilled, and firmly on the doorstep of racing headquarters at Newmarket. He quit the political arena in 'fifty-one, never quite making it to where they chuck you a peerage on the way out. He has Lydia for a concubine. Heads nodded knowingly, convinced the denouement when the Hall's secrets were laid bare would stick in the minds of the powers-that-be, yet nothing has happened. Apparently they're consigned to the skeleton-cupboard! Martin hasn't re-married, and Lydia seems happy to have re-invented herself in familiar mould, if longish in the tooth... She enjoys regular injections of oomph (if nothing else), clinging to Martin's tail as he travels around Britain's racecourses where he has come to enjoy the cutthroat rivalry over the sticks as much as the flat's flamboyance.

Often I'll sit and rage at England's rotten legal system where, if justice reigned, Martin would be knotted by the scrotum, strung up on Sissons's gibbet, and left there to rot – with *my* permission. I'd gladly tie the knots. I've agreed Henry uses and manages Briarsdale as he sees fit, as in wartime, until I find a solution, and shape my future, though I've 'privatised' the Lodge, and keep Carolean immaculate.

I'm never tempted to put out a feeler to Sissons about my pedigree: I trust mother keeps her trap shut too. I wouldn't want it dragged up. I've no reason to believe she'll do otherwise, though I've broken with home, and no longer know every local moggie due a litter.

With massive subsidy farming has again taken off, Bradbury's beginning to boom, and Henry runs an estate which is not merely doing well but trumpeting its success from the rooftops. Such is the nature of homo sapiens, locals are over the moon, greeting the transition with joy. Memories are notoriously short, and prosperity generates prosperity, creating work for the old firm of All and Sundry, after the angst-ridden years of tightened belts and empty gobs.

My hermit-like existence turned out surprisingly bearable at first, though the leathery features show the humps and hollows of a thirtyish something, accentuating the rain-channels running down to the chin. Romance belongs in the past. I see little of Estelle Fawcett, though I faithfully check her endeavours in the hunting fields of Rutland and Leicestershire, as she chases the well-bred hounds of the Belvoir, Cottesmore, and Quorn. She rides with the West Thorncliffe as well, never missing a meet at Bradbury or Little Downton. *Horse and Hound* has become my bible, the *Sporting Chronicle* next. I read every word, keeping tabs on Estelle, and on the racing endeavours of her evil, stand-in 'Daddy'.

It's impossible to describe my feelings, and harder still to convey the way Stella has played out the grisly farce. As you'd expect she's stuck to her guns, and to the outside world she and Noel are a notable couple, gracing the social scene as frequently as the sporting panorama enjoyed by the Midlands' elite. Prominent at county shows, county balls, and county fêtes, they figure regularly in the 'glossies', extending their activities to well beyond the boundaries of Middle England, doing a season in 'Town' as well as 'musts' like Henley, Wimbledon, Crufts, the Boat Race, and all the rest in the long list of Britain's regular bores. You name it, they're there.

But after a very few years, with no bairns in sight, they were soon in the dock for 'dereliction of duty'. Standard, hoary old suspicions were whispered though in this case they were bang on target! For all that the pair enjoyed a fair run of manufactured happiness, until the day the inevitable came about.

We've all seen the grizzled features of females swinging a leg over the back of a nag when well into their seventies, looking more equine than their mounts, but we don't get to see, nor hear, of the pathetic creatures terminally crippled, hideously disfigured, a limb missing, short of an eye, existence a curse to both themselves and to their faithful carers, just because they couldn't say 'no' to sitting up there, viewing the world from an elevated squat-point. Sadly, most were placed in invidious situations by the ruthless ambitions of parents desperate to scale the social ladder, keep up with the Foyles, the Fanshawes and the Foulenoughs, then end up caring for the sad remains of the bright young things they once rabidly pushed forward, and whose only highlights are patronage by the fit and healthy as they cringe in their wheelchairs at the local point-to-point.

Life turned out more or less the same as before, except Estelle not merely vanished for months on end, but had better things to do than pay me surreptitious visits on the rare occasions she came to Bradbury. That's not to say her visits were boring... and she argued vehemently she was there because that's where she wanted to be.

She'd come up to Briarsdale on Sugarfoot where I'd be waiting at the Lodge with the fire going, everything spick and span. After some initial hesitance she was as passionate as ever, more so really, and despite the basic resentment I loved her as much as ever. But the rats were gnawing and Noel must watch his step. Stella confided he was deep into a relationship with a male vet from Castle Ashworth who called regularly to have a look at the gee-gees... That didn't surprise me, but she saved the dynamite for later... she admitted to a hectic affair with the Master of drag-hounds, who was cheating the wife who bank-rolled him. She was quite open, yet bristled when I gently informed her I'd joined the club and negotiated an 'understanding' with a school-teacher from Downton who was winning plaudits for her work in protecting butterflies, and who, in any case, was free to roam.

Then came the day it happened. The spill that *wasn't* just a great big laugh! Out with the Cottesmore she was belting across a meadow on the outskirts of Edith Weston, with her husband upsides, when the nag in front jumped a ditch that wasn't there, crumpled on landing, giving Sugarfoot not a hope in hell of avoiding the flailing legs and the grounded rider. He overreached badly, went arse over head, sending Stella flying, then rolled right over, and on to her sprawling chassis. Her leg was trappped, her ankle shattered, and after several operations, and endless visits to Harley Street, she was destined to follow George into a life where legs no longer work in harmony. *One* goes alright, the other swings.

Twelve months later tragedy struck again.

On the eighth of May 1952, a B29, better known as a Superfortress, took off alone at precisely 10.40 from the local wartime base of the Americans, and still in use to answer the demands of a so-called 'Cold' War that had reached manic proportions. The plane was due to rendezvous with machines from Kings Cliffe, Mildenhall and Lakenheath, and join a massive flypast over Buckingham Palace to commemorate the end of World War Two – European division.

Three parts down the runway, its engines roaring and spitting, preparing to haul its enormous bulk into the air, the plane's nose lifted, it began climbing, when all at once something went disastrously wrong. The starboard engines exploded, turning instantly into balls of fire, the right wing dipped, the nose went down, then rose to almost vertical, the machine veered right, turned from its conventional take-off path to the west of Farndon, banked right-handed, lost height rapidly, then at ground-level hurtled in a dead straight line for the chimneys of Bradbury Hall. It clipped the roof of the shepherd's cottage, cutting off his ridge-tiles clean as a whistle, then pancaked smack on to the fabric of the infamous mansion eight hundred yards beyond. The result defies description, the consequences pre-ordained, but I'll do my best. The whole structure threatened to collapse, as explosion after explosion rocked the place, and every inch became enveloped in flames as smoke rocketed skywards, ten times higher than the tallest evergreens.

The crash was visible for miles, and the bomber's fuel-tanks were full... I could see the conflagration from Granleigh. I rushed outside, fearing the worst, but cursing myself for being such a bloody pessimist.

Accelerator hard to the boards the little Anglia responded nobly. We made for Little Downton in clouds of dust, my mouth dry, throat choking, heart going like a trip-hammer. On two wheels I somehow turned at the village pump, took the Belton road, then half a mile on cut across to the Farndon junction, better to approach the Hall via Briarsdale. In minutes I tore past 'our' ride-gate and breasted the familiar rise where all was laid out before me, my worst fears confirmed.

I learned how it came about from Ernie Tebbs, the shepherd, who fortunately was in the back garden with his missus when his tiles and chimneys went for a Burton – his neighbours were away. The facts were confirmed a thousand times by American airmen swarming, in total disbelief, over the grass like bees on buddleia but like the rest debarred from approaching the mansion, or getting close to the stricken bomber. No less than four fire-engines, and three ambulances from the Yankee base five miles off joined in the rescue. They got to work in seconds, creating the impression everything possible was being done to minimise the disaster. I eventually learned three maids had escaped the blaze, being close to an escape route, and a couple of men, though nobody knew their names. And no one around could give us a clue as to how many were trapped inside, or had been in the gardens when the plane went piling in.

My worries were many, but one was paramount – was it *remotely* possible Noel and Stella were here on a visit, and now lay helpless in that awful pile. I could only pray!

The devastation beggars description. Where before, clusters of tall chimneys had reached for the sky, now there was nothing. Everywhere masonry crumbled to destruction, the fires burning ever more fiercely – I could swear I saw stone ablaze. Our local fire engine, and one from Oundle, were already tackling the inferno from inside the paddock, another tried reaching the site via the main drive. They'd wasted no time in arriving. But the picture changed rapidly and soon the paddock, the fields beyond, and the roads in all directions, were jammed up with Yankee trucks, people on foot, and cyclists from all compass points, as hundreds more kept on arriving, but nothing could change the reality of the grim situation. An eerie, awesome picture – and *still* nobody could guess who might be inside, killed outright, trapped in impossible situations, or who had managed to get away. Some brave character had had the sense to open the stables and free the horses, then undo the kennels and let the dogs loose. I almost convinced myself Estelle must be in there, but Ernie told me he didn't believe so, though he couldn't be sure, and he'd seen several visitors arrive earlier, mostly VIPs judging by their limousines.

Slowly, very slowly, the assorted brigades began to achieve the one feasible goal – to contain the fire and preserve the cottages.

Onlookers were numb with shock, women crying openly, none could stand still for long, wandering aimlessly and staring in awe at the gutted manor house. I got as close as I could to the courtyard gates, wriggling up to an American ambulance with at least *one* victim aboard. It looked to be a gardener. He'd apparently been trapped near the stable-block until some hero heard his cries, and smashed through the collapsing wall. From what we could see it was impossible to think any of the bomber crew could have survived – not one! The mammoth plane sat flat on the rubble, a scorched, scarred, skeletal string of twisted metal girders like the remains of some long-dead dinosaur.

It was tea-time when the fire-crews decided nothing more could be done. The crowds drifted, the weary, smoke-scarred firemen began clearing up, and a couple of ambulances stayed on 'just in case'. I was still trying to glean information on how many had perished, how many injured, and if possible, who they were. It was the most futile exercise ever. But I persisted, and I'd poked my nose in, ostentatiously helping with the salvage. I had one big advantage – I knew exactly where I was, though many thought me a survivor.

The death toll was heavy, and tragic. I can do no more at present than mention those I either knew, or knew of.

Martin, Lydia, Henry, Doctor French, Sadie Thompson, Alan Stewart, poor Charles.

Tragedy on a giant scale, though cynics might think it deserved.

Epilogue

You'll have gathered Stella survived – she was safe in Market Harborough. So was Noel.

Six weeks after the tragedy I sat in the tiny garden looking at grass crying out to be mown and a hedge in need of a haircut. *The Chronicle* lay unread across my lap – I was thoroughly browned off, empty and gutless.

I heard a car draw up outside. I took little notice – until the gate clicked! Rubbing my eyes I went to sit up and promptly ended up on the grass, the deck-chair in bits around my legs, the rotted canvas draped across my shoulders.

"Can I come in?" She hobbled down the path, a case in one hand a bag in the other. She dropped them both and stood laughing her pretty head off.

"I'd *better* come in!" she added, between the guffaws.

"Stella! *Stella...*"

"I've come home Franz. For good! If you still want me?

"Darling..."

I'm still in tears.